FORETOLD

ALSO BY JANA OLIVER

The Demon Trapper's Daughter

Soul Thief

Forgiven

FORETOLD

JANA OLIVER

St. Martin's Griffin
New York

FORETOLD. Copyright © 2012 by Jana Oliver. All rights reserved. Printed in the United States of America. For information, address St. Martin's Press, 175 Fifth Avenue, New York, N.Y. 10010.

www.stmartins.com

ISBN 978-1-250-02184-7 (trade paperback)
ISBN 978-1-250-02183-0 (e-book)

First Edition: December 2012

10 9 8 7 6 5 4 3 2 1

To

Tyra Mitchell Burton

who found her very own

Georgia boy

Acknowledgments

Wow! I can't believe this is the fourth and final book in the series. The whole story is finished and yes, gentle readers, you will know how it all turns out for Riley and Beck. I hope you find the ending as joyful as I did.

There are many good folks to thank for helping me complete this book in record time. First and foremost, my thanks to my editor, Jennifer Weis, and a special shout-out to Mollie Traver, editorial assistant extraordinaire, who helped me smooth the rough edges and deftly find the best way to bridge the story between the Atlanta and Okefenokee scenes. And as always, a big thank-you to Meredith Bernstein, my literary agent.

Because of the short time I had to write *Foretold*, I needed lots of support, which was amply supplied by my dear friends Jean Marie Ward and Michelle Roper. They went the extra distance to keep me sane and managed to beta read my manuscripts in record time despite their busy lives. Also, a hug to my spouse who kept telling me, "It'll be okay." He was right, of course. He always is.

A special thank you to Steve and Jo Knight of Okefenokee Pastimes (www.okefenokee.com) for the extraordinary guided tour into the beauty and majesty that is Okefenokee Swamp. I've come to love that magnificent natural wonder as much as you two do.

Sometimes you just have to seek out a mortician's advice and this time it was supplied by Shane Burton, who made sure I didn't goof up the funereal parts. Thanks, guy. The Innis & Gunn is on me, my friend.

Once again I used the Scottish expertise of William MacLeod (just as I did in all the previous books) to ensure Grand Master Angus Stewart sounded authentic. Thank you, William. Because of you, Stewart is one of my favorite characters to write.

Finally, my gratitude to my readers, who have traveled along with Riley and Beck on their torturous journey and rooted for them every step of the way. The series would never have done so well if it hadn't been for you. You guys are truly #TeamDemonTrappers.

The two most important days in your life are the day you were born and the day you figure out why.

—MARK TWAIN

FORETOLD

ONE

2018
Atlanta, Georgia

"What could go wrong?" Riley Blackthorne muttered under her breath. That wasn't the kind of question she should ask while on a demon-trapping run in one of Atlanta's train stations.

What could go wrong? Everything.

She and two other trappers were stalking a Pyro-Fiend, a Grade Two demon whose Hellish job was to set fires. So far, it'd been having a grand time dropping fireballs in front of the MARTA trains, setting alight trash containers and, in one case, firing up a train car.

Usually Riley was all about capturing demons. Her late father, Paul Blackthorne, had been a legendary master trapper so it was in her blood. She should have been jazzed about this trapping run.

Not so much. Not when she was trapping with two guys who didn't want to be anywhere near her.

The pair were both in their early twenties, blond, and handsome, but there the similarities ended. The one to her right, her blue-eyed ex-boyfriend, wasn't quite as hostile as he'd once been. In fact, Simon Adler hadn't tried to splash her with Holy Water or accuse her of working for Hell once during the twenty minutes they'd been on-site.

Simon's battle with a ravenous demon had left him mortally wounded and if it hadn't been for the deal Riley had cut with Heaven, he'd be in his grave. Then one of Hell's most deceptive Archangels had played hockey with his mind and his deep Catholic faith. When he'd finally found out who'd been pulling his strings and about her deal with Heaven, Riley's ex had gone into free fall. The result was one confused guy who didn't know what to believe or who to trust.

At least you're not yelling at me anymore.

That privilege belonged to the guy on her left: Denver Beck, the muscled ex-military South Georgia dude who had served as trapping partner to Riley's father until his death. Beck was usually a cool guy to work with. Today he was opting for total butthead.

He glowered at them. "So what are we waitin' for?" he snarled. "Think the demon's just gonna come up and introduce itself to y'all?"

"It'll show up soon enough. They always do," Riley replied, trying not to lose her temper. Then Beck would win.

"Why would you think that?"

"Because I'm here," she said. "Demons can't resist trying to kill me."

That earned her a sidelong glance from Simon.

"Hey, it's true. It's not because I work for Hell, okay?" *Well, not entirely.*

"I didn't say a word," he murmured.

"You were thinking it."

"You two done?" Beck demanded.

Riley shot the senior trapper a scathing glare and it came right back at her. Beck had been this way ever since he'd tossed her out of his house in a fit of self-martyrdom. Just when they'd grown so close, something in his past had caused him to push her away. This time Riley wasn't going quietly, not when she knew she loved the guy.

Pushing ahead of the others, she worked her way through the crowd. It was a good time to be down here—in a few days the trains would be packed with people headed to or from the basketball games, all dressed in their favorite team's colors. Or in the case of Clemson University, orange-and-black tiger tails.

Folks waiting for the next train gave her a concerned look. That wasn't surprising since her face had been all over CNN and the newspapers in the last few weeks. It also might have something to do with the small white sphere she was carrying.

"You guys trappers?" someone called out.

"Sure are," Beck replied.

"Time for me to take the bus," the guy said, turning on his heel and heading for an exit.

Riley sighed. Maybe it would have been better to evacuate the train station, but if this turned out to be a false alarm there'd be hell to pay at City Hall.

As she continued down the platform, a train pulled in and passengers exited, including one man carrying a giant stuffed panda wearing a football helmet.

Sometimes it was best not to know the real story.

A thin plume of white smoke curled out of a nearby trash container, catching Riley's notice. Could it be the Pyro-Fiend? She shot a glance toward Beck and he shrugged in response.

The trappers positioned themselves on either side of the container.

"Ready?" Beck asked. When they nodded, he kicked the can over and trash tumbled out, along with a pile of burning napkins. Apparently someone had tossed a lit cigarette inside and now they had a mess to clean up. Plus MARTA passengers laughing at them.

Riley stomped out the fire, then kicked the junk back into the can. As she worked, Beck bitched under his breath about how this whole run had been a screwup. As she bent over to nudge an empty donut box into the container, she felt the prickle of something touching her mind. Something demonic.

Blackthorne's daughter, the voice called.

She shot up into a standing position. "It's close. It name-checked me." There was the crackle of paper at her feet and a red demon crawled out of the trash. It was about eight or so inches tall, with forked tail and sharp teeth. A flame flickered on its right palm.

"Trapper!" it cried and lobbed a fireball directly at Simon. He dropped and kissed the dirty concrete as the roaring flames shot over the top of his head.

"Hey, dumbass!" Beck shouted, but the demon ignored him, generating another flame to toss at Simon.

Riley stepped in its way, heaved a white sphere heavenward, and waited for the snow to fall. Instead there was a cracking sound and then a shower of sleet: The magic inside the sphere had misfired. Cold rain pelted down on them and it set the demon to howling. Distracted, the fiend dropped its ball of flame and it rolled across the platform like a fiery tennis ball, past a wooden bench and two startled onlookers.

Demon or flame? Riley ran after the fire, fearing it would spread throughout the station if she didn't contain it. Above her another snow globe cracked open and its contents swirled down like a North Dakota blizzard. The falling snow made the concrete slippery and she slid and cracked her knee. The flame ball kept rolling toward a train car and its open door.

Oh crap.

Panicking, she stripped off her jacket and threw herself on the ball of flame. The fabric immediately began to smolder from the intense heat and Riley pounded at it with her hands. The flames faltered and finally died.

Despite all the drama, people walked around her, one clipping her elbow as they hurried past to wherever they were headed. One couple laughed as she knelt there in the snow, her hair a mess and her jacket smoking. Someone began lobbing snowballs. After the train doors had closed, a small kid pressed his nose up against the window, eyes wide, watching her intently. She winked at him and to her surprise, he shyly waved back as the train departed.

Maybe life doesn't suck after all.

When she regained her feet, Riley found Simon holding a bait box containing the Pyro-Fiend and enough dry ice to keep it from playing firebug until they sold it to a demon trafficker. True to form, the thing was painting the station blue with its curse words.

A quick check around proved the train platform was devoid of gawkers except for a lone fellow with a cell phone busily recording the action. He'd probably have uploaded the video to the Internet before they left the station.

"That was sloppy," Beck complained, hands on his hips. It was his *I'm gettin' in yer face and you'd best listen* pose. "What's up with y'all?"

Riley would have loved to tell him exactly what was wrong if the guy with the cell phone hadn't been nearby.

Simon managed a weak "Sorry."

When Beck glared over at her, expecting her to apologize, Riley shook her head. She jammed her roasted jacket into his hands and whispered, "Bite me."

⁂

Once they were on street level and away from the phone dude, Riley flipped over her hands to check for burns.

Next to her, Simon took a sharp intake of breath. "Where did those come from?" he asked, eyes wide.

Oops. She'd forgotten about the dark inscriptions on both her palms. At this point she didn't care if the other trappers knew what they meant. Riley raised her left palm and pointed to the black crown. "This one's from Heaven." She switched hands. "And the flaming sword is from Hell," she explained. "Yeah, I know, it's wacked to have both."

When Simon frowned, she braced herself for another torrent of accusations about her being Lucifer's Minion of the Month.

Instead, his frown deepened. "Won't they ever leave us alone?" he asked, his voice trembling.

"Maybe someday," she lied.

⁘

Riley really wasn't playing attention as she walked to her car, eager to get away from Beck and his attitude before they got into a shouting match in front of her ex-boyfriend. That would be the ultimate humiliation.

She'd just reached her car when someone called out to her. When Riley turned, two girls were approaching. They were about her age, wearing modest dresses and coats in deference to the February chill, hair primly tucked into tight buns. Even more tellingly, they were loaded down with a Bible, a big bottle of Holy Water, and a cross.

This wasn't the first time she'd been confronted by someone keen to save her soul.

Though the Vatican and their Demon Hunters had tried to keep the cemetery battle off everyone's radar, in particular the whole Hell vs. Heaven part, Atlanta's citizens knew something major had happened. Some claimed to have seen angels, which was probably the case. You couldn't have a near miss with Armageddon without a few well-armed Divines flying around. Coupled with the recent demon attacks at the Tabernacle and the Terminus Market, all the blame seemed to stick to the trappers for some reason. Since Riley was always in the news for something or another, she'd become the focus of that wrath.

This duo was probably part of the team of girl exorcists who had arrived in Atlanta a couple of days earlier. From what Riley had heard, they'd been trying to cast out demons 24/7, including one supposed exorcism in the middle of a bowling alley.

"You are consorting with Hell and your soul is in peril," one of the girls said solemnly, a petite brunette.

Riley's soul was already the property of a certain Fallen angel, at least if Ori was still alive. She decided it was best not to mention that.

When she didn't reply, the girl tried again. "We have come to save you. We will exorcise your devil and free you this very night."

"Look," Riley began, "I appreciate what you're doing, but I trapped four demons today. People who work for Hell don't do that, okay?" *Well, actually they can but* . . .

"The Enemy is keeping you from God's grace," the girl replied, raising her cross.

Riley's enemy, Sartael, was currently in Hell—Lucifer's prisoner—but these girls weren't going to buy that. She didn't begrudge them their job, but she didn't want to get caught up in it.

"Sorry, gotta go," she said.

The chilly Holy Water hit her a moment later, drenching her face and hair. The cross was in her face next, along with some words that made little sense. It certain wasn't Latin.

These are wannabes, not the real thing.

When Riley wiped the water out of her eyes, someone grabbed her left hand, the one with Heaven's mark and the cross was pressed against it. There was no reaction. She didn't want to find out what would have happen if they tried it on Hell's brand.

Riley wrenched herself free and backed away. "Will you stop that!"

The girls seemed bewildered. Apparently they'd figured the combo of Holy Water and cross application would have caused her to cast out her devil like in some late-night horror movie.

Definitely wannabes.

"Riley?" Beck called out as he and Simon hustled up to the scene. "What's goin' on?"

When one of the girls tried to explain, Simon cut her off. "Just leave her alone. You worry about your own souls."

"You're working for the Devil. Don't you know that?" one of the girls called out.

"No more than you are," Beck replied. "Now get out of here."

Riley's tormenters retreated, noticeably disappointed they'd failed in their mission.

Riley slumped against her car, wiping her face free of mascara. If this kept happening, she'd have to buy the expensive waterproof kind.

"Thanks, guys."

"Sorry," Simon replied as if he'd been responsible for the fray.

"Part of the job, I guess," she replied, still mopping up her makeup.

Beck's cell phone rang and he stepped away to take the call. As he listened, his expression darkened. "Understood. I'll see she gets home safe."

Before Riley could ask what that was all about, he offered Simon his truck keys. "Follow us to Stewart's house, will ya?"

"Wait, you don't have to—" Riley began.

"Yeah, I do," Beck retorted. "Just get in yer car and don't bother to argue."

Simon took the keys and retreated.

Wish I could.

⁜

Beck drove, mostly because her eyes were still stinging and watering.

"Ya gonna be okay?" he asked.

"Yeah. I'm getting really tired of this crap."

"Ya were the one who put herself in the middle of it."

When his "you's" became "ya's" he was upset. But then so was she.

Riley glowered at him. "Why are you being a jerk?"

"I'm drivin' ya to Stewart's, aren't I?" Then he fell silent and glowered at the traffic.

Here we go again. Riley knew exactly where their problem lay and it wasn't her: It was his ex-girlfriend, the reporter chick, and whatever dirt she'd uncovered about his past.

"I don't see Justine backing off," she retorted. "You know, if you hadn't slept with her, you wouldn't be in this situation."

The second after she let her jealousy off its leash she knew it was a mistake. Beck reacted instantly, his foot jamming hard on the brakes as they reached a stop sign. Only the seat belt kept her from launching into the dash.

"Yer just like her, always tryin' to screw with my head," he said, the veins sticking out on his neck. "I'm startin' to regret the day I met ya."

That stung after all they'd been through. "You. Are. Lying. Tell me what Justine knows that has you so scared. Come on, spill it."

"It's none of yer damned business," he said, surging through the intersection, narrowly missing a slow-moving station wagon. "Give it a rest, will ya?"

Riley stared out the side window, surprised the glass didn't melt from her fury.

One of these days I'll know the truth.

TWO

Beck pulled into Stewart's driveway, then bailed out of the car though the engine was still running. Simon had barely pulled up to the curb when he was rousted out of the driver's seat. A moment later Beck turned his truck around in the street and drove away, without looking back at Riley.

What a drama queen.

Riley turned off the engine and gave herself time to calm down. These sorts of confrontations would continue until one of them cracked. If she was lucky, Beck would break first. If not . . .

She gazed up at Master Stewart's home while the car made funny *tick-tick* noises as the engine cooled down. Not every window in the grand Victorian structure was illuminated, but those that were gave off a welcoming glow. Her apartment seemed so empty now that her dad was gone. This place was full of life. With its fancy gable fretwork and the multistory turret, Riley swore this building had been transported to Atlanta from another century. Love felt real here, along with the promise that it could be nurtured and protected from a violent world.

Until the Vatican's Demon Hunters said otherwise, she was to remain under Grand Master Stewart's wing. It wasn't a bad thing; Stewart was nice, his house was huge, and his housekeeper was an awesome cook.

The master was in his sixties with silver hair and penetrating dark eyes. Behind his jovial smile was a clever mind and a ready wit. A member of the International Demon Trappers Guild, he'd lived in Atlanta for a decade, spoke a number of languages, and carried a lot of weight with both the local trappers and the Vatican's Demon Hunters. Riley's father had apprenticed with Stewart and had always spoken of him with genuine affection. Now she knew why.

After locking the front door behind her, Riley kicked off her shoes and laid the scorched jacket on top of them. She really didn't know why she'd kept it.

"Lass?" a voice called out, a rich timbre overlaid with a muted Scottish accent.

"Coming," she said.

It was a habit now: When she arrived home in the evening she would spend some time with Stewart before she went to bed. He'd be in that big den of his, sitting near the fire in the oversized stone hearth. They'd talk about school, about everything. It was something her father had done over breakfast every morning and she'd missed that so much after he'd died. Though this wasn't her dad asking the questions or gently guiding her through life's mysteries, she looked forward to this time.

As with previous nights she found the owner of the house in his favorite chair with a copy of a Scottish newspaper in his lap and a glass of whisky at his elbow. A pipe rested in a stand near a fat pouch of tobacco.

Though Riley was actually apprenticed to Master Harper, it was Stewart who had come to her aid when the Demon Hunters had arrested her, using his rank with the International Guild to plead her case. When the "Inquisition" was over, an agreement had been struck—Stewart was responsible for her behavior and would pay with his life if she strayed too far off the path.

Riley settled into one of the overly comfortable chairs, placing her backpack at her feet.

"Good evenin', lass."

"Master Stewart," she said politely. "Is there some reason you told Beck to drive me home?"

"The Guild received a death threat today."

If it'd been against the entire Atlanta Guild, Stewart wouldn't have called Beck.

"It was for me, wasn't it?"

"Aye."

What could she say to that? Someone hated her enough to threaten to kill her, all because she'd stood between the armies of Heaven and Hell and talked them out of the Big War.

"A few folks have figured out what happened and they're talkin'. Some still believe ya helped those demons attack the Tabernacle. Yer just too high profile right now."

"I won't hide," Riley protested. "I have to work to pay my bills."

"I know. We've passed the letter on ta the police and hopefully they'll find whoever is behind it." Stewart loaded his pipe with tobacco and then tamped it down. "Give me the run report," he added. "Harper's at an AA meetin', so I'll pass it on ta him."

It wouldn't do her any good to freak out about the threat, so she delivered her report.

"It wasn't a clean capture," she explained, "but we did trap that Pyro at the Five Points MARTA station."

"How did Simon do?"

"Okay. He didn't freeze up or anything."

"How about Beck? Is he still bein' a bear with a sore bum?"

He'd totally pegged Backwoods Boy. "Definitely."

"Are ya willin' ta tell me what happened between the two of ya ta make him that way?"

I swear this guy is psychic. "How'd you know it was about us?" she asked, puzzled.

"I'm good at readin' people. It's part of bein' a grand master."

Riley could try to avoid the question, but that wouldn't work as Stewart would get the answer out of her eventually. Maybe he could help her figure out how to break through Beck's defenses.

"We had a huge argument after the trappers' wake. I thought everything was fine between us after we..." Riley's cheeks warmed at the memory. "... kissed at the cemetery."

Sure they were both going to die, Beck had let down his guard, admitted he couldn't live without her, and delivered a heart-melting kiss that had completely rocked Riley's world.

"I was the one who told him not ta let the moment pass," Stewart said. "I told him he might not have that chance again."

"Oh, so that's why he did it," she said, disappointment welling up inside her. "I thought..."

"He took that bold step because he's verra fond for ya, lass. That wasn't a kiss between friends and ya know it."

"Noooo..." It had been epic. Everything she'd ever hoped for.

Her host was still waiting for an explanation.

"The morning after the wake, I went to see him. When I got to his house that skank of a reporter chick was just leaving. Whatever she said to him set him off. He was furious."

"Ah, Justine Armando again. Do ya know why she was there?"

"Beck said she's writing another article about him and he was really worried about it." Riley shook her head in dismay. "Then suddenly he tells me to leave, says that he doesn't want to see me ever again. At first I thought it was something I'd done. Then he said I deserved someone better than the bastard son of a drunk who couldn't read or wr—"

Oh crap. She'd let one of Beck's biggest secrets loose in front of a master. That was very bad. "Oh, man, you didn't hear that."

"I know he's semiliterate, lass," Stewart replied. "Yer father told me."

Riley sighed in relief. "He'd be way mad if he knew I said anything to you." Then she rolled her eyes. "Like it matters. He's pissed off at me anyway."

"Aye, and that troubles me. There's somethin' else goin' on or Beck wouldn't be treatin' ya this way. Not when he was so *keen* with ya at the cemetery."

"Maybe it has something to do with his mom."

"I'm sure he's upset about her illness, but it's more than that. Beck's a warrior at heart and he will always protect those around him. In yer case, it's even more than that, which makes me think the reporter knows somethin' he feels will harm ya. Or change yer opinion of him. Either way, his protective instincts would come inta play."

It was a shrewd analysis of the situation and a lot freer of emotion than Riley could manage.

"He won't tell me anything about his life before he came to Atlanta. It's like he's embarrassed or something."

"Paul told me a bit, but even he never got the full story." Stewart flicked his lighter and took a few puffs of the pipe. The sweet scent of caramel and lemon filled the air. "Anythin' else?"

Riley told him about the near-exorcism outside the MARTA station. He didn't seem surprised.

"Yer too visible right now. What with the threat hangin' in the air, I want ya out of sight for the next little bit. Beck's mother is much worse and he's leavin' for his hometown tomorrow mornin'. Harper and I both agree—we'd like ya ta go ta Sadlersville with him."

Riley shook her head. "I'm not the best choice. He's so mad at me I'll only make it worse."

"Beck has confided in ya more than any other person I know. Though he might be actin' like a total arse, he truly cares for ya." Stewart paused. "Even loves ya in his own way."

Riley's breath caught. Maybe it hadn't been her imagination.

"He's not real stable at present, and when his mother passes over it'll be worse. He needs ya at his side, Riley, even if he denies it."

She knew the master was right. It'd be ugly, but she'd been through that before and it'd get her out of Atlanta until things settled down.

"All right, I'll go." Luckily her black funeral dress was upstairs in the closet rather than at the apartment. There never seemed to be an end to the mourning.

"Bless ya," Stewart exclaimed. "That'll ease my worries a notch. Keep an eye on things down south. I want ta know more about Beck's background and what's causin' him so much anxiety."

Now I'm a spy. "He'll go ballistic when I tell him I'm coming with him."

"That's why I'll be the one doin' the tellin'."

⁜

As he materialized in a pitch-black alley in Demon Central, the angel wept in despair.

"No!" Ori cried, raising his fists in defiance. "Damn you, Lucifer! Why?"

He was *not* supposed to be alive. He'd been ready to journey into the nothingness that awaited a Fallen when they took their last breath. He had even agreed to Riley Anora Blackthorne's outrageous terms for her soul simply because he was convinced he would die that day and she would be free of Hell's chains.

But his master had denied him that solace. Though Lucifer could not create new life, he could sustain those who were in his thrall and he had healed Ori even as he'd begged to die. He could still hear the Prince's voice as he woke from what was to be his final rest.

You will die when I permit it and no sooner. Slay my enemies. Do not think to cross me again, for the peace of death will not be your reward.

"How dare you?" Ori cried, his fists tightening. He had willingly followed Lucifer into exile, cut himself off from the Light and the love of Heaven, and now he was being treated as if that sacrifice was nothing.

When Ori's eyes opened, he lowered his arms and ensured that his wings were no longer visible. There were no mortals around to see him at present, but that would change. They were far too curious for their own good. If he encountered one now, one who challenged him, he may well have to kill it.

Turning, Ori strode down the alley until he reached one of Atlanta's main streets. The city's populace flowed around him, unaware of what he was or who he served or the growing darkness within him. As he walked, he passed a necromancer bristling with magic, then a street preacher exhorting people to rid the city of devils.

He had no choice but to do his master's bidding, hunting rogue demons who defied the Prince's rule. Ori would never find the respite death offered as long as Lucifer reigned in Hell.

Perhaps it's time to change that.

THREE

Knowing Beck was an early riser, Riley pulled herself out of bed and hurried down to breakfast at seven. Mrs. Ayers, her host's housekeeper, promptly filled her to the brim with a cheese omelet, french toast, and bacon. Despite the woman's prodigious efforts, Riley really didn't enjoy the meal as much as she should have. She was too nervous.

Beck was a lot like her—she didn't like being told what to do even when it was in her best interests. He'd go supersonic when Stewart delivered the news and she knew who he'd blame—it wouldn't be the master.

She tried to distract herself with the newspaper—the biggest article was reserved for a guy named Reverend Lopez, an exorcist, who claimed he was going to come to Atlanta and rid them of their demon problem once and for all. From what she could tell he was the real deal, not one of the make-believe exorcists roaming around the city. If she was lucky, he would come and go before she returned from Sadlersville.

It was a little before eight when Beck arrived and promptly complained to the housekeeper that he wasn't pleased that Stewart had insisted on seeing him before he left town. Riley listened as his boots clomped down to the den and then began counting to twenty. It was at sixteen that Beck's voice rose in surprised indignation.

Backwoods Boy had just received the news that his trip to South Georgia wasn't going to be solo.

His outrage carried through the big house. "I sure as hell don't need some little girl along on this trip. She'll be nothin' but trouble."

Riley winced. *Time to go.* She raced up the stairs, collected her small suitcase, and then hurried outside in early morning sunlight. There was a topper on his pickup now, though it didn't appear to be new. She hadn't known he owned such a thing.

The topper was locked so she set the luggage down and waited. A moment later a crimson-faced Beck barreled out of the house and for a second it looked as if he were going to slam the front door, then thought better of it. As he thundered down the front stairs to his Ford, he scowled at her all the way.

Without a word he unlocked the truck topper, picked up her small suitcase, and slung it into the bed of the pickup where it landed with a jarring thud. She suspected he would have done the same to her if he could have gotten away with it.

Riley climbed into the truck and then they were off, peeling rubber as he backed out of the drive like all of Hell's demons were on his tail. She hastily fastened her seat belt, then gritted her teeth as she was forced back in the seat by the sudden sharp acceleration.

"Dude, you're serious cop bait," she complained.

A short time later he screeched to a halt at a stop sign, glowered at her, then turned the corner at a more reasonable speed.

"How long does it take to get down there?" Riley asked.

Deafening silence. She knew this drill and it didn't bug her as much as it used to. Beck was having one of his snits and he'd work through it eventually, hopefully before it was time to return to Atlanta.

To fill the time, Riley texted her best friend Peter, told him of her trip, and asked him the *how long before we're there?* question. The answer came back quickly because he was in front of his computer: Sadlersville, population barely nudging the meter above two thousand souls, was about five and a half hours from Atlanta. Not all of it was on the interstate.

HOW'S IT GOING? her friend texted.

BECK IS ACTING LIKE I DON'T EXIST

THAT COULD BE A BLESSING

She laughed at that, which immediately earned her a glare from the driver.

HEY, WATCH OUT FOR FIRE ANT MOUNDS, COTTON FIELDS, AND VIDALIA ONIONS

Peter was surfing again.

THX! CHAT WITH YOU LATER

GOOD LUCK. YOU WILL NEED IT

Once they were on Dekalb Avenue headed toward the interstate, Beck finally released his death grip on the steering wheel. He shot her a frown and then turned back to watch the traffic.

"I told Stewart I didn't want you along. This is too close to yer daddy's funeral and all . . ."

Riley wisely let his fib stand. Though she'd asked Peter about their destination, she tried to jump-start the conversation again.

"Where is Sadlersville?"

This time she got a reply. "A few hours south and east of Macon. It's near Okefenokee Swamp."

"What did you do with Rennie?" she asked, wondering who was watching Beck's rabbit.

"I took her to the neighbor's place. Mrs. Morton will keep an eye on her for me."

Then he went quiet again, buried deep in his own thoughts.

Once they'd passed the airport on I-75, the truck picked up speed. She wondered how much the trip was going to cost with gas now hovering at nine dollars a gallon. Better than the ten it'd been for so long, but still, a truck burned a lot of fuel. Hopefully the solar panel on the roof would help.

She put in her earbuds and clicked on her decrepit mp3 player. It worked most of the time and when it didn't she'd give it a sharp slap against her palm and it'd start again. Now that she had access to her dad's life insurance money she could have bought a new one, but somehow it didn't seem right. The thing was like an old friend and you never ditched a buddy just because he got wacky on you. If that had been the case, Beck would have been gone a long time ago.

Riley checked her backpack again to ensure her envelope of cash was where she'd stashed it. Soon she'd have her own debit card because just the day before, she and Beck had opened a checking account using her dad's life insurance money as seed. Also tucked in the backpack was the new laptop Peter had helped her find. It wasn't as fancy as his, but it was the best she could buy for under three hundred dollars. It was still so new she wasn't sure exactly how it all worked, even though he'd set up the e-mail account for her. Step by step, her life was changing and some of it was positive.

Beck clicked on the radio and the cab of the truck filled with a country song, which was all he listened to. To avoid a horrific mashup of Carrie Underwood and the Gnarly Scalenes, Riley clicked off her mp3 player and stowed it in her backpack.

It was time to get Beck talking again.

"So what's this going to be like?" she asked.

To her surprise, he lowered the radio. "Not good."

"Not good like hordes of rampaging demons or . . ."

He frowned at her. "Folks in Sadlersville don't remember me kindly and they're gonna figure we're, well . . ."

"Hooking up?" A nod. "So we'll tell them we're not."

"Tellin' them and havin' them believe it is two different things."

"Are we staying at your mom's place?"

He shook his head immediately. "No. We'll be at the motel. It's okay. I always stay there when I visit."

That was interesting. "Any other relatives down here?"

"Just me and her."

The radio's volume went back up, ending the conversation.

Other than a quick stop for a restroom and gas, Beck remained in silent mode from that point on. Eventually he pulled off the interstate and headed south on a state road and Riley found the scenery more interesting as Peter's prediction of fire ant mounds and cotton fields came to pass. She even spied a peach orchard, but no fields of Vidalia onions. The homes on either side of the highway were either really nice or totally run-down and there didn't seem to be much in the middle. For some reason folks stored their old stuff in their front yards, including dilapidated cars, broken lawn chairs, kids' toys, a garden tractor, bedsprings, you name it.

"Why do they do that?' Riley asked, gesturing toward one yard packed with items.

"All that metal is like a bank account. Might need it someday so the best place to keep an eye on it is in the front yard."

Ohhhkay . . .

Riley had hoped there might be a meal somewhere along the way and when they drove through a town called Waycross, she figured Beck would do a quick turn into a burger joint. It didn't happen. Luckily she'd had a big breakfast.

"How soon are we there?" she asked, fidgeting.

"Too soon," he replied, his fingers bleaching white as he gripped the steering wheel.

He's afraid. But of what? He's coming home.

Maybe that didn't mean the same thing to him.

✦

When Riley finally saw the Sadlersville's sign, she braced herself: She was about to see into Beck's past. As they swung into the motel's driveway and then under the canopy, she knew she'd entered another world. The place looked decent enough, one long white brick building with flaming red doors dotted along its length. The roof was red as well. Apparently the owner had a thing for the color.

Only a few moments after Beck disappeared into the small motel office his phone chimed on the truck seat. Riley checked the display and then wrinkled her nose in disgust. The reporter chick had sent Beck a text warning him that she intended to submit the article in the next day or two and if he wanted to offer any input, now was the time. The jealous beast that lived inside of Riley demanded she delete the message. It wasn't like he'd really be able to read it.

Not. Your. Call. She forced herself to behave.

When Beck climbed back into the truck he noticed her sour expression. "What's wrong?"

Riley pointed at his phone. "Justine. She's missing you."

He huffed and then promptly deleted the text. "Nothin' I hate more than a woman who doesn't know when it's over."

Was there a message for her in there somewhere?

He parked at the west end of the building and right before he got out of the truck, he tossed her a key, which meant she had her own room.

"Won't stop the gossipin', but it's the way it has to be."

As the door to her room creaked open, Riley prepared herself for the worst. Fortunately the room was better than she'd expected: an antiquated wall heater under the window, a small desk that hugged one wall, and two double beds with forest-green bedspreads. The carpet was generic brown. As Riley stepped inside she took in a lungful of that spray housekeepers use to scent the air. It made her cough. She placed her backpack on one bed and did a bounce on the other, the one closest to the door.

Not bad.

The bathroom had a shower and adequate space on the counter for her stuff. There was even a hairdryer.

"This works," she said.

"Glad you approve," Beck said from behind her. He dropped her suitcase on the extra bed and then sank down next to it. Ignoring his presence, she began to unpack, hanging her few clothes in the closet. At least with her own room he wouldn't claim she was hogging all the hangers.

"Gotta set some ground rules," he said.

Here it comes.

"You don't open the door unless I'm here and you don't go off on yer own. Be careful who you talk to and don't trust anyone."

He wasn't quite this crazy up in Atlanta. "Why are you so edgy?"

"Just bein' careful."

It was time to cut through all the BS. "But we're in the middle of nowhere. You have to give me a reason for all this paranoia."

Beck took a deep breath before he answered. "There's folks down here who don't like me. Some might think hurtin' you would be a good way to get even."

Whoa... "Are you going to tell me what hideous transgressions you have committed or should I wait for the movie?"

He ignored her as he moved to the connecting door and flipped open the lock. "Leave this open. That way if there's any trouble I can get to you quicker."

"Are we under siege down here?" she asked, his unease feeding hers.

"No, but it's still... we need to be careful."

"What about the demons?"

"We got a few. Sadlersville shares a demon trapper with Way-cross and mostly he catches the littler ones, but every now and then a Three shows up. For the most part, what problems we'll have will be with our kind, not them."

The outer door slammed behind him. A short time later he unlocked his side of the connecting door and opened it.

By the time she'd emptied her suitcase and stashed it in the closet, he had his clothes stacked on the end of his bed, tidy piles of jeans, T-shirts, socks, and underwear. His briefs were navy or black: no tighty-whities for him. His suit hung in the closet, all ready for his mother's funeral. It was the same one he'd worn to her dad's service.

As he tucked his clothes into the bureau, she flopped on her tummy on his spare bed, scrolling through her text messages. Nothing new other than Peter screwing up his courage to ask their friend Simi on a date. Riley sent him a text announcing she was officially in the middle of God Knows Where with a deranged country boy.

She became aware she was being watched and found Beck just outside his bathroom. "I'll be ready to leave in a minute or so."

Riley took the hint and headed for her room, finishing the text as she walked. Figuring she had a bit of time, she made a quick run to her bathroom to tidy herself up. She combed her long brown hair and then touched up her makeup, pleased to see that the bruises from the cemetery battle were well hidden and the dark circles under her eyes were nearly gone. She felt ready to meet Beck's mom.

When the toilet flushed in the other room, Riley slung her backpack onto her shoulder and stepped outside into the warm afternoon sunshine. The moment her eyes adjusted she saw the cop leaning against the front bumper of Beck's truck. His squad car was parked right behind it, blocking them in. The lettering on the side said this was the county sheriff who'd come to call.

If Riley had been expecting a stereotypical Southern cop she'd have been disappointed. This man was on the tall side, sleekly muscled, and apparently without an ounce of fat, his dark blond hair cut short. He was wearing sunglasses, a trooper-style hat, and his hands were crossed over his chest in a *piss me off at your own peril* pose.

When Beck exited his room, he halted in his tracks. His expression went unreadable in a heartbeat.

Uh-oh.

The cop took off his sunglasses and tucked them in his shirt pocket. "Heard you were back in town," the cop said in a soft drawl much like Beck's.

"Just got here," her fellow trapper replied, setting his backpack at his feet.

"Been to see your momma yet?"

"Headed that way."

"From what I hear it won't be long now."

"I hear the same," Beck replied, his jaw tight.

Hello? Am I invisible here?

As if the cop had heard her, his shifted his attention in her direction and tapped his hat in respect. "I'm Sheriff Tom Donovan." He looked over at Beck at this point. "Denver and I go way back."

Beck chuffed in disgust.

"I'm Riley . . . Blackthorne."

"You any relation to the master trapper in Atlanta?" the cop asked.

"He was my dad."

The man nodded now that he'd made the connection. "Pleased to meet you, Miss Riley. Since Denver here couldn't be bothered to pick up a phone, I had the pleasure of talking to your father every now and then." Another glance at Beck, then back to her. "Sorry to hear of your loss."

"Thank you."

"How old are you?"

"What? I'm seventeen. Why?"

"Just checking," the man replied. "Folks will hear that Denver's back in town and that he's got someone with him. He has a history with the local girls, so tongues will wag. I can shut some of that down by knowing the real story."

Beck took a step forward, a clear challenge. "Riley's not one of those. She's here to help with . . . *her*."

Donovan sobered. "It won't scald your tongue to call Sadie your momma."

"The hell it won't."

The sheriff shook his head and walked to his car. After he opened the door, he looked back at Riley. "Welcome to Sadlersville, Miss Riley."

"Thank you," she said, still unsure of what had just happened.

The cop car pulled out of the parking lot and headed up the road.

"So what was that all about?" Riley asked.

Beck dumped his backpack on the truck's seat.

"Just welcomin' me home," he replied.

FOUR

The center of Sadlersville was a curious mix of old and new. As Beck cruised along hunting for a parking place, Riley spied a kid with a laptop perched on a park bench, rocking away to something coming through his headphones. Right behind him was a barbershop with one of the old red-and-white poles. The town's water tower was the tallest thing around and most of the buildings were old, mom-and-pop shops rubbing elbows with the occasional chain store. There were none of the mini shops you found in Atlanta's parking spots. In fact, there were no parking meters so the street was full of cars and pickups. One vehicle had a giant sign in the back window proclaiming that Jesus was returning soon.

He's going to be really disappointed.

Beck noticed her studying the sign. "Folks take their religion serious down here."

"And folks in Atlanta don't?" she parried.

He shrugged, conceding that point. "It's different down here."

"Already figured that one out."

Once they were parked, Beck made a show of locking the truck's doors, on the alert, like he expected trouble with every step. He waved her up the street and they walked past a busy hair salon where necks craned to catch a glimpse of them, then a flower shop that still had Valentine's Day specials in the window and a thrift store.

Riley caught Beck's elbow. "I need a new jacket. I don't want to wear my mom's good one for trapping."

He didn't argue, but followed her inside and waited by the door as she found herself a replacement denim jacket for the one the demon had roasted. As she paid for it, Beck kept his attention on the street.

Once her purchase was complete, they returned to truck so she could switch out her mom's coat for the new one. It was then she saw the strange little wooden figure tucked underneath a windshield wiper. It was made of sticks, tied with green yarn, in the shape of a man.

When Beck saw it, his jaw tightened.

"What is that?" Riley asked. "Is it like some sort of warning?"

"No, it's someone tryin' to protect the truck." He carefully removed the stick man, and once he unlocked the doors he hung it from the rearview mirror.

"That's kinda weird, you know?" Riley said.

"Not if yer used to it. There's a couple wise women in town and they've taken a likin' to me. They probably figure someone will trash the truck if they get a chance, so they're letting them know that's not a good idea."

"So it's not all Baptists down here," Riley replied.

"No, not at all. The swamp has its own kind of magic and people have learned how to use it."

They retraced their steps. In time, Beck paused in front of the door to a diner, put on his game face, and then opened it to allow Riley to enter first.

The restaurant looked like it was right out of an old movie. Notices were stuck on the wall near the door—someone had a car for sale, another had free kittens to a good home. She and Beck had just missed Sandhill Crane Awareness Day. The floor was aged black-and-white-checked linoleum. A long table took up the wall to the left, covered by a blue vinyl tablecloth and loaded with old guys with newspapers and half-empty cups of coffee. Their average age seemed to be about seventy.

High-backed booths lined the walls and five tables formed a straight line down the middle of the room as lazy ceiling fans gently stirred the air above them. Along the back wall were shelves with row after row of mugs. Some had been personalized.

The moment the door shut behind them, heads turned and conversations stilled, every eye on them. When one of the old guys elbowed another and whispered something, Beck ignored the attention and selected the booth closest to the front window and the door. Riley slid into the other side.

A waitress wandered up to them, older, maybe forty, with large breasts that really demanded a better bra. Her makeup was overdone and her black skirt ended at just below the knee, followed by an expanse of tanned legs, pink socks, and red tennis shoes.

"I heard you were back," the woman said, her eyes totally on Beck. Then they moved to Riley. "I heard you weren't alone."

"Karen. How ya doin'?" he asked, politely.

"Not bad. You?"

A shrug. He didn't bother to flip open the menu, probably because he wouldn't be able to read it. "I'd like a burger and a double order of fries. Oh, and some black coffee, please."

Riley had to speed-read the offerings. Who knows what the food would be like in a place like this? She opted for the safest choice.

"A burger, some cottage cheese, and a glass of unsweetened iced tea."

The woman gave her a look like she'd ordered a plate of worms. "Unsweetened, huh? Where you come from?"

"Atlanta."

"Figures. All Yankees up there." The waitress took off toward the back of the diner and the swinging door that led to the kitchen.

Riley leaned over the table and lowered her voice. "We've been here, what, twenty minutes and everyone already knows it? What is it with these people?"

"Anythin' interestin' happens and it gets spread real fast."

"We're not interesting, Beck."

"Ya'd be wrong there, especially since yer with me."

His speech was already changing, reverting back to his roots, the drawl more noticeable now.

"Does all this *interest* have something to do with your history down here?"

He nodded. She beckoned for him to give it up. He shook his head.

"Okay, then I'll fill in the pieces." She lowered her voice so no one else would hear her. "You were a total horndog, right? If it was female, you were all over it."

To her surprise a lopsided grin appeared on Beck's face. "Some might say I was just bein' ... social."

"So how many did you date?"

"Only a couple. The rest were hookups."

Ohhhkay ... This guy definitely fell into the "no commitment" category.

The waitress reappeared, placing Beck's coffee in front of him and a tall glass of iced tea near Riley.

"Unsweetened," the woman said, shaking her head. Her tennis shoes *squeak-squeaked* across the linoleum as she headed toward another booth.

"So were you ... *social* ... with our waitress?" Beck shook his head. "Good. Then she won't spit on our food."

Before he could respond to that, the diner door swung open. His eyes rose to the newcomer and he tensed in recognition. It was then Riley realized why he'd chosen this spot: It was a quick way out in case of any hassles.

The newcomer made his way to their booth. He was about six feet tall, dressed in jeans and a chamois shirt with graying hair and a mustache that needed trimming. His eyes were a pale, watery brown and he squinted as if glasses were in his future.

The man smirked. "Denny Beck, well I'll be damned. I heard ya were back and here ya are, the Devil himself."

"Mr. Walker," Beck said, no warmth in his voice. He took a slow sip of his coffee, but she could see by the way he gripped the cup he was expecting trouble.

"It's been a long time. Where ya been? Prison?"

"No, Atlanta."

When he didn't get a rise out of her companion, the man checked Riley out. "I see yer still going after the ones too dumb to know yer trouble."

If this guy kept it up Beck was going to be all over him. Fortunately, the waitress provided the perfect diversion.

Riley gave Walker a hard stare. "Could you move, please?"

"What did you say?" he said, frowning.

She pointed behind him at Karen and her tray. "I like my food hot." *And you out of my face.*

The guy glowered at her, but backed off, grumbling under his breath.

The waitress delivered the plates, hiding a smile. "Anything else?" she asked.

"Not right now. Thanks," Beck replied.

Walker had found himself a seat at a nearby table so he could continue to glower at them. Beck ignored him, squirting ketchup, then mustard and hot sauce on his burger. He carefully rearranged the pickles, then picked up the burger, admiring it like it was a work of art.

"Was it his daughter?" Riley asked in a low voice.

A shake of the head. "Wife."

No wonder he's pissed. "How old were you?"

"Sixteen." He took a big bite of his burger. After he finished chewing and swallowed, he added, "It was right before I left town."

"Did you leave by choice or were you voted off the island?"

He dabbed at his mouth with a paper napkin. "Jury's still out on that one."

Riley did a quick mental recap—she was in some dorky small town with a local boy who had slept with just about every girl in sight, at least those of legal age. It was a good bet that every one of their fathers, brothers, or husbands would love the opportunity to have some serious face time with Denny Beck. She would be caught in the middle.

Lucky me.

Riley turned her attention to the burger and after a bit of doctoring she took a bite.

Ohmigod. It was incredible, juicy and rich with flavor, nothing like the ones she got at the fast-food places. She focused on her meal, ignoring the staring dude at the far table and the whispered conversations at some of the others. When anyone left they called out a good-bye to Karen or the other waitress and then took the long route around the diner so they walked right by their booth.

"Just ignore 'em," Beck said.

"Easy for you."

"Not really." When he finished the huge mound of fries he leaned back in the booth, content.

"How can you eat that much?" she asked, still picking at her own meal. The burger had been enormous and the cottage cheese was the extra creamy kind.

"I'm a growin' boy," he said.

"Well, you will be if you keep packing food away like that."

"It's better than starvin' yerself like you do." Beck lowered his voice. "You aren't like throwin' up in the mornin' or anythin'?" he asked, eying her closely.

That was one subject he'd skirted until now—whether her night spent with Ori the Fallen angel had resulted in her becoming pregnant.

"Nope, that's not going to be a problem."

His deep sigh told her he'd been worrying about that. "Well, there's some good news for a change," he said, followed by a long slurp of his coffee.

Someone moved up to the booth and for a moment Riley figured it was Walker back for more harassment. But it wasn't. This guy was a couple of years old than Beck and a little taller with dark brown hair and dark eyes. He was dressed in a navy blue T-shirt that showed off his muscles and a pair of criminally tight blue jeans. The smirk on his face was a like a billboard that announced I KNOW I'M HOT. Beck wore that same expression every now and then but this looked like it was the default setting for this guy.

The cold fire in Beck's eyes told her that this wasn't a friend. "Hadley," he said.

"Hey, Denny. I heard you were back."

Along with all the other Sadlervillians.

When Riley gave the newcomer another look over, he smiled back. *Cute.*

When her eyes drifted back to Beck's she found something new in them: raw jealousy. Maybe it was wrong, but part of her liked that a lot.

"I'm Cole," the guy said, sticking out his hand.

She shook it to be polite, though she knew Beck wasn't happy about it. "Riley."

Beck shifted out of the bench seat in one swift move. For a second she thought he was going to challenge the guy, but instead he scooped up the check and handed it and some cash to Karen as she walked by.

"Gotta be goin'," he said, picking up his trapping bag.

To Beck's obvious dismay, Cole followed them down the street. The vibes off this guy made her skittish, if nothing more than the fact that Beck's fuse was shorter than usual.

"What brings you to the middle of nowhere?" he asked.

Beck didn't reply, so she did. "His mom."

"You know her?" When Riley shook her head, he continued. "Well, then you're in for a surprise."

Wary, she shot a look over at her fellow trapper. The frown on his face was bone deep now. Riley swung her attention back to the guy walking next to her. Since Beck wasn't talking, she might as well be polite. "So how do you two know each other?"

"We used to hang together before he moved away."

She guessed *hang together* probably included all those sins Back-woods Boy didn't want her to know about.

So why are you talking to me? Are you trying to get under Beck's skin or is it something else?

They'd reached the truck now and Cole leaned up against a light pole, the smirk back again.

"See you later, Riley," he called out. "Don't let Denny take you into the swamp. That's a one-way trip."

Beck's growl echoed roughly in his throat. "Get in the truck, girl." The way he held himself told her not to argue.

Whatever was between these two guys was deeply personal.

"Sure, why not?" she grumbled. Riley took his keys and climbed into the pickup, making sure to slam the door to let Beck know she wasn't happy with his dictatorial attitude.

Though she tried to hear what was said, they kept it quiet. She was willing to bet it was Beck telling Cole to stay the hell away from her and Cole suggesting his old friend go screw himself. She knew her guess was right when the Cole laughed, winked at her, and then walked away.

You're cute, dude, but you're totally suicidal.

When Beck climbed into the truck, he looked ready to explode as his backpack thumped on the seat between them.

"So what's with him?" she asked.

"Nothing ya want to know," was the curt reply.

"Tell me or I'll ask Cole myself. You know me, I'll do it," she warned.

He heaved a sigh. "He's an arrogant SOB who will play all nice and then leave ya hangin' out to dry. Or in your case . . ." He shook his head. "Just stay away from him. He's bad news."

"Care to be more specific?"

"No, I don't. Ya have to take my word for it."

Strangely enough she would do just that. Beck had always been too overprotective, but he had a sixth sense when it came to trouble. If he said Cole of the Dark Eyes was bad news, then she believed him.

"Got it. I'll keep out of his way."

Beck gave her a bewildered look, as if he'd expected her to defy him. "Okay . . ."

"You've got enough going on without having to worry about that guy. I'm here for you, no one else."

Something changed in his face. "Sorry I've been really . . . mean. I'm not good with things down here. Too much bad stuff."

"Really? I hadn't noticed," she jested, then grew serious. "I don't care what you did or who you did it with when you were sixteen. It does not matter to me."

"I'd like to believe that. God, I would."

"Then when this is all over and we're headed back to Atlanta, you ask me if I think any differently about you."

"Fair enough," he said, putting the truck in reverse and pulling out onto the street.

FIVE

Beck insisted on driving her around so she could "get a feel for Sadlersville," which didn't tell her much other than he wasn't keen to get to the hospital. Another hint that his relationship with his mother was way complicated.

As Georgia towns went, Sadlersville wasn't very old, dating from early in the twentieth century. The founding father, Joseph Sadler, had been a railroad man and there was still a steady stream of trains lumbering through the city. Though it wasn't big, it did have churches—almost all of them Baptist. In Atlanta they would have combined them all into one megachurch, but down here each had its own little building and congregation. Add in a school, a hospital, a Laundromat, grocery store, and a funeral parlor and that was the sum of Beck's hometown.

"I couldn't handle this," Riley said. "No way. Too small. Nothing to do."

Beck snorted. "Oh, ya'd be surprised what kind of trouble you can find in a town like this."

"Oh, you mean trouble like picking up chicks who aren't smart enough to know your game?"

Beck frowned. "I'm sorry Walker said that. That wasn't right."

"Is his wife still with him?"

"Nah. Took off a few months after I moved to Atlanta with some guy who built swimmin' pools. Never came back."

"So why did you leave town?" she asked.

"Didn't have a choice. Walker got in my face one night when I was drunk. When I told him I wasn't the only one who'd had his missus he laid into me and I went after him with my knife. We both ended up bloody."

"Were you like stupid or what?" she blurted.

"Yeah, I was more mouth than brains back then." He grimaced at the memory. "Donovan threw Walker in jail to sober up. After a trip to the ER, he made me pack my clothes and then he hauled my butt to my uncle's place in Atlanta. Told me to stay up there if I didn't want to end up in jail, because if I came back home before a year was up, he'd make sure that happened."

"So *that's* what brought you to Atlanta. I always wondered."

He issued a lengthy sigh. "Time I go see the old lady. Can't put it off any longer."

"Won't she be pleased you're here?"

"I'm not countin' on that."

Riley's knowledge of Beck's mother was pretty scant—Sadie had never married, she had an alcohol problem, and treated her kid like he was dirt. And her son hated her for it. Or maybe he didn't, because you never knew with Beck. One thing for sure, he never referred to Sadie as his mother. That in itself spoke volumes.

Beck pulled onto the main drag, as he called it, and headed north. They passed another small restaurant, a dentist's office, a tire store, and finally turned into a long drive that led to a single-story redbrick building.

"Not as big as the hospitals in Atlanta, but they do a good job," he said. He hadn't said *like the hospitals back home.* That meant he still considered Sadlersville his home even though it appeared the residents might not agree.

Beck parked in the lot, hopped out of the truck, and then stopped dead in his tracks. Riley locked her door and walked around to him. He was leaning against the side of the pickup now, staring at nothing.

"You okay?"

He shook his head. "Ya should stay here."

Beck's proper "you's" had become "ya's" again. He was definitely stressing out about this visit.

"Sadie's not like yer momma was, Riley." He rubbed a hand across his face in agitation. "Nothin' like her."

"She can't be that bad."

Beck looked over at her. "She's a mean old cuss who likes to hurt people, especially me. If she can do that by hurtin' someone I . . . like . . . she'll be just as happy."

"Why does she act that way?"

"Some folks keep hatin' long past when it's best to let stuff go."

That still didn't explain why there was such bad blood between mother and son. Asking that question was sure to get her a load of grief, so she filed it away for later.

Beck made one more fervent request for her to remain in the truck, but Riley refused. "I'll deal, no matter what."

"We're both gonna regret this, I swear it," he murmured.

"My choice," she replied. *No way she's as bad as you say.*

They pushed through the double doors that led to the hospital lobby and Beck stopped at the reception desk to find out his mother's room number. The waiting room was empty, magazines stacked in neat piles on the end tables. To the right was a set of doors that led to the cafeteria and a couple of nurses were in there, holding coffee cups and chatting.

Beck returned. "They're pagin' her doctor now. I want to talk to him first."

Riley nodded, though this was proving harder than she'd expected. Her mom had spent countless hours inside a hospital for chemotherapy that hadn't worked until her body gave up. Just being in such a building brought up too many unhappy memories.

A tall, graying man in street clothes approached them. "Denver?" They shook hands. "Dr. Hodges. Thanks for seein' us."

"Sorry it's not in better circumstances."

Beck introduced her and then the doctor ushered them down the hall and into a smaller waiting room. He gestured for them to sit and after he closed the door, Hodges took a seat as well. Now that Riley could study him he really didn't look like a physician, more like a farmer with a wrinkled, tanned face and calloused hands.

"How much has your mother told you?" the doctor asked.

"Nothin'. It was Donovan who let me know she has cancer."

The doctor shook his head. "I tried to get her to call you, but you know how she is."

"How long?" Beck asked, his voice raspy.

"A few days, maybe less. I'm thinking the only reason she hasn't gone yet is she was waiting to see you."

"She doesn't care about that."

"Sometimes what people say and what they feel are two different things." The doctor straightened up. "Are you staying here in town?"

"We're out at the motel."

"Make sure the nurses' station has your phone number." He rose. "I'm sorry that we can't do more. Make your peace with her if you can. Time's running out."

Beck nodded and rose, shaking the man's hand again. After the doctor left, Beck closed the door behind him, then sank onto a seat, his head in his hands. Riley remembered what it had been like when the doctor had told her and her father the end was coming. The sense of utter helplessness. She put her hand on Beck's shoulder and it shook underneath her fingers.

"I always hoped . . . that we'd . . . find a way to get along." He looked up, his eyes brimming, then rubbed away the tears with the back of his hand. "But every time I tried she didn't want nothin' to do with me. She says I'm a total loser, not worth her time."

What kind of mother is she?

Riley laid her head against his, curling her arm around his broad shoulders, and gave him a hug. "She's wrong. You're not a loser, Beck. You're a very cool guy."

He sniffed once and pulled away, rising slowly out of his seat. Another swipe at the tears and then he donned his stone face, the one that wouldn't let the world see how badly he was hurting.

"Come on. It's time for ya to meet her."

⊹

Sadie Beck didn't have a roommate, her bed near the window. A moment before Beck stepped around the curtain he paused, like he was layering on additional defensive armor before engaging with the enemy.

She looked at least a decade older than her fifty years of age. Her skin was sallow, lined, her collar-length blond hair the same color as Beck's, except it was riddled with dull gray. She had an oxygen tube in her nose and each breath seemed to require a monumental amount of effort. Bloodshot brown eyes scrutinized her visitors. Her focus wasn't on Riley, but on her son.

"Damn, I must be dead and this is Hell," she said. "Why else would ya be here?"

Riley gaped. Maybe this was some kind of weird joke between them. She shot a glance at Beck and from the pained expression she knew it wasn't.

"Sadie," he said, his voice low. "Don't start. Not now. Not with what's happenin'."

The patient began to cough, a thick spasm that caused her to jerk on the bed. When Beck didn't move, Riley stepped closer, dug into the box for a handful of tissues, and handed them over. Sadie spat bright blood into the pristine white.

The patient gave her the eye. "So who's this? Yer latest bit of ass?"

What? "No," Riley replied. "I'm a . . . friend." *Maybe more than that.*

A snort. "Liar. He don't have no friends. Isn't that right, Denver?"

"Riley and I came down to be with ya and—"

Sadie waved him away with a bony arm. "Don't need ya. Never did."

"I know. But right now ya do."

She shook her head. "Don't worry, I'll be outta here soon enough. That's what ya want anyways."

"Ya know what I want," he said, his voice trembling. "Ya've known that since I was old enough to talk."

"It don't matter anyways." She coughed harder now.

"Mr. Beck?" a voice called out. The nurse at the door gestured for him to join her and he didn't seem pleased with the interruption.

Riley wasn't sure if she should follow him or not. Unable to make a decision, she remained rooted in place. He gave her a worried look from the door.

"Go on," Riley urged and Beck reluctantly followed the nurse down the hall.

Sadie issued a throaty chuckle. "Yer prettier than most of the ones he's been with."

"We're not dating. We trap demons together."

"I know. I read about ya in the paper."

If you can read, why didn't you teach your son?

"Then you know Beck saved some of the other trappers' lives."

The woman shrugged. "He's always played the hero. Never got him anywhere."

It was like suddenly discovering an alien species. Riley frowned, trying to wrap her mind around someone so callous, so self-centered that they couldn't see anything but themselves. It would be easy to believe that it was because of the illness, but the malice was so deep Riley felt that wasn't the case.

"I would think you would be proud of him," she said.

"Ah, ain't that pretty. Yer standin' up for him. Yer as stupid as I was. I believed everythin' guys told me and it was all lies. Ya'll learn soon enough."

"I've already learned that lesson," Riley replied. "Beck isn't that kind of guy."

"He's not told ya everythin'. He never will. He don't trust no one." Sadie's breathing grew labored. "Ask him about the time I dumped him in the swamp." The woman shook her head. "Only eight years old and I knew he was trouble even then."

"You left him..." Riley's fingers tightened on the bed frame. "How could you do that? He's your child."

"Because ya gotta cut 'em loose." She waved Riley off. "Now get the hell outta here and leave me die in peace."

Shocked, Riley hurried out of the room *It's the pain medication. Has to be.*

Riley found Beck at the nurses' station where he was giving them his contact information. He looked wiped, like the few minutes he'd spent in his mother's presence had drained him of his life force in some way. Riley felt the same way.

With a mumbled apology, she hurried past him and headed toward the front of the building, desperate to breathe fresh air. Maybe then she could sort out her impressions of the dying woman.

Beck caught up with her she as exited the building. "Riley? What happened?"

She kept walking. Sadie was just being mean, trying to psyche her out.

"What did she say?" Beck asked, catching her arm. He sounded panicky.

Riley turned to him, gazing up into the face of the man she thought she loved. What did she really know about him other than he'd grown up down here, been to the war, and came back a hero? That he didn't like commitment and he owned a rabbit. What else? He'd hidden so much of his past from her. From everyone. Was there a side to him that she hadn't seen yet, one that his mother knew so well?

"Riley?" he urged. "Talk to me."

She shook her head, trying to clear it of all the conflicting thoughts. "Your mother said she left you in the swamp, tried to get rid of you. Is that true, Beck? Did she do that?"

He lowered his eyes to the ground.

"Beck?"

He stepped back, his expression blank. "Just one of her crazy stories," he said.

He's lying. It was just like his mom had said. But why would he deny it?

As Riley waited for him to unlock the truck doors, some part of her was frozen inside. Sadie's poisonous words had wormed their way into her mind.

What if she's right and I really don't know the real Beck?

SIX

Beck took the side streets to Sadie's house, concerned about Riley's silence since they'd left the hospital. That was Sadie's trick, she'd get in your head and you'd find it hard to separate truth from lies. No matter what you said to the old lady, she sucked it up and spit it back at you as verbal acid. She was better at it than some of Lucifer's demons.

Why does she try to destroy everythin' good in my life?

He'd never hurt her. All he'd tried to do was to love her and she'd had none of it since the moment he'd been born.

As he pulled up to the curb in front of the homeplace, he felt his tension slowly uncoil. To him it was just a white house with faded black shutters that held few good memories. The shutters needed painting again, but he'd leave that to the new owner. It was small by most standards, dwarfed by the scraggly yard that surrounded it. An old well sat on one side of the house topped by warped boards and on the other side an aged magnolia tree dangled its massive branches onto the roof. There were no flowers or shrubs, nothing that indicated Sadie considered this her home.

Beck produced a key and opened the front door. The moment Riley stepped inside she began to cough. Now she knew why they weren't staying here: The lingering reek of cigarette smoke coated your throat with every breath.

"Better than it used to be. She quit smokin' over a year ago," he said.

As Riley inched farther into the front room, Beck tried to see it through her eyes: a worn couch, a matching chair, an end table. The floors were wood with an occasional throw rug and an old television sat on a stand in the corner. There were pictures on the wall, but they weren't of family.

This was Sadie's self-imposed exile. If she'd been decent to him, he'd have come to see her more often. Family meant everything to him.

Even when they hate you.

Beck glared at the couch. That damned plaid thing was still there, mocking him. He could remember Sadie sprawled on it during her many drunken stupors and most of the time she hadn't been alone. He made a mental note to burn the thing the moment she was gone.

He pulled his eyes away from it and scanned the rest of the room. Nothing much had changed though the ashtray was empty, full of candy wrappers now. Maybe if he'd cut off the money for the smokes sooner she wouldn't be dying.

When Sadie was younger and owned a car she'd spent her time at one of the bars in St. Marys or down in Florida. Sadlersville didn't have any watering holes, but that hadn't kept her from being a full-time alcoholic.

There was a deep frown on Riley's face now, telling him she didn't like what she was seeing. *Damn, girl, why didn't you stay in Atlanta?* He felt naked, like he'd stripped off all his clothes and she was seeing every one of his flaws.

"You lived here as a kid?" Her voice quavered.

"Yeah. My granddaddy bought the house for Sadie when she got pregnant with me. I think he hoped she'd settle down, get married. Stop drinkin'." He shook his head. "Just wishful thinkin'."

Riley paused to peer into the run-down kitchen and then moved into the hallway toward the two bedrooms. She halted at the second one.

"Was this your room?"

He nodded. At least when he was older and someone finally gave him a bed. When he was a kid he'd sleep on the bathroom floor, on top of the dirty clothes, because it was the warmest room in the house. But Riley didn't need to know that.

"I had a Chris Hemsworth poster too," she said, smiling in recognition. "He made a totally hot Norse god."

Beck mumbled his agreement. He'd left the poster behind when he'd gone up north. He could have taken it with him, but there hadn't been time to pack much. For some reason Sadie had never pulled it down.

"I thought he was kinda cool," Beck said. Maybe it was because the guy was strong, good looking, in control of his life—everything Beck had always wanted to be.

Riley returned to the kitchen, took off her jacket, and laid it across a chair. When she checked out the sink, she grimaced at what she found.

"Sorry," he said.

"Not your fault," she replied and turned on the water. "What are you going to do with the house once . . ."

"Sell it, I guess, once I get it cleaned out."

"I'll help you," she said, then began moving dirty dishes out of the sink onto the counter.

"Riley, I . . ."

She turned toward him, her hands dripping. "It's not that bad, Beck. A little messy, but not horrible. It's just so . . . sad, you know?"

He knew what she meant and it had little to do with dishes. The place had never been full of love like her family's house. Even after Riley's mom had died, her dad had made sure their tiny apartment was a home.

Beck had no idea what that was like. Once he knew Sadie didn't care about him, he'd made his own life, separate from hers. He never stepped away completely—he couldn't do that—but tried to insulate himself from her as much as possible. She always found ways to hurt him.

He scooped up a pile of mail off the couch, took it to the kitchen table, and spread it out. He'd like to think it was because that was the best place for the sorting job, but in truth it had something to do with being closer to Riley.

Beck laid his jacket over the top of hers and then pulled out a chair and sank into it. As she placed the clean dishes on a towel on the countertop, Riley hummed to herself. The song sounded like one of Carrie Underwood's tunes. He couldn't help but smile.

Out of habit he studied each envelope, hoping that one might be *the one*. He'd always dreamed of getting a letter from his father and when he was a kid he ran to the mailbox every day as soon as the mailman came by. He was never sure if Sadie would burn any message from that source, so he hadn't taken the chance.

That letter never came, at least not while he had lived in Sadlersville.

Beck silently cursed himself. He should have given up that fantasy years ago, but here he was, still scanning the envelopes like he had when he was a kid and could barely reach the mailbox.

Looking up he found that Riley was scrubbing the counters. She was attacking the task with a vengeance, probably her way of burning off her disgust at the woman in the hospital. By the time he'd finished with the mail he realized Sadie was overdue on a few of the bills, including the one for the phone. In fact, it'd been disconnected. Apparently the money he'd been sending her hadn't been going to the right places.

Another hassle.

Riley was washing one of the cupboard doors now, up on her tiptoes. For a second he forgot his problems and settled back to admire the view. She really was a fine girl. It was going to be the worst day of his life when she turned her back on him and walked away.

✢

An hour later the kitchen was tidy, except for the floor and the stove.

"Make sure I got these in the right piles, okay?" Beck said, pointing to the mail on the table.

Riley checked through them, her fingertips wrinkled from the water. The tattoos on her palms were stark in their simplicity—black against pale flesh. She saw him staring at them.

"You got them right," she said, handing over envelopes.

"Good. I've been payin' them for some time so I can usually recognize them."

"Why would you pay her bills?"

He blinked at the question. "Why not?"

"Because she hates you?" Riley ventured.

"Don't matter. She's family. Ya'd do the same."

Riley opened her mouth to argue and then shut it again. He was right—if her aunt Esther needed help, she would be there even though she couldn't stand the woman.

"I'll go back to the hospital tonight, check on her," Beck said. "She won't stand me bein' there too long, but at least I can see her for a time."

"Do you want me—"

"No. I'd rather you stay in the truck. Yer not used to her like I am."

"Okay." *At least for tonight.* Eventually she'd have to confront the woman again and she'd want to be ready for whatever came out of Sadie's mouth. Beck's mom had worked her over once. The next time it wasn't going down like that, even if the woman was terminally ill.

Riley yawned, then apologized.

"Yeah, let's call it a day," Beck said. "We'll start sortin' through the rest this stuff tomorrow."

"Does she know you're doin' this?"

"I'll tell her tonight. That's another reason I don't want you there. She's not gonna be happy with this."

⁜

As Beck walked toward the hospital's main entrance, Riley fired up her phone, pleased there was decent service. In fact, she had more bars than in some places in Atlanta.

"Hey, Riley, how is nowhere land?" Peter called out.

"Bizarre, but I had the best hamburger evah at lunch today."

"Really? So what's it like down there?"

"It's a tiny version of Atlanta with a lot more *y'alls*. What's weird is that everybody knows everybody and what they're doing. Not like at home. Oh, and most of the town doesn't like Beck because, well, they just don't."

"Sounds like a blast. So what are you two doing tonight?"

"Beck's visiting his mom right now. He'll be tired by the time he gets out of there. We'll probably find food and catch some TV."

"*Demonland* is on at eight. You don't want to miss that."

"There's so much wrong with that show I don't know where to start."

"Then don't," Peter said. "Leave my delusions intact, okay? So how are you and Beck doing?"

"One minute he seems pleased I'm here and then the next he's being an asshat. I'm cutting him some slack because of his mom—who is a real piece of work, by the way—but one of these times I'm going to go medieval on him."

Peter's chuckle echoed down the phone. "Well, you're missing some epic weirdness up here. Some reverend has announced he's going to exorcise *every single demon* in Atlanta, all at the same time. Can you believe that?"

"I saw that in the paper. All he's going to do is piss them off and guess who will have to clean up that mess?" *Me and the other trappers.*

A figure emerged from the hospital entrance moving at a brisk pace.

"Ah, here comes Beck. He's not looking good. I'd better go."

"Hang in there, Riley. Call when you need to vent. Or if you need bail."

She laughed. "I will. Talk to you later."

Beck climbed into the truck, slammed the door, and jammed the keys into the ignition. Then he banged his fist against the wheel. Once, twice, three times.

Riley held her breath.

"Why do I even bother with her?" he growled.

"Want to talk about it?"

"Hell, no."

⁜

Once back at the motel, Riley followed him into his room, hoping that he might want to talk if given the opportunity. Beck dropped his backpack on the first bed and began stripping off his clothes like he'd forgotten she was there. Right before his jeans came off, she cleared her throat and that pulled him up short. He retrieved clean clothes out of the bureau drawer and headed for the bathroom. The door shut, then the shower came on.

Realizing that a heartfelt conversation wasn't on the menu, Riley retreated to her room. She needed a shower as well. It was as if some thick choking tar had coated her skin since she'd met his mother and the house hadn't helped either.

What would it be like to live with her? It was a sure bet that nothing anyone did would meet with Sadie's approval. Maybe that was what had sparked her father's interest—the fact the young man had never had a chance. Now her dad had left Beck in her care, though Backwoods Boy thought it was the other way around.

I promise, Dad, I won't let him fail, no matter what.

To her relief, the shower had pretty decent water pressure. After she'd dressed, she sat on her bed and toweled her hair dry.

Beck peered in at her. "We can go for pizza if you want." He was back to using proper English so he *was* feeling better.

"That works. I'm really hungry."

"I'll order it ahead so it's waitin' for us. Anythin' you hate?"

"Green peppers," she said. "They're totally vile."

He dug on the nightstand for the card with the local pizza place's number and punched it into his cell phone. Then hung up. To her surprise he brought the information to her.

"Better if you order it," he said. "Make it *to go* with yer name on the order."

She wanted to ask why, but his expression did not invite questions. Using her own phone she called the restaurant and put in the order, along with a request for a six-pack of soda.

"Thanks," he said, then stepped outside to make a call, as if he didn't want her to hear what he said. It was another *I don't entirely trust you* moment and her patience was wearing thin.

"You are so jonesing for it, dude," she muttered.

⁜

Riley should have seen it coming: Beck gave her the money and sent her in to get the order. After settling the bill, she gathered up the pizza and the plastic bag that held the soda. As the restaurant's owner pushed open the door to help her out of the store, he spied Beck's truck.

"Hell, if I had known it was for that bastard I'd have never taken the order."

She glared up at him. "Why?"

"Ask him. Maybe he'll tell you where they are."

"They who?" The door banged shut behind her.

Why won't anyone say what's going on?

SEVEN

Riley shifted the hot pizza box on her lap. The smell was driving her crazy. Maybe after they ate she could quiz Beck about what the pizza guy had meant.

"Where are we going?" she asked.

"Somewhere near the swamp."

Exactly where Cole had told her not to go with Backwoods Boy. *Paranoid much?*

He didn't choose a picnic spot, but a road out in the middle of nowhere. If this hadn't been Beck she'd have been way nervous.

"Where are we?"

"We're south of town on one of the roads near the federal park land. Okefenokee's over that way," he said, pointing west toward the setting sun.

"Why here?" she said, unbuckling her seat belt.

"Because it's not *in* town," he said. "I've had enough of people starin' at me for one day."

Riley could relate. She opened the door and peered down at white sand. That was different. Trusting he knew what he was doing, she waited for him to pull a blanket from behind the seat and then followed him to the back of the truck. There he fixed up a little place for them to eat on the tailgate.

"Sort of like a picnic," she said, trying to make the most of it.

"Yeah," he replied, but she could tell his heart wasn't in it.

Riley crawled up on the gate and then eagerly opened the box. Her mouth watered instantly. She scooped up a couple of napkins and a thick slice of pizza. Beck did the same.

While she chewed, Riley checked out the scenery around them. Tall pine trees stood in the distance and in all directions were these strange plants with spiky leaves. They were about three or four feet off the ground, curiously uniform in height.

"What are those?" she asked, pointing with her free hand. "They look like baby palm trees or something."

"They're saw palmetto. They're all over this part of the country."

"Why are they all the same size?"

"Must have had a fire, burnt them all down. Now they're growin' back." A half smile filled his face. "When I was eleven Donovan took me out to the swamp. He said it was high time I learned how to survive on my own since it was clear even to a blind man Sadie wasn't goin' to take care of me."

"So what did you guys do?"

"We'd take off for a weekend and camp, just the two of us. He taught me how to not gettin' eaten by the gators, how to catch a snake, skin it, and cook it. Taught me all sorts of stuff. I really liked spendin' time with him. He didn't judge me like everyone else."

"That's cool."

"Oh, and I won a fishing contest once. I caught a bowfin, a real big one. Donovan took a picture of it. I got thirty dollars' prize money."

"What did you spend it on?"

"Boots. A real nice pair. Never had any decent ones like that before."

"So there was some good in your life." Most of it seemed to be connected with the sheriff. *So why are you two thumping heads now?*

"Doesn't balance out the bad, though."

Riley heard skittering in the brush to her right. "Are there . . . any alligators around here?"

"Might be, though they'd rather be closer to the water." Beck grinned. "Yer such a city girl."

"Sure am," she retorted, defiant. "I like buildings and pavement. I like stuff that I can understand. This"—she did a sweep of her hand—"is pretty, but I feel out of place here."

"I like the country," he said, softer now. "It's quiet and I can think. The city jams up my mind sometimes."

She popped open a can of soda and took a long drink. "So now that your mind is unjammed, tell me about Cole."

Instant frown. "Why do you want to know about him?"

Riley couldn't resist. "Because he's totally hot and I want to run off with him and have his babies."

Beck's eyes widened in surprise. "Riley—"

"Look at you!" she said, playfully slapping his arm. "You're easy to set off."

The frown didn't retreat, but she could tell she'd made her point.

"You don't know him like I do," he replied.

"Well, now is the time to fix that. Tell me why you can't stand him."

He huffed. "When I was in school I dated a girl named Louisa. Lou and I were real tight. Cole made sure to break us up. He dated her for a few weeks then dumped her, his way of sayin' he could steal away any girl I cared for."

"Okay, so Cole is a total scumbag. I can go there. But that's a long time ago, Beck. You're still carrying a grudge?"

"Yeah, I am," he admitted. "Lou was special and she was the only good thing in my life at that point. Now he's eyein' you and I don't like that one bit."

Yup, he's jealous. "Did you have any other girlfriends?"

"Why do you wanna know?"

"Because I'd like to get to know you better?"

He launched off the back of the truck and walked a few paces down the road. "Why the hell do ya do this to me?" he demanded.

"What?" Riley asked, startled.

"Ya can't be part of my life. When are ya gonna understand that?"

She slammed down the soda can and hopped off the truck gate. This moment had been brewing for a long time and when it was over, he'd either accept she was on his side or she was out of here.

"You're the one who keeps moaning about how nobody will give you a break because you're some hick loser. Just let someone actually *care* about you and you can't handle it."

"Ya have no idea how bad it can get down here," he said, shaking his head.

"Really?" she said, advancing on him. "As bad as having two dead parents or dealing with the Vatican and their Inquisition Lite? How about that whole Armageddon thing? Just how bad is this going to be, Beck? Let me know the worst."

His mouth had dropped open. "Ya don't understand," he sputtered.

She took a deep breath, trying to calm her boiling emotions. "Then tell me the truth. I want to know why everyone hates you and why I had to order the pizza. I want to know why Cole warned me not to go into the swamp with you."

"Just let it go."

"Tell me, Beck! What is this black secret that Justine's uncovered? Did you get some girl pregnant? Or run someone over with your truck when you were drunk? What is it that has you so worried?"

Beck was silent. Around them birds began to nest in the trees as the sun set.

"It's all about trust," she said, quieter now. "I shared my darkest secret with you. Now it's time for you to do the same."

He looked away, both fists clenched.

Come on. Let it out. You want to, I can feel it.

Beck's fists unclenched as his face took on a haunted expression.

"They all think I . . . killed . . . two boys in the swamp. That I hid their bodies so they'd never be found."

Oh, God. That, she hadn't expected.

To buy time Riley retreated to the truck, her stomach churning. Could Beck have killed them? *No.* At least not the man she knew today. What about a young Beck? He'd said he was a hothead and he'd tried to carve up Mr. Walker with a knife. *Could he have . . .*

"When was this?" she asked, leaning against the tailgate to try to calm her suddenly jittery legs.

"Seven years ago, right after Christmas."

Riley held her breath, waiting for the rest.

"It was the Keneally brothers, Nate and Brad. Nate was older than us by a year or so and he was pretty wild. He'd gotten some whiskey and dope and asked me to come with them to the swamp so we could party."

"Isn't that kind of . . . dumb? The swamp is a dangerous place."

"Yeah, it was big-time dumb, but not many of the kids would talk to me because of Sadie, so I thought it was cool they'd asked me along."

"You were what . . ." She did the math. "Fifteen?"

He nodded. "We took their daddy's boat out and found a place to set up camp. Then we got totally wasted. I didn't touch the drugs—never liked that stuff." He hesitated.

"Don't stop now. I want to know all of it."

Beck nervously cleared his throat. "It was goin' okay. Nate was braggin' how he'd scored somethin' that would keep him in money for the rest of his life. Then they started raggin' on me about Sadie and sayin' stuff about Lou I didn't like. So I told them to—well, ya know—and I went back to the boat." He rubbed his chin in thought. "It was nearin' dark and I was *so* sick. After I stopped puking, I climbed in the boat, pulled a tarp over the top of me, and passed out."

Beck returned to the truck and sat on the tailgate. After a drink of soda, he began to talk again, like he was desperate to tell the story now that the floodgates were open.

"Come mornin' the boat was driftin' in the canal. I thought that was odd, but sometimes they come untied. It took some time to get it back to where we'd landed and then I went to find the guys. I was still feelin' like crap and I was hopin' they'd be ready to go home."

"But you didn't find them."

"No. All their stuff was there at the campsite, but Nate's gun was gone so I figured they'd decided to do some poachin'. I tramped around for over three hours, callin' their names. No sign of them."

"Do you think an alligator might have got them?" Riley shuddered at the thought.

"Maybe, but it'd only take one of them. Besides, Nate could have shot it. Same with a bear or anythin' like that."

"What about a demon?" she asked.

"Possible. There are some really nasty ones out there if yer on yer own. Anyways, I took the boat back to the dock and then hot-wired Nate's truck and went to the sheriff's office. They searched for five days, but they never found either of them."

Now she knew why the folks in Sadlersville hated Denver Beck. They thought he was a double murderer.

"Go on, ask the question," he said, challenging her. "Everybody does."

"I am not going there," she said firmly.

"Ya won't ask? Then I will." He straightened up, tormented by vicious memories. "Did ya kill those boys, Denny Beck? What did ya do with those bodies? Was it some kind of Say-tanic ritual or a weird cannibal thing?"

My God.

"If it wasn't an animal," she said, intentionally keeping her voice calm so as not to feed into his anger, "it had to be a person. Who do you think did it?"

"Why not me?" he retorted, glaring at her as if she was making the accusation. "I could have killed them both, easy."

Riley shook her head. "Not your style. If you'd been really pissed off you might have beaten them up, but you would not have murdered them."

"Maybe I accidentally killed one of them and then had to take out the other because he was a witness," he argued.

Beck was only parroting back what had been said to him over the years.

"You would have loaded up the body and brought him and his brother back to the sheriff. Even at fifteen, you would have taken whatever punishment you deserved. You would not have left those boys' parents never knowing what happened to their sons."

He began to protest, but she cut him off.

"Whoever did that was stone cold, Beck, and that's not you."

He huffed. "Depends on who ya talk to."

A thought popped into her mind that was absolutely treasonous. "I really hate to say this, but Justine might be doing you a favor."

"What? How do ya think that?" he said, irate.

"She's got people talking about the missing boys. I know that's not what you wanted, but you should push it now, insist the sheriff reopen the case and find out what really happened."

"Ah, hell, yer crazy," Beck replied, shaking his head vehemently as he jumped off the back of the truck again and walked a few feet away. "They could charge me with murder."

"Seven years later?"

"Doesn't matter. I'd be in prison for life ... or facin' execution," he replied, his back to her now. It was as if he was trying to shield himself from the truth.

"Convict you based on what evidence?" she said. "They don't have any or you'd be in jail right now."

"I don't care. Let them think I'm a killer. It doesn't matter."

Yes, it does. This is what's been holding you back all these years.

This was the point in Beck's life where everything could change for the better. If he continued to run from his past, he would have no future.

Riley prepared herself for what was to come. This was going to hurt both of them.

"You're going to be just like your mother someday, you know? I can see it already."

Beck swung around, infuriated. "Don't ya dare say that!"

"No? You told me she took everything good and twisted it until it was dark. Well, you're doing the same thing. You have people who care for you and you push them away, because you don't want anyone to get too close. You're afraid to ask for help because you're convinced everyone is your enemy."

His eyes blazed. "Careful, girl. Yer goin' too damned far, even for Paul's daughter."

He had to hear it all. "You're setting yourself up to fail. If Justine's article keeps you from becoming a master, you'll claim the world is out to get you. You'll hate everything and everybody." Riley shook so hard it was difficult to form the words. "Then it'll be easy to drink it all away because nobody ever thought Sadie Beck's bastard was worth a damn. You'll be proving them right."

She hammered home the last nail. "You'll die just like her—old and bitter and lonely."

Beck shook as well, but she didn't think it was in fury. It was time to stop using words as weapons. Riley slowly approached him, unsure if what she was about to do was wise.

She carefully laid her hand on his heaving chest. "Inside here is the heart of a good man, an honest man. A hero," she said in a hushed voice. "He'll rush into the flames, risk death to save others." She looked up into tortured eyes. "Isn't it time he saved himself?"

Beck sucked in a breath like she'd socked him in the gut.

"God, ya go for the throat, don't ya?" He looked over her head into the distance. "Ya think this so-called hero is worth savin'?"

"Of course he is," she said, giving him a tentative smile. "But he has to be the one to demand the truth, no matter the risk. He has to *believe* he's worth saving."

"I don't know where to start," he admitted.

Riley reluctantly moved her hand. She had liked feeling his heart beating under her palm.

Her practical side took hold. "Someone knows what happened. Come on, these people can tell you how many pieces of toast their neighbors had for breakfast. Someone saw something. We need to kick over the rocks and see what crawls out."

"If someone did kill them, this could get bad," Beck said.

"I know, but you have a chance to make it right. You have a chance to make sure those boys' parents know the truth."

Beck lowered his eyes, but didn't reply.

"Look, if you really don't want to do this, I'll back off. I'll pack up my stuff and go home tomorrow. It's your decision. It always has been."

"I . . . ah hell," he said, jabbing the toe of his boot into the sand. Another one of his defensive walls cracked and collapsed with a low rumble. "I really want ya here with me."

Beck's eyes rose to meet hers. "But I'm afraid, Riley. Yeah, ya heard me right. I'm scared of what's comin' down, because somethin' is. I can feel it in my bones. I don't want ya hurt."

"Whatever is coming, we'll face it together. We've done that before and we'll do it again."

A half smile formed on his face. "Yer fierce, like yer momma. Paul said he knew he could survive anythin' as long as she was walkin' beside him."

"I'm not my mom," Riley said, wistful. "I wish I was, but I'll do what I can to help you."

"Oh, God . . . Okay, then, we go for broke. All or nothin'."

"That's the Beck I know," she said, smiling.

He frowned and stomped one of his feet. "Damn, I got sand in my boots. I hate that."

It broke the tense moment and so she kicked more sand at him.

"Hey, stop that!" he said, kicking a cloud back at her. Then they paused and studied each other.

"Ya might regret stayin' down here with me," he said soberly.

"I might. But if I was in Atlanta, I'd be worrying about you every minute until you came home."

"Ya . . . you care that much about me?"

"More."

"I have no idea why," he said, quieter now.

"Makes two of us," she replied, "but that's the way it is."

He seemed comfortable with that explanation.

As they walked back to the truck Riley felt her tension ebb away. Her outburst could have backfired badly, but instead it seemed that was what it had taken to reach him.

As twilight deepened around them, Beck ate a slice of pizza in silence, no doubt working through what she'd said. Then he wiped his hands on a napkin.

"There was another girl I was in love with. We met in the Army. Her name was Caitlin."

He'd mentioned her once before. "The one who didn't sound like a Southerner."

"Yeah. Caitie was real sweet." He looked at Riley now. "We fell for each other so quick. I even asked her to marry me, but it didn't last." He shook his head. "She decided I wasn't the right guy for her."

Riley had never known he'd been that serious about a girl.

"Why not? What's wrong with you?" she asked, indignant. "You don't snore in your sleep. At least not much."

"Nothin' like that. I brought her down here to meet Sadie and that was it. Whatever the old lady said, Caitie walked away. She'd never did tell me why."

Riley had a good idea of exactly what had happened: Sadie had run the same game on her son's fiancée as she'd tried on Riley. It'd worked in Caitlin's case.

"Were you serious about anyone else?" It seemed important to know how many times he'd given away his heart.

Beck shook his head. "It was easier to hook up when I felt the need. That way, well . . ."

"You didn't get hurt," she said.

He studied her more intently now. "You know how that goes, don't you?"

"The endless hooking up part? No." That wasn't her style. "The getting hurt part?"

All too well.

⬩⬩⬩

As Beck drove through the increasing darkness, his mind kept circling around all that Riley had said. She'd infuriated him, gotten in his face, but no matter how much he wanted to deny it, she'd spoken the truth. If he really didn't care about his future, why was he trying to learn how to read and write, work so hard to build a new life?

The sheriff would help him clear his name: Donovan had never slept easy after those boys had disappeared. Riley was good at ferreting out secrets people wanted to keep hidden. He'd seen that when she'd cracked the Holy Water scam. He had two strong people in his corner, folks who believed in him. Maybe it was time to find out what really happened to Brad and Nate; then maybe he'd sleep easier at night as well.

What if we can't figure it out? What if the truth remained hidden and the National Guild used that to deny him from getting his master's license?

He felt a surge of defiance. If the Guild screwed him over, he'd go freelance. It wasn't as honorable as working in the Guild, but he had to make a living. Maybe Riley would join him and they could trap together.

He shot a quick glance over at her and then back to the road. He wasn't quite sure how to handle a girl—he corrected himself—a young woman who believed in him so completely. But first there was Sadie to deal with, then he'd try to right an old wrong, both for his sake and for the missing boys.

EIGHT

After Riley changed into her bedclothes—she'd gone for the T-shirt and shorts look since she wasn't going to let Beck see her panda pajamas—she found her guy in his own bed, under the covers, a book in his lap. It was the same one she'd seen in his house the night he'd been hurt in Demon Central. By the bookmark's location he hadn't made much progress.

Too busy fighting the bad guys.

Beck painstakingly mouthed every word, one finger tracing along as he read. Every now and then he'd pause and consult the sheet of paper her father had given him, the one with the definitions. Then he'd go back to reading. When he realized she was watching, he thumped the book closed, embarrassed.

"Go on," she said. "It's a good book."

"How do you know?" he asked, instantly defensive.

"I saw it in your bedroom that night I stayed at your place. Dad was helping you with it, wasn't he?"

Beck's wariness vanished at the mention of her father.

"Yeah. He'd tell me the words that I didn't understand, write them out for me. Then he'd have me copy them over and over until I could spell them right."

"That's how I learned," she said, sitting on the edge of the bed.

"Yer smarter than me."

"I'd argue that." She pointed at the book. "Anything I can help you with?"

For half a second she thought he'd say no to cover his ego, but instead he nodded. "There are some words I just don't get."

Riley took the book from him and checked her dad's list against the page Beck was reading.

"Twining?" He nodded. "That means twisting something together, like thread or pieces of rope."

"Twi . . . ning. Okay. I got that."

She went through five more words, ensuring he understood them. If he didn't, he asked more questions.

"I think I got them," he said. "This book's a lot harder than the ones I usually read. It's takin' forever."

"But you're getting through it," she said.

"I suppose. I don't think I'll ever read like most folks."

"At least you're trying. That's what counts."

He didn't go back to the story, but stared off at nothing, the book forgotten in his hands.

"Beck?"

"Hmm?"

"Did your mother leave you in the swamp? I need to know the truth."

So I know if she's a liar or truly evil.

He sagged against the headboard, then rubbed his eyes. "Once I start down this road, Riley, there is no stoppin'. There's so much."

"I can handle it," she urged. "Talk to me, Beck. This is eating at you like the cancer is your mom."

He looked up at her. "Never thought of it like that." Beck placed the book on the nightstand, his jaw set. "I was eight. She'd been drinkin' and we had one helluva fight. It was the first time I stood up to her." He sighed. "I called her a . . . whore because I caught her with some guy she'd brought home from a bar. She'd said she'd stop doin' that and there she was with the bastard on the couch and they were . . ." He shook his head at the thought. "Well, you get the picture."

Riley bit her lip.

"I kept thinkin' my daddy would come back to us someday and if he saw her like that . . ."

He'd leave again.

"The next afternoon, right after school, she has me get in the car and we went for a long drive. I had no idea where we were headed. When I asked she said it was a test to see if I could be trusted."

Riley struggled to hide the whole-body shiver that shot through her.

"Sadie drove over to the west side of Okefenokee, to the state park and then into the swamp. She seemed to know where she was going, so I didn't say anything. I thought this might be somethin' fun for a change, it bein' Friday afternoon and all."

Riley could just imagine what it'd been like for him, out for a ride with his mom. He'd have been so excited, especially after such a big fight. He'd have thought things were getting better between them.

"Sadie parked the car and then we started walkin'. I don't know how far we went, but it wasn't easy. We kept goin' deeper into the swamp. After a while I got scared, but she kept urgin' me on. Then she stopped."

He fumbled with the sheets.

"I still remember the look on her face. It was so . . . cruel." He cleared his throat. " 'Stay here, Denver,' " she said. " 'If ya stay right here and ya don't cry, I'll tell ya the name of yer daddy.' "

Riley's mouth dropped open. "And you believed her?"

"Hell, yes," Beck snapped. "I was a kid. All I wanted was for her to love me and if that meant staying out there, I'd do it."

"Oh my God," Riley said, her blood running cold. Sadie had used the one lure that her son would never resist. The woman *was* evil.

Beck's hands were clenched on either side of him now. When he realized it, he forced himself to let them fall slack on the covers.

"Sadie said she was teachin' me how to take care of myself because no one else would."

"How long were you . . ." Riley barely choked out.

"Two days and three nights. By the second mornin' I knew she wasn't comin' back for me, so I set off on my own. It was right before sunset when the park ranger found me."

"How did he know where to look?"

"He didn't, but by then Donovan knew I was missin' so they'd put out an alert." Beck ran his hand over the sheet again, smoothing out the wrinkles.

"Why the hell isn't she in jail?" Riley demanded. When he didn't reply, the truth hit her. "You didn't tell them what really happened, did you?"

Beck shook his head. "I said I ran away. Donovan knew better, but he didn't have any proof. They couldn't charge Sadie for anythin'."

"But she left you to die!" she protested, outraged that this horror had been allowed to stand.

"I know," he said, his voice trembling. "When you want someone to love you, you'll do anythin'. Even lie for them."

Then she never told you about your father. What a cold-hearted bitch.

Now Riley understood that profoundly sad expression in his eyes. He'd been betrayed by the one person who should have always been there for him.

As if exhausted by the confession, Beck shut off the reading light and curled up with his back to her. That's what she would have done if she didn't want him to know she was crying. He might be nearly twenty-three years old, been to a war and back, but he was still that little boy in the swamp. He would always crave acceptance from the one woman who would never give a damn.

"Beck?"

"Yeah?" he said, his voice muffled.

"Sadie hates you because you were better than her from the moment you were born."

He rolled over, a sheen in his eyes. "You really mean that?"

"Yes. And I'll trash anyone who says different," she said defiantly, her fists clenched.

"You might have to back up those words if we stay in this town much longer."

"Then let's do what we have to and go home," she said.

With a murmured "Yeah," he rolled over again, crawling back into his shell.

She looked down at him, all rumpled in the bed, his hair askew. He was so lost she really wanted to hug him and never let go. Every time he let down more of his defenses she discovered his hopes, dreams, his hidden pain. Every revelation made her love him that much more.

Riley left the doors between their rooms open, more for him than her. She never wanted Beck to think that she didn't trust him, especially not now.

As she curled up her own bed, tears formed in her eyes. Some were for her parents and the gaping hole their deaths left inside her. Most were for a little towheaded boy who'd nearly died trying to prove he was worthy of his mother's love.

Riley woke to the sound of someone talking, murmuring over and over. The murmuring grew louder, then Beck cried out in terror. She swung her feet out of her bed and hurried into his room.

"Beck?"

He was bolt upright in the bed, his whole body shaking, breath labored. Beads of sweat glistened on his forehead.

Nightmare. She knew how those went.

Riley sank on the bed next to him and waited until he was more awake.

"Bad?" she asked quietly. A nod. "Trapping?" He shook his head. "The war?"

"Yeah. It's always the same one."

"Want to talk about it?"

He shook his head again. "Maybe someday."

Without hesitation, Riley wrapped her arms around him and hugged him. After a time, when she started to let go, he wouldn't let her. This wasn't just about the nightmare. He was defenseless down here, and he was scared, like he'd said.

Riley wasn't sure she knew how to dispel the darkness, but she'd do the best she could, just by being there. She made him lay back down, then curled around his back, hugging him tightly and remaining there until he fell into a deep sleep.

⁙

Morning brought noises: the sound of a shower running, then the buzz of an electric razor. Riley finally blinked open her eyes. Through the connecting door she spied Beck standing in front of a full-length wall mirror, clad only in a pair of tight black briefs as he addressed the stubble on his face. If he was worried about her seeing him in his underwear he would have shut the door.

Riley sighed in appreciation as she scoped out the scenery, running her eyes from the top of his head all the way to his calves and then slowly back up again. Her attention hung on the long jagged surgical scar on his left hip. It didn't look like a demon wound.

Probably from the war. Her eyes edged upward. Backwoods Boy had one of the finest butts she'd ever seen and his chest and shoulders were sculpted with just the right amount of muscle. He was definitely worth the scrutiny.

Then her eyes met his in the mirror.

"Like what yer seein'?" he called out, grinning.

Busted. "I'd like it better if it had clothes on," she said, then pulled the covers over her head so he wouldn't see her blush.

"You lie," he replied and then laughed.

There was the sound of a drawer opening, then the slide of clothes on flesh. A short time later the bottom of her bed indented. She peeked out to find him sitting on the edge, pulling on his thick socks.

"What time is it?" she mumbled.

"A little after seven." He put on a boot and expertly laced it up. "Pretty late by my way of thinkin'." The second boot went on and he double knotted it like the first. "How about I find us somethin' to eat while yer gettin' ready?"

"That works." *Come back in a couple hours . . .*

"Would a breakfast sandwich work for you? How's about some orange juice?"

It was obscenely early to be talking about food. "Whatever."

"Coffee?"

"Tea. Hot."

"Won't be gone long so don't go back to sleep, you hear?"

Riley mumbled a swear word under her breath. Even her dad had understood it took her a while to get going in the morning. The door to her room closed and a few seconds later Beck's truck roared to life, headed toward some fast-food place. She rolled over, savoring the peace and quiet. Riley was just drifting back to sleep when her cell phone rang. Plucking it off the nightstand, she didn't bother to check the display.

"Hello?" she growled.

"You want hash browns too?" Beck asked, amusement in his voice. He'd done this on purpose. "Riley? I didn't wake you, did I?" Then he laughed again.

Jerk.

Riley turned off the phone and dropped it on the nightstand. "All right!" she snarled. "You win! I'm up!"

As she hauled herself to the shower she knew one thing for certain: If Beck had a nightmare tonight and expected her to be sympathetic, he was seriously out of luck.

✛

Bent over a book, it took Stewart a moment to realize he was not alone. He glanced up and his eyes locked on the figure in the library doorway.

The Fallen angel that had seduced Paul's daughter studied him soberly.

"Yer alive, then," Stewart said, shutting the book. "Why have ya dared ta enter the house of a grand master without his permission?"

In lieu of a reply, Ori tossed him one of Stewart's own swords. The master caught it one-handed and rose in a swift motion, despite his damaged leg.

"If yer thinkin' about tryin' ta kill me, it'll not be in this room. I'll nay have yer blue blood soakin' into my fine books."

"I'm not here for you, Angus Niall Stewart."

"Why the blade, then?"

"I thought it might comfort you in my presence."

Stewart snorted in derision. "God, yer as arrogant as yer master." He gestured. "If yer not here to fight, have a seat, angel."

Ori pulled out a chair and sat across from the master. He looked much the same as he had in the cemetery, but there was something subtly different now. The dark eyes seemed colder, more feral. *Haunted.*

"Does yer boss know yer makin' a social call?" Stewart asked as he placed the blade on the table between them.

No reply.

"Look, yer on borrowed time here. I'm not takin' kindly ta havin' ya in my house, so ya'd best start talkin' or I will be needin' this sword."

"So much for that famed Scottish hospitality," Ori replied. "Hell is in turmoil. Sartael remains in chains, but his supporters have not given up."

"And?"

"It is only a matter of time before those supporters free their master."

"While the Prince has his back turned? That I doubt. If Sartael is freed, it is because Lucifer wishes it so."

"The Prince is losing control. There are those who wish a . . . change. There are some that believe I should take my master's place."

"Really?" Stewart replied. "Looks as if I *will* have ta kill ya today."

"You can try," the angel replied evenly.

"Since we're layin' it all out here, do ya hold Riley Blackthorne's soul?"

"Yes. I accepted it during the battle at the cemetery. The fact I have not offered it to Lucifer is part of the disagreement he has with me."

That caught Stewart off guard. "Why haven't ya done so? It's customary."

"Riley set her own terms: Her soul is mine, but I am not permitted to give it to anyone else, including the Prince. If I die before her, she will be free of Hell's debt." At the master's puzzled expression, he added, "I swore on the Light. I cannot break that vow."

Stewart leaned back in his chair, thoughtful. "Well, no wonder yer havin' problems with yer boss. But this isn't all of it." He frowned. "Something else has happened."

Ori's expression darkened. "I sought death and it was not granted to me. I am Divine and yet I am treated no better than one of his unholy demons."

"I see. Ya still have not told me why yer here."

"Because I execute those who are traitors to Lucifer, any mortal's soul I have taken is in peril. The demons will seek to destroy that person to gain revenge against me. In the past, I immediately gifted any soul I owned to my master to spare the mortal's life because the demons were less likely to harm them if Lucifer was involved."

"But not with Riley's soul."

"Indeed. When she made her bargain, I saw a way out. I would die and she would be freed. Since I am still alive and the terms of our agreement do not allow me to give her soul to anyone, she is in great danger."

Stewart stroked his chin. "If I didn't know better, I'd swear I was talkin' ta one of Heaven's crew rather than a Fallen. Yer kind is not known for keepin' yer word."

"I do keep my vows," Ori replied hotly. "That is why Riley must . . ." He sighed. "To stay alive, she will need to sacrifice even more than her soul. She must dedicate her life to survival, learn how to destroy my enemies when they come for her."

"I could just kill ya. That would free her."

"Even if you could, she would still be in danger. She has to know how to fight Lucifer's foes. I'm the one to teach her."

"So that's the real reason yer here." Stewart sighed. "When would this trainin' begin?"

Ori closed his eyes, as if trying to discern the thread of Riley's life. "Once she's finished with the trapper. Providing she is still alive."

NINE

"Furniture shop and funeral home?" Riley asked, peering up at the worn sign above the old brick building. "So you can pick out a casket and a new sofa at the same time?"

"Don't judge us by yer big city ways," Beck said, displeased. "Down here folks have to do more than one thing to get by."

"I'm not judging anyone, Beck. I'm trying to understand it. You have to admit it's a bizarre combination."

"It's not that uncommon. A couple centuries ago the guy who made furniture also made the coffins."

"How do you know that?" she asked, puzzled.

"Saw it on some TV show."

Riley followed him into the building and found it was like any other furniture store with a decent selection of sofas, chairs, tables, and even a few big-screen televisions. All the kinds of furnishings you'd find in Atlanta, only in a smaller space.

The owner, a middle-aged guy with heavy jowls, watched them approach.

"Denny. I heard you were back in town."

Riley issued a silent groan. *If one more person says that I'm going to scream.*

"Hey, Bert. How's things goin'?"

"Been okay. Who's this young lady?"

Beck gestured at her. "This is Riley Blackthorne. She's helpin' me with Sadie."

"Bert McGovern," the man said, offering her a hand. She shook it, not knowing what else to do. The moment she touched him, an odd feeling came to her. Probably because he was an undertaker.

McGovern turned his attention back to Beck. "What can I do for you?"

"I need to get some funeral plans squared away."

"I understand. I lost my mother last year. It's hard," the man said, nodding in sympathy. "Are you thinking about internment or cremation?"

"Burial. She has a plot in the cemetery."

"Okay, then come on back and I'll show you what I have. I've got both plain and fancy coffins, depending on what you think she'd like."

"Plain," Beck said. "We trappers don't get paid that much."

Riley followed the guys through the floor displays into a room with somber beige walls and a highly polished wood floor. Seven coffins were carefully arranged in a neat row, lids open, their shiny white linings looking like the inside of a cocoon. She took one step into the room and then her knees locked up, refusing to move her forward. Vivid memories of her father's funeral filled her mind though she desperately tried to halt them, followed by images of his busted coffin after he'd been stolen from his grave.

Beck had been right—maybe it was too soon for her to face this. She'd pushed a lot of the grief aside to keep going and now it threatened to engulf her.

Her eyes met his and he knew what was happening without her saying a word.

"I'll be done in a little bit if you want to wait outside," he said softly.

Riley gave him a nod of gratitude and hastily retreated. Then she immediately felt bad: She was supposed to be here to support *him*, not the other way around.

She picked a chair near the front window so she could watch the townsfolk as they passed by, anything to keep her mind off the industry of death. A few of the locals gave Beck's truck the once-over, talking among themselves after pointing at the vehicle. She could pretty much imagine the conversation, all beginning with, "I heard Denny Beck is back in town."

Beck and the store owner were finished in about five minutes. Apparently it was going to be a really simple funeral.

"Have the hospital call when it's time," McGovern said. "Don't worry, we'll give her a good send-off."

"That's all I ask," Beck replied.

⊹

Beck fell into one of his funks after his visit to the funeral home. Instead of pressuring him to talk, Riley followed him around a dinky grocery store buying cleaning supplies. As she bent over to inspect a bag of sponges a twitch crept across her shoulders. Then a small voice whispered, "Blackthorne's daughter."

Gazing upward she found two red eyes peering at her from around the handle of a floor mop. It was a Klepto-Fiend, one of Hell's little cat burglars, but not the one that lived in her apartment.

"Hi there, demon," she muttered. As she moved down the aisle she swore the thing was following her. Probably one of Lucifer's hench-fiends keeping an eye on her for its Big Boss.

As she picked up a bottle of drain cleaner she heard Beck's voice, low and tense. When someone responded she knew why. *Cole.* She didn't think he was the kind to hang around a grocery store, which meant he'd tracked them down on purpose.

"Yer a total sleaze, Hadley."

"Why are you being a jerk?" Cole asked. "You can't still be pissed about Lou. Get over it, man. That was years ago."

"Not to me."

"That's your problem. What's the score with the cute chick? She's a little young for you, isn't she?"

Riley shook her head in dismay. What was it about testosterone that made guys so stupid? Cole was purposely goading Beck, like some kid who'd found the world's largest hornet's nest. He couldn't resist poking it with a stick to see what he could stir up. It was time to shut this down before it got ugly and someone (Beck) landed in jail for assault.

Riley walked around the corner as if she hadn't been listening in.

"I got some window cleaner and paper towels." She looked over at the other guy. "Cole," she said, then walked past him. Maybe if she acted disinterested he'd take his stick and play somewhere else.

"How about you and me go for some ice cream, Riley?" he called out.

In February? "No, thanks. Got too much work to do," she said, and kept walking.

Beck said something under his breath and then joined her.

After they'd paid for their supplies and loaded the truck, Cole watched their every move from the sidewalk.

"He's strange," Riley said under his breath.

"He's more than that," Beck replied, slamming the truck gate and locking the topper. "He's big trouble."

✦

When Beck dialed the hospital to get an update, the nurse said Sadie was weakening—but he had bills to pay and the sheriff to visit.

"How about I sit with your mother while you do whatever you need to do," Riley offered. "I should be there if you're not."

"You sure?"

She nodded in return.

Riley might be, but he wasn't so sure this was a good idea. It'd be an act of faith to let Paul's daughter anywhere near *her* again. Or extreme foolishness. Despite Riley's assurances, there was a good chance that when he picked her up after his errands she'd be crying and ready to return to Atlanta. Desperate to leave him behind, much as Caitlin had.

No. Not like Caitie. Riley was younger than Caitlin but she'd survived more hell than anyone he knew. Caitie believed Beck to be her white knight, the one who'd carry her off to his castle and keep her safe forever. Riley wasn't like that. She was tough and had scars, both inside and out, and she'd earned every one of them. She'd learned that good guys could screw her over just like bad ones.

✢

Beck reluctantly dropped Riley off at the hospital, muttering under his breath the entire time that she was going to regret this gesture of kindness. He was probably right.

What Riley didn't say was that she had her reasons for wanting private time with Sadie. To better understand Beck, she had to decipher the riddle that was his mother.

When she entered Sadie's hospital room, Riley steeled herself before she stepped around the curtain. She'd done that every time she'd visited her own mom in the last week of her life. This wasn't much different, except this patient wasn't eager to see her.

Sadie's labored breathing emanated from a body that seemed more a skeleton than a creature of flesh, her skin stretched across her bones like a pale sheet of parchment.

"Why are ya here?" she said, eyeing Riley. "Wanna see what a dyin' person looks like?"

"No," Riley said, refusing to be baited. "I already know about that: My mom died of cancer."

Sadie's glower faded. "So why are ya here?"

"You shouldn't be alone."

"I've always been alone. Doesn't matter now."

Only because you wouldn't let anyone close to your heart.

"Why ya hangin' around the boy? He got nothin' to give ya."

Except his love. But that wasn't something she'd tell his mother.

"He's a great guy who treats me well and doesn't try to screw me over. Do I need any other reason to hang with him?"

"He hides things, keeps things secret."

"We all do," Riley replied. "You included."

The woman's face wrinkled into a frown. "Ah, I see. He sent ya here to see if I'd tell ya the name of his daddy."

"I'm here because I want to be, not because he asked me to." Riley sucked in a hasty breath, the anger building. "You use his father's name like a weapon. That's not right. It's just mean."

"No respect for the dyin', huh?"

"I'll respect you when you do the same for your son."

"Ya got a sharp bite." The woman wheezed. "But ya only know part of it. That son of mine has done some bad stuff, but yer not willin' to hear about that."

Though Riley knew she should probably cut this woman some slack, that's what people had been doing Sadie's whole life, never calling her on her half-truths and how she'd cruelly manipulated her son.

Someone has to stand up to her. Stand up for Beck.

"There you go, again," Riley replied, shaking her head. "Trying to freak me out so I'll take off. That might have worked for the other girls, but not this time." Before Sadie could respond, she went on. "I don't know all of Beck's secrets, not yet, but he already told me about the two guys in the swamp. So I'm not buying into your head games."

The woman coughed long and hard. "I don't frighten ya. Why not?"

Because I've stared Hell in the face and you're not in their league.

"You just don't."

"Yer not like the other one he brought home."

"Caitlin?" A nod. "Why did you run her off?"

Sadie's eyes rose to hers. "Had to find out if she was tough enough. She wasn't."

"Tough enough for what?"

"Denver doesn't need some sissy-ass girl. He needs someone hard as nails to watch over him, keep him from goin' bad."

It appeared that Beck's mom had been vetting his girlfriends in her own peculiarly sadistic way. It was probably best that her son never knew that.

Riley switched directions. "What do you think happened to the Keneally brothers?"

After a long coughing session, Sadie finally answered. "I don't think it was some critter that got 'em unless it had two legs."

"It wasn't Beck," Riley said flatly.

"I know."

Then why didn't you stand up for your own son?

Unaware of Riley's mental tirade, Sadie adjusted the oxygen cannula in her nose. "Talk to Lou Deming. She's still in town. Married now, gonna have her first kid." A pause. "She was okay."

That was the closest to praise Riley had heard from this woman. "Until Cole took her away from Beck, you mean?"

Sadie's expression flattened. "Yeah. She should have known that bastard was nothin' but trouble. Denver got worse after that happened."

Riley made a mental note to hunt up Beck's former squeeze and see what the *okay* ex-girlfriend could tell her.

"Cole Hadley's a lot like his daddy," Sadie added. "He was a troublemaker too. I should know. Don't trust that boy. He's bad seed."

"I already figured that out."

Cole didn't have a chance with her, even if he grew a set of wings and claimed that she was the love of his life.

Sadie's eyes drifted shut, worn out from the intense conversation. "When ya see Denver, tell that boy to get his head out of his ass . . . do somethin' right for a change. He's runnin' out of time."

"Time for what?"

There was no response.

Riley left the room wiser than when she'd entered. This time she was even more determined to help Beck find the truth.

TEN

Beck's first stop was the sheriff's office—Donovan was out of town so he left a message with the surly Deputy Martin. His next stop was the bank, then the post office to mail the bills. Every stop involved whispers from the townsfolk. He ignored them as best as he could, more worried about how Riley and Sadie were getting along.

His last stop was the funeral home where McGovern promptly ushered him into his office, a fairly tidy space with a selection of urns high on a shelf.

"Here's a grand down on the bill," Beck said, placing a cashier's check on the desk. "I'll need a receipt."

"No problem," McGovern replied. He quickly scribbled it out and handed it over.

A document was placed on the desk in front of Beck and he cautiously bent over to study it as if it were a coiled snake. He couldn't read it.

"What's this for?"

"To authorize the burial. Just sign there and there," McGovern said, pointing at two separate lines.

While he did the deed, the undertaker puttered around the room.

"Did you hear that there's been some lady reporter down here asking questions about the Keneally brothers?" McGovern asked.

Justine. "She's been doin' the same up in Atlanta."

"I don't think that's a good thing, you know? Best to leave sleep-ing dogs lie."

Beck finished the last signature and dropped the pen on the desk. "Easy for you to say if yer not the one bein' blamed. Hell, I can't even buy a pizza in this town because folks are sure I'm a murderer."

McGovern walked to a filing cabinet behind him and slid open one of the drawers, dipping his hand inside. "So who do you think did it?"

"Who knows? Maybe it was the guy who gave Nate the money for the booze and the drugs. He said if the dude didn't do what he wanted a ton of hurt was goin' to come down on him."

"Huh. It's a pity Donovan never figured out who that was."

"Yeah, well, now he might get a chance," Beck replied. "I'm gonna ask Donovan to reopen the case, get this figured out once and for all. I want this damned thing off my back no matter who it takes down."

McGovern turned toward him now, his expression guarded. "Don't think that's wise, Denny."

"Well, it's not yer call. Are we done here?"

McGovern shut the drawer. "For now. I . . . might need you to come by later."

"Okay. I'll see you soon enough."

⁜

Beck met Riley in the front lobby of the hospital where he searched her face for clues. It didn't look like she'd been crying, so that was a good sign.

"How is she?" he asked.

"Asleep. It won't be . . . much longer, Den."

"I figured. So . . . how'd it go?" he asked, fearing the answer. If Sadie had been her usual nasty self . . .

"It went okay," Riley replied as they stepped outside into the sunshine. "Neither of us tried to kill the other. I think that's a good start."

He shot her a quick glance. "She run her game on you?"

"She tried. I shut her down. Your mother doesn't think you killed those boys."

"She never told me that," he replied. "Not once."

"Well, she has now, at least through me. She says you should pull your head out of your butt and do the right thing for a change."

"What does that mean?"

"No clue."

There was more that Riley wasn't telling him, but since she wasn't really upset maybe things had gone fairly well with her and Sadie.

That's a freakin' miracle.

He could still remember Caitlin's shattered expression when he'd returned from buying something for supper. She'd only been with the old lady for a half an hour, but in that short time Sadie had offloaded a ton of lies and ruined everything.

Riley isn't Caitlin.

Maybe Sadie had met her match for the first time in her life.

⁜

A short time later they pulled into the house's driveway and Beck geared himself up for another round of boxing up the old lady's stuff. With each room they cleared he felt his old life giving way. Layer by layer, old memories were being washed clean or tossed in the trash, leaving his hellish childhood behind. If he ever had kids, he'd be damned sure they wouldn't feel the same about him.

They tore into the cleaning like possessed people and by the time Riley checked the clock, it was nearing five in the evening. They'd just begun to make plans for dinner—Beck thought a quick trip over the state line might be a good idea since no one would know him there—when his cell phone rang. He looked at the dial and his face went ashen.

"Beck." A few seconds later he said, "We'll be there." He scooped up his backpack and jacket and was out the door without a word.

There was no need to ask where they were going—Sadie Beck was about to meet her Maker.

✛

The instant the truck came to a halt in the hospital parking lot, Beck turned it off and bolted toward the front entrance. Riley retrieved his keys and made sure the vehicle was locked.

Please, let his mother say she loves him. Just once.

Riley had always known she was at the center of her parents' lives and she'd felt that love from the start. Beck never had. He'd always been an afterthought, a nuisance, a child to be abandoned in the swamp like a sack of garbage.

Riley found the grieving son at his mother's bedside, Sadie's thin blue-veined hand engulfed in his larger tanned one. He shot a look over at Riley, then back at his mother.

"I'm here, Sadie," he said. "I won't let you go alone."

The woman muttered something, then closed her eyes. From Beck's despondent expression it wasn't "I love you."

With each gasping breath Sadie appeared to suck more life out of her only child, as if somehow their lives were physically intertwined. Through it all, Beck stood resolutely by the bed, refusing to move. Time crawled by. Five minutes, then ten. The nurse came in and checked the patient, then left on silent feet.

There was a groan from the bed and Sadie's eyes lit on Riley, reflecting a wild panic, as if she'd finally realized this was the end. Riley moved closer and took the woman's other hand.

Her mom had died peacefully, surrounded by her loving family. Sadie fought every last breath, as if she was too proud to admit that her time had come. Or too frightened of what she would face when she was no longer on this earth.

Riley bent down near the woman's ear. "Please, make it right, for both of you."

The woman weakly shook her head, each breath tighter. "Keep . . .

him ... safe ..." When Riley didn't reply, Sadie gripped her hand tighter. "Promise."

Riley bowed her head. "I promise."

Sadie Beck took her last breath and died.

+‡+

When Beck realized she was gone, emptiness overwhelmed him, as if it had poured out of the lifeless body and sought refuge inside him.

He'd pleaded for only two things—her love and the name of his father.

Sadie had taken both to her grave.

Tears swarmed down his cheeks, shaming him, visual evidence of what he'd lost and what he'd never had. He collapsed into a chair, no longer having the strength to stand as the bitter dampness on his cheeks scalded his face. All those years of hoping, praying that he'd been wrong, were over. *She never loved me.*

Someone touched his hands and when he peered through the dark mist it was Riley, kneeling next to him.

"I'm here, Den," she said, lightly touching his face. Her touch was so soft, so caring. Riley was at his side, and though he was afraid to admit it, she really cared for him, maybe even loved him. She would guard him, protect him. Keep the darkness at bay.

"It's over," she said, wiping away one of his tears with a fingertip. "You did everything you could for her."

He knew what she really meant. Sadie could no longer hurt him.

"It doesn't ... feel that way," he whispered. "Why didn't she tell me who he was?"

"Do you think she knew?"

Beck jolted at the question. He shouldn't have. He'd asked it of himself enough times. "I don't know." *It'd be like her to lie to me.*

To his surprise Riley tentatively placed a kiss on his cheek.

"I'm sorry, Den. I really am."

⊹

It took some time for Riley to dry her own tears. They weren't for Sadie, but for her son. When Beck offered her the truck so she could return to the motel, claiming he could catch a ride after the paperwork was done, she declined. Riley heard the false bravado behind his words. She'd used that same tactic after her dad died.

"I'll wait for you outside," she said.

His grateful expression told her it'd been the right choice.

⊹

As she leaned against the truck, Riley groaned to herself. *I promised to watch over him.* The vows she'd made in the past had always come back to haunt her but maybe this one would be different.

Why did Sadie trust me to watch over her son? If his mother hadn't loved him, why did she care what happened to Beck after she died? *Maybe she didn't know how to tell him she cared.* Or maybe she thought love was a weakness.

Riley dialed Stewart and he answered on the first ring.

"Beck's mom has passed away," she reported. It sounded so clinical.

"I'm sorry ta hear that. How's the lad doin'?"

"He's hanging in there, but it's really hard for him."

"Aye. Anythin' else I should know about?"

It wasn't her place to tell the master about the Keneally brothers and Beck's supposedly sordid past, so she mumbled, "Not really."

She wasn't sure if Stewart caught the fib or not, but he didn't press her on it.

"Call me when ya have the funeral arrangements in place. Harper and I will be sendin' flowers."

That was nice. "I will. That'll mean a lot to Beck."

A lengthy pause. "So what was his mother like?" the master asked.

"Cold and hard, like she'd been hurt so many times she hated everyone, no matter how good they were to her. I understand Beck better now. Which is why you wanted me to come down here with him, wasn't it?"

"I'm that transparent?" the man said.

"Not usually." Nevertheless, Stewart rarely did anything that didn't have at least four layers of strategy behind it.

"Things are gettin' unruly up here. I'm in the mall right now and there's magic flyin' all over the place. It's good yer down there, lass."

"It depends on your point of view, sir."

ELEVEN

Stewart stood at the far end of the shopping mall near two magic users he now considered friends: Mortimer Alexander, a summoner, and Ayden the witch. They'd been called to put a stop to a magical duel and this was their second such call today. "Any idea how this started?"

"Trash-talking, probably," Mort said, his navy summoner's robe hanging loosely from his shoulders. It looked like a tent on him as he was as wide as he was tall. "Ever since Lord Ozymandias raised those demons, there's been hell to pay."

He ducked a particularly poorly aimed spell and it struck the front of a New Age shop. Every single crystal inside lit up like a Christmas display.

"Witches can't aim worth a darn," he said to their other companion.

Ayden cranked an eyebrow at the summoner, her auburn hair and full-cleavage tattoo commanding attention no matter what clothes she wore. "You necros aren't any better with that aim thing," she said, gesturing toward a gaping hole in the mall's ceiling.

"True, but——"

They both jumped as a blast of magic impacted a few feet from them, generating a swarm of tiny armor-plated butterflies armed with swords. A counterspell enveloped them and the winged warriors turned to brightly colored confetti.

"Time to shut this nonsense down," Stewart said.

He stepped forward and planted his feet to prevent himself from being toppled by the magical waves rippling through the structure. "I'm Grand Master Stewart of the Atlanta Demon Trappers Guild. Cease and desist this instant!" he roared.

The duelists—a younger witch and an older summoner—ignored him. A wave of magic clawed its way up the walls, causing them to turn transparent, revealing the pipes and wiring underneath.

Mort joined the master. "Hey!" he shouted. "Knock it off!"

The guy in the pale green robe opened his mouth to argue, but then clamped it shut, no doubt noting that Mort's robe was darker than his. The darker the robe, the more power. This guy was out-classed and he knew it.

"Ah, only if the witch stops," the necro called out, clearly nervous now.

"Your turn," Mort murmured.

Ayden took her place next to the other two. "It is time to end this," she said.

"He started it!" the witch called back, slowly working a spell between her hands.

"You're not three years old. Lobbing spells around makes us look ignorant and we don't need the bad press."

"But—"

"There are people who believe we work for Hell and would love to kill us because of that. We're trying to get them to think other-wise," Ayden replied, her voice tighter now. She gestured at the de-struction, including the line of fizzling magic playing along the rafters. "This is *not* helping. You understand me?"

"But he's summoning demons," the witch protested, pointing at her foe.

Mortimer's face grew a frown. "Is that true?"

"No!" the other summoner shouted. "It's not me. I saw what

Lord Ozymandias did to Summoner Gregson. I don't want to die that way."

"Then who *is* summoning demons?" Mort asked.

The man paled. "Ah..."

Mort took three steps forward, blue magic swirling around his hands now. "Who is it?" he demanded.

"Ah...oh God. It's...Cantrell. He called one up last night and it got loose on him. He can't call it back."

"Well, that's just cheery news," Stewart rumbled. "As if we don't have enough of the damned things ta deal with already."

The guy mumbled an apology, sweat running down his face now.

"Go home, people. Stop bein' stupid. Do not start a war ya canna win," Stewart commanded.

The combatants frowned at each other, then they headed in different directions, trailing magic in their wakes.

"What will happen with the guy who called up the demon?" Ayden said.

"Lord Ozymandias will deal with the problem," Mort replied.

"How?"

"Let's just say that when he's done there won't be enough ashes left to bury."

"My Goddess..." the witch replied.

"Tell your lordship I'm pleased ta hear he's bein' so keen on policin' his own," Stewart said. "The last thing we need is for any of the summoners ta side with Hell, either by choice or by coercion. It's one thing ta meet demons in battle. It's another to face a bunch of yer lot slingin' magic around."

"He understands the danger. That's why he's being so... forceful." Mort sighed. "You know, my mother wanted me to be a dentist." He allowed the magic to drain away from his fingers and then began to roll up the sleeves of his robe. "Instead, I just had to be a summoner. Look what it got me."

"A steady job," Stewart replied, more relaxed now that the duel had ended. "Someone has ta clean up the magical Hazmat and yer good at it."

"Don't remind me." Mort looked over at Ayden. "You ready?"

She nodded and began extracting various witchy supplies from the tapestry bag on her shoulder, including candles, crystals, and magical chalk.

"I'll leave ya ta it then," Stewart said.

As he walked away, he heard them discussing the best place to set the circle from which they'd disperse the residual magic. There was some professional disagreement, but it was good-natured, not confrontational. It appeared that the battle at Oakland Cemetery had forged a bond between them, one of mutual respect.

Pity the rest of yer kind didn't get the memo.

⁜

A few minutes after McGovern arrived at the hospital with the hearse, Sadie's body was rolled out on a gurney. Beck followed behind, then stood near the hearse, head bowed and hands at his side, until his mother was loaded inside.

Riley's lower lip quivered and her heart ached to see him like this. Once the undertaker had finished, Beck headed in Riley's direction. His mask held until he reached the truck.

"Can you drive?" he asked, a glimmer of tears in his eyes.

"Sure." It took some time to get the seat adjusted right. Throughout the process he stared out the side window, his jaw clenched.

At Beck's mumbled request they made only one stop, at the convenience store. When he climbed out of the truck, eyes followed him inside. One guy flipped him off, but he didn't seem to notice.

He just lost his mother, you ass. Riley forced herself not to return the gesture.

After some time inside, Beck returned with a bag of ice, a six-pack of beer, and some BBQ potato chips. A guy's idea of a balanced meal. A second bag came her way and inside was a turkey sandwich, some dried fruit, and a can of soda. Her dinner, it appeared. Even in grief, he was still thinking of her welfare.

Once they were back at the room he put his trapping bag next to the bed and tossed his wallet inside. The ice went in the sink, followed by four of the beer bottles. He tucked the fifth under his arm, twisted the top off the sixth bottle, and headed back outside. She trailed after him, concerned.

Beck dropped the tailgate and hopped up onto it.

"You want to be alone?" she asked. When he shook his head she climbed up next to him.

He took a swig of beer. "I always hoped she'd get over herself long enough to act like I was her son, but she never could."

"Was she always this way?"

"Pretty much. Right after I was born my gran took me to north Georgia. She was worried Sadie wouldn't take care of me proper. I stayed up there until I was three and then they brought me back down."

"Why didn't they keep you?"

"Sadie was on the wagon. They thought she could handle things." He took a long swig of beer. "She promised them she could, but she started drinkin' a short time after I came home. I was too much for her to handle."

He's blaming himself again. "If she couldn't handle a kid, she should have gotten help or taken you back to your grandparents."

"Not her way." He tracked a UPS truck along the highway until it was out of sight. "She'd go out at night, leavin' me on my own. She told my gran everythin' was fine and they believed her."

"How old were you?" Riley asked, surprised he was being this open about his childhood.

"Four."

Riley gaped. "God, Beck. It's a wonder you're still alive. You could have set the house on fire or something."

"Mostly I watched television," he said.

"How did you eat? I mean, did she leave you food?"

"Not really. I remember being really hungry one night so I climbed up on the counter and got a can out of the cupboard, but I couldn't get it open."

"What did you do?"

"I took it to the neighbor next door. Mrs. Welsh was always really nice to me. I made her promise she wouldn't tell Sadie I'd taken one of the cans or I might get a whippin'. She said it'd be our secret." He smiled at the memory. "She gave me the can back and then fed me from her own cupboard. That way I wouldn't get in trouble." He sighed. "She died a couple years back. I do hope she's in Heaven because she deserves everythin' good in the next life. She was a saint."

Unlike your mother.

He cleared his throat. "I knew when Sadie came home it was time to hide. Mostly she was too drunk to know I was there, but every now and then she was mad drunk and if I did anythin', I'd get a lickin'. Sometimes she'd bring some loser home with her." He shook his head. "Didn't understand it all until later, but I knew it wasn't right."

His fingers tightened around the beer bottle. "I kept hopin' that one of those guys was my daddy, but I don't think any of them were."

"I don't know how you made it. I would have taken off." Then she realized why he hadn't. What if his father had returned while he was gone?

"Sorry, you don't need to hear all this crap. Doesn't matter now."

It does or you wouldn't be talking about it.

"Did you tell anyone else about this?"

"Donovan knew most of it. He wanted to put me in foster care, but I told him I'd run away. I found out later that he was the one who paid for my school supplies. It sure wasn't Sadie."

Just like a father would do. Her mind flashed back to the first time she'd seen Donovan—the close-cropped blond hair and muscular build. A lot like an older Beck.

She wanted to ask the question, but now didn't seem like the right time. Besides, wouldn't they have settled all that a long time ago if Donovan and Sadie had ever hooked up?

"Don't be a martyr, Beck. Your mother wasn't worth it."

He looked over at her and she wondered if she'd gone too far. Instead, he blinked back tears. "Yer so damned good to me."

"Easy to do when you're not pushing me away."

"I never did it because I hated you or anythin'."

"I know."

He drained the first beer. "I'd like to sit out here and think for a while, on my own, if you don't mind."

Taking that as her cue to leave, Riley hopped off the end of the tailgate. She placed her hand on his knee. "You sure you're okay?"

"I'm gettin' better," he said, his voice quieter now. "You helped me a lot."

"Well, it's cold so don't stay out here too long. And if you get drunk, you are sleeping in the truck, mister," she said, giving him a mock glare.

He cracked a grin and then snapped a smart salute. "Yes, ma'am."

She returned the salute, picked up the empty beer bottle, and headed to her room, relieved. As long as she kept him talking, he'd be okay.

⊹

Riley took a shower and dressed for bed. A peek out the drapes proved Beck was sitting where she'd left him, nursing a beer and his deepest thoughts. Ravenous, she demolished the sandwich and the fruit. Neither were half bad. Another check on Beck. He hadn't moved.

This might take some time.

Flipping open her phone, she sent a text to Peter letting him know the situation and that it'd be a day or two before she returned to Atlanta. When no reply was forthcoming, she began to doze. The sounds of "Georgia on My Mind" filtered in from the parking lot signaling that someone had called Beck. There was muted conversation.

Probably somebody in Atlanta.

Yawning, she crawled under the covers and was nearly asleep when the truck roared to life. By the time she reached the door, Beck was headed up the highway toward town.

Maybe he needed some space. Or the sheriff was back in his office and Beck went to talk to him about the missing boys.

Still, as she crawled back in bed to await his return, a nagging sense of unease tugged at her.

Maybe I should have gone with him.

⁜

By the time he was halfway to the funeral home Beck realized he'd left two things behind: his trapping bag and his wallet. He debated about turning around and fetching them, but Riley was probably asleep and that would just wake her. That was the reason he'd not bothered to let her know where he was headed in the first place.

When Beck had pressed McGovern about what was so important at nearly nine at night, the undertaker claimed he had yet another piece of paper for Beck to sign and that it just had to be done tonight. Then he'd asked Beck to park in the rear of the funeral home, which had seemed odd until the guy said something about a freshly mopped showroom floor.

Shaking off his gloom, Beck walked to the back door, hoping to deal with whatever problem McGovern had dreamed up so he could get back to the motel. If he was gone too long Riley might wake up and worry about him.

He knocked but there was no answer so he tried the knob and the door swung open.

"Hello?" he called out. "Hey, McGovern! You in here?"

There was no reply so Beck walked through the garage area and into a long corridor toward the interior of the building. His irritation rose with each step. He'd had a helluva day and he only wanted to get back to the motel and climb in bed. Not that sleep would make it any better.

"McGovern," he called. When there was no answer, Beck swung around and headed back the way he came. He was halfway through the garage when the undertaker appeared between him and the outer door.

"Where have you been?" Beck demanded.

"Waiting for you," McGovern replied. "The girl out in the truck?"

That was a weird question. "No, she's at the motel. Let's get done whatever you need, okay? I'm not in the mood to jack around."

"I agree."

As Beck grew closer he saw something in the man's hand and it took him a moment to realize exactly what it was. He ground to a halt midstep, his full attention on the Taser.

"Hey, look, man, what's this all about?"

McGovern moved closer. "It's all about payback, Denny."

"Payback for—"

Twin projectiles hit Beck in the chest, delivering a sharp electric shock that took him down. As he lay on the floor trying to control his twitching and suddenly uncooperative muscles, McGovern walked up to him.

"You should have left it alone, boy."

The second jolt from the Taser turned Beck's vision to black.

TWELVE

A thundering headache brought Beck back to consciousness. It felt like a hangover, at least until he tasted the blood in his mouth and the trembling ache in his muscles. He slowly became aware that his hands and feet were tied and a piece of thick tape covered his mouth. With a groan he tried to roll over but was unable to complete the maneuver, encased in something.

What the hell is this?

He thrashed and it got him nowhere as the sharp stench of plastic nearly made him gag. One of the last things he'd seen right before he'd gone unconscious was a stack of body bags in the funeral home's garage. It was a good guess he was inside one of them now.

From the sounds around him, he was in the back of a vehicle, maybe even his own truck. He could hear the radio playing in the cab. There was something else rattling with each bump in the pavement, but he couldn't sort out that noise.

A cold chill sped up his spine. Was he was being taken somewhere for a little country justice? All it'd take was a bunch of drunken locals eager for that payback McGovern had spoken of. A quick toss of a rope over a thick tree limb and Denny Beck would be no more. When the sheriff tried to figure out who'd killed him, there'd be no witnesses willing to say what they'd done to Sadie's murdering son.

Beck kept wiggling around until he could get one of his fingers close to his mouth. He tensed and ripped off the tape, then swore at the pain as his lips burned in protest. Next he had to get the ropes off. If he was lucky he'd be free when it came time for them to hang him. How he'd fight off a lynch mob he had no idea, but he wasn't going down easy.

He was still working on the ropes around his feet when the truck slowed and made a turn. From the change in tire sounds they were no longer on the highway, but traveling on one of the side roads, which meant they could be anywhere.

Sweating at the strain, he nearly cheered when the bonds around his ankles came free. Fearing he was running out of time, he dug frantically at the ones on his wrists, using his teeth as leverage. His jaw muscles clenched in protest, but he kept gnawing at the ropes.

The truck pulled up and halted. A minute later he heard the topper swing open and he knew he was out of time. Beck kicked out at the plastic and shouted his outrage.

"Figured you'd get that off," McGovern said.

"Why ya doin' this?"

"Because it's the way it has to be," the man replied.

Did he find my gun? Beck kept it in his glove compartment so it wasn't like it was hidden.

He was hauled to the edge of the truck gate and unceremoniously rolled off the edge. Before he could react, he landed hard, his shoulder and skull slamming into the ground. Woozy from the blow, his head swam in protest.

The Guild's doctor had warned him about this, cautioning him to be careful after the head injury he'd taken a short time ago. He had been careful; he'd just not planned on being kidnapped by Sadlersville's only undertaker.

What was missing was a tangle of drunken voices boasting about what they planned to do to that no-good SOB Denny Beck. Had he gotten it wrong? Maybe this wasn't country justice but something else entirely.

As McGovern dragged the body bag across the ground, he groaned in discomfort. With considerable difficulty his captor maneuvered him up, then into something that moved, a boat perhaps. Through it all, Beck's head continued to pound in time with his heart.

"Where are we goin'?" he called out, his mouth dry.

McGovern didn't answer.

Why is he doin' this? Beck had never had a problem with the undertaker and the guy should have no beef with him. Maybe it was something with Sadie. Still, that was no reason this man would risk jail time if there'd been bad blood between the two of them.

Beck tried to concentrate on the little details. Besides the sickening plastic stench there was another smell, one he knew as well as any: They were somewhere in the swamp. His mind narrowed down the possibilities. There were only a few entrances to Okefenokee and the one south of town had a main gate that was locked at sunset. The next closest entrance was Kingfisher Landing, north of Sadlersville, the one locals called Poachers' Landing because it was open to everyone and the easiest way to slip into the swamp unnoticed. Beck bet that's exactly where they were.

With the roar of the boat's motor in his ears, he forced himself to rest. If he was lucky he'd be given a chance to escape. If not, this was going to be a one-way trip.

⁂

As best he could tell, hours passed. The body bag didn't allow much personal freedom and so his back ached where it met the uneven bottom of the boat. He kept working on the ropes, but only managed to make his mouth sore and his lips bleed.

How far are we goin'?

When the boat slowed and then the motor cut out, Beck knew the moment was near. He'd given up on trying to loosen the bonds around his wrists. Those were there to stay. At least he had his feet free and that meant he could run if McGovern hauled him onto solid ground. Swimming wasn't going to be an option.

What if he throws me overboard? Beck would drown before he could claw his way out of the bag. Something told him that wasn't McGovern's plan or he'd have done the deed already.

The boat rocked as his captor climbed out. Probably tying it off to a tree.

"Ya still haven't told me what this is all about," Beck said, trying to sound like he'd given in to the inevitable.

"It's nothing personal. It's just something has to happen."

Keep him talkin'. "That's not making me feel good here."

A chuckle. "Always did like your sense of humor. Don't worry, I'll make sure your mother has a good funeral."

Beck's fury grew and he struggled to keep it in check. "Ya let me go and I'll not say a word to the cops."

The only response was McGovern manhandling him out of the craft and onto the bank. Water splashed around the bag, but it remained intact. More dragging, but this time it wasn't as easy as his body passed over branches and other swamp debris.

"Yer gonna kill me, aren't you?"

"Yeah, it's come to that. Sorry."

Nothing would prevent McGovern from killing him while he was still inside the bag. Beck had to get him to unzip it.

"Then at least let me see the sky one last time. I don't want to die staring at the inside of some damned black bag."

His captor kept hauling him onward, farther from the boat.

Beck forced his pride down in an effort to gain one last chance at survival.

"Come on, man. I'm . . . beggin' ya here."

There was a resigned sigh and the dragging halted.

That's it. Open the bag.

As McGovern fumbled with the zipper, Beck prepared himself. He needed to make an explosive leap and tackle his kidnapper before the man had the opportunity to react. He'd never get another chance.

Suddenly McGovern yelped in terror. There were noises Beck couldn't place, then two rapid-fire gunshots split the air. He grimaced, waiting for the searing pain, but it didn't come.

"This is mine!" a voice cried out.

McGovern shrieked and then there was the sound of someone crashing through the brush in a blind panic.

What the hell just happened?

The body bag continued its journey across the ground, in the direction he'd originally been headed.

Beck called out. "Hey! I thought ya were gonna open this bag."

"Not yet," the new voice said. "In time."

"Who are ya?"

A low laugh turned his blood to ice. "Sleep, Denver Beck," the voice said. "For there will be little of it when you awake."

Beck opened his mouth to protest, but his brain shut down before he had the chance to form one word.

✦

Riley woke with a start, blinking open her eyes. The clock on the nightstand said she'd been asleep for over two hours. Beck should be back and in bed by now, but the light was still on in his room.

Probably reading his book.

She crawled out of bed and stuck her head around the door. Beck's bed was untouched and the bathroom empty. She plodded to the window and pushed back the curtain—his truck was still gone and his trapping bag was where he'd left it. He wouldn't go that far without that, even in his hometown.

Where are you?

Three hours in she dialed his cell phone. As she waited for it to ring, Riley tried to figure out what she was going to say to him. She suspected it would start with, "Where the hell are you?"

It rolled over to voice mail. It was close to midnight now and he would never leave her alone for that length of time, not with how paranoid he'd been about Sadlersville.

Maybe he's at a bar somewhere. The moment she considered that she knew that was wrong. Beck could go bar hopping in Atlanta with no hassles, but down here it was a surefire way to land him in a fight. He wasn't looking for that kind of trouble, not with all the extra responsibilities that came with his mom's death.

Something is wrong. She fumbled through the phone book until she could find the business number for the sheriff's office. The radio dispatcher wielded a deep Southern drawl like a blunt-edged weapon and it took Riley a bit to understand what the woman was telling her: The sheriff was out of town. What did she need?

Riley explained the situation and was relieved when the dispatcher said she'd send a deputy to the motel. Only then did Riley notice she was still in her nightclothes so she quickly changed and took a position near the window. Fifteen minutes later there was the crunch of gravel as a cop car pulled into the parking lot. Riley hurried outside, tucking her jacket around her.

The deputy took his time hauling his butt out of the cruiser, like a missing person was no big deal. He was clad in a thick coat, which was open at the front and he had a slight paunch.

"You the one who called the office?" he asked in a lazy drawl.

"Yes. I've got a friend who is missing. I need you to find him."

"You're the girl with Denny Beck, aren't you?"

"He's the one that's missing," Riley replied, walking closer. She nervously gave him the details of what had happened and why she was so worried.

The deputy clearly didn't share her concern. "He probably ran out of beer."

"No! There are four more bottles in the sink and he left his wallet here."

"You been drinking any of that brew, missy?" the man asked, frowning now.

"What? No, I haven't. I don't like beer." Besides the fact that she was underage.

"He'll probably be back in the morning with one helluva hangover.

That's his style." The deputy began to fold himself back into the car.

"Wait! What are you going? He needs your help."

"He always took off, even when he was a kid. If he's not back by tomorrow night, call the office. We'll get you to the bus station. You wouldn't be the first girl he ditched after he's done with her."

He thought she was Beck's squeeze. "We just trap demons together. He wouldn't leave me here on my own."

The man chuckled. "You trap demons. That's a good one."

Before she could retrieve her trappers' license and jam it under this idiot's nose, he drove away.

"You . . . moron," she shouted, kicking gravel at the departing car. She stormed into her room and slammed the door, then felt bad for the people trying to sleep next door.

What could she do? Call Stewart? That wouldn't help much since the master was in Atlanta. With the sheriff unavailable and her without a ride, she was stuck here until morning.

Frightened of every sound now, Riley retrieved Beck's steel pipe and climbed into his bed. It smelled of his aftershave but that did nothing to calm her. Tucking a pillow close to her chest, she closed her eyes and prayed that her worst fears were all imaginary.

✢

Blinking in the dark, Beck found himself propped against a tree, a thin sliver of a moon visible through the trees above him. He shivered in the cold, despite his leather jacket.

The good news was that the ropes on his wrists were gone. He rolled his neck around and felt it cramp on the right side in protest. At least his vision was okay so maybe he'd avoided a concussion. It was only when he moved his legs to stand that he discovered the bad news: A log chain, heavy with rusted links, stretched from the tree to his left ankle. A battered padlock mated him and the chain together in an unmovable union.

"Oh, sweet Jesus," he said, his panic rocketing off the charts. A jerk on the metal proved his ankle would snap before he broke free. He dug his fingers underneath the links, trying to force it off his boot. It was too tight.

Beck rose on unsteady feet and studied the tree behind him. It was a cypress, one of the aged sentinels of the swamp, smooth and thick. It was so large that it would take three of him to get his arms around it. He cinched up the chain, braced his feet against the trunk, and pulled hard. Heat spread across his arms and back muscles, but the restraint held. He returned to his feet, wiping his hands free of the dirt and rust.

"Ya bastard!" he shouted, his voice echoing in the wilderness around him. In the distance an owl hooted in reply. Who had done this? Why attack McGovern just to steal him and chain him to a tree?

Beck tried to slow his breathing, think it through. If he didn't find a way to escape this was going to be short and brutal: If one of the swamp's demons didn't take him down, he could die from exposure. A bear or snake could get him, or an alligator would tear him free of the chain and carry his ravaged body into the water to stash in its larder.

A rustling in the undergrowth pulled his eyes in that direction. He had no weapon, so Beck reeled in the chain and held it between his hands. If he was lucky, it was a foraging raccoon.

Not with all the noise I've been makin'.

When there was no further rustling, Beck forced himself to relax. If he remained on the ground he'd be more vulnerable, so he tried to scale the tree. That was a major fail: The slick bark wouldn't give him any traction. Swinging up, he managed to dislodge some Spanish moss from a long branch above him and he kept kicking until a thick pile of it hit the ground. At least that would help him stay warm tonight. Come morning he'd have to find a way to break free or he'd never see Riley again—and he realized now, that was the one thing he wanted more than anything in the world.

✛

Riley was out of bed at a little before seven in the morning, though there had been scant sleep overnight. Every noise jerked her awake, reigniting her hope that it was Beck and that he'd finally returned. But he never had.

He'd been gone for ten hours now. She'd promised his mother she'd keep him safe and the woman wasn't even in her grave yet and Riley had already broken that vow.

She didn't bother with makeup, not caring what she looked like. After using her laptop to figure out where the sheriff's office was located, she bundled up in her warmest clothes, hoisted her backpack, and began the hike into town. The cold morning air nipped at her nose and ears. Every time a car passed her she'd turn to check it out. One old guy pulled off the side of the road and offered to give her a ride, but she refused. There was no way she could trust anyone at the moment even if they had more wrinkles than a shar-pei. Adjusting her pack, she kept hiking.

Five minutes into her walk she'd worked up the courage and dialed Stewart. She needed backup.

"Lass, good mornin' ta ya. How's it goin'?"

He sounded in good spirits and she was about to ruin that. When she gave him a rundown of the situation she heard a long sigh down the phone.

"Ah, damn," he said. "Where are ya now?"

"I'm going into town to talk to the sheriff. He seems to like Beck so he'll help me find him."

"That's a good plan. Things are in a mess up here so I canna come down, but I'll see who I can spare. Keep me in the loop. Ya be verra careful, ya hear?"

"I will. Thanks."

She hung up and kept walking.

Thirteen

She reached the outskirts of Sadlersville just as the town was stirring to life. When Riley walked past the diner she wasn't surprised to find the old guys already lined up at the long table, coffee and gossip in abundance. One of them was the dude who'd offered her a ride. Once she'd checked in with the sheriff she'd come back and have some breakfast, try to tap into the town's rumor mill.

It has to be good for something.

According to their Web site, the county sheriff's office was housed in a single-story building located next to the courthouse. Riley pushed open the front door and then paused to get her bearings. The moment she crossed the threshold into the sheriff's office the aroma of fresh coffee teased her nose. It reminded her of the old Starbucks where she attended school.

"Hello?" No reply. Since there wasn't anyone in sight, she moved to the closest desk, put her pack down, and plopped into a chair. Clearly the city wasn't a hotbed of criminal activity. About a minute later a deputy wandered out from the back of the building, coffee cup in hand. He was young and had a suntanned face. His name tag proclaimed he was Steve Newman and he'd been a cop for the last three years.

"Morning," he said. "Can I help you?"

"Hi, is Sheriff Donovan here?"

"No. He'll be back later today. What can I do for you?"

At least this guy is nice. "I'm looking for Denver Beck. He's missing."

"Are you the young lady who called the dispatcher?"

"Yes. Would you have any idea where he might be?"

"No, I don't," he said, shaking his head. "Deputy Martin said you were worried about him not coming back to the motel. Tell me what's going on."

That sounded good so Riley laid it all out, point by point. At least this time the cop took notes.

"What makes you so sure he's in trouble?" the young man asked.

"Beck left his wallet behind and he never goes anywhere without his trapping bag. That's one of the first things we're taught—carry Holy Water at all times or you're demon food. He left it in his motel room, along with the steel pipe he uses for protection."

The deputy blinked. "You're a trapper too?" Riley nodded.

Newman took another sip from his mug—it had a picture of a collie on it. "I heard his mother died yesterday. Maybe he wasn't thinking clearly."

She picked at a fingernail in nervous frustration. "Beck was upset, but we talked it out. Look, I know him, he wouldn't leave me on my own. He's like a . . . big brother. He's always worrying about me and he was really spooked that something might happen while I was down here with him."

The deputy nodded in understanding. "Truth is, I can't file a missing person's report on an adult until twenty-four hours have passed." At her protest, he added, "But I'll put the word out. Give me a description of his truck. Someone must have seen him."

She gave him the information, along with her cell phone number.

The cop finished his notes. Looking up, he issued a reassuring smile. "The sheriff is due back in town in a couple of hours and I'll make sure he knows about this. Maybe by then Beck will have shown up."

If he does, he better have one amazing excuse or he's a dead man.

"Thanks."

"Do you need a ride back to the motel?"

"No, I'm headed to the diner." She rose from the chair. "Thanks. I really appreciate it."

"We'll see if we can find him."

That's all I want.

⌖

Dawn brought a raging thirst and the realization that this wasn't a bad dream. By now Riley would be freaking since she knew him well enough to realize something was wrong. He knew she'd be smart: She'd call Donovan and Stewart for help and between them they'd figure out what happened to him. Riley would be okay. If anything, he needed to worry about himself.

It'd been a rough night, especially since he was the main course for the voracious red bugs that lived in the Spanish moss. Northerners called the things chiggers and they'd found him a great feast. The old swampers would use smoke to kill them, but Beck was a few matches short for that. Soon those bites would start to itch, but it was that or hypothermia.

When Beck rolled over his bladder kicked in so the first order of business was to maneuver the chain around the back side of the tree and take care of that problem. Then he returned to his original position to survey his surroundings.

In most people's minds, a swamp was one big watery mud hole, but that wasn't the case with Okefenokee. It offered a variety of terrains and Donovan had shown him every one: the prairies, hammocks, cypress bays, lakes, and bogs. As swamps went this was a big one, over four hundred thousand acres, opened to the world by a series of man-made canals. It was teeming with wildlife and included remote sections that rarely saw a human.

This time of year was a mixed blessing: There were fewer tourists floating up and down on the tour boats so Beck's chances of being discovered were reduced. On the other side of the coin, the colder weather worked in his favor when it came to the gators: They weren't as active. Or as hungry.

Plenty of other things that can kill me.

There'd been no sign of whoever had stolen him away from Mc-Govern, and though it really was tempting to panic, he fell back on his survival training. He began by excavating a hole to about foot or so deep using a stout branch. Since the swamp was pretty much just floating ground, the hole would fill with water and he'd need something to drink soon enough.

Once that was done and he'd wiped his muddy hands on his jeans, he began to examine the loops of metal that held him prisoner. The chain was old and rusty and looped through a large ring. The ring itself was corroded and had a half-inch break in it, though not big enough for him to force a link through to gain his freedom. The gap gave him hope. If he could work on that weakness, maybe he could break free. He'd still have the chain attached to his leg, but at least he could travel.

"I'd kill for my steel pipe," he muttered.

The hairs on the back of his neck rose. Something was watching him. He swept his eyes over the landscape, looking for the threat and found two red eyes peering at him from around a tree.

Demon.

"Trapperrr . . ." the fiend hissed as it stepped out into the open. It was short, about three and a half feet all, totally hairless with glitteringly sharp teeth and wicked talons. The locals called them swamp devils and they weren't like the fiends in the city: Hellspawn were good at adapting to their surroundings.

It's not a Grade Three. Those were hairy and didn't have much of a brain except when it came to food. A Pyro-Fiend was considerably smaller and this one didn't seem to have an obsession with flames.

"What kind of demon are you?" he murmured to himself.

The creature hunched down in a crouch, observing him. "The kind that always wins," it said.

He knew in an instant. "Yer a Four, one of the Mezmers." The fact that it spoke decent English told him it was an older Hypno-Fiend, but not as powerful as some he'd met. Still, it had been strong enough to put him to sleep and haul him away like a bag of Halloween candy.

Instead of sifting through his brain and making him do its will, this one would have to worry on him like a dog on a bone. If he became desperate enough, hungry enough to make a deal, it'd claim his soul. In the meanwhile Beck was just food tied to a tree for any predator.

"You do not want to tangle with me right now," he declared.

The fiend's strange barking laugh echoed around them, telling Beck how much it considered him a threat.

"You put McGovern up to this?" he demanded. He could think of no other reason for the undertaker's bizarre behavior.

"No. I do not know of that mortal." The demon rested its elbows on its knees and it appeared as if it had nothing else to occupy it for the remainder of the day. Or the next month, for that matter. It gestured toward the chain. "Your freedom for your soul."

"No deal."

It scratched behind an ear in thought. "Blackthorne's daughter will not come for you."

"Of course she will," Beck retorted. That was a given.

"No. The Fallen lives and has claimed her as his own. She will do whatever he says. She has no need of you, trapper."

"Yer lyin'." *God, I hope you are.*

"You will die here," the demon replied.

"Might happen. Might not. No way I'm going to Hell."

The fiend tried on a friendly smile, the effect ruined by its pointed teeth.

"Time will tell, Denver Beck," it said, then slunk off into the bushes.

✛

Riley's stomach was rumbling by the time she approached the diner. It seemed traitorous to be hungry what with Beck missing, but she knew she had to eat. As she paused to open the door to the restaurant, someone caught her arm. It was an older woman with bright white hair and twinkling eyes and she wore some strange symbol around her neck.

"He wants you to find him," the woman said. She boldly took hold of Riley's hand and pressed something into the palm. Something cold. "This will help you," she said, smiling.

Spooked by the lack of personal space, Riley backed off, and stared first at the woman, then the object in her palm.

"It's a . . . rock." A polished one, but a rock nonetheless.

"It's a seeker stone. It'll help you find him. Just don't give up. If you do, he's lost."

"Are you one of the wise women?"

There was a quick nod and before Riley could ask how a rock was going to be of any use, the woman hurried away. Shrugging, she tucked it away in her backpack, figuring it couldn't hurt.

The diner was bustling so she had to wait for a couple to leave one of the booths before she had a place to sit. The waitress wasn't the same from the day before—she was closer to Beck's age and frowning even before Riley took her seat.

Probably one of his hookups.

"What do you want?" the girl asked, clearly in a hurry to be somewhere else.

"Hot tea, please." Riley opened the menu and gave it a quick glance. "I'll have the eggs and bacon special with wheat toast."

Her breakfast was uneventful as long as she ignored the whispering and the naked stares. This wasn't fair—she'd figured she'd be anonymous down here, not like in Atlanta after all the demon business. Now she was Denny's *whatever* and everyone wanted to check her out.

As she was finishing off her tea, wondering how to question the dinosaurs at the old guys' table, Cole entered the diner and headed straight for her.

How did he know I was here? It wasn't like Beck's truck was parked out front.

Without asking if he could join her, he slid into the booth across from her.

"I hear Denny's gone," he said. "Is he back in Atlanta?"

"Not likely."

Cole flagged down the waitress and ordered a cup of coffee. The girl seemed to like him, so she was all smiles. Riley even scored a refill on her tea with minimal hassle.

"Lots of rumors flying around," Cole said. "What I'm hearing is that you two were knocking boots, then Denny decided he couldn't deal and left you behind. Stuck you with burying his mother and paying the funeral bills."

Riley rolled her eyes. "Whoever is saying that doesn't know Beck." *Or me.*

"I doubt he's changed much. He always was unreliable."

Before she could get in his face, Cole's phone rang and he pulled it from a jacket pocket.

"Yeah?" A long pause. "Sure, I can do that." Cole's eyes shifted to Riley and a cunning smile appeared. "I'll be there in an hour." The smile grew wider as he ended the call.

"Why are you here, Cole?"

"Wanted to help you find Denny."

Liar. "Not buying that."

"It's the truth." He ramped up his bad-boy smile and it gave Riley the creeps.

"Shut it down," she said. "I know what you did to Beck and his girlfriend so you have no traction with me."

"I see," he said, momentarily off his game. "Damn. Here I thought I had a shot at you. Looks like I'll have to work for this: How about if I find Denny for you, then you take me to dinner to celebrate?"

"Oh, God, listen to you," a voice said. "Don't you ever give up?"

The newcomer was about Riley's age, dressed in faded jeans, a

long forest-green T-shirt, with a heavy navy vest layered over the top.
Her blond hair had wide streaks of white and was blunt cut at her
chin, a little longer on the right than on the left. A single ruby stud
adorned her nose.

Her brown eyes bored into Cole with naked disgust.

"Sammie," Cole said, looking up at her. "Get kicked out of
school again?"

"You're such a dickhead, Hadley," the girl replied. Her attention
went to Riley. "The name is Samantha, but you can call me Sam.
Uncle Donovan said to let you know he's looking for Beck."

Riley sagged in relief. If the sheriff was on the case then they had
a chance.

"Have a seat," Cole said, offering a small space next to him.

"No way. Hit the road, jerk," Sam replied, angling her thumb
toward the exit.

"No wonder you don't have a boyfriend," Cole said, grinning. He
took down the last of his coffee, dropped some cash on the table to
pay for his drink, then rose and delivered a mock bow. As Sam took
his place, she flipped him off.

"Let me know if I can be of any help, Riley," he said and then
headed for the front door, humming to himself.

Sam clunked her cell phone on the table. It was one of the expensive smartphones, the kind that wouldn't survive a week in a trapper's
life.

She pushed Cole's coffee cup out of her way as if it were toxic.
"He's such a loser. He even tried to get my mom horizontal. Can you
believe that?"

"You live here in Sadlersville?" Riley asked, figuring that might
be a safer topic.

A shake of the head. "Tampa." That explained her deep tan.
"I'm . . . here on spring break."

In February? Riley let it pass. She put money on the table to cover
her meal, plus a tip.

"You have wheels? I really could stand a ride." Sam nodded immediately. "I want to talk to one of Beck's exes. Her name is Louisa . . . Deming. You know her?"

"No, but I know someone who will."

As Sam made a phone call to check with her source, Riley walked up to the long table of retired folks.

"Hi, guys." There were a few mumbles in her direction. "Denver Beck went missing last night. You know anything that can help me find him?"

Looks were traded down the table.

An older man with a bushy gray mustache squinted up at her. "Saw his truck last night on Main Street. Probably about nine thirty or so."

"Was he driving okay?" A nod. So that meant Beck wasn't drunk. "Anything else?"

A table full of head shakes. Riley pulled a napkin over and wrote her cell phone number on it. "Call me if you hear anything." She looked at each one of them in turn. "Please . . . I really need to find him."

"You might as well go back home, girl. He's taken off again," one of them replied. "He always did that. Like that time when he was a kid and he ran away."

"I remember that. They had the cops out looking for him," another man added. There were nods from some of the others.

It was time to set some of Beck's record straight.

"Oh, you mean the time his mother took him into the swamp and left him there . . . to die?" she asked.

The mustachioed guy shied back in his seat. "That's not how I heard it. You sure about that, girl? Not right to say bad things about the dead and all."

Riley pushed her phone number closer to him. "But it's okay to tell lies about the living?"

She left them muttering to themselves.

✦

Sam's ride was a maroon sedan with seats that warmed one's behind. Riley decided if she ever had money she'd buy herself something like this, though it was doubtful a Three would fit in the trunk.

"So what year are you? Sophomore or a junior?" Riley asked.

"Junior," Sam replied.

"Like me then."

"Is it true that you guys go to school in abandoned buildings?"

"Yup," Riley replied. "Mine's a Starbucks. Before that it was an old grocery store. Who knows where the next place will be?"

"That's so bizarre. I go to a regular school. Well, most of the time when I'm not..." She shot Riley a glance. "Okay, Cole was right. I'm on suspension."

"What hideous offense did you commit?" Riley asked.

"I kicked a guy where it counted. He was feeling me up and when I told him to stop, he didn't. So I nailed him."

Riley gave her a thumbs-up. "Works for me."

"Yeah, well, I got another lecture about not being combative and how I should have ratted the octopus out to the teacher and had the school deal with it."

"Was this his first offense?"

"No. He's groped other girls. Each time he gets a lecture from the principal and keeps on doing his grab-ass thing."

"How about after you nailed him?"

Sam shook her head. "Word is he's dialed it way down." She turned onto a side street. "Of course, my mom went ballistic. My uncle, not so much. He says I have to learn when it's best to fight and when it's best not to."

"Your school would not like me," Riley said. "I'm pretty peaceful, but sometimes I've found you just need to kick butt."

Sam smiled at that. "So that's my story, why I'm in the middle of... nowhere... bored out of my skull. Well, except I still have homework."

Riley groaned at that. Her homework was piling up at home. "I'm here to help Beck with his mom."

"You two hooking up?" Sam asked.

"No," Riley said wistfully. *Maybe someday.*

"Don't worry, my uncle will find him. He likes Beck a lot. Oh, and he said we should trade phone numbers in case you need to get around town."

It sounded as if Sam didn't mind that assignment.

⊹

Beck's "okay" ex-girlfriend's house was well maintained with a sizable flower bed that still had plenty of color, an indication that frost wasn't a constant visitor in Sadlersville. Unlike Sadie's place, this looked like a home.

Riley pushed the doorbell, then looked back over her shoulder. Sam had opted to remain in the car, texting a friend at her school. It was cool to have someone Riley's age to talk with, someone who didn't think Beck was a waste of life force.

The door opened and she found herself staring at a young woman with a heart-shaped face, pale cheeks, and fine blond hair. Louisa's pale blue eyes were wide and expressive, adding to the china doll look. Riley guessed her to be at least eight months' pregnant. That and the wedding ring signaled that Beck's ex had definitely moved on.

"You're Riley, aren't you?" the woman asked. At Riley's expression of surprise, she added. "Denny told me what you looked like."

"Is he here?"

"No, I haven't seen him, but I'm glad you came by. He said he wanted me to meet you."

Riley was waved inside. The house was toasty warm and smelled of cinnamon and baked apples. Louisa guided her into a small front room where Riley settled in a chair. Her hostess eased herself down on the couch next to a skein of pale pink yarn and a pattern for a baby blanket. The work-in-progress lay nearby.

"I have to sit here," Louisa explained, placing a protective hand on her bulging stomach. "If I sit in one of the chairs I can't get up."

"When are you due?" Riley asked.

"Three more weeks. It's a little girl." Then Louisa smiled and held up the crochet work. "As if you couldn't tell."

Riley smiled back. She could see why Beck had really liked this girl. She had no pretense to her.

"Denny called me the other night," Louisa added. "He said he was going out for pizza with you. He sounded really tired, but he had it together. Now I'm hearing people think he took off on you." She shook her head, frowning. "That's not like him."

"Did you call Beck last night about nine?" Riley asked, hoping for find out who had lured him away from the motel.

"No. Is it true Denny was going to ask the sheriff to reopen the investigation?"

"Who told you that?" Riley asked, astounded at how fast news traveled in this town.

"The cashier at the grocery. I thought it was a good idea. Now . . ." Louisa stirred uneasily on the couch. "I never believed he was guilty, you know? What if Denny's disappearance has something to do with that?"

So Riley wasn't the only one thinking in that direction.

"What do you remember about the weekend Beck and those guys went into the swamp?"

Louisa's expression darkened. "Denny and I had an argument a couple days before. He was ducking some things he needed to take care of and I called him on it. He didn't like it. When I asked if we were going to do anything for New Year's, he told me he already had plans and they didn't include me."

"Smooth move, Beck."

"You could say that," Louisa replied. "He wasn't easy to get along with back then and most of that was his mother's doing. I had no idea he was out in the swamp with the Keneally brothers until Cole told me."

"Cole? How did he know?"

"He said he'd heard it somewhere, but I found out later he was selling drugs to Nate Keneally."

Now we're getting somewhere. "Could Cole or Nate have told anyone else?"

"Maybe. I think the only reason Cole told me was to make me mad at Denny. He was always working on our heads. Eventually he broke us up."

"Beck still carries a grudge about that."

"Yeah, so do I." Louisa patted her baby bump fondly. "I wonder what would have happened if we'd stuck together. This little one might be Denny's and . . ." She looked up, embarrassed. "I'm not saying I don't love my husband, it's that sometimes I think of what might have been."

"No harm, no foul," Riley replied. "I do the same every now and then."

"Are you two . . ." the girl ventured.

"Close friends, but . . ." Could she admit the truth to Beck's ex? "I want more. I want what you've got. Well, not the baby right off but . . . you know."

Louisa smiled broadly, then it faded. "You have to find him, you hear? Don't let him disappear like those boys."

"I'll try." *No, I will find him.* She couldn't live with anything less.

By the time Riley left the house, she'd been given a picture of Beck from when he was fifteen. He lounged against an old car, clad in worn jeans and a black T-shirt, his summer-blond hair spiky and unkempt. His half smile barely disguised his damaged life.

It only made her miss him more.

FOURTEEN

As the temperature rose, Beck took the opportunity to strip out of his jacket and shirt so he could shake out the red bugs. Once he thought the clothes were less critter-filled, he put them back on.

All the while his mind was working through options. The lack of food was an issue and there wasn't anything within reach that would be of help. He'd pointedly ignored the bugs skittering around in the underbrush. He wasn't that desperate . . . yet.

He really needed to find the right stone or thick branch to use as leverage to widen the gap in the ring. Then once he freed himself from the tree, he could arm himself with the chain and make a dash past the demon toward the canal. From there he'd have to figure out which direction to walk to reach civilization, but he'd done that before and lived to tell the tale.

As he buttoned his shirt he found himself staring at the next tree over. It had a chain as well, a twin to the one holding him prisoner, probably left over from when they used to log the swamp.

If he could get that other length of chain free, maybe he could use it in some way, if nothing more than as an additional weapon against the demon. Beck walked over as far as his leash would allow, within ten feet of the tree, but couldn't cover the space. He went down on his knees, then on the ground, angling himself for maximum stretch. Clawing across the leaves and debris, he edged closer.

As he moved, he uncovered beetles and other crawly things. Beck shuddered and kept working forward inch by inch. And fell short. There was no way he'd be able to retrieve the other chain.

Swearing, he rolled over on this back and stared up at the sky. It was a brilliant blue, quite pretty, unless you were trapped in a swamp. *Think, dammit! There has to be a way to get free.*

His right shoulder blade began to complain about the uneven ground so he rolled up into a sitting position. Hoping to score a rock, he dug with his fingers, but instead unearthed something metal. *Even better.* Scooping away the dirt revealed the business end of a rifle and he excavated it from the ground.

Brushing it off, he felt a thrill of hope. If there was still a cartridge in the thing, maybe he could find a way to weaken the chain. He knew better than to try to shoot off the padlock; that only worked in movies. Beck struggled to his feet, knocking dirt out of the barrel, then opened the chamber. There was no bullet.

"Of course not," he muttered. At least now he had another weapon. It would only be a matter of time before some small critter got too close to him and the rifle would make a great club. If it came to eating raw squirrel rather than dying of starvation, he'd find the will to do it.

Exhausted, his muscles jittery, Beck rested. He caught sight of an anhinga observing him from its perch. The locals called them snake birds and when they dove into the water their feathers would became saturated. They'd have to sit in a tree until their feathers dried so they could fly again.

Beck's eyes lowered to the weapon in his hand. It seemed in decent condition other than the damaged stock which had suffered from too much moisture. He scrubbed away on the wood with a thumbnail, then froze. The wood had a skull and crossbones imprint and the initials NTK.

Nathan Tate Keneally

"Oh my God," he whispered. He knew this gun. He'd fired it once.

He looked up to find the demon watching him from a respectful distance, resting on its haunches again.

"Is this some trick of yers?" Beck demanded.

The fiend shook its head. "It has been here since *that* night. Do you remember?"

There was no way he could ever forget *that* night. It had played havoc in Beck's nightmares for years, switching back and forth with the one from the war.

"What really happened to them?" Beck asked, his throat tight.

The demon cocked its head. "Your soul for the answer."

"I've lived seven years without it, I can go a bit longer."

"So you'd like to believe," it replied, then crept off into the brush.

⁂

After her visit with Beck's ex, the next stop was Sadie's house. Though Sam offered to help with the cleaning, Riley declined the offer. This was her job, her way of thanking Beck for everything he'd done for her over the last few months. Besides, she needed time to think things through.

"When do you want me to pick you up?" Sam asked.

Riley checked her phone for the time. "Make it three hours. By then I'll be tired of cleaning. Meet me at the funeral home, will you?"

"Okay. I'll be here."

⁂

Riley blew through the remaining rooms in Sadie's house like a robot at warp speed, mostly because the work was mindless and the cleaning products smelled a lot better than stale cigarette smoke. As she scrubbed and dusted, she tried to look at Beck's disappearance from all angles. Cole was at the top of her list of suspects, but that was because she couldn't stand him. Still, it wasn't like the guy would make off with Beck just to get a chance to hook up with her. That meant this had something to do with the missing boys.

I hope Donovan can figure this out or Beck's screwed.

By the time Riley had finished nearly all the cleaning, she'd reached the one task she'd been putting off. Digging in someone else's closet made her feel like a voyeur, especially when that person was dead. It was no surprise to find that Sadie's clothes weren't fancy, mostly jeans, shirts, a few tank tops, and a jacket or two. Nothing you'd want to be buried in.

Riley kept moving clothes around until she found something promising. The dress was navy and had a slight sheen to it, probably knee length on its owner. If Sadie had done something with her hair and makeup, maybe added a few dozen pounds, she would have looked good in it. At least before she'd taken ill.

Riley laid it on the bed, wondering what had led Beck's mom to buy the dress in the first place. Was it for someone special? She dug around a little longer and discovered a pair of high heels. A check of Sadie's jewelry box didn't turn up much: The woman wasn't into bling. Feeling it was best to go simple, Riley picked out a cross and a plain pair of earrings. She packed everything up in a grocery bag and set off for the funeral home.

⊹

McGovern solemnly accepted the bag of clothes. "Thanks. I was wondering who was going to handle this now that Beck's gone."

"He's not gone, he's just . . . missing," Riley replied.

"Hope he hasn't done something stupid," the man continued.

"Like what?"

The undertaker hesitated. "He said life wasn't worth a damn now that his mother was dead. Said he wasn't sure how he could go on."

"What? When was this? At the hospital?" That certainly hadn't been a topic of conversation at the motel.

McGovern hesitated. "Last night. I called him and he came by to sign some papers. He said he was going to buy some beer and get hammered."

"What time was this?"

"Ah, about nine fifteen or so."

No way. Beck was too careful about driving drunk, worried he'd lose his truck.

"Did you tell the cops about this?" she demanded.

"Didn't seem that important," McGovern said, shrugging. "Denny was always out of control."

A low growl formed in her throat. He was lucky he was the only mortician in Sadlersville.

"Anything else you need?" she asked.

"Not right now. You headed home soon?"

"No, I'm not going anywhere until I find Beck."

When she reached the front door, she looked back. McGovern's eyes were narrowed and he was watching her too closely.

He's lying about something.

✦

Sam was in the parking lot, right on time. Riley had barely reached the car, about to offload about McGovern's stupidity, when a cop car pulled up next to her. It was the deputy who'd come to the motel, the one named Martin. His side window rolled down.

"Need you to come with me," he said.

"Did you find him?" Riley asked.

"We found his truck," was the terse reply.

"But what about Beck?"

"Just get in the car."

Riley's chest tightened. Had they found Beck's body and Donovan wanted to tell her the news in person? "Give me a sec."

She turned her back on the deputy and leaned over to talk to Sam. "Can I trust him?" Riley whispered.

"Yeah, he's on the level. He just lacks social skills."

That Riley could handle. "Thanks. I'll let you know what's going down."

"Hopefully it's good news," Sam said, but she didn't sound convinced.

Riley hopped into the cruiser and buckled the seat belt. "Where are we headed?"

"South of town."

As they made the drive, the deputy asked questions while Riley responded with noncommittal answers. She'd learned that skill from her time with the Vatican's Demon Hunters. As she saw it, if the cop wasn't willing to tell her anything, that could go both ways. Finally he gave up.

That works.

⁘

Their destination was the eastern edge of the swamp, somewhere near where Beck had taken her for their pizza picnic. The location looked like an impromptu parking lot with two other cop cars, some sort of state vehicle, and an ambulance.

Oh God.

"What is all this?" she asked, her fear growing.

Martin gave her a dispassionate look. "We found a suicide note and—"

Riley was out of the car before it came to a stop, her feet pounding toward the ambulance, kicking up sand as she ran.

No. Beck wouldn't do this to me.

Donovan stepped into her path, causing her to skid to a stop. "Hold on!" he called out.

"Where's Beck?" She searched for the familiar face, the one she longed to see, but he wasn't visible. Then she spied a man on the stretcher being carried over the sand by two EMTs.

"Beck?" she cried and took a few steps forward.

Donovan caught her arm. "It's not him," he said.

Then why am I here? As the stretcher rose to enter the back of the ambulance, Riley caught sight of a head crowned in dark hair and a face covered in blood.

It was Cole Hadley.

A short time later, the ambulance was rolling across the sand toward the main road, lights and siren engaged.

"What happened?" she demanded.

"Hadley's been shot," Donovan explained. "Don't know if he's going to make it or not."

"Who shot him?"

Martin joined them at this point. "Beck, who else?"

"We don't know that yet," Donovan retorted.

"Works for me. He gets Hadley out here—probably told him he wanted to buy some drugs from him—then he shoots him and takes his wheels. Not that I'm upset he did it or anything."

Could Beck have shot Cole? He certainly hated him enough.

Riley shook her head at the thought. "Shooting him puts Beck in jail and then he can't bury his mom or go back to Atlanta." *To his rabbit and his job and all the stuff that matters to him.*

She felt the shakes coming on so she took a couple of deep breaths to calm herself. "What's really going on here? He"—she angled her head toward the deputy—"said you'd found a suicide note."

With a glower at his subordinate, Donovan waved her forward toward the back of the pickup. The topper was open and the tailgate down. "Tell me if anything's missing or seems out of place. Newman's still dusting for prints so don't touch anything."

Riley stepped closer and peered into the bed of the Ford. She wasn't sure what she'd expected but there was nothing out of the ordinary. Fortunately there was no blood.

"It looks like it did last night," she said.

"What about in the cab?"

She moved around to the passenger door, which was open like the driver's side. As she peered inside, Newman sprinkled black powder on the steering wheel. Beck's keys sat in the ignition and the glove compartment door was hanging open.

"There should be a steel pipe and two blankets behind the seat. Well, maybe not the pipe. He gave one to me about a week ago and he might not have replaced it yet. They're expensive."

"What about inside the glove compartment?" Donovan asked.

"His trapper's manual, truck registration stuff, and . . ." She looked up at the sheriff. "He keeps his gun in there." *And a box of condoms.* She wasn't going to mention those or face ridicule from Martin.

"The gun is gone," the sheriff replied. "We found this on the seat." He handed over an evidence bag, like the kind on the cop shows. A piece of paper was inside, a note it appeared.

They were right. I killed Nate and Brad. What with my mother gone now, I hear them in my mind, calling to me. Demanding retribution for my sins. So I've settled my score with that asshole Hadley and I'm out of here. No one will miss me. Just like when I was alive.

Riley looked up at Donovan, her mind whirling. "What? This is total crap. He didn't write this."

"Tell me why you think that," the sheriff replied, watching her closely.

"Beck never called Sadie his *mother.* There was too much bad blood between them." She sighed, unhappy to give up one of Beck's closely guarded secrets. "That line, 'demanding retribution'? That's not Beck. He can barely read and write. Though the signature kinda looks like his handwriting, the rest of it isn't. It isn't even close."

"You sure about that?" Martin challenged.

"Yes, I am. I know his writing. This isn't it."

"Someone might have helped him with it," the deputy countered. "I know a few in this town who'd be happy to see him gone."

"Beck has everything to live for now. He's been invited to Scotland to meet some of the grand masters in the International Guild.

For a trapper, that's a *really* big deal." She speared the deputy with a look. "Does that sound like someone who's jonesing to kill himself?"

"Not unless the guilt got to him," Martin replied sullenly.

"No way," she said, shaking her head. "He wanted to clear his name. Someone doesn't want that to happen."

Riley's phone rang. Irritated at the interruption, she pulled it out. It was Beck's number.

"Ohmigod, it's him!"

"Put it on the speaker," Donovan ordered.

More fumbling, but she got it done. "Beck? Where are you?" she cried out. "Are you okay?"

"Go home," a raspy voice said. "It's over."

A second later, the sound of a gunshot split the air.

FIFTEEN

Donovan snatched the phone from Riley before she dropped it. As he strode away from her, he jammed a finger in one ear and tried to listen to the sounds coming through the speaker. There was silence, a clunking noise, and rapid breathing. Then the call ended.

He closed the phone. When he turned back, Riley was on her knees in the sand, rocking back and forth, sobbing, a strained, high-pitched wheezing sound issuing with every breath she took. Martin was on his knees, trying to reassure her.

Donovan knelt on the other side of her. "Take it slow. Breathe in, then out. You're okay."

"He . . . shot . . . himself. . . ."

"No, I don't think he did."

Riley's tear-tracked face rose to his, desperate. "But . . . I heard . . ."

"Just relax your breathing. That's what's important right now."

Riley closed her eyes and made an effort to slow each breath, making them deeper, less panicky. Then she frowned. "Beck wouldn't do that to me. That was cold. Cruel."

"I agree," Donovan replied. "If Beck shot himself . . ." He hesitated, his eyes meeting his deputy's. "It probably would have been in the head. His gun is a nine millimeter, which would have taken him down instantly. I should have heard a body hitting the ground or some noise to indicate he was incapacitated. Instead there was rapid breathing for at least seven or eight seconds, some other sound, maybe the gun being put down, then the call was disconnected."

"Beck can't hang up a phone if he's a corpse," Martin said, frowning.

"Exactly."

Fury built on Riley's face as she struggled to her feet. "What kind of sick creep fakes someone's suicide over the phone?" she demanded, her fists balled.

"The kind of person I want to see behind bars," Donovan replied. *Because if he's going to all that effort, he's hiding something big.*

When he placed his hand on Riley's shoulder, he felt her tremble. "Can you wait for me in my squad car? I'll drive you back to town in a little bit."

After she collected her pack from the deputy's car, Riley headed toward his cruiser. Though she held her head up and her back straight, Donovan could tell she was scared. She had a right to be. Someone had taken this situation to a new and sadistic level.

Martin watched her closely. "You sure it wasn't Beck?"

"I am. No way he'd do that to any girl. Especially not *that* o..e."

"So what do we do now?"

"Canvass the neighbors down here and see if they heard anything. Then pull Beck's and Cole's phone records, check who they've been talking to over the last few days. I'll swing by the hospital, see if Hadley is in any shape to tell me who's behind all this."

"That'd be like one snake turning on another," Martin replied.

"That's exactly what I'm hoping for."

⁜

Donovan waited until they'd reached the main road back to town before he opened up a conversation with his passenger. "You better now?"

She nodded soberly. "What about the truck?"

"As soon as we're done with it I'll have it delivered to the motel. Sorry, but the fingerprint powder makes a real mess."

"I'll deal."

"You planning on staying until we have this sorted out?"

"That's a definite," she said, her words clipped. "There's something you should know about the undertaker."

After he listened to Riley recap her conversation with McGovern, he made a mental note to have a talk with the man.

"Thanks. I'll check it out." He cleared his throat. "How much you know about Denver's past?"

"Some, but not much. He's pretty closed about it," she admitted.

"Then I'll give you a little background. When the brothers disappeared Denver was just holdin' his own. Sadie had a new boyfriend, a guy named Vic, and he used to beat on the kid. I never could get Denver to say a word about it and Vic was smart enough to hit where the bruises didn't show."

"He wouldn't have told you. He never left his mom because he was sure his dad would show up someday."

Donovan nodded his agreement. "I figured that was what was going on. Up to that point he'd listen to me, take my advice, then the brothers went missing. Louisa and Denver broke up and he spun out of control. After he was in a knife fight I sent him north."

"You did the right thing. Beck's turned his life around."

Donovan pulled past a camper and then cut back into the lane.

"I was really worried about him up there since his uncle didn't really give too much of a damn about the boy and both his grandparents were dead by then. When your father called me we talked for a long time. I realized Denver had himself a champion, and one he might respect. Over the years Paul and I kept in touch. That's how I learned the boy had been wounded in Afghanistan."

"My dad really cared about him." She looked out the window. "I don't have anyone left except Beck," she murmured. "I can't lose him. He's . . . too important to me now."

From the yearning in her voice it was more than friendship.

"Don't worry, we'll find him. One way or another."

She swung back toward him. "You didn't find those other boys."

"That's why I won't stop this time until I bring him home."

⁙

Beck was pleased to see that the hole he'd scooped out had about three inches of water in it. He knew it'd taste awful, but dehydration was his second biggest threat right after the demon. He cupped his hand and brought the liquid to his mouth. As it trickled in, he nearly spat it out, but forced himself to swallow it.

"God, that's awful."

"All the water you wish can be yours," the demon said. It was back in its usual position, scrutinizing him like a teenager does a freshly baked pizza.

"I know the drill," Beck replied, then took another long sip. "Ya'll give me everythin' I want in this world as long as I sign up to be yer slave in the next life."

"What is it you wish for, Denver Beck?"

"For you to go away," he replied. He went back to the task at hand—trying to free himself from the chain. Bashing the padlock only made his foot ache, so now he was trying to widen the gap in the ring. Where had the demon gotten the padlock in the first place?

"They hated you," the fiend continued. "Those two who died. They brought you out here to make fun of you."

Beck's nerve faltered. "I know that now." He looked up. "Why are you here? Why would a demon be playin' tag with the gators?"

The fiend's eyes flared. "Punishment, they said. For not honoring the Prince in the proper way." It spat in disgust. "For not heeding his commands."

"Not a fan of old Lucifer, huh?" Beck said, seeing if he could get a reaction.

The demon winced at the use of its master's name, but it didn't cry out in anguish like most of them did.

Beck sensed weakness. "Let me guess, yer one of Sartael's crew but somehow you didn't show up for the big battle. You thought that crazy old Archangel was going to knock off Lucifer and you wouldn't have to be there to help out. Now yer here. A traitor exiled from a bunch of traitors."

The demon moved faster than Beck thought possible. He brandished the rifle for protection, but the fiend had already struck and retreated. Beck staggered backward, scowling in pain. Keeping an eye on the demon, he warily bent down to touch a hand to his left leg. It came away bloody. Within an hour or two he'd start to feel the effects, first a fever, then, as the infection worsened, he'd begin hallucinating. If left untreated with Holy Water, the wound would kill him.

"Now you have no choice, Denver Beck," the demon snarled. "You will give me your soul or you will die here and no one will find your bones." It smiled and gestured toward the patch of ground in front of the other tree. "I'm sure the brothers will embrace you in death."

⁜

The body of the slain trapper lay at his feet, the victim's sightless eyes gazing upward in bewilderment as his lifeblood pooled in the sun's harsh glare. Ori shook his head at the man's stupidity. It was as if the fool had wanted to commit suicide.

He blamed the Creator for mankind's hubris. In this case, the insane belief that a lone demon trapper could battle a Divine and live to tell the tale. It did happen, but it was extremely rare. It had not happened today.

Ori had known the man had been tracking him for some time, then finally allowed him his moment of gruesome glory. The newly deceased hadn't been one of the local trappers—they knew better than to challenge one of his kind—but had come from another city in a brazen attempt to gain fame. In the end there was no fame, only death.

With a swipe of his hand the body flamed and then disintegrated, but the fire did nothing for the coldness within the angel's soul. Too long had he slain rogue demons for his master with scant praise. Even now, he was being pressed to kill more of them, and with no additional help. But that would change when Riley Anora Blackthorne returned to the city. Ori would make sure of it. He felt something close to impatience—an utterly human emotion—as the moment drew closer.

He picked up the faint scent of his prey, a rogue Archfiend, in the mortal city of St. Louis. Ori vanished, on the hunt once again. In many ways, he thought the dead trapper was lucky. That man had chosen the moment and manner of his death. As long as Lucifer reigned in Hell, Ori would have no such solace.

SIXTEEN

Riley knew she was being stubborn and wasting money by keeping the unused motel room, but the moment she packed up Beck's clothes and moved them into her room she'd be admitting he was gone. Maybe forever.

Restless, she called Stewart to let him know the latest, but he wasn't at home. According to his housekeeper he was attending yet another meeting between the witches and necromancers, in an effort to tamp down the tensions brewing between them.

So life sucks even back home.

She left a detailed message and then began to pace from room to room, unsure of what to do next. The helplessness was driving her crazy. Beck was somewhere and he needed her help but what could she do without wheels or any notion of where to turn next?

A knock on her door paused her pacing. If this was Beck she'd hug him first then shout. Then hug him again and never let go.

She checked through the privacy portal and found twin blue eyes gazing back at her.

Simon? He was the last person she'd expected to see in Sadlersville. She opened the door, not knowing what to say.

"Riley," he said, clearly as uncomfortable. "Master Harper sent me down to help you find Beck."

"Ah, okay." *Now what?*

Simon didn't move. "I know this is hard for you, but . . ."

"We'll work it out," she said, waving him in. "You can stay in Beck's room."

Simon didn't remark about the fact the rooms were connected and that the door between them was open. Luckily the housekeeper had made Beck's bed or it'd look even worse.

Riley opened a drawer and gazed down at the tidy piles of Beck's socks and underwear.

"I haven't moved his stuff because I thought . . ." She froze, her hands trembling. "It'll just take me a minute and . . ." Riley looked up at the ceiling, tears stinging her eyes. "Oh, God, Simon, what if . . . he's . . . dead?"

He turned her around gently. She wanted him to hold her, but with what had happened between them, was that even possible? Apparently he was thinking along the same lines.

"Stewart said we're not to come home until we find Beck," he murmured.

"But what if . . ."

"Then we'll find who hurt him and introduce them to Hell . . . *personally.*"

Shocked at the malice in his voice, Riley took a step backward. This wasn't the Simon she knew, the one who used to apologize to demons when he caught them.

Oblivious to the reaction he'd caused, he gestured toward the open drawer.

"Leave Beck's things where they are. I'll work around them. He can pack them up when he gets back."

That was a thick slice of hope and she clutched at it greedily.

"Yeah," she said, "let him do it. No way I'm touching his underwear."

Simon gave her a nod and a painfully thin smile.

Riley left him to unpack. As he moved around the other room, he was on the phone to Harper reporting that he'd was in Sadlersville and ready to take up the hunt. Though it made sense that he'd be the best trapper to send down to help her—all the journeymen would be too busy—it was hard to be close to him without remembering their past. She saw Stewart's hand in this, even though Harper had been the one to send her ex down south.

Riley had just turned off her computer when Simon stuck his head into the room. "I came down on the bus and I haven't eaten yet. You hungry?"

Riley really wasn't, but to humor him she nodded. "How'd you get out to the motel?"

"I hitchhiked. Couldn't seem to find a cab."

"Tell me about it." *Maybe we can get a ride.* She dialed Sam's number and when the sheriff's niece answered, she explained the situation.

"The new dude. Is he a hottie?" Sam asked.

"Totally."

"I'll be there in ten."

"We got a ride," Riley called out, not bothering to explain it was because of Simon's appearance.

⁜

A screech of tires in the parking lot announced their driver had arrived. As Riley and Simon walked to the car, Sam rolled down the window.

"You're right, he is a babe."

Riley groaned. *Just shoot me now.* "Simon, this is Samantha, aka Sam." *Who has no idea of how to monitor that mouth of hers.*

"Pleased to meet you," he said politely.

"Yeah, real fine," the girl replied and beamed.

Riley had Simon take the front seat, knowing that Sam would spend the entire drive with her eyes on him. If he was sitting in the backseat, that could get dangerous if they actually encountered any significant traffic.

"So what's it like?" Sam gushed. "Being a trapper I mean. Is it all kick-butt stuff, like the TV show?"

"It's unique," Simon replied diplomatically. Then he deftly changed the subject to Sam's life and away from his. Their driver didn't seem to notice. As she kept talking, Simon made conciliatory noises, but Riley could tell his mind was elsewhere.

"So where can we eat?" Riley asked. Now that she was out of the motel room she was hungry.

"There's an Italian place. That work for you?" Sam asked.

"Sounds good," Riley replied.

It didn't work for any of them as the restaurant was closed for a private party.

"God, it's like being exiled in Siberia," Sam grumbled.

Like moths to a flame, they ended up at the diner and chose a booth in the back. When Sam made sure to sit next to Simon, he seemed bemused by the attention. To her surprise, Riley didn't feel a bit of jealousy. Whatever she'd felt for her ex-boyfriend had been put to rest, reinforced by a drenching in Holy Water.

At least he doesn't hate me now.

As Sam inspected the menu, Simon dug two newspapers out of his pack and set them in front of Riley. "Sorry, I should have given you these at the motel. Stewart wanted you to read them. They're by the reporter Beck was . . . dating."

Dating? That wasn't what Riley would call it, but she didn't bother to correct him.

"Thanks," she replied and pulled the papers closer. She started with yesterday's newspaper. The article was not on the *Atlanta Journal Constitution*'s front page, which was a blessing, but buried inside. Beck's photo was decent and though she didn't want to give the Stick Chick any credit, the article was well written. There was nothing inflammatory until you read the last paragraph when Justine began to pose questions about Beck's early years in Sadlersville. In particular, his role in the deaths of the Keneally brothers.

Which meant the masters and all of Atlanta now knew Beck's darkest secret.

Grumbling under her breath, Riley switched to the next paper, the one that had been published that morning.

IS THIS DECORATED WAR HERO A STONE-COLD KILLER?

Her eyes lifted to meet Simon's. She could tell he was concerned about her reaction.

"I'm good." *I will be, right after I rip her lungs out.*

Riley skimmed over the article. Justine had made only one error, claiming Beck had been sixteen rather than a year younger. Still, it didn't answer the question, but laid out the pros and cons of the case. At the end there was another teaser:

Was Denver Beck the scapegoat for someone else's heinous crime?

"Stewart thinks the reporter is using Beck to flush out the real murderer," Simon observed.

"If that's the case, the killer would go after him, not her, which might just have happened." Riley folded the paper, thinking it through. "I need to make a phone call," she said, slipping out of the booth.

"What do you want to eat?" Sam called out.

"I don't care. Just order something with potato chips." It was time for fat, salt, and something crunchy.

Riley stepped outside the diner into the chilly night air. The town was quieter now, few cars on the road. Down the street the cop shop was lit up, three cars parked in front of the building. Donovan was still on the case.

Riley scrolled through her incoming calls until she found the one she wanted. As it rang through, she made a fist of her free hand. *I hate you, you lying skank. You hurt the guy I love, but if you can help me find him I'll . . . I'll . . .*

"Justine Armando," the lyrical voice announced.

"It's Riley Blackthorne. I'm in Sadlersville. I need you to help me find Beck."

"I don't understand."

"He's missing and the cops think he shot a local guy, then killed himself," Riley said.

"That's nonsense," Justine retorted. "Tell me what has happened."

Riley laid it all out for her, including the fake suicide call. "You were using Beck as bait to find the real killer." It wasn't a question.

"Not as such, but my articles may have served as a catalyst. I am in Florida conducting research on a collateral story. As soon as I am finished here, I'll come to Sadlersville." A lengthy pause. "However, in return I want the truth of what happened at Oakland Cemetery."

She never stops. "I can tell you about the battle with the demons, but that's it."

"I need to know it all."

"Not happening. I'm under orders from the Vatican." That wasn't quite the truth, but closer than Riley would care to admit. "Here's the deal. Your articles started this mess so now you're going to help me get Beck back. If you try to screw us over, you will have an enemy for life."

Justine huffed. "You are hardly a threat, girl."

Riley's mind conjured up the favor Lucifer owed her.

"In that you would be wrong," she said and then hung up.

⁜

Riley's ham sandwich and potato chips were waiting for her, but her stomach churned so badly it was hard to eat. She didn't like having to threaten people, even the skank.

Simon put down his hamburger and gave her a worried look. "You okay?"

"I just made a deal with the Devil," Riley said. When he registered surprise, she shook her head. "Not that one. The reporter chick.

Justine is going to help us. She knows this case as well as the cops but she can't get to town for a few hours."

"Then what do we do while we wait?" Simon asked.

"God, I don't know." Riley bowed her head. "I feel so useless. If he's being held captive somewhere, he'll be counting on me to find him." *Rescue him.*

Sam's tanned hand stretched across the table and gently touched hers. "Hey, you're not alone here."

Riley knew that. But Beck might be. *Or he's dead.* She had to prepare herself for that moment when everything good in her life ended. When there would be no more Backwoods Boy to harass. No cocky smile, no more kisses. His will left everything to her: his house, his rabbit, his money, but without Beck there to share it none of that would matter.

The rest of the dinner was quiet, even Sam sensing now was not the time to chatter. When they returned to the motel, Beck's truck was parked in front of their rooms, a note stuck in the door saying the keys were in the office. Riley checked in with the front desk guy to claim those and an extra room key for Simon.

As they headed to their separate rooms, her cell phone rang. "Hello?"

"Miss Blackthorne. This is McGovern at the funeral home. I'm ready on this end so we can hold the service tomorrow morning. That way you don't have to stay down here any longer than you need. I'm sure your family is eager to have you back home."

He'd pushed a *don't go there* button.

"Beck *is* the closest person I have to family," she said hotly. Simon leaned in the doorway now, listening in, caught by her sharp tone. "I'm not leaving until I find him. I'm sure his mom can wait a few days."

Riley winced at what had just come out of her mouth, but it was true. Sadie was past caring.

McGovern sighed. "This isn't like Atlanta, Miss Blackthorne. Not everyone wants Denny found," he replied. "You'd be best to back off or it could get unpleasant."

Was that a warning?

"I'm staying, Mr. McGovern. I don't care what happens. I'll find him, one way or another."

There was a lengthy silence.

"Well," he began, "since Denny's not here, I'll need to have you review the arrangements for his mother's funeral. Can you come by the funeral home tonight? Say about ten?"

"Tonight?" That seemed odd.

"I'm busy right now with funeral arrangements for another family. Come in the back door. I'll have everything ready."

I don't want to do this.

She gave in. "Okay, I'll be there." Anything to get this guy off her case.

SEVENTEEN

Despite her misgivings, Riley would have gone to the funeral home on her own, but Simon refused to let that happen.

"No, I'll go with you," he said. "There's something about this town that makes me nervous."

"Like what?" she asked as she cleaned the seats and steering wheel with hand wipes. The fingerprinting stuff seemed to be everywhere.

"I don't know. It's just . . . wrong in some way. Or maybe it's me. I'm not real trusting right now."

"I know how that goes." She pulled out one of the blankets Beck kept in his truck and had Simon spread it over the seat. That was the best they could do until she could find a car wash.

As they headed into town Simon fidgeted. That wasn't his style.

"What's wrong?" she asked.

He seemed startled she'd noticed. "Just a lot on my mind."

She waited him out.

"I've been meeting with a counselor. He thinks I'm suffering from posttraumatic stress disorder."

"And you think . . ."

"It's more than that. I'm so short tempered. I can go from cool to furious over nothing. Whenever I'm talking to someone, I wonder what their real agenda is."

Riley slowed to a crawl behind some guy in a battered Chevy. "I've been second-guessing stuff I've done." *Like trusting Ori.*

"You mean like agreeing to Heaven's deal to save my life?" Simon asked.

That she hadn't expected. "When I was really, really mad at you, yes. I wondered why I'd bothered. The truth is, I had to do it. You were a nice guy. You deserved to live."

" 'Were,' " he said. "Not 'are' a nice guy."

His depressed tone worried her. "Are you doing okay, I mean, you're not ... thinking ... of ..."

Simon shook his head. "Suicide is a sin and I have enough of those to deal with. I don't think I'll ever find peace again, not like I once had."

Riley halted at a stop sign, knowing he needed support, not condemnation. "You will and when you do, it'll be good again. Hell won't get a second chance at you."

"Maybe. Or perhaps they've already won and I don't know it."

⁜

Riley parked behind the funeral home, as McGovern requested.

"This guy is driving me nuts," she said. "He's making a bigger fuss than he needs to."

As they exited the truck, Simon's cell phone rang.

"It's my mom," he said, glancing at the dial. "I better take this. She's really worried about me right now and if I duck the call, she'll freak."

"Say hi to her for me. I'll be back in a bit."

The rear entrance led to the funeral home's garage where the hearse was parked on one side, its back door open. An empty body bag lay next to it.

That's creepy.

Maybe she should have waited until Simon had finished his call so she wasn't on her own.

Stop being a wuss.

"Hello?" she called out. When there was no reply, Riley continued on until she entered a hallway. She passed a couple of doors, but those were closed. Funeral homes had always unnerved her, but this one especially. Sometimes it was cool to see behind the curtain, know how things worked. Mortuaries were not included on that list.

Some instinct made her stop and turn. McGovern was behind her, standing in a patch of dimly lit hall.

"Oh, there you are," she said, trying to relax, but failing.

He moved toward her. "I'm sorry you had to come here, but I had no choice. Especially when the next of kin has committed suicide."

The last word hung in the corridor between them.

The hairs on the back of Riley's neck rose. How did he know about the note or the phone call? Was it small-town gossip or something else?

Beck had come to see this guy right before he disappeared. An undertaker could haul anyone out of town and no one would notice. They'd just assume it was a corpse.

Hello? This is not a horror movie. Get a grip.

"I've got the paperwork here," he said, beckoning her closer.

As he moved into the light she realized he wasn't holding any papers. Instead, he had a Taser and it was pointed directly at her.

✢

"Hadley," *Donovan said,* standing at the side of the hospital bed. "How's it going?"

Cole frowned back. His breathing tube had been replaced by an oxygen cannula and his color was better, but he still had more wires and tubes than a space shuttle.

It looked as if the loser was going to live, which was perfect for what Donovan had in mind.

"Who shot you?" he asked.

"Beck," he croaked.

The sheriff leaned over the bed in such a way as to ensure Cole saw his face clearly. It was time to get tough.

"You're talking bullshit. If Beck had shot you, you'd be dead. So who pulled the trigger? One of the pukes you sell to?"

No reply.

"Doesn't matter. The drugs we found in your pocket are your ticket to prison."

"What drugs?" Cole demanded, shocked. "I wasn't carrying."

That sounded like the truth and opened up a whole new set of possibilities.

"Oh, but you were. Cocaine. You're going down, Hadley."

"I wasn't carrying," he insisted. Then the patient's eyes widened. "That son of a bitch! He planted those drugs on me."

"That sucks," Donovan said, trying to keep the grin off his face. "Beck doesn't mess with that kind of stuff, so who set you up?"

Cole's face was bright red now and his breathing sped up. "That bastard McGovern."

Donovan's world spun once and then settled down in a new position. *McGovern?* That was the last person he had on his radar. He kept his tone mellow. "Why would he do that? Did you stiff him on a deal?"

"No, I saw him in Beck's truck the night Denny went missing."

"Where?"

"North, on the highway. He lives up that way. I was..." He halted in self-preservation.

"Out making a delivery, no doubt," Donovan guessed. "When was this?"

"About ten or so."

"You tried to blackmail him, didn't you?"

Hadley swallowed hard. "We just had a friendly talk," he muttered.

"Until he shot you." Donovan shook his head. "So where is Denver?"

"In the swamp. McGovern said it was the perfect burial ground. That whoever goes in there never comes back."

Donovan pounded a fist on the bed rail, startling the man. "Damn you, if you'd come to me sooner we might have had a chance to find him alive."

"I didn't have anything to do with that," Cole protested.

"You covered up a crime, and that's just as bad in the eyes of the law."

"I want to do a deal. You hear?"

"Then start talking, son."

⸎

Riley edged backward along the hall. "Why are you doing this?"

"It's nothing personal."

Like that helps. "This is what happened to Beck, isn't it?"

A nod. "It had to happen."

"Why?"

"Because he was the best one to take the fall."

Take the fall for what? "People know I'm here."

"They might, but come morning they'll think you headed back to Atlanta."

He moved closer, forcing Riley to continue her blind retreat. "That lie won't hold."

"Just needs to hold long enough for me to get on a plane out of the country."

She reached a door. Where did it lead?

"That's where the bodies are kept," McGovern said. "There's no way out."

He's lying. She twisted the knob and bolted for freedom. If she could get outside, she and Simon could escape, go to the sheriff, and . . .

To her relief, there was an exit on the other side of the room, leading to the garage. Once she was in the open space, she sprinted for the outside door, about twenty-five feet away. She'd made it about half that distance when something slammed into her back.

Then the pain came and Riley fell forward, her knees and elbows and face kissing the oil-stained concrete.

Had he shot her?

Riley's muscles twitched and her bones screamed in agony like they were being ripped away from the muscles. She fought to regain her feet, to run, but her body wasn't cooperating. It was as if someone had cut all the strings to her limbs.

McGovern stood over her, the Taser pointed at her. He had a gun stuck in his waistband and she bet it was Beck's.

"You should have left when I told you to," he said, shaking his head. "You had to stay for that damned loser."

"Where's . . . Beck?" she gasped.

"Gone. In the swamp. Probably in a demon's belly. You'll be joining him soon enough." He raised his hand again to deliver another jolt.

Before she could cry out, someone mowed McGovern down. Simon's lithe figure struggled frantically with her captor, the Taser scooting away from them on the concrete. He slammed a fist against the man's face as McGovern tried to throttle him. As they exchanged a flurry of blows, they rolled into the rear wheel of the hearse, then tumbled back into the center of the garage.

McGovern regained his feet and pulled the gun free from his pants before Simon had a chance to react. He pointed it at Riley.

"Stay put or she's dead."

Her heart nearly stopped. Simon slowly regained his feet, breathing heavily and his eyes filled with unrestrained rage. If he went after her captor, he was going to get both of them killed.

"Police! Drop the weapon, McGovern!" someone shouted.

Donovan and the two deputies spilled into the room. Martin and Newman fanned out on either side of their boss, their guns drawn. The sheriff's was out as well.

"Put the weapon on the ground. Do it!" Donovan bellowed.

Her captor didn't move.

"Now, McGovern! I swear I'll take you down."

The undertaker slowly lowered the gun, then bent over and placed it on the garage floor.

"Step back!"

As he complied, he caught Riley's eye. "Damn you, girl, you should have gone home. Then it would have been all right."

EIGHTEEN

As she sat in the sheriff's office, people bustling around her, Riley was sure she'd been flattened by a truck. Her joints and muscles ached down to their individual cells, her head throbbed, and there were two points on her back that felt as if someone had driven spikes into them. She'd refused a trip to the ER. She could imagine what the National Guild would make of that insurance report: Apprentice demon trapper nearly electrocuted by crazed mortician. She had enough notoriety as it was.

Simon sat next to her now, an ice pack pressed against a cheek that was already darkening, the beginning of a spectacular bruise. His shirt collar was ripped and his lip was cracked and bleeding. He had a dressing on his right hand and his knuckles were skinned.

As she'd tried to recover from the attack, he'd filled in the missing pieces: The longer he sat in the truck, the more anxious he'd become, so he decided to see what was going on. When he found McGovern standing over Riley's body, he'd lost it. Fortunately, the sheriff and the others had arrived just in time.

"When are we leaving for the swamp?" she pressed.

"We can't until morning," Martin replied. "We have no idea where Beck is, so we need daylight to try to track him. I know you're frustrated. So am I and I don't even like him."

Not until morning. This would be Beck's second night alone. *He must think I'm not coming for him....* If he was still alive.

Simon touched her arm. "You okay?"

Riley shook her head, the tears burning. She swiped them away, angry that she had no way to stop them.

"We'll find him. We'll bring him home," he said.

She nodded and then dug for a tissue in her pocket as Donovan entered the office. He laid numerous evidence bags on his desk.

"McGovern had Beck's phone and his gun. He's asked for a lawyer so we won't get anything more out of him." The sheriff sank into his chair. "But why?" he asked, his voice rising in frustration. "What drove him to kidnapping and attempted murder? What is McGovern hiding?"

"Perhaps I can shed some light on that darkness of yours," someone said from the office doorway.

Justine.

"She's back . . ." Riley mumbled. Her jealousy raised its muzzle and scented blood.

The reporter looked perfect as usual. Her emerald green eyes lacked dark circles underneath, her pants suit didn't display one wrinkle, and her hair cascaded down her shoulders in smoldering red waves. Justine chose a chair next to Riley, probably so everyone in the room could make the comparison between *together* and *total mess.*

"Have you found Beck yet?" the reporter asked.

"No. He's somewhere in the swamp," Donovan replied.

The reporter frowned. "I know the undertaker's secret and why he has turned violent as of late. In return, I want an exclusive on the story."

Riley ground her teeth. She might hate Justine Armando, but the reporter was very good at her job. If anyone could unearth secrets and lies, it'd be the Stick Chick.

Donovan didn't hesitate. "You've got a deal. Talk to me."

Justine retrieved a notebook from her expensive leather bag and opened it. Running down a page of notes with a polished fingernail, she began.

"A decade ago a necromancer in Jacksonville began paying a few Florida undertakers to supply him with bodies suitable for reanimation. These bodies were sent for cremation by families who didn't want to sit vigil at the gravesite." She shifted to another page of her notes. "In late 2009 two Georgia undertakers joined the scam. Bert McGovern was one of them. He served as the collection point for corpses in the southern half of state."

"Go on," the sheriff urged, sitting up in his chair now, his attention captured.

"Instead of being cremated, bodies that were in good condition were transported to the summoner in Jacksonville. McGovern filled the urns with concrete dust so the families had no idea their loved one was being auctioned off to the highest bidder."

"My God," Riley murmured. That was too close to home after her father's death.

"One of the bereaved relatives saw their deceased sister in Orlando a few months after she'd died," Justine continued. "When the police checked it out, the summoner stonewalled them. My reporter friend heard about this and he began investigating the story."

"The Jacksonville Police Department know about all this?"

"Yes. They arrested the necromancer earlier today."

Justine closed her notebook, her brows furrowed. "I have no direct evidence, but I believe there is some connection between McGovern and the missing boys."

"There is now." Donovan chose a file from a stack and flipped it open. "In November 2011 the Keneally boys broke into three businesses in Sadlersville and stole mostly small stuff to satisfy their growing drug habit. The sheriff at that time worked out a restitution plan, and they got a juvenile record out of the deal in exchange for returning the goods they'd stolen."

"A juvenile record," Justine murmured, nodding in understanding. "No wonder I couldn't find the connection. The boys' parents said nothing about that, of course."

"They robbed the tire store and the video shop and ... the funeral home. McGovern never reported the break-in and our office only found out about it after the sentencing. He claimed they'd not taken anything so he hadn't felt the need to file a complaint."

Justine tapped her notebook with a gold pen. "If the brothers had found evidence of the corpse-running scheme during the break-in, McGovern would be eager to pay them off to keep them quiet."

"With drugs and booze from Cole Hadley," Donovan added. "McGovern was one of Hadley's *customers*."

"That doesn't explain why they went missing," Martin argued. "McGovern would have had to know the boys were in the swamp that weekend to kill them."

"Cole did," Riley said, finally seeing the pieces fit together. "He told Beck's girlfriend he knew where the boys were going. Maybe he told McGovern."

"So the undertaker kills the two boys, but doesn't know Beck is along for the trip because he's asleep in the boat. Which still works in McGovern's favor as there's someone to take the blame," Donovan said.

"But why shoot the drug dealer?" Simon asked.

"Cole saw him in Beck's truck the night Denver went missing so he tried to blackmail McGovern," Donovan replied. "Cole didn't plan on an undertaker pulling a gun on him."

There was quiet for a time as each of them digested the news.

Riley closed her eyes. "So how do we find him? Can the park rangers help us?"

"The feds won't authorize a chopper until four days have passed. We'll do it ourselves," the sheriff explained. "There'll be three teams. One will go in the east entrance, just in case he's down there, and the other two at Kingfisher Landing. Of those two teams one will take the canal to the west and the other to the south."

The time for waiting was over. Now they'd be able to do something, even if it was nothing more than bringing Beck's body home for burial.

⁘

The fever and body-wracking chills struck Beck with a ferocity he'd not anticipated. There'd been numerous demon wounds over the years and after the first, they'd been mildly annoying. This time was different. He had no Holy Water to neutralize the toxin and his body was running on empty, the lack of food and abundant clean water taking their toll.

When he opened his eyes there was someone watching him. It was a young Indian, a Seminole, indistinct in the night air. Donovan had said the ghosts of the swamp's dead would sometimes appear. The brave inclined his head and then walked away into nothingness.

I'm dyin'. There was no hysterics involved in that realization, because it was the truth. He'd been there before, after that roadside bombing in Afghanistan. Somehow he'd survived.

But this time . . .

The chain wasn't going to magically break or a buffet appear at his elbow, so that left two options: Continue on to the grave or accept Hell's bargain.

Another chill rolled through his body, clouding his sight. Beck curled up in a ball, shivering so intensely his muscles ached and his teeth chattered. In his fevered mind he saw Riley in the coffee shop in Atlanta, laughing with Ori. She wasn't looking for him. She'd left him behind.

"Riley will . . . come . . . for . . . me," he whispered. "She won't leave me here."

"She doesn't care, trapper," the demon whispered in his mind. "Don't die because of your pride. Accept Hell's mark and live. You can take your revenge against all those who hurt you."

"No."

"Paul Blackthorne gave us his soul. So can you. There is no shame in it. Your life is precious," the demon said.

"Paul . . . isn't in Hell now. He out . . . witted y'all." Beck issued a dry chuckle at the thought.

"You're mine, trapper. You will raise my stature in Hell, and I will find favor with the Prince again. You *will* give me your soul."

"Go screw yerself, demon."

The fiend laughed, a sharp biting sound. "You mortals always say that, until the *very* end."

✛

It was nearly eight in the morning when Riley arrived at Kingfisher Landing, still aching from the night before. Her guide, a guy named Ray, was hurrying as much as possible, but it took time to do things right. What little patience Riley had was history: She wanted to be actively looking for Beck rather than cooling her heels at the dock.

Ray was in his early fifties and said he'd been conducting tours of the swamp for over a decade. That was reassuring. Donovan had warned her the journey would be at least five hours long, then it'd take that much time to get back out to civilization. If Beck was in bad shape he'd need food, water, and first-aid supplies, not counting Holy Water if he'd tangled with a demon. An early morning trip to the convenience store had netted those supplies and now they were packed into Beck's duffel bag and Riley's backpack. Everything was ready, but they were missing someone, a man named Erik. So far he'd been a no-show.

"What about the other teams?" she asked.

"They went out half an hour ago."

Like we should have.

Simon was on one of them and, to Riley's surprise, Justine was on another. The reporter had refused to stay in town, saying she'd always wanted to see what a swamp was really like.

Maybe an alligator will carry her off.

Ray dialed a number, then spoke with someone. His brow creased in frustration, then he ended the call. "Erik has backed out of the trip. It's just us unless I can find someone else."

Surprise. "No, let's hit the water," Riley replied. "Beck's running out of time. We need to go now."

Ray didn't argue, but helped her into the boat and then pointed out the blankets underneath her seat. "It'll get cold when we start moving."

Riley unearthed one of the heavier ones, draping it over her knees. Fortunately she'd thought ahead and had added a few layers under her jacket and bought a stocking cap. As Ray did something with the motor, she studied the area around her. The water was a perfect mirror, reflecting the tall trees and brown grasses along its edges. Birdsong reached her ears and every now and then something would flit from treetop to treetop. There was a unique smell in the air, part decay, part fresh earth overlaid by abundant moisture.

"I'll use the outboard for a while, then switch to the electric motor," her guide explained. "That way we'll be able to hear Beck if he calls to us."

"Why not use it right now?" she asked, concerned they might go right past him if he was injured.

"It's slower. As I see it, if I was going to get rid of someone in the swamp I sure wouldn't leave him close to the dock."

Ray had a point. "What about the demons? Have you ever seen them?"

"Yes, off and on over the years, but the swamp can play tricks on you when it wants to. If you're out here on your own, I've heard they can be dangerous. Usually I'm guiding a group so I've not had much trouble."

Riley readjusted the thick blanket around her to stave off the chilly breeze blowing across the water. What would it be like for Beck? They really had no clue where to look and McGovern had refused to help them by narrowing the search area. They were on their own.

Maybe we're not. She dug out the strange polished rock the woman had given her and held it tightly. At this point she'd do anything to find her missing guy.

"Keep an eye on either side as we move along," Ray advised. "If you see broken branches or signs someone might have been hauled onto the bank, call out. I'll try to do the same, but with the water level being lower than normal I'll need to watch for submerged logs."

He started the motor and they began to move down the canal. As Riley scanned the banks only one word seemed to apply: *primordial.*

Okefenokee tolerated humans, at least for brief periods of time. Someone had dug the canal they were using—it was too straight for nature's efforts—but those same people had failed to tame the swamp. Just the opposite: The land of the trembling earth had tamed them.

Riley couldn't quite understand how something so beautiful could be so alien. Thick cypresses grew on either side of the forty-foot-wide canal, massive giants with the roots buried deep in the water. Cypress knees, bizarre knobby monoliths, had formed around the base of the trees like small children. Even the water itself was strange, tea-colored, and reflective. She stared down at it, unable to see very far under the surface.

Ray called out over the sound of the motor. "The water has tannic acid in it from the rotting vegetation. It's perfect for the alligators. They can hover just beneath the surface and wait for the right moment to grab a meal."

Riley immediately leaned back, away from the edge of the boat. She didn't see any gators, but that didn't mean one of them wasn't scoping her out.

Sometime later Ray cut the throttle and switched over to the electric motor and sudden stillness enveloped them like a shroud. As he studied the water in front of him, he gave her more of Okefenokee's history, how a canal system had been dug in the late 1800s to try to drain the swamp and that the project was eventually abandoned. Then came the loggers who cut massive amounts of timber. The canal they were floating in was constructed in the 1950s to dredge peat. Now the place was federal parkland.

In the distance Riley spied a huge bird sailing over the water to land in a pine tree. "Wow. Look at him! What is he?"

"That's a great blue heron."

As they drew closer, the bird took to the air again, swooping a short distance and then landed along the bank. She guessed its wingspan to be at least six feet wide and its faint blue coloring seemed to blend in with the grayish Spanish moss. Once again, it took flight moving farther down the canal, as if it was guiding them. A harsh croak floated across the air, the bird announcing its territory.

Near the bank an alligator surfaced like a living submarine, then pulled itself onto solid ground with its stubby front legs. It was at least ten feet long, big enough to take down a man.

Ray pointed out another lounging on the far bank. "As the temperature warms up they'll pull themselves out of the water onto the bank to sun," he said. "This time of year they're still sluggish. They'll get livelier as the temperature rises. In the summer they're really active."

Riley's hope began to fade. What chance did they have of finding one guy in the middle of this vast wilderness? What if Beck was injured and nowhere near the canal; would he even know they were searching for him?

She called out his name and there was no reply. "Do you think he can hear me?"

"Who knows? Maybe we'll get lucky. If you see anything odd, let me know and we'll check it out."

It all looked odd to her, but she tried her best. As they moved deeper into the swamp there were more basking alligators and the occasional turtle on a log. The trees appeared to be in mourning with heavy veils of Spanish moss. It would have been eerily captivating if the guy she loved wasn't out here somewhere.

Time passed and so did long stretches of swamp. They glided by a fork in the canal that led north. Riley would call out every now and then, but other than the occasional response from a bird there was no sign of Beck. As the hours moved by them like the slow water, her heart grew heavier. Ray pulled up to the bank a few times, checking for signs that someone had exited a boat. He shook his head each time.

Where are you?

⁜

At five and a half hours into the search Riley's throat was raw and there had been no sign of Beck. When Ray broached the subject of turning around, she nearly cried. Instead, she reluctantly agreed as dark would come soon. Behind her, she heard Ray calling the sheriff to give him a report. When he finished, she asked if the other teams had had any luck.

"No," he said, shaking his head sadly. "They didn't find him."

The last time she'd seen Beck he'd had been sitting on the back of the truck, beer bottle in hand, grieving for his mother. She'd never told him she loved him. She'd never told him a lot of things that she had sheltered inside her heart, believing they still had time to be together.

Oh, God, please, no. It can't end this way.

As they floated back down the canal, another heron kept them company, flying ahead a short distance, landing, and then waiting as they caught up. Riley would have enjoyed it if she didn't feel like it was mocking them.

When they drew closer, the heron held its position. As they passed it, the heron squawked and Riley turned to study it. Where the creature stood the bank looked different. She blinked, her eyes so tired she was sure they were playing tricks on her.

It's nothing. There's been nothing for the last five hours.

The bird squawked again. It was refusing to move on.

Her instincts took over. "Ray, we need to check something out."

He must have heard the urgency in her voice. "Okay. Show me where."

Ray turned the boat around in a lazy arc and returned to where the heron still roosted. When they drew near, it flew off after one loud squawk.

As the boat moved toward the bank, Riley held her breath.

Please let us find him. He wants to come home to me.

NINETEEN

Ray cut the motor and they drifted. He gave her a quizzical look. "What did you find?"

"There . . . see that?" she said, pointing at a break in the brush. "It looks different."

The area she pointed at appeared as if something had been dragged across it, bulldozing small branches and leaves out of its way.

"Could have been an alligator, but we'll make sure." Ray rose, using a long pole to maneuver the boat slowly toward the spot.

"Looks clear. I'll tie us up." He crawled out and after securing the boat he examined the stretch of bank she'd indicated. "There's no gator tracks here." He knelt and then pointed. "But that's a boot mark and it's pretty fresh. We need to check this out."

Riley felt a thrill course through her body.

Something made her uneasy, as if someone was watching them. Was it a demon? Ray had mentioned seeing them in the swamp on previous trips. Ill at ease, she extracted a bottle of Holy Water from her pack. Maybe she was being paranoid, but most times that was the best way when dealing with Hellspawn.

Riley handed out the heavy backpack, then Beck's duffel bag. It was just as heavy, fully loaded with bottles of water and food.

"We could leave these here," Ray tactfully suggested.

"I have this feeling we'll need them."

"Okay," he said, hefting Beck's duffel on his back. "Follow right behind me and watch where you step. I'm searching for more footprints, scraps of fabric, anything. If you see something, tell me, but don't go after it on your own. I'll do that."

She filed all that away as they began the painstakingly slow hike through the swamp. The ground was uneven: Tree roots and broken branches were everywhere. Critters moved in the brush around them. Riley didn't want to know what they were but she figured they were all keen to nosh on trapper. Something above them began to make an unholy hammering noise.

"What is that?" she asked, scanning the trees.

"Pileated woodpecker." Ray halted and then pointed at something. "What does that look like to you?"

She peered around him. In the dirt was a footprint, but it wasn't human.

"It's a demon. See the claws?" she said. "It looks like it was dragging something."

"Maybe it was our missing trapper," Ray replied.

The farther they walked, the more Riley could hear the clock ticking. Dusk would be coming soon and they had to find Beck tonight. She called out every now and then but other than the sounds of the swamp, there was no reply.

Ray put up a hand for her to halt and then he pointed again. Sitting near a log was snake, a big one, though any reptile seemed huge in the middle of the wilderness. It began a dry, ominous rattle.

Riley gulped. "Is it poisonous?"

"Yes. Pretty, isn't it?"

She had to admit it was kind of cool all coiled up like that, gray with sort of black chevrons. "What kind is it?"

"Canebrake rattler. We'll just wait until it wanders off. They're not aggressive unless we get stupid."

Hope the snake knows that.

After letting them know it wasn't amused at being interrupted, the creature slithered away, five feet of reptilian beauty.

As Riley waited for her heart rate to drop, something came across the wind, faint and distant.

"Wait," she said, touching Ray's arm. She closed her eyes and concentrated, trying to separate the sound from everything else around them. Then she smiled. "It's Beck. He's singing. Can you hear him?"

Ray shook his head.

The voice stopped. Had it all been an illusion? Was she so desperate she was hearing something that wasn't real? Or was it a demon luring them deeper into the swamp?

The singing started up again and this time she knew she wasn't hallucinating.

"It's him!" she cried. "It's a Carrie Underwood song. He plays it in the truck all the time."

They moved forward faster now, but still with that caution that came with not knowing what might be underfoot. The voice faded in and out. Finally it stopped.

"Beck?" she called out. "Beck!"

They kept going forward hoping to hear the song again, until they entered a broad clearing, an open space with a few massive cypress trees. It took her a moment to find Beck in the scene, his light brown jacket serving not only as a cover, but as camouflage. He was propped up against a massive tree, his bearded face crimson and sweaty, his hair matted down and eyes distant. He stared up at her in bewilderment.

"Get away from me, demon!" he croaked, flailing his arms at her.

That wasn't good news.

"Ya can't have my soul," he said, then began coughing so hard it was difficult for him to breathe. "Yer not Riley. She's not here."

"Oh, yes I am," She hurried forward, not caring if there was any kind of creature in her path. The moment she dropped to her knees next to him, Beck swung at her.

"Stop it!" she commanded.

He blinked at her, his eyes still not focusing properly. "Yer real?"

"Sure am."

"No, you can't be. Yer with that damned angel . . ."

Ray hunched down near the trapper, laying the duffel bag on the ground.

"Hey, guy, we found you," he said, smiling broadly. "Just in time, I think." He traded a worried look with Riley.

"Ya *are* for real. Oh, thank God," Beck murmured, then began to shake. "I thought ya'd forgotten me."

"Never," Riley said, touching his burning hand. "We'll get you back to the boat, then to the hospital. You'll be okay."

"I'm . . . not goin' nowhere," Beck said, shaking his head, each movement exaggerated. When he gestured toward his left foot, Riley stared in horror at the thick log chain around Beck's ankle.

"What the hell?" Ray blurted.

"Demon did it," Beck said. "That damned McGovern was gonna kill me . . . and . . ."

"We know. We'll get you out of here, don't worry," Riley said, more for his benefit than because it was the truth.

She noticed a dark stain on Beck's jeans below the left knee and knew what it was on sight: The fiend had injured him. That explained his fever and his disorientation.

The demon must not be that powerful if it had to resort to such a bizarre trap. With Beck unable to escape, it had given him a wound, one that would keep pumping toxins into his system. Even if he was hallucinating, he could still hand over his soul and it'd be a one-way trip to Hell's front door. Trappers would no doubt rate special treatment down there.

That's not going to happen. Not to him.

"Any way we can get that chain off?" she asked, the joy of having found her guy fading.

"I've got some tools in the boat," Ray said. "I'll go fetch them. One way or another we'll get him free."

That's what she'd wanted to hear.

Riley pulled a Holy Water sphere out of her backpack and handed it to the guide. "If the demon gives you any trouble, hit it with the sphere. The Holy Water will burn it like acid and it'll back off."

The man nodded and headed toward the canal.

"Hang in there, Backwoods Boy."

Beck's eyes were closed now and he was quaking with the fever. Seeing him so ill freaked her out. It'd probably been the same for him when he'd found her dying in her apartment after she'd tangled with a Three. Riley pushed down her fears and began laying out supplies to treat his leg. Once that was done, she'd try to get some water into him before they began the long trip back to the landing.

When Ray returned there was nothing in his hand but the sphere. His troubled expression wasn't comforting.

"What's wrong?"

"The tools are gone. Every one of them." He looked around, nervous. "And my cell phone isn't getting a signal. That's not normal. What's going on?"

Riley did a quick check of her phone. Same issue. "It's the demon, it's messing with us."

It took a moment to locate it near one of the trees, a mud-colored and hairless monster with those blazing red eyes she'd come to despise.

The fiend moved a few steps forward, its head cocked. "Blackthorne's daughter," it hissed.

"Give us back those tools. Now!" she demanded.

It laughed, shaking its head. "The trapper is mine. Leave him or you will die."

"We'll have to get some help," Ray whispered, his attention never wavering from the Hellspawn.

Beck stirred. "Get out of here," he said, waving them away. "Leave me some water and . . . I'll be fine." As if to prove he was lying, his body began to quake from another spike of fever.

By the time we come back, you'll be dead.

There was only one way to do this.

"I'm staying here," Riley announced. "Please go get us some help."

Ray stared at her like she was a lunatic. "That's crazy," he protested. "I can't move through the water that fast in the dark. It could be tomorrow morning before I can get back. I know you're a trapper, but spending a night in the swamp with one of those things is . . ."

"What a trapper does," Riley replied, her voice amazingly calm. "Beck won't make it on his own. I can treat his wound and keep him alive while you get those tools."

"You sure about this?" the guide asked.

She nodded, her insides fluttering like a bird trapped in a cat's claws.

"Ah, damn," he said, agitated now. "You both better be alive when I get back."

"It'll be okay," she replied. *Now I'm sounding like my dad.* "You should get going. It's almost dark."

With one last look at Beck, Ray began to edge his way out of the clearing. The fiend tensed, hissing again. The moment it launched itself at the guide, Riley was on the move, her Holy Water sphere arcing toward the rushing Hellspawn. The demon shrieked in agony as the sacred liquid impacted its chest, scalded its skin, and with a snarl it whirled and vanished into the undergrowth.

"Go!" she cried.

Ray took off at a run toward the canal, feet pumping and Holy Water sphere in hand. If he didn't make it to the boat, she and Beck were in big trouble.

Knowing she didn't have that much time before the fiend returned for round two, she dug in her backpack. Tucking a bottle of Holy Water under her left arm, she used the steel pipe to inscribe a circle in the dirt around Beck and the tree. She made it at least fifteen feet in diameter to give her room to move. Every few feet she'd pause and fill in the circle with the liquid, building a sacred barrier as she went. It was hard going. Her back cramped, her knees trembled, but she kept at it.

Beck roused and began to sing about a good old boy who went to war and whose family made moonshine, his voice cracking at the higher notes. Riley smiled at the tune, but kept constructing the holy barrier.

About halfway around she ran out of Holy Water. After collecting another pint, she kept digging in the dirt, pouring the liquid, over and over. Another bottle gone and she'd only brought four. Once the circle was completed, she took the third bottle and walked the line, filling in any gaps. When she was sure the Holy Water barrier was as strong as she could make it, Riley sank on the ground near Beck. As long as there was only one Hellspawn, it'd hold. If it brought back friends, it would get ugly.

In the distance she heard the sound of a boat motor revving up, signaling Ray had made it to the canal. Or it was the demon making her think help was on the way.

We'll know in the morning.

✛

Riley twisted open the lid on a quart bottle of water and offered it to Beck. He grabbed onto it with both hands and began to drink in earnest.

"God . . . that's good." Another long swig.

With her knife, she cut the seam of his left pants leg, beginning at the ankle. The demon wound was a long slice on the outside of the calf and Riley shuddered at the copious drainage. Once the wound was completely exposed, she gave him the warning.

"I need to treat this with the Holy Water. You ready?"

He gave a faint nod and she let a stream of the liquid drop onto the wound. As the infection bubbled in reaction, Beck sucked in a sharp gulp of air. Then he swore, long and loud.

Sorry.

Once the wound looked fairly clean, she rinsed it with clear water, then applied a light bandage. She'd be repeating the task every two hours until the infection was gone. After she stashed away the supplies, Riley insisted he take some aspirin and finish off the water. He still had a high fever, but that would disappear with the infection.

As Beck dozed fitfully and the night deepened, Riley sat vigil, her nerves on a razor's edge. She was prepared for the demon's return, the magical knife her friend Ayden had given her in the sheath at her waist. The steel pipe sat to her left and a Holy Water sphere to the right. Now that she'd found the man she loved, there was no way Hell would have him.

I will die first.

But wasn't that what love was all about, the realization that someone else mattered more than you and that you'd do anything to keep them safe? Even if they didn't love you in return.

⊹

When Beck struggled back to consciousness, he was pleased to find he felt better. He raked his nails over his chest in broad swipes. His fever was dropping and he was hungry, all of which was good news. But when he saw Riley, he growled under his breath.

"What the hell are ya doin' here?" he demanded, cloaking his concern in anger. "This isn't some damned picnic."

She ignored his question and fired one back. "Why are you itching?"

"Bug bites. The things are in my shirt, eatin' me alive."

"That I can fix," she replied.

Between them they managed to pull off his jacket and shirt. After shaking her head at the mass of red marks on his chest, she handed over a packet of hand wipes. Beck was going mad from the itching, so he gave in. Though the wipes were cold, they felt good and he used them to clean his hands, face, arms, pits, and chest. Riley did the honors to his back. By the time she was done, he was shivering in the chilly night air, his skin dotted with goose bumps.

Riley pulled off her jacket, then a sweater, revealing a heavy sweatshirt. It was one of his and as it came off her shirt rode up and the edge of a pink bra peeked out. He knew better than to mention it. Riley helped him dress and the sweatshirt felt good. It smelled of her and for some reason he liked that.

"Stealin' my clothes while I was gone?" he asked.

"Only the sweatshirt," she replied. "Your jeans didn't fit that well."

God, he'd missed her humor. She wasn't freaking like some girls would. Instead, she was meeting the challenge head-on.

As he studied her, he noted fresh bruises on her face and he asked about those.

"McGovern," she replied. "He wanted to bring me out here to keep you company because I wouldn't stop trying to find you. He's in jail now."

Beck felt a ball of fury ignite in his gut. It was best that the bastard remain behind bars or he wouldn't be aboveground long if Beck had his way.

"What the hell was this all about? He wouldn't tell me."

"He was covering his tracks." Riley leaned back against the tree and spun him the whole tale. The longer she spoke, the more he worked out for himself.

"He killed Nate and Brad, didn't he?"

"That's what Donovan thinks," she replied. "He would have killed you too if he'd known you were sleeping it off in the boat. You would have just disappeared like the other two boys."

Beck moved his gaze to the far tree. Were their bodies under those leaves? Had the demon done them all a favor without intending to?

When she offered him his jacket, Beck shook his head. "The critters are in that too. They're from the Spanish moss."

"Okay . . ." Riley set the garment aside and unpacked a large, silvery, thin blanket from her backpack, then laid it out about five feet away from where he was sitting. "Let's move you over here. This will keep you warm and get you away from the bitey things."

Though he was already too warm from the fever, it seemed like a good idea. He made it to his feet with her considerable help and then hobbled over to the new location, his leg throbbing with every step. The moment he was settled she tucked the silver blanket around him.

"What about you? It's gonna get colder," he said.

"I'll be okay." She wouldn't be in a couple of hours, but they'd cross that bridge later.

"So what else ya got in that pack of yers. Any food?"

"I thought this wasn't a picnic," she retorted, arching an eyebrow.

He frowned at her. Why did she have to challenge him all the time?

"Ya scare me when ya do this kind of crazy stuff, girl."

"I scare myself too," she admitted.

A few moments later he had an unwrapped power bar in his hand. It vanished within seconds, followed by a handful of orange slices and some beef jerky. He took a healthy chug from a bottle of sports drink, then leaned back against the tree in relief. His stomach wasn't happy that he'd eaten so fast, but that couldn't be helped.

"So what's the story with the rifle? Is it McGovern's?"

"No, I found it here," he said, unwilling to get into whose it was or what that might mean. "No ammunition, so it didn't help me much."

He closed his eyes and he could hear her moving around, then he caught the scent of wood smoke. She'd lit a fire without his help—he didn't think city girls knew how to do that. After a time he dozed, images of his mother and the dead boys haunting his dreams.

TWENTY

When the demon returned a few hours later it was evident the Holy Water had hurt it. Its chest looked like it'd been attacked with a flame-thrower and every now and then Riley could hear a whimper cross its lips.

"You will die here," it growled, glaring at her. "You will pay for my pain."

She ignored it, refusing to allow the thing to get a foothold in her mind.

"Remember, Denver Beck? Remember how I told you of her angel lover?" the fiend taunted.

"Give it a rest, demon," Beck mumbled.

"Has she told you of her soul? How it is ours now? How she gave it to *him* . . . forever?"

There was a rapid intake of breath behind her as Beck digested that bit of news.

"Thanks for that," she muttered. Riley had intended to reveal her secret when the time was right, if there ever was such a thing. Now it was out in the open, flopping around like a dying carp.

"Tell me it's lyin'," Beck demanded.

She couldn't meet his eyes. "No, I gave my soul to Ori."

"Oh, girl," he murmured.

The demon barked in triumph. "Why is she here? Is it for you, trapper, or for her demi-lord? Did he order her to find you? Did he order her to *kill* you?"

Riley exploded off the ground. "Where do you come up with this stuff? Do you losers have a giant book of lies and you choose which ones sound good?"

She took a couple of steps forward, her knife out of the sheath now. Then she halted. The demon was baiting her, trying to get her to break the circle.

"Is that what's happenin' here?" Beck asked. "That angel tell ya to kill me?"

He's sick and this damned thing is playing with his mind.

"No."

"How can I believe ya?"

She shot a look over her shoulder at the wounded man. "But you'd believe this piece of Hell crap?"

The fiend chortled to itself, then blended into the brush. It had sown the seeds of doubt and now it just needed to let them grow.

You're history, demon. I don't how I'm going to do it, but you're dead.

Beck went silent after that, refusing to talk to her. In time, he fell back asleep, but he wasn't resting easily. He kept jerking awake, his eyes wide, then he'd close them again. She'd just stoked the fire when he lurched out of a dream, his eyes darting around, wide with fear as his breath came in short pants.

"Beck? What's going on?" she asked, moving closer.

"Demon. It keeps pushin' on my mind. I hear it over and over tellin' me what that damned angel did to ya and—" He jammed his palms against his ears. "Oh, God, make it stop!"

Panicking, she knelt next to him. Singing country songs to block the demon's mind games wasn't going to do it. They needed something stronger than Hell's lies.

Love.

Riley didn't know whether he loved her, but she knew he adored her father. She gently guided his hands away from his ears. "Beck, hey, look at me." His eyes tracked to hers, pleading. "Tell me about my father. You know, how you met and what he was like."

"What?" he said, bewildered.

"Talk to me about my dad," she ordered. "The demon can't screw with you when you're thinking about someone you love." She wasn't sure if that was true or not, but it was the only weapon they had against the dark voice in Beck's mind.

"Yer playin' with me, tryin' to get me to—"

"No! I'm trying to help you. Please listen to me. I would never do anything to hurt you, Beck. I swear that on my father's grave."

He blinked, then nodded his head, the message getting through to him. "I did love Paul. He was so good to me. He was like the daddy I never had."

"Tell me about the first time you guys met. It was in class, right?"

Beck gritted his teeth as if the demon had tried to cut across his thoughts. "It was . . . in American history class. I'd only been in school a few days and I was still pissed at Donovan for haulin' my ass up to Atlanta."

Riley sat next to him, tucking her jacket around her for warmth. "Go on, I want to hear it all." *Keep talking . . .*

Beck took a deep inhalation then let it out slowly. "I told Paul that I didn't do any effin' homework, that there was no point. He said I should stay after class. I figured I was goin' to the principal's office and then maybe get detention. If I did that enough times they'd kick me outta school and then I could do what I wanted."

"Then what happened?" Riley executed a quick demon check. It had to be out there somewhere.

"Instead of bustin' my ass, Paul sits me down and asks me a bunch of questions—where I'm from, what TV shows I like, stuff like that. I couldn't figure out what he was doin'."

Beck grimaced again.

"Don't listen to that other voice. Tell me the story," she urged.

"I . . . I told Paul to go screw himself. I figured that'd get me tossed out of class, maybe the school. Instead, he gives me an assign-ment: I was to write a paper about the one person in the whole world I thought was awesome. I told him there wasn't anyone like that. Then he said I should write down what that person would be like if there was one."

She remembered this part—her father had said he wasn't sure if he'd ever be able to reach the boy. Then, after a solid week of pres-sure, Beck had finally turned in the assignment, six barely readable sentences, riddled with misspellings.

"Did yer daddy tell you what I wrote?" he asked.

"No." He'd taken that secret to his grave.

"I wrote that all I wanted was somebody who wouldn't judge me for who I was and where I came from. I just wanted a chance like everyone else." He leaned back against the tree and gazed upward at the stars, as if he could see her dad in Heaven. "Instead of laughin' at me, Paul said he'd be happy to give me that chance, but in return I had to earn it."

"He was amazing," Riley said, the loss pulling at her heart. Both of her parents had been so great.

"Still is. Probably teachin' angels a thing or two." He looked over at her, pensive now. "I gave him hell for another week or so and then we started workin' together, after school. Most of the time I fought him for every inch of ground, but he didn't give up. By the time I joined the Army I could sorta read and write, just slower than most." Beck blinked in surprise. "Hey, it worked. I don't hear that damned demon no more."

"Go you," she said and gave him a thumbs-up.

He peered out into the darkness. "It'll be back. It won't leave us be."

"We only need to make it through tonight," she said, refusing to believe that morning wouldn't bring help. If she started thinking that way Hell would have won. "How's about some more food?" Ri-ley rummaged around in the pack and unearthed a small bag of bar-becue potato chips which she dropped in his lap. "Sorry, I don't have any hot dogs."

He wasn't looking at her again.

"What's wrong? Is it the demon?"

A shake of the head. "You told me you didn't give up yer soul that night when the angel . . . Why did you lie to me?"

"I didn't lie to you, Beck. I signed over my soul during the battle at the cemetery, when I de-statued Ori. That way he would go after Sartael."

"He can give it to anyone in Hell, even Lucifer."

She shook her head. "No, he can't. That was part of the deal. Only he has control of it."

"You believe him?" he asked, incredulous.

"Yes. Ori swore on the Light, and that means everything to him."

The bag of chips lay forgotten in his lap. "If you hadn't made that deal we'd all be dead. Millions . . . would be dead."

There was nothing she could say to that.

"Dammit! That demon had me goin'," he snarled. "They tell you lies and then sprinkle in just enough truth to make it sound right." He shook his head in despair. "Sorry. I should have known better. Yer Paul's daughter. You wouldn't go down easy."

Which was what she'd told the angel.

"You want a banana?" she asked, hoping to change the subject.

"No, you have it."

Riley didn't eat it, though she was hungry. They might need it in the morning, or the next morning if someone didn't come to get them. Instead, she listened as he crunched his way through the bag of chips. When they were gone, he finished off the sports drink, then leaned back against the cypress, thoughtful.

"I've never had a woman in my life that believed in me as much as you do."

She touched his hand fondly and he immediately grasped it. They held hands for a time, then he curled up under the silver blanket. He was quiet for a few minutes, then she heard, "Thank you, Riley."

"You're welcome, Den."

He slid into sleep and this time he wasn't restless. She tucked the blanket up around his shoulders and then gently bent over and kissed his cheek. He wasn't quite so hot now and that meant he was healing.

She returned to tending the fire, scanning the darkness for the trouble that was sure to come. The demon had failed in its latest gambit. It would try again.

⁙

Beck rose from his bed a few hours later, slightly dizzy, mumbling something about having to take a *walk around the tree and deal with all that water* he'd consumed. When he hobbled back, he appeared more alert.

"How are you doing?" she asked.

"Better. Time to work on the leg again?"

She treated the wound and was pleased to see it was already beginning to heal. Within a day or so it'd be a long red line, yet another one of the many scars that graced his body.

"You get some sleep. I'll keep watch," he offered.

Riley wasn't comfortable with that idea, but he sounded in control so she agreed. He insisted she curl up under the silver blanket and they switched places. She handed over her jacket, worried he'd get cold. It wouldn't fit, but at least he could put it around his shoulders.

"Wake me up in a couple hours," she said, then burrowed down and let sleep claim her.

Something stirred her awake a few hours later, but it wasn't Beck. The fire had died down and he was asleep on the ground next to it, lightly snoring.

There was movement within the circle. Riley shot out of the blanket, fearing it was the demon, but instead it was a curious raccoon shuffling across the ground. When it saw her, it growled, then took a run for it, hurrying across the leaves and into the night.

Beck roused, then sat up and yawned. "What's wrong?"

"A raccoon came into the circle and woke me up."

"Huntin' for food, most likely."

"It wouldn't have screwed up anything, would it?"

"Not unless it dug at the circle or somethin'. Just crossin' the Holy Water wouldn't make a difference." Beck groaned and stretched. "God, my back hurts."

He poked at the fire and added more wood. Then he blew on it. When it sparked back to life, he rose and walked back to the tree, dragging the chain. Riley remained on the alert.

"What's botherin' you?"

"Something doesn't feel right," she said. "Not like before."

Riley began to walk along the inside of the circle, studying the ground. Suddenly, she halted.

"Beck! I need Holy Water, quick!"

He never got the chance to retrieve it. All he saw were the bright red eyes and talons as the demon charged directly at him. Lightning fast, Riley was in its way, coming up into a fighter's stance, the knife in her hand. He'd never seen her move that quickly.

The demon skidded to a halt. "This soul will be mine," it said.

"He's not yours, not ever," Riley retorted, the blade glowing silver-blue in the faint moonlight.

Beck reached the end of the chain, but he couldn't get near them. "Back up toward me, real slow," he said.

She paid him no attention.

"You think I will not kill you because of your demi-lord," the demon replied. "You are wrong."

"Leave this circle or you die," Riley said evenly.

In a blur the Four leapt at her before Beck could shout a warning. Riley caught it by the throat and slammed it into the ground, the knife piercing its chest and driving deep into its heart.

She rose, like an ancient war goddess come to life as the black demon blood coursed down her blade. The fiend's lips were moving, mouthing curses, but no sound came forth. Then it died.

What the hell was that? Beck hadn't trained her how to do hand-to-hand combat and he doubted Stewart had.

Slowly the wildness that had claimed Riley drained away, leaving her confused and unsteady on her feet.

"Are you okay?" he asked.

Riley shook her head. "I feel weird." She stared down at the fiend and the bloody weapon in disbelief. "I killed it?"

"Seems so," he said, trying not to let his panic bleed through his voice.

After that, she went on autopilot, cleaning the knife and replacing it in its sheath before she dragged the demon's body outside the circle and into the brush. After rebuilding the Holy Water barrier where it'd been breached, she rejoined him at the tree. Despite her assurances she was unharmed, he checked for wounds and found none.

The Riley he knew never would have been able to destroy a demon with such cold-blooded precision. Clearly, her angel had extended his protection to her. How else could she survive a head-on attack from a rampaging Hellspawn?

Riley stirred. "I don't remember killing it, Beck. What's wrong with me?"

"Nothing," he soothed. "It happens like that in battle." Fortunately, she accepted the lie.

He insisted she join him inside the blanket, anxious as to what was going on in her head.

"I should keep watch," she murmured, but he could tell that wasn't going to happen. She needed to rest.

"We won't be bothered again. That corpse will tell any of the others that they don't want to mess with us." *With you. Because yer Fallen will make sure of it.*

"Okay," she said, then snuggled up against him. "Sorry, I smell like dead demon."

He stroked her hair until she fell asleep. What did that liar Ori have in mind for her? Why keep her alive instead of claiming her soul?

He'd know soon enough. If they ever got out of here he was going to hunt Ori down and have a little chat with him. If Beck didn't like the answers, Hell might come up short a Fallen angel.

✢

The sound pulled Beck out of a solid slumber somewhere near dawn. It sounded like a harp. For a moment he wondered if he was dead and someone was welcoming him to Heaven.

"My phone," Riley mumbled. Apparently the demon's death had restored their means of communication with the outside world.

She dug under the blanket and came up with it. Then she dropped it on his chest.

He took charge. "This is Beck." He grinned when he heard the message. "Sounds good. See you soon." He hung up and laid the phone outside the blanket. "That was our ride. They're about thirty minutes out."

A lazy smile came to his companion's face. "Good. Wake me when they get here."

For once Beck wasn't in any mood to hurry out of bed. No, he was fine where he was, other than the fact that his leg throbbed and his back ached. He tucked Riley up against him, enjoying the feel of her next to him. It was a miracle they were both alive.

I've been an idiot. No other way to look at it. He'd been so convinced that the only way to survive his past was to keep his present away from it. That had only managed to get him backhanded every time he tried it.

No more. Riley had been right—he should have trusted her, should have known she wouldn't turn away from him. All he'd ever seen from her was a fierce need to protect him, a need so strong that she'd risked her life for him in the middle of an accursed swamp.

When he was young, his granddaddy had told him that someday he'd find a woman that would be his equal, one that would complete his soul, and that she would be there for him when life got rough and stick by him even when he was being a dumbass. If Beck ever found that woman, and kept her close, he'd be twice the man he would have been without her.

His granddaddy knew a thing or two about that—he'd been married to Beck's grandmamma for forty-five years until death finally broke that bond. They would have easily made fifty if his heart hadn't given out on him.

Did Beck have that special woman in his arms? Was Riley the one who would stay with him? It made Beck anxious to think that might be the case. If so, everything he did from this moment on was vitally important. He dare not screw it up.

Beck sighed in resignation, knowing they had to get moving. "We should get goin'," he nudged.

"Why?" she replied, still mumbling. "I like it here. Well, not in the swamp. You know what I mean."

He did. "I like it too, but that was Simon on the phone. How well is he gonna take it that we're all tangled up together?"

"That's his problem."

He grinned. "Come on, lazy girl. We need to be ready to leave when they arrive." When she didn't budge he used the one lever that would get her up. "Who knows, they might have a reporter with them. It'll probably be Justine. She'll take some pictures and they'll put them right on the front page of the paper."

Riley was up in a heartbeat, running a hand through her tangled hair in horror, scowling.

"You're evil, Denver Beck."

"So I've been told." He retrieved a wet wipe and handed it to her. "You have demon blood on yer face."

"Yuck. . . ." That set off a frenzy of cleaning and hair brushing. To him, she was beautiful without all the effort, but he knew she wouldn't believe him if he told her.

When Riley was done, he borrowed her brush and tried to get himself in good shape. Who knew? There just might be a photographer.

They had the campsite tidy, trash bagged, and the remaining supplies packed within a few minutes. The demon's body was noticeably missing.

"Probably some scavenger," Beck said. Her silence told him she wasn't buying that.

Riley did a quick bathroom run, fretting about snakes the entire time, but returned unbitten. As they waited, they shared some of the beef jerky and the last banana.

"Why did you come out here?" he asked. "Yer not a country girl. You could have left it to someone else."

Riley tossed the peel in the trash bag, thinking through her answer.

"I knew if anyone was going to find you, it was me," she said. "But to have you vanish, forever . . ." She shuddered. "I couldn't deal with that. It was bad enough to lose my parents, but you . . . you're . . ." She looked away as if embarrassed at being so open. "You're part of me now, Beck. You always will be."

He didn't know how to respond to that. He tried on a number of words, but they seemed inadequate so respectful silence seemed to be the best option.

In the distance there was a shout and Riley answered it. In a short time a team entered the site: Donovan, Ray, and Simon.

"No photographer," she said, shooting Beck a mock glare.

"Could have been," he said, smiling.

"God, it's good to see you, Denver," the sheriff said, crouching down next to Beck. "Damn good." They grasped hands firmly.

"Same here," Beck said. "Now please get this thing off me."

He groaned in pain as the guide worked the bolt cutter between his boot and the tight chain. Ray applied pressure and Beck's face went red. Finally the chain fell free.

"Thank you, God," he said. He unlaced his boot and when it and the sock finally came off, his ankle proved to be bruised and raw.

Simon noticed the dried demon blood inside the circle. "Bad night?"

"Yeah. I had to kill a Mezmer," Riley said.

He gave her a strange look, but didn't reply.

Riley broke open the first-aid kit. While she dealt with the wound, Beck pointed to the rifle near his duffel bag. "Got somethin' for you, Donovan," he said. "It's Nate's. I recognized it right off."

The sheriff inspected it and then nodded. "Where'd you find it?"

"Over near that other tree," Beck said, angling with his head. "McGovern was headed this way before the demon caught up with him. I think Nate and Brad are here somewheres."

"You didn't tell me that," Riley protested.

"I didn't want to spook you," he replied.

Donovan crossed the space and then began to sweep away the leaves and debris with the tip of the rifle.

With Beck's foot properly bandaged, Riley carefully eased the sock back on, then his boot. He laced it loose, watching Donovan out of the corner of his eye. The sheriff knelt, dug around in the dirt, and unearthed something white. He studied the object for a moment, then held it up. It was a bone, possibly a rib.

"Sweet Jesus," Beck murmured. *The demon was right.*

Simon crossed himself.

"I wonder which one of the boys it is," Donovan said as he returned the bone to where he'd found it, then covered it over with leaves. "I'll call the forensic team. They're going to love this location."

Beck limped to his feet with Riley's help. "Get me out of here," he said, suddenly more emotional than he cared to be. Nate and Brad hadn't been good to him, but they deserved better than to die out in the middle of nowhere.

As Ray helped him down the path, Beck paused long enough to look back.

Rest in peace, guys. Sorry I wasn't there for ya.

TWENTY-ONE

Though Riley really wanted a nap on the way back, she was treated to a euphoric Beck who was surfing the *I can't believe I'm alive!* wave.

"This is the third time this swamp has tried to kill me," he announced, triumphant. "Still, it's a glorious place, isn't it?" He pointed toward the far bank. "I mean, look at those yellow flowers. They're so pretty."

They were pretty now that Riley wasn't fearing for his life.

"You know, maybe someday I'll come back here and take a canoe through the place. Stay overnight at one of the shelters. You could come with me. Just the two of us."

Riley wisely didn't reply.

⁂

When the boat abruptly slowed, Riley woke to find herself covered in a blanket, her head on Beck's lap. He was sound asleep and she nudged him awake. She slowly sat up and then stretched, her muscles weighing in one by one. In the distance she could see the dock along with news vans and one familiar redhead. *Justine.* Somehow the alligators hadn't eaten her.

Donovan and Simon's boat docked first and quickly unloaded.

Once Ray pulled their boat up to the shore, the sheriff offered Beck a hand to help him out.

"Best not to say what happened out there," he said in a lowered tone. "Don't worry, your story will be heard."

"Just as long as it is." Beck hobbled up the concrete ramp, then stopped, eyeing the ambulance. "I'm guessin' that's for me."

"Sure is," the sheriff said. "Once you're done at the hospital we'll take your statement at the office." He looked back at Riley. "You can pick him up there in a few hours."

"Will do." That'd give her time to have a shower and maybe a longer nap. Then it'd just be the two of them. She wanted nothing more than for her and Beck to curl up together and the rest of the world to leave them alone.

"Where ya been, Denny?" someone called out. "Been playing with those dead boys' bones?"

Beck bunched his fists but kept walking, the sheriff by his side.

A reporter got in their way. "Is he under arrest? Mr. Beck, tell us, what happened out there?"

Donovan pushed him aside. "No comment."

By the time Riley reached the top of the ramp, the center of everyone's attention was in the back of the ambulance. Beck gave her a nod, then lay on the stretcher. The doors swung closed.

As if on cue, the crowd's attention turned toward Riley. Two reporters were in her face and there was the constant click of camera shutters. To her surprise, Justine wasn't in the fray, but stood some distance away, as if she was above such juvenile drama.

As Riley and Simon climbed into the pickup, questions flew, along with catcalls and ribald comments about what she and the wounded trapper had been doing in the swamp.

"How can they say things like that?" she demanded, slamming the passenger door.

"Because they're idiots." Simon fired up the truck and made sure to spin sand and gravel out of the parking lot, raising a cloud of dust that swirled around the knot of reporters, causing them to cough and shield their eyes.

Riley grinned and gave her fellow trapper double thumbs-up. "That was awesome!"

"I didn't do anything," he said, but there was rare mischief in his eyes. "I'm not used to driving a truck."

Riiight . . .

✧

As they neared town, Simon caught her up on the phone call he'd made to Atlanta on the way back to Kingfisher Landing.

"Since we found Beck, Harper wants me back home tonight. I called Sam and she can take me to the bus station after I grab my stuff at the motel."

Maybe he wasn't finding Donovan's niece too much of a flirt after all.

"Why do they want you back so soon?" *Please tell me there are no more zombie demons.*

"Harper needs every trapper he can find, what with all the calls coming in. The hunters left yesterday so it's all on the Guild now and there aren't that many of us left."

Riley felt a twinge of regret. Though she held mixed feelings about the Vatican's team, she had wanted to say good-bye to a couple of them.

"I don't get it," she said. "Why didn't Rome just tell everyone what really happened at the cemetery? How close we came to the end? Maybe then they'd all get a clue and start doing things right."

"Because not everyone is happy that the world didn't end."

"What? It would be a horrific thing. Zillions of people would die. Who would want that?"

"It depends on what you believe. If you're looking forward to the Rapture and being summoned to Heaven, then you'd be disappointed when it didn't happen and maybe angry at the one who stopped it."

That would be me. "Are you . . . angry?" she asked.

A frown creased Simon's brow. "I'm not sure," he admitted. "A month ago I would have been. Now?" He gave a half shrug. "I've learned that nothing is that clear-cut. The End of the World I believe in might not be the one that actually happens."

Amen.

‡

By the time Riley finished her shower and dressed in fresh clothes, Simon was packed and waiting to say good-bye. In the past she would have given him a kiss, but now everything had changed. She could still feel the Holy Water soaking into her clothes, hear his furious accusations and that betrayal had cut deep.

Hell had drawn first blood from both of them.

Still she owed him something. "Thank you, Simon. You saved my life the other night."

He seemed troubled at Riley's gratitude, which confused her.

"It's not that simple," he replied.

He crossed to Sam's car and hopped in like he was eager to escape. With a wave Sam drove away.

Now you're weird again. What is it with this guy?

‡

Riley's plan to swoop in and collect Beck from the sheriff's office was foiled by the one woman she'd hoped she'd never see again: Justine. Sitting at one of the deputy's desks, the Stick Chick was in full reporter mode, notebook and tape recorder in full view. Beck sat nearby, a cup of coffee in his hand, his sore leg propped up on the seat of another chair. Someone had found him some clean clothes as he was in a pair of sweatpants and a white cotton T-shirt now. Above all, he appeared at ease, as if Justine no longer posed a threat.

Riley's resentment immediately stirred from its fitful slumber.

What was it about this woman that pushed every single one of her buttons? Justine was female antimatter in high heels and crushed silk. Though Riley worked hard to keep her expression neutral, when Beck caught her eye he smiled, as if he knew what was going on inside her head.

Yeah, I'm jealous. Just deal.

Riley noted that his tone wasn't friendly, but measured, and he answered Justine's questions crisply and without any extra words, like he was testifying in court.

Grudgingly, she shoved the Jealousy beast back into its cage and slammed the door, denying it the power it craved to ruin her life.

"I'll wait outside until you're done," she said.

Justine's emerald eyes appraised her. "This will take some time. I'll drive him to wherever he wishes to go once we've finished our interview."

The beast howled in torment, rattling the cage's steel bars, wanting to rend and maim.

"That work for you, Beck?" Riley asked, her jaw so tight it was difficult to speak. When he nodded, she left the pair of them behind before she did something stupid.

The instant she was in his truck, she pounded the steering wheel much like he often did, and then glowered at the building.

I go all the way into the damned swamp and save his butt, and then she swoops in . . .

How long would the interview take? When it was done, would they go for drinks and then . . .

The jealous howls in her mind grew frantic and only tapered to a petulant whine when she finally reached the motel.

⁘

Ninety-eight minutes later Justine delivered Beck to the motel. Not that Riley was counting or anything. There was some brief conversation outside Beck's hotel room, which Riley couldn't really hear. Instead her caged beast helpfully filled in the details.

Beck: *Let me ditch the kid. Then we'll knock boots until dawn, baby.*

Justine: *Oh, Beck, you're such a stud.*

Riley thumped her forehead with the palm of her hand to halt the jealousy soundtrack. In reality it was probably more like:

Beck: *Ya've had yer damned interview, now we're done. Hit the road.*

Justine: *(pouts)*

The door to Beck's room opened and then closed. The first stop was the bathroom, then he hobbled into her room, aided by a cane.

"Washing off her lipstick?" Riley asked before she could stop herself.

"Yup. Didn't want you to get jealous or anythin'," he shot back. Then he sank on the end of the bed. The medicine they'd used on his chest and arms had bled through the cotton T-shirt in little blue splotches.

"Donovan found another undertaker willin' to handle Sadie's funeral. It'll be two days from now."

Which meant Riley needed to finish cleaning the house and get all that fingerprint dust out of the truck before then.

Beck continued on, oblivious to her mental list making. "Donovan's having a press conference tonight. He's gonna lay it all out so folks know who's to blame." Beck cleared his throat like he was going to say something more, then shook his head. "I need some sleep."

"Beck . . . about Justine . . ."

"Don't go there."

A few moments later he was in his own bed. She couldn't leave it like that, so she made her way into his room and sat next to him. His eyes opened and then his hand trailed over to touch hers.

"Sorry," he said.

"I was good for it," she said. "The skank makes me crazy sometimes."

"Only sometimes?" he asked.

"All right, every time I see her I want to tear her head off. Are you happy?"

She got a lopsided grin for that admission.

"Now you know how I feel when I think of that damned angel." His hand left hers to pull back the covers. "Stay with me until I go to sleep. Just behave yerself, you hear?" he said, a smile lightly gracing his face.

"Are you kidding? You've got a bad leg, you're a mass of bug bites, and you look like a Smurf. None of that makes me hot, Beck."

"Figured."

She kicked off her shoes and curled in next to him. He put his arm around her. "That's better," Beck murmured. Less than a minute later he was sound asleep.

As Riley listened to the beat of his heart under her ear, she knew that things would never be the same between them. For the first time her in life, she was eager to see what the future would bring.

⊹

The next day was a blur of activity. As per Beck's instructions, Riley had donated Sadie's clothes, the kitchenware, and most of the furniture. His request that she leave the sofa in the house didn't make much sense, but she did as he asked. Sam had insisting on washing the windows while Riley scrubbed the floors. As they raced through the final few tasks, her new friend had traded texts with a certain apprentice trapper in Atlanta.

By nightfall everything had been completed and to celebrate, Riley picked up a pizza and took it to the motel. This time the restaurant owner didn't give her any grief. In fact, he threw in a free six-pack of soda and asked how Beck was getting along.

After supper, Beck was unnaturally quiet, but she didn't push him to talk. He was trying to read his book, but she could tell his head wasn't into it. Finally he set it down.

"I want to stay down here a few more days."

That was unexpected. Riley had figured he'd want to be out this place the instant the funeral was over.

"Okay." What else could she say?

"I'll take you to the bus after the funeral. Jackson will pick you up at the station."

Clearly this had all been planned out without her input.

"Some reason you're so eager to get rid of me?" she asked, her feelings stinging a little.

"Got things to do and things to think about. Can't do them if yer here," he said. "We'll talk once I get back to Atlanta."

Talk? She was hoping for a whole lot more than that. "What's this about?"

"Not yer concern," he said, testily.

Now her feelings were really hurt.

"Whatever, Backwoods Boy," she said, and retreated to her room for the night.

+‡+

The day of her father's funeral Beck had cooked her breakfast and driven her to the cemetery. In all ways he'd been respectful of her loss. It was Riley's turn to show Beck that same respect. She made sure his truck was clean, inside and out, which took over an hour because of all that fine fingerprinting dust. She pressed his dress shirt, tidied his suit, and polished his shoes. He never said a word as they drove to the cemetery, but she knew he'd noticed it all.

The graveyard was small but there were a fair number of people gathered near the funeral tent. Given Sadelia Beck's reputation, it was a good bet most of the attendees were just being nosy. To Riley's relief, Deputy Martin was screening the mourners, keeping the majority of the press away.

Thank you, she mouthed as they drove by him. He nodded in return.

Once she parked the truck, her eyes zeroed in on Justine Armando talking to one of the townspeople.

Beck followed her gaze. "I told Justine she was welcome to come to the funeral if she wanted," he said, swinging open his door. "Don't read anythin' into that, okay?"

"I won't."

While the reporter was dressed in all navy, with a stylish hat, Riley was in *the dress*, as she'd come to think of it, the one she'd worn to both her parents' funerals and to all the services for the dead trappers. If worth could be calculated in sorrow, this garment would be priceless.

Once Beck climbed out of the truck, cane in hand, Riley joined him. His face was tight, his emotions under considerable restraint.

"We'll get through this together," she said quietly. It was exactly what he'd said to her before her father's funeral. He nodded, but gave no reply.

Donovan stood near the coffin under the blue tent. He was in a suit, not his uniform, and the similarities between him and Beck were more noticeable now. When they stood next to each other, their height was about the same, though Beck's hair was sandier than the sheriff's and he had broader shoulders. The funeral director they'd brought in to handle the services stood next to Donovan, a thin man with a pinched face.

"Denver," Donovan said solemnly.

"Tom. Thanks for comin'," Beck replied and they shook hands. He turned his attention to the undertaker. "Thank you for steppin' in and gettin' everythin' ready, Mr. Bishop."

"It was the least I could do given the unfortunate circumstances," the man replied.

The pleasantries over, Beck chose one of the chairs near the front of the tent as other mourners filed in around them, including Sam and Louisa. Riley recognized some of the faces from the diner, including a few of the old guys.

Though the preacher did his best to warn them about the dangers they faced if they didn't keep their eyes on Heaven, Riley lowered her eyes to the twin inscriptions on her palms, knowing the man's warnings were too late for her.

When he finished his sermon, he looked toward Beck expectantly. Puzzled, Riley watched as Sadie's son took his position in front of the coffin. Beck's face was pale and lined, the emotional strain almost too much to bear.

Why is he doing this to himself? He doesn't owe his mother anything.

Beck shifted his weight uneasily. He knew everyone was watching him, but he had to sort out the battle inside his heart. His eyes moved to Riley and he felt a sense of calm envelop him like a loving embrace. What was it about Paul's daughter that made him feel like that?

She gave him a nod of encouragement, though she had no idea what he was about to do. Beck cleared his throat and made sure to look at the far end of the tent, over the faces of the mourners. In particular, he avoided looking at the red-haired reporter.

"The preacher said some fine words for Sadie. I need to say a few more." Another throat clearing. "Some of ya . . . you knew Sadie when she was younger. I've heard she was a great deal of fun and had a sense of humor. By the time I showed up that was pretty much gone. Leastways I never saw it."

His heart pounded inside his chest. Why was he up here? Why did he feel driven to do this?

"The Sadie I knew wasn't a good woman. She was mean as a snake and lived in a bottle. I don't think she ever met a guy she'd turn down."

A couple of old ladies gasped. Maybe he'd been too honest, but somehow he knew Sadie wouldn't disagree.

"By the time I was sixteen and had to leave town I'd seen so much of the bad that I didn't think there was much better out there. I was sure I wasn't worth a damn. Some of you here tried to help me along and I'll always think well of you for that." His eyes were on Donovan now.

"The one thing that Sadie taught me was that I didn't want to be her. I wasn't gonna become someone who hated life so much that I'd destroy all the joy in it." His eyes moved to Riley now. "I was lucky—I met some good folks in Atlanta and they showed me a much better way." He heaved a sigh. "They taught me I was worth a damn and that Sadie was the one who was missin' out. So I guess what I'm sayin' is that even if Sadelia Beck wasn't a good person or even a good parent, she taught me more than she ever realized."

His legs began to shake: He tried to control them and failed. "So I thank you for comin' here today. I doubt she'll find peace where she's headed. That wasn't her way, but at least we said a proper good-bye."

Beck made it back to his seat, but not a moment too soon, his stomach roiling and sweat beading on his forehead.

Riley leaned over and whispered, "I never could have done that."

"I had to," he whispered back. "I'm leavin' all of it behind, here in the dirt with her. I'm startin' over from now on. Nothin' is gonna hold me back."

Riley slid her hand into his and squeezed it. "God, you're awesome, you know that?"

"No, I'm just me." *And for today, that's enough.*

The preacher ended the service with another prayer, though he seemed rattled by Beck's candid farewell. Mourners trailed by the open coffin and then stopped to speak to him and Riley, one by one. Louisa dropped a kiss on his cheek. Then Justine was in front of him, her deep emerald eyes glistening with moisture.

"Often the worst times of our lives are the ones that shape us the most," she said. "I am truly sorry for your loss, Beck."

She didn't kiss him, but touched his arm fondly, then departed after he murmured his thanks.

When it was only the two of them, Beck made his way to the coffin where he gazed down at the face of a woman who had given him life, and then made it a living hell.

Why couldn't you have loved me? I was never that bad.

A sob lodged in his throat. "Rest in peace, Momma," he whispered and then placed a kiss on her cold forehead.

I don't know if I can ever forgive you, but that doesn't keep me from lovin' you.

TWENTY-TWO

After they'd changed clothes at the motel and Riley's luggage was stowed in the truck, Beck drove her to the bus station in Waycross.

She bought her ticket and then returned to wait with him until the time came to board. This was his opportunity to show her how much had changed between them. If he hadn't just buried his mother, Riley would have expected a blazing kiss. At the least she expected some acknowledgment that he felt the same as she did.

"Thanks, for everythin'," he said. He took hold of her shoulders, gave them a squeeze, and then placed a chaste kiss on her forehead.

Riley felt disappointment, then anger in rapid succession.

"So that's it?" she said, her voice shaking. "After all that happened between us, that's *it*?"

"For now."

Her mouth closed with a click of her teeth, her jealousy roaring again.

He seemed to know what she was thinking. "This isn't about Justine or that angel. It's me. I need some time to get things sorted out, get my head on straight. That's why I'm stayin' down here until I do."

"There's nothing to sort out, Beck," she replied. "It's all been settled."

"Not in my mind. I can't go forward until ... I know some things."

What was there to know? I love you. You care for me. Why make this hard?

"Okay, then when you finally get that head of yours straight, give me a call. Who knows, maybe I'll answer the phone," she said, then whirled on her heels and marched toward the bus. As she climbed the steps, out of the corner of her eye she saw Beck staring at her. He wasn't angry. If anything, he looked lost.

Riley slumped into her seat, feeling like a jerk for going all ugly on him. In an instant, she knew what had to be done. Rushing down the aisle, she nearly collided with the driver as he entered the vehicle.

"How soon do you leave?" she asked.

"Five minutes," the man said. "Don't go too far."

"I won't."

Riley hurried down the stairs and then crossed the lot to where Beck was waiting.

"What's wrong?" he said, straightening up.

"You." Riley grabbed onto his collar, pulled him forward, and kissed him with as much ferocity as she possessed. She put everything into that kiss, all her wild hopes, all her dreams.

When it ended, Beck's eyes were glowing with desire. He quickly took in a huge rush of air.

"Damn, girl," he murmured.

Now that she had his attention . . .

Riley carefully tidied his collar and then looked deeply into those bottomless brown eyes.

"Remember when we first came to town I told you to ask me if I felt any different about you when it was all over?"

He nodded warily. "Do you?"

"Yes, I do. Get your head straight and come back to Atlanta. Come back to me. Because I'm not giving up on you. I can't. . . ." Her voice broke from the emotions careening inside her.

He has to know.

Riley carefully touched her forehead to his, like he had in the cemetery, her hands lightly caressing his forearms, feeling the muscles beneath his shirt.

"I love you, Denver Beck," she whispered. "I have for a long time." Then she stepped back. "Now it's your turn to decide if you love me."

As Riley walked back to the bus, her heart hammered and her mind whirled. *Ohmigod.* She'd told him she loved him. There was no going back now. Either he felt the same about her, or it'd all turn to ashes like it had with the others.

She climbed aboard with shaking legs, without looking back. In truth, she was too frightened to do so. It wasn't until Riley returned to her seat that she looked out the window. Beck's mouth had dropped open in shock. He blinked a few times and closed it.

When the bus pulled out, he was still there, watching her depart. He hadn't taken off, not like she'd feared. Instead, he'd held his ground despite her actions.

Riley waved good-bye and he returned it along with a tentative smile.

Then she was on the road to Atlanta, leaving behind the man she loved more than life itself. Only time would tell if he felt the same about her.

✦

The bucket of fried chicken setting between them was mostly empty. The bottle of Jack Daniel's was mostly full. That said a lot about the pair of them: Donovan wasn't much of a drinker and Beck was still too hungry to waste time sucking down booze when there was food at hand.

They sat on Sadie's rickety back porch, which overlooked a long stretch of open ground. In the distance a hawk soared above the field in hopes of a meal. Sadie had never cared for the porch, which is why Beck had spent countless childhood hours out here. He could dream that he was on a pirate ship or exploring some strange new country, anything to be away from the woman who despised him.

To his right sat an old battered metal box, the one he'd had

Donovan fish out of a heating vent where it'd been hidden from Sadie's eyes. If she'd found it, she would have tossed it in the trash. She'd always been that way when it came to anything he valued. Now his personal treasures would be going to Atlanta with him.

Sitting about fifteen feet in front of them was that damned couch, reeking of gasoline fumes, courtesy of a can of fuel. At Beck's feet was a rolled-up newspaper and a box of matches. At his request, the sheriff had already let the proper people know that a visit by the fire department was not going to be needed.

"Some reason you're going all Viking funeral on this piece of furniture?" Donovan asked, his face crinkling in humor.

"I hate the thing. When Sadie had been drinkin', she'd come home and pass out on it. Usually she'd have some guy with her."

Donovan sobered. "I talked to her about that, told her it wasn't the right thing to do when she had a young son. She'd never listen to me."

"At least you tried."

With the sheriff's help, Beck lit the newspaper and then hobbled over to the remaining source of his nightmares.

"Burn, you bastard," he muttered, then threw the lighted paper onto the center of the couch. The fumes ignited instantly and began to consume the fabric in thick, greedy waves.

Beck returned to the porch and sat down, watching the inferno build. "Been wantin' to do that since I was ten."

"Surprised you waited."

That did make Beck grin. "I was gettin' into enough trouble without being a fire bug."

"That's the truth." Donovan retied a shoelace. "We have a plea bargain in place with McGovern. Once the feds are done with him, they'll go directly to the sentencing phase."

"Any chance of the death penalty?"

"No. That was part of the bargain. That won't sit well with some folks, but that's the way it went down."

"If I was him, I'd let them kill me rather than spendin' the rest of my life in some damned cell," Beck said.

The sheriff took a quick slug of whiskey. "If it wasn't such a mess around here, we could go fishing."

Beck smiled. "I'd have liked that, but I'll have to get back to Atlanta. Maybe sometime down the line." He leaned forward, elbows on his knees. *How do I do this?*

Something must have shown on his face as Donovan leaned forward as well, adopting the same pose.

"What's on your mind, Denver?"

"Got a question and I don't know how to ask it."

"Does it have something to do with Sadie and me?"

Beck's heart skipped a beat. "Yeah, it does. I'm not the only one who thinks you and me look a lot alike."

"Figured that would come up one of these days. In fact, I'm surprised it hasn't until now."

"Part of askin' the question is maybe gettin' an answer I won't like. I wasn't willin' to take the risk," Beck admitted.

"But you are now." Donovan picked up the bottle of whiskey, but didn't take a drink. "Your mother and me were together for a few months right before I went into the Navy. When I came back four years later she's got this little blond-haired boy. Sweet fellow with big brown eyes and a smile that would own your heart."

Beck jammed his lips together.

"I asked her if you were mine and she said you weren't. Now by that time she was drinking heavily and not known to tell the truth, so I kept an eye on you as best I could." He paused. "When she left you in the swamp I was so damned mad I had Doc Hodges do a paternity test while you were in the hospital, on the sly. I never told Sadie about it."

Beck sat up, his breath caught. "Yes or no?"

"It was negative, Denver. You're not my son. I can tell you that wasn't what I wanted to hear. I had so hoped you were."

"Ah hell," Beck murmured, his hopes crushed. "I always thought..."

"So did I. I'd hoped you were mine so I could sue for custody, get you away from your mother."

"All those years I wasted dreamin' you might be my daddy."

"No, not wasted. It gave you something to hope for, something Sadie couldn't destroy. That's why I never told you. As long as you held that hope you had a reason to keep moving forward."

Beck ran a hand over his face. "Guess I'll never know who he is."

"Well, one thing's for sure, he must have had a great deal of courage or his son wouldn't be as good a man as he is."

Beck shrugged.

"I'm sorry that wasn't the answer we both wanted." Donovan sighed. "In some ways I regret that Sadie and I didn't work out. Maybe she would have stayed out of the bottle if she'd had someone to look after her."

"Probably not." Beck squared his shoulders. "Well, as far as I'm concerned I had two daddies—you and Paul. I couldn't have asked for better."

"That means a lot," Donovan replied, clapping a hand on his shoulder.

"Before I leave, I want to see Louisa again and meet her husband. Tell him what a lucky guy he is. Once that's done, I'll be headin' home."

"Don't forget your roots, son. They're important. And whatever you do, don't let Riley get away from you. She's just what you need."

It was heartening to know Donovan thought so highly of her.

"Yeah, I'm workin' on that. Not to worry."

"Good. She never gave up on you, not once. That's the kind of woman a man wants by his side."

Beck nodded. "I was thinking the same thing."

His time in Sadlersville was drawing to a close. Everything was settled now.

With a sense of accomplishment, Beck leaned back to watch the couch, and his past, vanish in a sea of flames.

✢

Atlanta lay beneath them like a conquered city, but the view from the roof of One Atlantic Center did not impress the angels. After you'd witnessed the beginning of the cosmos, the mortals' cities were like a child's toy.

The Divine standing next to Ori was the pensive kind, the kind that saw the future with disturbing clarity. It was one of the reasons he'd asked Gusion to join him tonight.

"Where will you stand if war comes?" his friend asked.

Ori raised an eyebrow. "Where do you think I should stand? What do you see of our future? You're known for that talent."

"All I see is blood," the other Fallen angel replied solemnly. "Nothing is clear beyond that."

That wasn't the response he'd expected. "Whose blood?" Ori asked. "Mortals or angels'?"

"Both." Gusion turned toward him. "Do not go to war against Lucifer. He will destroy you and all you hold dear."

"What if that's exactly what I want?" Ori parried.

His old friend shook his head despair.

"I have a favor to ask of you, Gusion. You have every right to refuse."

Then he laid out what it was he wished, how his fellow angel may well have a role to play in the days to come.

Gusion ruffled a wing in agitation before he answered. "You ask much."

"But will you do it if the need arises?"

"I shall, though it is not of my nature."

"What of the other Divines? Where do they stand?" Ori asked.

"They are undecided. Though many do not hold you in high regard, they are displeased with the way you have been treated."

Ori nodded his understanding. "Lucifer hopes to pit Sartael against me to destroy us both. He has lost sight of what is important."

Gusion did not argue that point. "Where is this soul you hold, the one that has made our Prince so angry?"

"Blackthorne's daughter has just returned to the city."

"Does she know of the danger she faces, how so many would view her as a means to destroy you?" Gusion asked.

"Not yet. Riley Anora Blackthorne will learn soon enough."

"Is she strong enough, this soul of yours?"

"She had better be."

⁂

As Beck promised, Riley found journeyman trapper Chris Jackson waiting for her outside the Greyhound bus station in Atlanta, leaning against the front bumper of his truck. Jackson's build was on the thin side and he was one of her favorite trappers: He'd been in her corner from the moment she'd joined the Guild.

"Welcome back to the big city," he called out, a welcoming smile in place.

"Hi, Jackson. How'd you get stuck with picking me up?"

"Volunteered," he replied.

He hefted her small suitcase into the back of his truck and then they were headed north into the heart of Atlanta. Since Jackson's trapping bag took up space on the seat between then, Riley placed her backpack at her feet.

"How's Beck?" he asked.

"Doing okay. You hear what happened?"

"Yeah. It's been in the papers." He shook his head in sympathy. "I can't imagine him having to carry that weight on his shoulders all those years."

"It was really hard. Now they know he's as much a victim as the other guys."

As Jackson took a corner, her backpack flopped over onto her feet and she readjusted it. "So what's happening up here? Am I still on someone's hit list?"

"Nope. The cops caught up with the dude. He made the mistake of sending threats to the mayor, the governor, and a state senator. He's done for."

"Wow, the company I keep," she said wryly.

"Besides that idiot, we've got a bunch of new folks who want to join the Guild. A good portion of those are *very* scary. Most of them actually." He took in a breath. "Oh, and the *Demonland* film crew arrived yesterday. They start filming tomorrow evening."

"Why would they come here after everything that happened?"

"Ratings is what I hear," Jackson replied. "They really want to know what went down at the cemetery so they can work it into an episode. Harper has threatened to gut anyone who tells them a peep about the battle."

She could see her master doing that.

"I never got to thank you for what you did at the cemetery," he continued. "I don't know how you stood up to those angels."

"I had no choice," she said. "Sometimes when you're cornered you do the impossible."

"Is it true Heaven made a deal with you to save Simon's life?" Jackson asked, looking over at her now.

Apparently that bit of truth was in the wild now. "Yes, they did."

Jackson whistled under his breath. "I've only seen him a couple times since the battle and he's not looking good. I think the guilt is getting to him."

"Yeah, it is."

"How's about some good news: I passed my master's exam."

"That rocks, Jackson!" she said. "Wow, you have to be jazzed."

His grin told her he was. "Now I have to do my thing with an Archfiend and I'm good to go."

"You're not going to try to capture one of those things, are you?" she asked, worried.

"After what I saw at the cemetery, no way. I'm just going to kill it before it kills me."

Riley totally agreed. "You sure Harper will sign off on you to become a master?"

"He says he will. He's less of a . . . jerk now that he's clean and sober. The National Guild has waived its restrictions about the number of apprentices per master. Harper has two new ones to train now." Jackson gave her a look. "You're going love these guys."

"Bad news?"

"Clueless."

She laughed. "They'll feel right at home with me, then."

TWENTY-THREE

The next morning brought a hearty breakfast courtesy of Mrs. Ayers and a scrawled note from Master Stewart that welcomed her home and told her that she was expected at Harper's new office by ten. He even supplied the address.

No rest for the damned.

Since she'd crawled out of bed late, Riley had no time to fly by her apartment though she knew the mailbox would be jammed full by now. She moved that task onto the "later" list and followed Stewart's directions to her master's new home.

When Riley pulled into the graveled parking lot she knew she'd found the right place. Like his previous location, Harper had opted for a car repair business that had fallen on hard times. At least this one was in better physical condition than the old one after a Grade Five Geo-Fiend had torn it apart.

The new place was constructed of tan brick. One side of the building was two stories and the other—the garage portion—just one. The garage's twin overhead doors weren't peeling or warped. In fact, it looked as if they'd recently received a fresh coat of paint.

"Much better," she said, nodding her approval. Maybe Harper's new sobriety was carrying over into other aspects of his life. *Or he got tired of living in a dump.*

Despite Jackson's observation that her master was better behaved now, Riley was still apprehensive. She and Harper had shared a rocky relationship, including a history of bruises he'd left on her during his blistering tirades. Now that she knew him better she understood where that anger had come from, but that didn't mean she trusted him.

Right before the battle at Oakland Cemetery, he'd promised that if they made it through the end of the world he and Riley would have a little chat and that she wouldn't like what he was going to tell her. She suspected that conversation would conclude with her handing over her trapper's license.

I made the deal with Hell. He won't have any other choice.

She steeled herself and pushed open the front door to the building. The interior smelled more of garage than it did demon, but that would change over time. Harper's new office was bigger than the old one and her master had positioned his battle-scarred desk so he could take advantage of the space. Some of his old furniture had made the move—the battered filing cabinets crouched in a corner—but there was a new office chair. The grubby recliner was gone and Riley did not mourn its loss.

The door to her right led into the old service bays. The hydraulic lifts were noticeably absent, probably sold for scrap by the previous owners, and in their place were four cages that were specially designed to hold Grade Three demons. All were occupied and the demons set up a chorus of howls when they spied her, including their usual *Blackthorne's daughter* greeting.

Harper looked up and grunted at her arrival. He was in his late fifties with a long wicked scar running from his left eyebrow down the side of his face. Given the warmer weather, he was in a T-shirt and the skull tattoo on his arm was partially visible. A full bottle of water sat next to him now, instead of a bottle of booze. Next to it was his can of chewing tobacco, telling Riley that he'd not abandoned all his vices.

"Blackthorne," he said evenly.

That was new. Usually he called her Brat.

"Master Harper." She gestured at the space around them. "I like this place. It's nicer than the old building."

"So do I. It's got a couple decent rooms upstairs so I can spread out."

Then he leaned back in the chair and studied her intently, like a lion waiting for a gazelle to make a fatal error. "I hear you killed a Four down in the swamp. That true?"

"Yes."

"You killed it on your own?" When she nodded, his expression grew pensive.

It was time to end this one way or another.

Riley placed her trapper's license on the desktop. He eyed it, then looked back up at her. "Giving up?" he asked.

"You said we were going to have a little talk if the world didn't end. Well, it's still here, so . . ."

"If I take that license away you'll go freelance, right?"

She nodded. "I have to make money somehow."

"Damn," he muttered, then shoved it back her way. "We'll have that talk when I'm ready and not until then."

"But—"

"Stewart and I will be keeping an eye on you." He leaned forward now, the scar standing out on his jawline. "You go dark on us . . ." He left the threat unspecified. It was far scarier that way.

"Understood." All she had to do was stay on the straight and narrow and maybe she could avoid being shipped off to the Vatican for punishment. Or worse.

As Riley returned the license to her backpack, Harper shuffled some papers.

"That TV show will start filming tomorrow night. I need you there. Reynolds will be there too. Watch yourself with those people and don't tell them a thing about what went down in the cemetery. You got that?"

"Yes, I got it." The last thing she needed was for Hollywood to do their version of the showdown between the Archangel Michael and Lucifer. Knowing them, it'd involve a car chase and a trashy love scene.

Harper pushed a trapping order across the desk. "There's a Magpie at the convention center. Good luck with that one. The place is huge."

She sighed and took the order.

"I've got two new apprentices, they'll be here pretty soon. Tomorrow we'll go down to Demon Central. I'll have you and Adler show them what it means to be a trapper."

Riley opened her mouth to protest that he was going to spook the newbies too soon, but he waved her off.

"Might as well have them see what's it's really like. If they can't stomach it, we need to know that now."

Before she could reply, the front door swung open and two young men entered. The taller of the pair had curly brown hair and dark glasses. His T-shirt was something like her friend Peter might wear, proudly proclaiming ACTUALLY, IT IS ROCKET SCIENCE. The other guy was shorter and had a little more meat on him. His hair was about the same color, but it was straight and ended at his collar. Both were in jeans and work boots.

The newbies.

Harper pointed at the taller one. "That's Fleming. The other is Lambert." His finger veered toward Riley. "This is Blackthorne. Listen to her and you might live through the first week."

While Fleming seemed taken aback at Harper's blunt pronouncement, Lambert adopted a bored expression.

He's going to be the problem child. There was always one in every crowd.

"Start them *at the bottom,*" Harper ordered. His grin told her exactly what he meant.

"Come on, guys," she said, waving them toward the garage. "Let me show you the wonders of demon poop."

⊹

The old Starbucks' parking lot was nearly full up by the time Riley pulled in, and, to her relief, she was a few minutes early despite all her fretting about being late. Harper had been right—finding a

Klepto-Fiend in the middle of a peach producers' convention had been anything but a slam-dunk. Three hours in she'd finally caught the little fiend as it'd slowed down long enough to collect some glittering peach pins at one of the producer's booths. On the plus side she'd scored four jars of peach preserves. Those would be yummy on Mrs. Ayers' homemade scones.

Peter sauntered over the moment she exited her car. "The wandering Riley returns," he said. "And look, no gator bites either."

A magnificent bruise encircled his left eye, shading from brown to green. "Peter! What happened?" she demanded.

"Your stalkery ex said something I didn't like and I told him to jam his head up his butt. It didn't end well."

"Allan? I warned you he'd try to get even for you dissing him," she said. "Why didn't you tell me about this?"

"You had enough going on down south you didn't need to know about my problems."

Getting in Allan's face felt like a plan right now. He couldn't hit her best friend and not incur her wrath. Riley's eyes swept the various knots of students as they clustered around talking or texting before class began.

"So where is the jerk?" she asked.

"He's suspended until Thursday. I only got a warning."

There was only one reason Peter might receive that. "You hit him back?"

"Sure did," he said, holding up his skinned knuckles as evidence. "My dad gave me props once he heard what happened. He said he was proud of me, but it had to be top secret so Mom doesn't come unstuck." He waggled an eyebrow. "Simi thinks I'm cool because of it."

"She's jealous of your hair," Riley replied, pleased her barista friend had finally begun to take Peter's interest seriously.

"Maybe, but she thinks I'm so cool we're going to the dance together."

That works. Simi would encourage his wilder side while he mellowed her out. Then the other part of his statement registered.

"What dance?" Riley asked, hefting her backpack on a sore shoulder. Her muscles still felt as if someone had stomped them into a pulp.

"It's the annual citywide 'dress like an adult' thing. It's this Saturday." Peter fell in step next to her as they walked toward the building.

"You mean the prom?" Of course he did.

With the school system bankrupt, the dances were sponsored by local businesses. To accommodate all the kids in the city, there were a series of proms and it appeared theirs was going to be way early this year.

A pang of envy shot through her. She would have loved to go but . . .

"You guys have fun." She would probably be trapping smelly demons in a MARTA station or in the bowels of Demon Central.

"You can come, you know?" Peter suggested. "I'm sure I could spare a dance for you."

"No. It's . . . It wouldn't feel right."

"So ask Beck to the dance."

"What?" she sputtered. "No. Not happening."

"Ah, I got it. You're chicken. You'll take on a horde of demons but when it comes to the one guy you're really hot for—"

Riley glowered at him. "Don't. Go. There. The subject is closed, Mr. King."

Peter raised his hands in surrender. "Whoa, you are grouchy. I was looking forward to seeing you . . . why?"

"You don't understand. It's complicated with me and Beck."

"Bogus!" he said. "It's totally simple: You guys have to stop being idiots. You're driving each other crazy along with the rest of us."

"I don't think it's salvageable, not after I—"

"After you what?" he pressed.

Tugging her friend away from the stream of students headed to class, she related exactly what had happened at the bus station and how she hadn't heard a thing from Beck since she'd left Sadlersville. That it was all her fault.

"A public display of affection? Awesome," Peter replied.

"No, I spooked him big-time. He'll back off. I know it."

"I'm guessing he won't. Trust me on this."

Maybe Peter was right. "I hope so. If not I looked like a complete dork."

"Time will tell on the dorkdom."

When Riley followed him inside the old coffee shop, nothing much had changed since she'd been gone: same lovely ground coffee aroma, same Mrs. Haggerty, same mismatched desks and students. No, there was one difference: The desk that Allan had used was empty.

Her mood soared. She might not have a date to the prom, but the bully was gone, at least temporarily. Peter had proved he wasn't a wimp. A few months earlier he wouldn't have had the courage to take on a bully.

Her former nemesis, Brandy, shifted around in her chair once Riley was seated.

"Have you met the *Demonland* actors yet?" she asked, her eyes sparkling. "Is Jess Storm as smoking hot as he looks on TV?"

"I'll be seeing them tomorrow night. I'll let you know."

"Don't forget the autographs. I've told all my friends I'm getting one," the girl gushed.

It was nice that things were so insanely simple in Brandy's world.

"Autographs, photographs, the works. I promise," Riley said.

At that point she was waved up to the front of the classroom. Riley's buoyant mood promptly deflated when she was handed her assignments from the time she was in South Georgia.

"You did all this when I was gone?" she asked, astounded at the thick stack of papers.

"No, but I figured the way your life is going you might like to get a little ahead," Mrs. Haggerty responded.

Riley dragged herself back to her desk and dropped the assignments into her backpack on top of the Holy Water spheres. As the teacher began to take roll call, she slumped back in her creaky chair and wondered how many more days of school were left before summer vacation.

⁜

By the time class ended, Riley was suffering serious withdrawal symptoms and the only known only cure was the Grounds Zero. Since it was close to six at night, the coffee shop was fairly empty. Simi, her hypercaffeinated barista friend, wasn't working, so Riley collected her beverage and headed for her favorite booth, the one she and her dad had often shared.

She checked her phone again like she had at least a million times over the course of the day. No call from Backwoods Boy. She was good enough to slog into a swamp to save his butt and now he was too busy to let her know what was going on. All because she'd unloaded the truth on him at the bus station.

Beck's instinctive response would be to retreat behind those massive defenses of his, just when she'd finally gotten him to take a few steps outside those very shields.

Why did I do that? That was so dumb. He'd say she was being *goofy* again. Beck didn't know it, but this time the rules were different. This was the endgame: If he didn't step up and accept her love, she was done.

I will not make a fool of myself again.

Riley popped one of the chocolate curls into her mouth and sighed in relief. Life was manageable if she focused on the things that made sense: excellent hot chocolate, homework, and trapping demons. Not that the last two always did.

Just after she'd taken a long sip of her drink, a tremor ran up both arms and lodged at the base of her brain, like a primal warning system. When her eyes rose she gasped and nearly dropped the cup.

Ori strode toward her like some dark knight.

The angel's black leather jacket, T-shirt, and jeans were the same as before and his ebony hair was secured in a ponytail. He sat across from her, acting as if she hadn't held him in her arms, watched him dying after the battle.

"Riley Anora Blackthorne," he said, his voice crisp. "Do I need to remind you of your vow to me?"

She shook her head. Somehow she'd known it would come to this moment.

"Lucifer kept you alive," she said. A curt nod returned.

Riley studied him anew. His eyes were guarded, not as caring as they had once been. Whatever had happened to him after Lucifer had vanished him from the cemetery had altered the angel in some elemental way.

"So how does this go?" she asked. "You going to haul me off to Hell right in front of all these people?"

Ori leaned back in the booth, dark brows furrowed and arms crossed over his chest. "Nothing so dramatic."

"Then what am I to do? Polish your boots? Tell you just how awesome you are every minute of the day?"

No reply.

"Well, whatever it is, I will not try to take anyone's soul for you."

"*I* set the terms. You abide by them," he replied, his tone chillier now.

"You don't scare me, angel. I'm doomed no matter what. I refuse to hurt anyone because you expect me to."

"Once again you try to dictate terms when you have no leverage."

"The only leverage I have left is my conscience," she retorted. "I will not sacrifice that."

Stormy eyes glared at her. "You may find that a difficult promise to keep."

Concerned that someone had to be overhearing this conversation, Riley gave a quick look around. No one seemed to notice them. "Tell me what happens next," she insisted.

"As I am your demi-lord, you are mine to command. My job is as it always was: to destroy those of our realm who defy my master," Ori continued. "You will aid in that task."

"Me? How?"

"I will summon you when it is time to do battle against the rogue demons. You will fight at my side."

"Are you crazy?" she said in a forced whisper. "I am not some cosmic warrior."

"You will be my second nonetheless."

"If you want me dead, just zap me with a lightning bolt and get it over with."

"You *will* serve as my second," the angel insisted, rising from the booth in a fluid movement. "Beginning tonight."

"This is payback. You're pissed I didn't beg to hand over my soul like the others."

"No," he said, flatly. "This is survival, Riley Anora Blackthorne. For you, at least."

He turned on a heel and strode out of the shop. Unlike in the past, none of the women noticed, as if he wasn't really there.

Riley found her hands locked around her cup in a death grip and she pried them off. Ori hadn't done this kind of thing with her father. Just her.

All because I wanted to be loved.

TWENTY-FOUR

Nestled in her bed at Stewart's house, Ori's summons came in the middle of the night, a clarion call that interrupted her dreams and pulled Riley awake in a heartbeat.

Dress. Or fight unclothed, he ordered deep in her mind.

She'd barely managed to pull on her jeans, shirt, and high-tops when the room around her faded. Her new surroundings came into focus: a broad, open field of green grass, the moon fat and full in the midnight sky.

I know this place. This was all angelic illusion, like the romantic picnic they'd shared when Ori had been trying to seduce her. This time there was no tasty watermelon or wine, only her and Lucifer's assassin. He was in full-angel mode now, wings visible, his jet-black hair pulled back and secured with a leather cord. There was a feral light in his dark eyes, one that made Riley shiver.

"Sleep in your clothes from now on, unless you wish to fight nude," Ori said brusquely. "I will call you at a moment's notice."

Great. "During the day too?"

"Perhaps."

"Someone will notice if I just disappear."

"I'll ensure they don't. Now extend your hand, the one with my master's inscription upon it."

Riley did as he asked, wondering what he had in mind. The question was answered the instant her right palm flared to life in brilliant white flames. Crying out, she tried to wave them away, but failed. There was no pain, but it freaked her to see her hand engulfed in fire. The flames gradually spread down her fingers and became a sword, a petite version of Ori's blade.

"How do you do that?" she asked, staring at it in wonder. It was so bright it hurt her eyes.

"I am sharing some of my Divine essence with you."

Riley gave the blazing blade a couple of test swipes through the air. It was kind of cool.

This wasn't a good idea. "Look, I am not a warrior. I can try to watch your back, but I'm not good at killing demons."

"You did well enough in the swamp."

The blade ceased its lazy arcs. "You know what happened there?"

"Of course. I'm your demi-lord. I knew exactly what was going on."

"Then why didn't you help me find Beck?" Riley demanded. "Why did you let me do all that on my own?"

"It was your test, not mine," he responded. "Now I shall show you some basic sword techniques and then we'll go hunting."

Hunting? This was getting out of hand. "What can I possibly do other than act as bait?"

The angel nodded agreeably. "I see you understand your role perfectly."

⁜

When it was over and Riley had returned to her room, the clock indicated only an hour had passed. To her it felt like half a day. Her clothes were clean now, though they'd been soaked in demon blood only minutes before. Her muscles ached, but not as badly as when she'd been in the middle of the fight. Somehow Ori had shared some of his angel mojo to help her recover.

As she'd warned him, she'd done very badly her first time out, unable to handle the blade. Their prey, as he'd called it, had been a quartet of rogue Threes, those who had defied Lucifer. Ori had shouted commands at her, reprimanding her when she didn't parry the blows or move fast enough. It had been a nightmare.

At the end of the killing, there was a pile of corpses which he'd burnt with his angelic fire. Through it all, he'd shown no emotion as he'd cut them down. The caring Divine who'd made love to her was gone, subsumed by the grim executioner.

⚜

The next morning Riley found herself in Demon Central with Simon, their master, and the two new apprentices. She was sure Harper would see she was different somehow, call her out for hanging with one of Lucifer's dudes, but he hadn't said a word.

In contrast to the demons Ori had slain, the single Gastro-Fiend they were trying to trap was one of the younger ones, plump, with only one row of teeth. It stood about four feet tall, with black fur and glowing eyes. Currently it gnawed on a pawful of garbage, one of its usual food sources in Demon Central.

This time there was no fancy sword or angelic backup, so one of them would serve as the "lure" while the other wielded the Holy Water. If the trapper with the sphere missed, the lure was in line for the demon's fangs and claws.

Troubled, Riley looked over at Simon. Did she trust him to throw the sphere accurately? Would he change his mind at the last second and let the fiend attack her?

Simon was frowning as well. *He's wondering if I'd do that to him.*

"I'll be the bait," she said. It seemed to be her lot in life. "You're better with the spheres than I am."

Her former boyfriend shook his head. "No, I'll do it."

Riley was taken aback. He trusted her after all that had happened between them? "Simon, you don't—"

"Yes, I do," he insisted. "You'll hit it first time. I know you will."

She wasn't sure about that.

"Get it done," Harper called out from where he and the newbies were tucked behind a Dumpster. If the trapping went wrong, the master was the backup plan if the demon got the upper hand. It'd be his job to keep the thing from eating them, if possible.

"Ready?" Simon asked, testing the grip of the steel pipe in his left hand.

When she reluctantly nodded, he moved closer to the beast. Since one of these things had nearly killed him, this was an act of supreme courage. Simon's fingers clenched the bag of chicken entrails and his breath came in quick gasps.

You're scared out of your mind. He had to be reliving every agonizing second of the attack at the Tabernacle. Riley certainly was. When Simon lifted up a bag of chicken entrails, the fiend dropped the handful of garbage and howled in delight. From its perspective, it'd gone from Dumpster diving to two trappers on the hoof with a chicken appetizer.

Once Simon tossed the entrails toward the beast, he didn't have to wait long for the fiend to make its headlong rush at the offering. The chicken was gone in a gulp and then the Three began to size up its next meal. This one was still a little green in the trapper-killing business. An older, more seasoned fiend would have already begun its run.

Riley edged into a better position and her movement caught the demon's notice.

"Blackthorne's daughter," it grunted. Then those laser eyes sheered back to her fellow trapper as if she wasn't on its menu. This was the second time a demon had ignored her and chosen to target Simon. Was it because it knew Ori was her demi-lord?

"Chew yourrrr bones!" the fiend cried and began its lumbering run toward her fellow trapper.

Riley forced herself to wait until the beast was within range and then threw the Holy Water sphere. It proved a perfect delivery as the glass orb hit the beast square on its ugly face. As the liquid soaked in, it roared in agony, then crumpled to the ground in a furry heap.

Riley cried out in enthusiastic relief. As they crammed the rank fiend into one of the steel mesh bags, she whispered. "You trusted me. Why?"

Simon snapped the closures in place, then his vivid blue eyes sought hers. "Because I had to take the first step out of this endless darkness. That meant trusting someone I once thought had betrayed me."

Riley was stunned. "I could have missed the thing, Simon."

"It was a risk that I had to take."

My God.

Before she could respond, Harper and the new guys joined them, the master explaining exactly what had gone right and what would have happened if Riley's sphere hadn't contacted the Three. Why having a steel pipe with you at all times was vital for survival.

"Would it really eat you?" Fleming asked, his eyes wide like he'd just stepped into a horror movie.

"It'll make a meal of you in about fifteen minutes. Or less," Harper replied. "Their claws are filthy so if you get hurt, treat it with Holy Water pronto. If not, you start dying." He pointed at Simon. "Ask Adler how that feels. Or Blackthorne for that matter. Both have been there."

Though Fleming paled, the other apprentice didn't seem troubled at all.

Harper noticed. "Any questions over there, Lambert?"

"That demon didn't seem that scary," the guy said. "You'd have to be pretty dumb to get ripped up by one of these things. Why are we wasting time? Why not go for the bigger demons right off?"

Simon was on his feet in an instant, spoiling for a fight. When he took a step toward the smirking apprentice, Riley grabbed onto his arm.

"No. He'll learn the hard way," she said.

"Don't worry, Lambert, you'll get your chance at a Three in a month or so," Harper said, frowning. "If you're still my apprentice, that is."

As the trio walked away, Fleming peppered the master with questions. The other guy didn't seem to care.

"What is wrong with him?" Simon asked, frowning. The flush of color on her fellow trapper's cheeks stood out against his pale skin

"He's a hotshot. If he's not afraid of a Three, he won't make it very long."

"Thanks for stopping me. I would have . . . well . . ."

Totally nailed him. That wasn't the old Saint Simon she knew. Riley hated to admit it, but she liked the new one better.

⁜

The moment Beck pushed open the door to his house and turned off the alarm, he felt better. In the past when he'd returned from Sadlersville it had been with extreme relief. No visit to Sadie had ever been good and the horror of the Keneally brothers' disappearances had dogged his every step. Now that was all behind him and for the first time in his life he was a free man.

He immediately collected his rabbit from Mrs. Merton, the neighbor next door. She prattled on about how much she'd enjoyed watching over Rennie and then offered her sympathies about his mom. He took it all in good stride, thanking her, then retreated to his house in search of solace. After checking his messages, he settled onto the couch, his bunny at his side. Beck savored this rare moment of tranquility as his mind tumbled with possibilities, unlike in the past.

"I got a situation, Rennie," he said. Though he was sure it was crazy, he often talked to her because she always seemed to understand. "Paul's daughter is in love with me. Can you believe that?" He shook his head in amazement. "Now I gotta decide what to do."

Did he try to build a life with Riley or was it better to step back and not get hurt again? He'd argued both sides all the way back to Atlanta, for and against.

When Rennie gave a gentle tug on his shirt to remind him she was in need of some attention, he hoisted the small rabbit onto his lap and petted her. In her own way, she'd helped him find the right path.

"You know, yer right. We all deserve love," he murmured.

Even me.

⟊

The Demonland location shoot was easy to find—all Riley had to do was follow the string of tractor trailers into the heart of Demon Central. There was a line of them, some with generators to power the lights required to make Hollywood magic. Farther on, she passed a portable trailer that housed the toilets and then one for costuming. It was like a mini city had set up residence inside Five Points.

Riley was stopped by an off-duty Atlanta cop and her trapper's ID checked. Once she'd been vetted, she kept wandering around until she spied Lex Reynolds near a table stocked with coffee and pastries. Reynolds wasn't like most of the other trappers: He could easily pass as a surfer with his deep tan, shoulder-length blond hair, and full beard. He was one of the nicer guys in the Guild and Riley was pleased to spend some time with him. Like any trapper, he was unlikely to miss this opportunity—not if there was a paycheck and free food.

"Riley," he called out as she approached, half a plain donut in hand. "How was South Georgia?"

"Memorable," she said. "So what's going on here?"

"Not a whole lot. They're getting ready for Blaze's next scene." He angled his head toward a knot of people near one of the cameras. "She's over there. Man, she's totally hot."

Riley suppressed a groan. The show was Hollywood's idea of demon hunting though they'd completely ignored the Church's role and their rules (no girls) and instead created a team of hunky guys and "totally hot" Blaze running all over the world killing Hellspawn in unrealistic ways. No surprise, the show was a hit and annoyed the Vatican to no end. In this case, Riley agreed with Rome. Because the show was a hit, the public thought that demon hunters were the same as the trappers. *Demonland* just made Riley's job that much harder.

Now that she saw her, Blaze seemed prettier on screen. That never worked when someone filmed Riley: She was usually covered in something vile and smelly.

Let her take on a real demon and see what happens.

Since the Vatican wouldn't deal with these guys, the trappers had been asked to help increase the "accuracy" of the show. Yet time passed and there was no request for assistance or advice.

Riley huffed in annoyance. "Why do I think we're here just to build up the show's street cred?"

"I got that impression too. Well, at least we're being paid for our time." Reynolds studied the surrounding area. "They've got some stones setting up in the middle of Demon Central. A Three could do a lot of damage to their fancy equipment."

He was right. "You think we should split up, keep an eye out for trouble?"

"Yeah, I do. The Threes are getting more aggressive, working in teams now."

"What? I thought that was because of Ozy—" She paused, aware that someone might overhear them discussing the necromancer-enhanced Hellspawn they'd battled at the cemetery. "I thought we had that all sorted out."

"We did, but the everyday demons learned from the others. They've adopted new tactics."

"Thanks, Reynolds," she muttered. "You've made my night."

With a sigh, Riley trudged to the far side of the set so between them they would have a clear field of vision in case of trouble. Crew hurried past her, doing whatever folks did on a television series. It made no sense to her, but the end result was weekly episodes of a show that her friends adored.

After more discussion with a goateed guy in a *Demonland* T-shirt— Riley pegged him as the director— Blaze took her place in front of the cameras. She seemed displeased, but so would anyone forced to wear stiletto boots, butt-hugging jeans, and a chokingly tight spandex top. She was joined by a male actor and it took Riley a bit to recognize him: Jess Storm, the one Brandy thought was so babelicious.

He was sort of cute, but he had nothing on Beck.

The thought of Backwoods Boy made her frown. She'd expected at least a phone call, a "Hi, how ya doin', Princess?" Instead she'd been given the silent treatment for daring to speak from her heart.

"Jerk," she grumbled. Riley pulled her attention away from the actors, scanning the surrounding area for anything furry and ravenous. There was something that fit that description under one of the catering tables—a sleek rat. Her father claimed they were like canaries in a mine: As long as the rodent wasn't freaked, things were good. They did seem to have a sixth sense when it came to Threes, mostly because they were high on the fiends' menu choices along with trappers and fat pigeons.

The director joined the actors, an assistant at his elbow. You could always tell that species—a clipboard was a required fashion accessory.

"Okay, let's get this in the can," their boss ordered. "In this scene you two are going to argue about the previous night's near tryst, then Jess rescues you from a demon."

"Come on, Arnold," the actress complained. "Raphael rescued me last week and Jess the week before. I'm not liking where we're headed here. I used to take down demons on my own."

"The ratings show the female demographic likes the guys saving your ass," the director replied. "Besides, it's more realistic."

Riley nearly gagged. *Realistic? You have got to be kidding me.*

When Blaze actually growled under her breath, she smiled. Maybe the actress wasn't such an airhead after all.

The first take went down in flames—Jess flubbed his lines. From the whispered remarks of a couple of crew members, it was a common occurrence.

Three more takes and it still wasn't going right. Tempers were growing short and the poor guy portraying the demon was having trouble with his costume since one of his clawed feet kept falling off.

Hollywood magic at its best. It was best her friends never knew about this side of the show.

They were partway through the fourth take when one of the main lights snapped off, causing the director to swear in colorful terms. Clearly this wasn't something that happened that often.

Riley did another quick rodent check and found that it had dropped its morsel and was on its hind feet, peering into the night, nose twitching frantically. Then with a squeak it took off, bolting for the nearest hole.

She set off along the perimeter of the set, pulling out a Holy Water sphere and the steel pipe as she maneuvered her way over the tangle of electrical cables. When she caught Reynolds' eye the other trapper gave a nod and began moving in a giant circle, in the opposite direction from her. Blaze and Jess remained in the center, bickering among themselves as they waited for the lighting problem to be sorted out.

"Come on, people. Get it together," the director called out. "We've got to get this scene done before—"

The light came back on and Riley shielded her eyes to keep it from destroying her night vision. A second later a low-pitched snarl came from somewhere nearby as a Three lumbered out of the darkness near a crumbling brick wall. It paused, sized up the competition, and then bellowed, "Blackthorne's daughter!"

This was the real deal.

This time, the demon headed right for her at top speed, claws making sparks on the pavement. Reynolds sprinted toward her, a steel pipe in hand. They didn't need to talk strategy, there wasn't time.

The Three sped up, claws glistening in the remaining lights, drool streaming down its furry chin. To Riley's astonishment, Reynolds put himself between her and the demon. He gave it a solid blow to the left shoulder, but it managed to wrap its claws around the pipe, attempting to pull the trapper into its other set of claws.

He wisely turned the pipe loose and the demon flung the weapon at her, the cylinder tumbling end over end. Riley executed a quarter spin to avoid the missile, then flung her sphere, which crashed directly in the center of the demon's face. The fiend howled, took a few steps forward, then did a solid face-plant into the ground, scattering dust and debris in the process.

"Yes!" Reynolds shouted, executing a fist pump. He sprinted for his pack and dashed back with one of the steel mesh bags in hand and between them they shoved the Gastro-Fiend into the steel prison as quickly as possible. He'd just engaged the clamps when the demon stirred and began to yowl like a banshee.

"That was damned fine work," her fellow trapper said. "You're really good with those spheres."

Usually she wasn't. Did this have something to do with Ori's protection?

Shaking, Riley rose to find the entire production crew staring at them. Most of them wore an *Ohmigod, that was for real* expression.

Blaze broke into a genuine smile. "Gee, Arnold," she said. "Looks like girls can trap demons. How's about we make that happen on the show?"

The director frowned.

"That rocked," Blaze pressed. "Admit it."

The man reluctantly nodded. "We'll duplicate the scene, but without using those weird spheres." He turned to his assistant. "Have all that broken glass swept up and we'll do a walk-through." Then the director shot a look toward Riley and her fellow trapper. "You two, get off the set and take that beast with you."

"It appears our one minute of fame is over," Reynolds said.

Riley issued an unladylike snort.

Knowing Reynolds would handle the Three, Riley made her way to a canvas chair, desperately needing to rest. The whole takedown had been too close. If she'd missed with that sphere . . .

But I didn't. That's what counts.

Something made her look up and at the edge of the set she spied a familiar figure, one whose blond hair and handsome face she'd dreamed about often enough.

Beck turned and limped up the street before she had a chance to call out.

Why are you avoiding me?

She suspected the answer didn't bode well for their future.

⁘

Jackson had taken her place at nine thirty as the shoot was running late and Stewart didn't want her in Demon Central in the wee hours of the morning. It was nearly ten when Riley reached her apartment complex. As she feared, her mailbox was jammed full and it took her some time to retrieve all the bills and advertisements. While she hiked up the two flights of stairs to her place, she sorted them according to importance. One in particular caught her notice—a letter from the landlord, no doubt reminding her that the rent was going up soon.

After she let herself into the apartment, clicking on the light revealed that no helpful fairies had dropped by and magically replaced the third-hand furniture with something that looked decent. The packing box that served as a coffee table was still in place in front of the lumpy couch and the concrete block and two-by-four bookshelves were there as well.

Even though it was nothing more than an oversized hotel room with a dinky kitchen, it was home. It still held memories of her dead father, though even those were fading with each passing day. Like when she'd dropped one of his favorite coffee mugs and it'd shattered. She'd wept as she'd swept up the ceramic shards.

Riley engaged the door locks, stashed her backpack on the floor, and dropped the mail onto the kitchen table. After making herself a cup of hot chocolate and finding there was only one carton of yogurt in the fridge—staying at Stewart's had definitely cut into her grocery buying—she began opening the envelopes. She put the bills in a pile and then ripped open the one from the landlord. Two words immediately snagged her attention.

Eviction Notice

There had to be a mistake. She'd paid the rent on time.

Further study proved the notice had nothing to do with the rent payment but complaints that Riley was disturbing her neighbors because of her profession. That she was keeping demons in her apartment and her neighbors were afraid that one of those might kill them all some night while they were asleep in their beds.

She put her face in her hands, feeling the urge to scream and cry at the same time. The demon that lived in her place wasn't the *I'm going to slit your throat and eat you* kind but the stealthy variety that stole other people's shiny stuff. Sure, her father had stored Grade One demons in the apartment, but that had been with the management's approval. *Who complained?* It certainly wouldn't be Mrs. Litinsky, her next-door neighbor. She had no issues with Riley's profession.

Mrs. Ivey. This had the old bat's name all over it. She'd bitched up a storm about her missing hearing aid and now Riley was going to be kicked out because her demon roomie had a thing for bling. The fact her name had been in the media nonstop certainly hadn't helped the situation.

Riley groped for her cell phone, then stopped. Her first instinct had been to call Beck, but what could he do? Shout a lot and hope everyone would play nice? She could contact Fireman Jack, the Guild's lawyer, but he'd already done so much for her.

Riley reread the notice more carefully now, but there were no loopholes, no mention of "you have the opportunity to challenge this eviction by such and such a date." The only date on it was seven days from now and that's when she and her possessions had to be out of here.

"This SUCKS!" she shouted. The universe didn't disagree.

Then it hit her: She'd be leaving behind the last place she and her father had shared. Yet another big chunk of Paul Blackthorne was breaking away, like an iceberg in an unseasonably warm Arctic spring. It would float off and the physical memories of him would be lessened. *Again.*

Riley rubbed her eyes, not because of tears but because she was tired of all that life kept throwing at her. Whenever she thought it was getting better, it didn't.

Her mom would have reassured her that this was what growing up was all about, leaving places and things behind. It wasn't like Riley was going to live in this apartment forever, make a shrine of it to her dead father.

With a remorseful sigh, she headed for her bedroom to begin the job of sorting through her and her dad's closet. She'd done this same thing at Sadie's.

This time every item she touched would be special.

TWENTY-FIVE

As usual, Riley found Master Stewart in his den, but instead of having a newspaper on his lap, there were forms from the National Guild. Her father used to work on those in his spare time.

The older man smiled at her approach. "Good evenin', lass."

"Master Stewart." She choose her usual chair and settled into it, but wasn't keen to tell him just how her day had gone. Not like in the past.

When she didn't speak, he raised an eyebrow. "What's wrong?"

"I'm being kicked out of my apartment. Someone complained. My neighbors are sure that I'm going to bring demons and destruction to the place so they want me out."

"I was worried somethin' like that might happen. Ya've been in the press too much as of late." Stewart set the papers aside. "If yer of a mind, yer welcome ta stay here, make this a permanent arrangement, even after the hunters remove their restrictions. Like a live-in tenant or somethin'."

That she hadn't expected. "Thanks. It's just..." Riley adjusted herself in the chair to give her time to think it through. "I can't keep crashing in your house without helping out. It's not right. If I'm not in the other place, I can afford to pay rent. Well, not much but..."

Stewart pondered that for a time. "Aye, I think we can come ta some arrangement. Ya'll need a bigger room. There's a large bedroom just off the turret on the third floor. Those two combined will give ya plenty of space. It'll be like yer own home."

"The turret?" *Now that would be cool.* "I'd like that."

"I'll put tagether some figures and we'll do some hagglin'," he said, winking. "I'll be more than fair with ya. Mrs. Ayers and I have found ya ta be verra pleasant company." He picked up his pipe and began to pack the bowl. "I heard from Beck this mornin'. He's back in town."

Riley ground her teeth in frustration. "I saw him at the *Demonland* set. He avoided me like I have the plague or something."

"Give him time, he'll get it figured out." A match flared to life and the tobacco caught fire. "Now get some rest. Ya look knackered."

She had no idea what that last word meant, but she was probably good for it.

Riley rose. "Good night, sir."

"Good night, lass. Tomorrow will be better for ya. I'm sure of it."

Not likely.

⟑

After breakfast the next morning, Mrs. Ayers took her up to the third floor. Riley had never gone up there before and according to the housekeeper, Master Stewart's bum leg meant he didn't make the journey very often.

"This was his late wife's office," the woman said as she headed down a hallway that led toward the front of the house. "I came to work for them when she became ill. Died of cancer. Lolly was a lovely soul and he took it right hard when she passed over."

Riley was embarrassed to admit she didn't really know that much about the man who'd taken her in. It was time to fix that. "He has some kids, right?" She knew that much from the pictures in his office.

"Three sons and a daughter. Anthony, the eldest, is a trapper. The others have picked less dangerous professions."

The door swung open and they entered a large and airy room, the wood floor creaking under their feet. It was a feminine space with eye-catching floral wallpaper and a high ceiling with ornate cornices. The double doors in the far wall beckoned to her. When Mrs. Ayers swung them open, they revealed a broad, circular room. The turret. It was at least twenty feet in diameter and studded with windows.

"This is amazing," Riley said, walking along the wall, checking out the view of the city in the distance. "It's so big."

"You can have your bedroom in here or in the other room, which-ever feels best to you."

Riley scrutinized the layout. "No, I want this to be like a living room. It's so bright." She could put her "desk" in front of one of the windows and watch the world go by as she did her homework.

"Then that's the way it'll be," Mrs. Ayers replied. "There's a bath down the hall and you'll not be sharing it with anyone."

Riley was still in *wow* mode.

"This is really going work, isn't it?" she said in wonder. "I was so mad about being evicted and now . . ."

"Sometimes we just a need a shove to send us into a new direction," the woman advised. "I'll come up this afternoon and give it a good cleaning. You can move in anytime after that."

"Thanks. I can't wait." *Oh yeah, this is perfect.*

Maybe Master Stewart was right and things were really going to get better.

⊹⊹⊹

Beck's day had flown by, though in truth he knew he was stalling big time. He'd taken a trip to the bank, spent some quality time with his friend Ike at the homeless shelter, and then dropped by to check in with Stewart. He had to see Riley eventually, and the longer he put it off, the angrier she'd be. She wasn't the kind who'd cut him much slack.

It was after six in the evening when he paused at the bottom of the stairs to her apartment, gathering his courage. Stewart had warned him that Riley's temper was shorter than usual and that it wasn't just because she had to move.

"Tread carefully, lad," Stewart had cautioned him. "Ya should have called her the moment ya got home. Now ya have ta pay for that mistake. Tell her where yer heart lies. That's yer only chance."

With a long sigh, he headed up *those* stairs. They would always remind him of the night Paul had died. At least, once Riley moved he'd never have to take this journey again. After the second flight of steps, he paused in front of her door as her words still echoed in his mind:

I love you, Denver Beck. I've loved you for a long time.

He'd been shocked, though he shouldn't have been. She'd been showing her love in so many ways, only he'd been denying it.

"All or nothin'," he murmured.

Beck rapped on the door, his throat suddenly dry and his heart pounding. "Please, God, don't let me screw this up," he whispered.

The door opened only as far as the security chain. Riley studied him soberly, her eyes puffy from crying.

"Hi there. Thought ya . . . you might need some help."

When she didn't let him in, his worry escalated.

"Sorry I didn't call. I just got a new phone today—Donovan's still got my old one for evidence—and, well . . . I'm here now," he said not willing to go much further into the groveling department.

"You didn't need a phone to talk to me last night. You were at the shoot."

Damn. She'd seen him.

"Didn't look like a good time. Besides, you handled the trappin' really well. You dropped that demon like a pro."

"That's no excuse."

He couldn't back down now. "I came to help you. And I've apologized. So where do we go from here?"

Riley mumbled something under her breath and when she pushed the door closed, he'd thought he'd lost everything. Then she unfastened the chain and let him into household chaos. Boxes sat everywhere, some full, most empty. There was an open space in the middle of the living room with belongings piled all around it where she'd been sorting her possessions.

"Sorry yer havin' to move," he said, growing more uncomfortable.

Riley turned toward him, eyes glinting. "It's so . . . hard. I thought I could just weed through this stuff really quick, but everything has a memory attached to it." She picked up a picture frame adorned with orange kittens from off the couch. "Like this. My dad and I bought it at one of those dollar stores. It was so silly we thought it was perfect. Now it's . . ."

"Goin' with you. Take what you want to keep. Start over. Paul and yer momma would understand."

She peered up at him solemnly. "I can take the small stuff, but things like my mom's favorite pie pan and roaster, what do I do with those?"

"Pack them and give them to me and I'll store them in my garage. I've got plenty of room now that Harper's salvaged metal is out of there."

When her face brightened he knew he'd said exactly the right thing.

"You sure?" Riley asked.

"Totally sure. Maybe someday you'll make me some of yer mamma's roast beef and her awesome peach pie."

Their eyes met and her cheeks tinted crimson. "If you're going to tell me I was being all goofy at the bus station, just say it and then . . . get out."

She thought he was going to tear into her again, like he had in the past.

"I heard a pretty girl tell me exactly what she thought. I didn't see anyone bein' goofy, did you?" he replied.

"Oh, I . . . thought . . ." She fidgeted with the picture frame.

Knowing it was best not to push any further, he slipped off his jacket. "Tell me what to do, ma'am. I am yer slave."

Her grin told him she really liked that idea.

✢

As Riley sorted through her father's books she could hear Beck packing up the kitchen. She'd pulled out a few things she wanted to keep, then turned him loose and he was moving right along, having emptied the upper cupboard. Now he was digging around under the sink while complaining about just how many half-full boxes of laundry detergent he'd found.

His grumbling made her smile. If things had played out differently in the swamp she might have never heard that again.

Exactly where they stood was unknown. He hadn't shown up at her door, swept her off her feet, and made passionate love to her amongst the packing boxes. Neither had he told her to back off. They resided somewhere between those two extremes.

A few minutes later the microwave dinged and then he joined her, two cups of hot chocolate in hand.

"Figured you needed a break."

She took the cup and they retired to the couch. "How's the leg?"

"Sore," he replied. "The demon wound is all healed. The top of the foot is the problem. My boot rubs on it."

"You could wear tennis shoes until it healed."

"Nope. Not my style."

"Your pain." She tapped a stack of papers on the arm of the couch. "These are the newspaper articles about you and the Keneally brothers. I kept them in case you wanted me to read them to you."

"Thanks, I would," he replied. "Donovan called this afternoon— the crime scene people found two partial skeletons. He figures critters made away with the rest. They'll do DNA tests, but given the size of the bones and the bits of clothing they found, it's Nate and Brad."

"It could have been you out there," she said, softer now.

"Yeah, I keep thinkin' about that. But it turned out okay. Mc-Govern took a plea bargain and Cole's goin' down too. He'll never get to buy you that ice cream he kept promisin'."

"I'm crushed," she said.

It took a bit of unearthing and then she handed a bank envelope to her guest. *Now comes the hard part.*

He peered inside at the stack of bills. "What's this for?"

"It's all the money you loaned me. I'm paying you back. Thanks for helping me out when it counted."

"Riley, I . . ." he began.

"You didn't trap for a week and you have your mom's funeral to pay for. I want to do this, okay? It's important to me."

"You gonna give me loads of grief if I don't accept this?" he asked.

"Count on it."

Beck gave a nod and tucked the envelope away. "Thank you. Glad I could help out."

He went for it? She'd expected a major hassle.

Beck took a wary sip of his beverage.

"What's up with you?" she said, pointing at his drink. "You don't like chocolate."

"No, but I like the company, so I'm willin' to suffer a little," he replied, a twinkle in his eyes.

"Huh?" That hadn't made much sense.

"I'm hangin' with my favorite girl. My granddaddy would have called this . . . courtin'."

Courtin'?

Before she had time to process that, he continued. "You doin' anythin' Saturday night?"

"Ah . . . no." She certainly wouldn't be going to the prom, that was for sure.

"I thought we could do somethin' together."

"Let me guess—trap demons," she said.

"No, that wasn't what I had in mind. I figured we'd act like normal folks for a change."

"And do what?" she asked suspiciously.

He tugged his jacket off the end of the couch and retrieved a flyer

from a pocket. "I can't read all of this, but I think I got most of it."
He handed it over.

Probably some country-and-western concert.

Riley unfolded the paper and read the top line, then her eyes
stalled in surprise. There had to be some mistake.

She looked up. "You want us to go to the prom together?"

"Yeah. That's what normal folks do."

If Riley's brain had been a computer, it would have just gone to
blue screen. Overwhelmed, she hastily pushed the reset button and it
whirred back to life.

"But this is . . . I mean . . . we'd have to dress up. No jeans, you
know? We're talking suit for you and really nice dress for me."

"I know," he said patiently. "We could make an evenin' of it. Go
out to dinner somewhere special and then to the dance."

Beck is asking me out on a date.

"Ah . . . ah . . ." *Ohmifreakingod. He asked me to the prom.*

"I know it's short notice and all, but I think it'd be fun," he said,
still pitching. "I'd get to see you all dressed up. That'd be real fine."

Why is he doing this? Does it matter? Don't be an idiot.

"Ah . . . okay . . . sure . . . yes." *Yes! Yes!*

His smile told her he was very pleased. "Good!"

"Can you dance?" she asked before she could stop herself.

"I can," he said, affronted. "I'm really good with the *slow* songs."

Riley's cheeks began to burn at the thought of the two of them
pressed up tight against each other. Then reality kicked in. "Oh, I'll
need a dress and my hair and . . ."

With a chuckle that said he was enjoying her minor freak-out,
Beck rose and placed his nearly full cup on the bookshelf. "Then we
got a date. Sorry, but I need to get going. I'm meetin' Jackson down
in Demon Central for a little trappin'. Need to build up my bank
account." He tapped the envelope underneath his jacket. "This
helps, though. Thank you."

"Thanks for all the packing," she said, gesturing toward the
kitchen.

"No sweat. You helped me out with Sadie's stuff. When you need the truck to move, let me know."

Riley followed him to the door, still trying to wrap her brain around all that had happened. Then it got awkward, at least for her. *What to do now?*

Beck solved the problem by leaning close and placing a quick but soft kiss on her lips.

"See you soon, Riley."

She locked the door behind him and hurried to the window, trying not to trip over the packing boxes. When Beck reached his truck, he gazed up at her and waved. She returned it. Then, on impulse, she blew him a kiss.

He grinned as if he'd won the lottery.

I'm going to prom with Denver Beck.

The moment his truck left the parking lot, Riley dove at her cell phone. She needed serious backup.

Simi answered on the first ring. "It's me. So talk already."

"Ohmigod! You are not going to believe this!"

⁜

Though overnight she'd acted as Ori's sidekick, Riley's day was consumed by the apartment. She and her dad had never owned that much stuff, not after the condo fire, but it seemed as if somehow all her possessions had given birth to twins or triplets. Her clothes weren't an issue but her father's were. What did she do with them?

Once she gave them away another part of him was gone. Still, it was silly to keep them when other folks might find them of use. After an "I'm losing it here" convo with Peter, she followed his advice and pulled out a few of her dad's favorite garments and laid them aside. The remainder were lovingly packed into boxes to be donated.

It was close to four and Riley was head deep in the tub, scrubbing, when the knock came at the door. Muttering under her breath about crappy timing, she opened it as far as the security chain. Then did a double take.

"Hi," Blaze said. "Ah, is now a good time?"

It wasn't, but Riley's curiosity got the better of her. *Why would a TV star visit me?*

Blaze was in blue jeans and a Bon Jovi T-shirt, but nothing as tight as was required for *Demonland*. She had little makeup on, her hair back in a ponytail, sporting black-rimmed glasses and bright red tennis shoes. In short, she didn't look at all like the "totally hot" demon slayer.

Riley let the actress into the apartment after warning her it was a complete mess.

"Moving, huh?" Blaze said, clutching a manila envelope in her hands.

"Evicted. The management is sure I'm a threat to civilization because of my job."

"What? That sucks," the woman replied. Then she abruptly stuck out her hand. "The name's Susan, by the way."

They awkwardly shook. The manila envelope came Riley's way.

"Those are the autographed photos you asked for. I threw in some special stuff too. Figured your friends might like that."

"Wow. Thanks. They'll be jazzed."

"I noticed you didn't ask for anything. I'm guessing that's because Blaze is not your idea of a demon hunter."

"Ah, no, not really," Riley replied diplomatically. "You see, I've met the real dudes and . . ."

"That's why I'm here. The Vatican won't deal with us, so I wanted to talk to you about what it's really like trapping or killing Hellspawn. I'm trying to get Arnold—he's my director—to make our show something more than a total frat boy fantasy."

Riley's suspicions kicked in. "I'm not going to say much about the battle in the cemetery, if that's what you're after."

Susan shook her head immediately. "I don't want to know about that. I want your perspective on being a female demon trapper. Can you do that?"

"Sure. Do you mind if I pack while we talk?"

"Even better, I'll help you."

Over the course of the next hour they packed boxes while Riley laid out what it was like to be the lone female in a male-dominated profession. She spoke of the good parts and the bad, the amazing support she'd received and the hate she'd encountered. She was careful not to use names, but in her own way she gave Blaze . . . Susan exactly what she needed.

"How do you face that every day?" the actress asked, busily taping closed a box of history books.

"I just do. It's nothing different than what other women go through. They get out of bed every morning, they do their job. Mine happens to be trapping demons."

Susan set the tape dispenser aside. "This is exactly what I need to know. I get letters from so many girls who want to do what I do in the show. That's why I want Blaze to be a bit more real, you know?"

"Can Hollywood *do* real?" Riley asked.

"Sometimes. We'll still be pretty out there with the demon hunting techniques, but I'd like to have the show layer in more of the hassles, the reality of the job. I think the listeners would like that." She glanced at her cell phone. "Oh, I better scoot. I'm supposed to be in makeup in half an hour."

As Susan opened the door to leave, she hesitated. "You guys need to be careful. I've . . . heard rumors that the show's producer has a mole in your Guild. The guy is trying to get the skinny on exactly what happened in that big battle. They want to make it into a special miniseries."

Susan had just ratted out a superior. That deserved respect.

"Thank you. I'll pass the word along *without* using your name. As far as I'm concerned, we just packed boxes and traded girl talk."

Susan smiled. "Good. You rock, by the way. Just thought I should say that."

"So do you," Riley replied and meant it.

A short time after the actress left, Riley called Harper and let him know they had a problem, without naming her source.

"Figured somebody would try a stunt like that," he replied. "National's background check isn't worth spit."

"Do you think it's Lambert?"

"Could be. Or Fleming. Or one of the new ones Stewart will be training in a couple of weeks. Don't worry, we'll find the guy and kick his ass to the curb. Thanks for the tip."

After she hung up, Riley realized this was the first time Harper had thanked her for anything. She was willing to bet Lucifer and his demons were donning ice skates now.

TWENTY-SIX

Though a glittering array of gorgeous gowns hung on the rack in front of her, Riley shook her head mournfully.

"You're sure none of these would work?" Simi asked, exasperated. Which was warranted since they were on their fourth shop, the evening was drawing to a close, and Riley still hadn't found *the perfect dress.* Or if she'd found one that was close it was too expensive.

"They're not right for me."

"Explain, please," Simi replied, grumpy as she'd not had any coffee in the last hour and that was like a full day for most people. Not even Blaze's signed photograph had helped her withdrawal symptoms.

Knowing her friend's patience was about to snap, Riley treaded carefully.

"I want something so cool it'll make Beck's head spin, but I can't afford two hundred dollars. It has to be under a hundred." She had her dad's life insurance settlement, but that was supposed to last a long time, to help pay for some of her college expenses. There was no reason to spend so much of it for one dance, no matter how important it was.

Simi's brow wrinkled in thought. "Okay. Let's blow out of here. We'll get some caffeine and then we'll go to this used clothing place I know."

"This was supposed to be easy," Riley complained as they exited the store.

"Nothing about you and the trapper dude is easy, girlfriend. So why should this be any different?"

"What are you wearing?"

"I found this incredible black and white dress. It's way sexy and Peter will love it. I'm just having trouble finding the right color tights."

Knowing Simi those tights would not be black or some other normal color.

Probably Day-Glo orange.

+‡+

The clerk at the secondhand shop sized up the situation, including the cash restrictions, and took charge.

"Strapless?" Riley shook her head. "High or low neck?"

"Low is fine, but not so much that I look slutty."

"Classic or frilly?"

"Classic." That'd been her mom's style.

"Color?"

"Anything but black." She'd worn that color too much in her seventeen years.

Like magic, gowns appeared in the dressing room. The first was really chic, a red silk number, but it was a little tight. The next was too flashy for Riley's taste. Three gowns later she felt a thrill of hope.

The clerk slid the next choice over Riley's head. The zipper in the back went up, she turned toward the mirror, and ...

She'd found *the perfect dress.*

Rich royal blue velvet clung to her body in ways that astounded her, with tiny satin ribbon rosettes edging the neckline. It revealed the right amount of cleavage, draped over her hips, and was the proper length for a pair of low heels.

She looked anxiously at Simi. "What do you think?"

A purple thumb shot up. "That's it. You look ah-mazing."

"How much?" Riley asked, crossing her fingers.

"Seventy-five," the clerk replied.

That left enough cash to buy a long slip and maybe a pair of pantyhose. Giddy, Riley executed a test swirl in front of the mirror.

The princess had found her gown for the ball.

✝

Beck leaned against the wall of Riley's new bedroom, trying to catch his breath.

"You just had to be on the third floor, didn't you?" he wheezed.

She would have razzed him about being some old guy, but she was too busy trying to breathe as well. The worst was over: The mattresses, headboard and frame, and dresser were up the stairs now. That left some boxes and her clothes, stuff she could handle on her own.

Beck wiped sweat from his forehead. "If you move again, it'd damn well better be into a place without a lot of stairs, like my house."

It took Riley a bit to realize what he'd said. Had it been a slip of the tongue? You never knew with him.

"I'll keep that in mind," she said, trying not to read too much into his words.

Digging in his backpack, he came up with a pile of papers. "This is the back part of yer daddy's trappin' manual. You've pretty much blown past all that, so I thought you should have it so it'll be complete."

She took the pages and thanked him. After they assembled the bed, Beck took off, limping more than usual. He had stuff to do, he said, but she knew better than to ask exactly what that might be.

Maybe someday you'll let me all the way across that moat of yours.

✝

Beck's first stop after the move had been a florist shop where he needed to determine exactly what kind of flowers Riley might like and where she'd wear them. The choices were mind-boggling. After that harrowing decision, he moved on to the next stop: a new suit. Stewart had recommended a store that wasn't too expensive, but would make sure he received a proper fit.

This datin' business isn't easy. He'd never gone to this trouble with Louisa, but back then there hadn't been money for a suit or flowers or any of that. Lou had been heartbroken when he'd not asked her to the prom, but deep down she knew why. Instead, she went to the dance with Cole. It was the same night Beck had gotten into the drunken knife fight with Mr. Walker, and been exiled to Atlanta for his sins.

Now he had a chance to reclaim a part of life he'd missed and he'd be damned if anything, or anybody, would ruin it.

⊹

The final part of the move was the hardest part: scrubbing out the old apartment so Riley could get the damage deposit returned. It took her over five hours and she even vacuumed the heating vents. Once the apartment was tidy, she hauled the cleaning supplies down to her car, then made the final trip back inside the building.

Riley stood at the open door, studying the empty apartment. No lumpy couch, no cat hair fluff balls on the floor. What would the next renter do with the space? Paint the walls something other than industrial tan? Would they share as much love as she and her father had?

She walked into the middle of the living room and began to catalog those memories, filing them away, one by one. Without thinking, she touched the demon claw necklace where it rested under her shirt. Beck had given it to her here. Simon had been here as well, taking her out for hot chocolate. Even Justine had woven her way into the weft of this story.

She heard a gentle cough behind her and turned to find her neighbor, Mrs. Litinsky, at the door. Max, her cat, sauntered into Riley's apartment and parked himself for a paw wash.

Mrs. L had watched over her when she'd been so sick with the demon wound and the cat had comforted her after her father's death. They were part of her life.

"All done?" Mrs. Litinsky asked.

"Yes. I . . . it's so hard to leave," Riley said, the sadness welling up again.

Max began to nose around the empty room. She'd really miss him and her little demon roommate, who had mysteriously disappeared right after the events at the cemetery.

"You will come and visit us, please?" the old woman said. "We'll miss you."

"I will, I promise."

They shared a tender hug and at the end of it, the old woman touched Riley's hair with fondness. "Your father would be very proud of you."

Riley's eyes brimmed. "Thank you for watching over me," she said. She looked down at Max who was now batting at her shoelace. "Both of you."

A short time later, Riley had handed over keys, survived the super's fussy inspection, and received the damage deposit refund. Now, as she sat in the car, she took one final look at the building that had been her home.

"Good-bye past. Hello future. I hope it's way better."

⚜

It was nearly ten in the evening before Riley had everything exactly the way she wanted it. It'd taken forever because she'd move something into a new location, then move it back to where it had been before. It was good that Beck wasn't here or he'd have lost his mind.

She'd placed her parents' pictures on the top of an old bookcase Mrs. Ayers had scrounged from the attic. On the shelf below were two trapping manuals: hers and her dad's. In between was the cat framed picture of the two them, then a picture of Riley and her mom. She placed the teenage Beck photo right next to that.

That works.

"Need some plants," she mumbled, adding that to a list she had on her computer table. As long as she remembered to water them, they'd thrive with all the sunshine in the turret.

Her phone rang. It was Beck. "Hey, guy. How's it going?"

"Just fine, Princess. How's the new place?"

"Good. I like it here. It feels right."

"Glad to hear that. Jackson and me are headed to some buildin' in south Atlanta. Neighbors said somethin' about a Three down here so we'll check it out."

"You guys be careful. I do not want you to be all chewed up for the dance."

"I'll make sure I'm not," he said, then laughed. "You sleep well and I'll see you tomorrow night."

Smiling, Riley set herself and the phone on the couch. Lounging back, her arms behind her head, she sent a longing gaze at the formal dress hanging in a door frame. She was going on a date with Denver Beck. Simi's stylist was going to do her hair and nails. This was really going to happen.

"Please, let everything be awesome," she prayed. "No demons, no weird Allan. Let it be wonderful, okay?"

Just once she'd like everything to go right, for her and Den to have the most beautiful evening together. The kind of night other girls got without having to pray.

As she daydreamed of what that might be like, something caught her eye. Looking over, she spied the tiny form of a Klepto-Fiend creeping along her new bookshelf, loot bag over his shoulder. It was the demon from her apartment and since Stewart didn't ward his house with Holy Water, it'd apparently moved along with her.

"Hey!" she said. "Are you nuts? This is a grand master's house."

The little Magpie paused, then shrugged like it was no big deal.

"Try not to steal anything he'll miss, okay? I don't want him to kick me out."

A series of high-pitched noises returned, probably the Hellspawn version of "Whatever." With a sudden blur of motion, her perpetual roomie was gone.

Now the place felt like home.

✛

The swirling Chicago snowstorm nearly blinded Riley, but it seemed to have no effect on the angel standing beside her.

"I can't see a thing," she complained. Or feel much for that matter as the chill seemed to drill right into her bones.

"Use your senses," Ori retorted.

"My senses can't see anything, either, okay? What kind of demon is out in this kind of weather anyway?"

"The kind that we need to kill," Ori replied. "It is a traitor to the Prince."

A second later a shrill shriek ripped through the storm, a high-pitched scream of mortal terror.

"Where is it?" she demanded.

The angel didn't reply, but let her fumble through the swirling flakes like an idiot. Another shriek rent the air, one that tore through her skull. Panicking now, Riley closed her eyes and trusted those senses Ori was always talking about.

Very quickly the strong stench of demon filled her nose, nearly making her gag. Opening her eyes, she hurried forward. Then she saw it, a four-foot-tall lumbering form covered in snow and ice. Chicago's version of the abominable snowman.

The Gastro-Fiend had two teens cornered. The terrified boy had positioned himself in front of the girl, trying to hold the demon back with his computer bag. That made her think of Peter. The girl was crying into a cell phone, begging for someone to help them.

Riley moved closer and let her sword erupt from her hand. She had to admit it looked really badass.

"Hey, demon!" she called out. "Yeah, you."

The fiend whirled, its twin glowing eyes piercing the snow veil. It howled her name.

Remember what I taught you, Ori whispered in her mind.

The Three charged immediately, moving with a speed she'd not expected. She slashed at it, wounding its arm as it surged past. In response, it bellowed and swiped at her with one of its razor claws, gashing her cheek. Riley bit back the cry of pain, trying to keep her balance on the slippery pavement.

With a roar, the demon launched itself at her again. This time she managed to do exactly as Ori had taught her: Step to the side at the last minute and catch the demon full on in its chest.

The blinding blade cut true and the Three went down into the snow, blood steaming like a cauldron. As she struggled to catch her breath, the boy called out his thanks. She waved them off and the pair of them fled into the night.

"Did they see you?" she asked, straightening up.

"No. They won't remember what you look like if anyone asks," Ori replied.

He gestured and the demon burst into flames, a grisly bonfire for a bitterly cold winter night.

Once her sword had vanished, Riley touched her face where the demon had cut her. It stung and her jaw was sore.

"Hold still," her demi-lord instructed. His hand brushed her face, causing the wound to heal. In that instant she remembered that night in the mausoleum, how he'd made love to her.

"What happened to you, Ori? Why are you different now?"

"It does not matter," he said, but the angel's eyes grew sad, as if he too remembered that night and what they'd once had.

It does to me.

Then she was in her room, but the cold and the feeling of loss were hard to shake.

✛

It was nearly noon and the parking lot outside the old Starbucks was crowded with students, all in their little cliques, chattering away. Riley stifled a yawn, not quite ready to take on the noise yet. With each one of these nocturnal hunts the guilt within her grew. She had to tell Beck what was going on, but what if he lost it? Decided not to take her to the prom?

I'll wait until after the dance and tell him. Yeah, that will work.

Ahead of her were four hours of class to make up for the time the schools had been closed during the zombie demon crisis. No one wanted to be here, not with the prom tonight. Even those who were blowing off the dance were talking about it.

That included Riley, whose mind was still racing with all the things she had to complete by the time Beck picked her up at seven. Her hair and nail appointment was at five thirty, then she had to rush home and begin the process of transforming from a scruffy demon trapper girl to the princess that her date imagined her to be. She had all her clothes laid out, but still it was going to be tight.

To curb her rampaging nerves, Riley made her rounds of the parking lot, handing out the collection of autographs, photos, and whatnot from the *Demonland* cast. The reactions were instant: When she received the personalized photograph from Jess Storm, Brandy went ballistic with one of her supersonic whoops. As Riley distributed the other goodies to Brandy's friends, they celebrated their good fortune, comparing photos and signatures.

"You rock, Riley," one of the girls said.

I do. She'd come through as promised.

"Is Blaze as smoldering in the flesh as on TV?" Peter asked, studying the glossy photograph in his hand. The actress had added a lipstick kiss in the lower left corner next to his name.

"Sort of. She's pretty nice. Not a ditzy airhead like I figured."

"I'll ignore that you dissed my fave actress."

"Probably best."

"Allan's back," he said. "The Neanderthal overheard me talking to Brandy, so he knows you're going to the prom."

Before she could tell him how much that sucked, her cell rang. It was Beck and she needed to hear his voice. "Hey, guy. You getting ready for our night together?"

"Ah," he said, his voice strained. "It's just . . ."

"What's wrong?"

"We got a pack of Threes in Little Five Points, near Mort's house. They don't usually go there so this is somethin' new. Jackson, Reynolds, and me are to take them down. Tonight."

You wouldn't dare bail on me. "Tonight? Can't they do it?"

"Not without backup and no one else is free. I promise, I'll be there at the dance, but our fancy supper is history."

Peter was staring at her now, probably because of her darkening expression.

"Tell them you have a date," she said through clenched teeth.

"Don't worry, I'll be there for the dance. I'll not leave ya hangin'. I gotta go now. See ya soon, girl. I can't wait." Then Beck hung up, as if he knew any longer on the phone might be life threatening.

"Ah . . . I think I'll go inside now," Peter said, edging away.

"He's going trapping," Riley snarled. "The one night we're supposed to be together and . . ." She jammed her phone into her backpack. "He's going to meet me at the dance. Won't that look special?"

"You need a ride?"

She nodded, feeling the sting of tears. "I swear I'm going to kill him. I'll wear my new dress to the trial and no jury would convict me. They'd probably give me a medal or something."

Allan came out of nowhere. She knew what would happen next, just like it was scripted or something.

"I'll take you, Riley," he offered. "I won't ditch you like that hick did."

As she began to walk away, he caught her arm.

"Come on, get real," Allan said. "Stop being an idiot. He's not your kind of guy."

"How many times do I have to tell you? I want *nothing* to do with you. Leave me alone!"

"Riley—"

She got into his face, which was always dangerous. "Back off, Allan. I swear I'll tear you apart if you keep messing with me."

She felt the familiar tingle in her right hand. With little effort her right palm would ignite into a fiery sword and slice this miserable excuse for humanity into sushi. Riley forced herself to take a deep breath in an effort to calm down. Hanging with Ori was starting to affect her in ways she didn't like.

Peter gave a low whistle and headed for the door, sensing retreat was the best option. Muttering choice Hellspeak curse words, Riley followed him. Fortunately Allan held back, her anger having stunned him into silence.

Her special night was a ship foundering on the rocks in a heavy gale.

Why am I surprised?

TWENTY-SEVEN

With his romantic dinner plans trashed, Beck fell into a foul mood. He'd planned it so carefully and a damned trio of Gastro-Fiends had screwed it all up. There was no need to check the time on his phone: He was way late and Riley would be furious.

He'd had no choice. This pack had gone after a couple of senior citizens and only luck had kept them from becoming a meal. Now those same rampaging demons were all lined up in steel bags, howling like the world was coming to an end. One of them was bleeding and Beck took credit for that.

"Ah, shut the hell up!" he shouted.

"Man, did you go medieval on that thing or what?" Reynolds asked, pointing at the Three with the busted arm. "Something bothering you, Den?"

Though he knew it wasn't the others' fault, Beck spewed out his frustration at the screwed-up plans, what the evening was supposed to be like.

Reynolds and Jackson traded looks.

"The prom? That's cool," Reynolds replied.

"No, it's not. I'm late and she's gonna be totally pissed."

"Then get your butt out of here," Jackson said. "We'll take care of these things."

"You sure about that?" Beck asked.

"Take off!" Reynolds said, giving him a playful shove. "Go have a life, dude. You can buy us a beer down the line for our trouble."

"Thanks, guys, I owe you!"

Despite his sore foot, Beck took off at a run.

⁜

As she dressed, Riley's emotions boiled like a pool of lava. It was silly, but she'd dreamed of floating down the long staircase at Stewart's house as her handsome beau waited for her. She'd even made a test trip down the stairs to judge how much the dress would be a problem with her heels. When no one else was around, of course.

Now there was no Beck.

"Damn!" she swore, tugging her pantyhose into place.

The dinner would have been so cool, but the dance was the big event. How stupid would she look if he didn't show up? It was a good bet Allan would certainly notice and he'd be all over her about it. He wouldn't back off no matter what she said.

Why did Beck have to go trapping tonight? Why couldn't he have refused?

⁜

Once home, Beck raced through his shower, did a quick shave, threw on his suit, hastily knotted his new tie, and fled out the door. It was pure torment not to exceed the speed limit, but with his luck a cop would pull him over and he'd get into an argument and end up in jail.

I'm like some kid on his first date.

He felt like it too. Riley made everything seem new and shiny and he wanted that feeling to last, but his first big chance to make a good impression was falling apart before his eyes. He hoped this wasn't a harbinger of their future together.

✛

Riley had been so caught up in her own misery that she hadn't noticed the car had come to a stop in the hotel parking lot. Simi and Peter looked over the front seat in unison, concerned.

She sighed. *You have a gorgeous dress and a ticket to the dance. Suck it up.*

She followed her friends toward the hotel's entrance, trailing beside them. As Riley drew near, Peter took her hand. Then he ran his arm around Simi's waist.

"Hey, look at me. I've got two hot girls with me tonight."

When Riley didn't smile, he sighed. "Beck will be here. That guy would walk through fire to spend time with you."

"What he said," Simi added.

"I hope you're right," Riley replied. "I only want to see his face. Know he's safe. I'm mad at him but . . ."

God, I have it bad.

Riley shuffled through the line and checked in, then followed her friends into the hotel's courtyard. It was an open area with skylights that offered a magnificent view of the clear night sky. Real trees sat in huge containers, decorated with miniature white lights. Flagstones paved a trail among the trees with benches interspersed here and there. Couples wandered down the paths, the girls clad in a rainbow of colors, like a flower garden in motion.

"This is so neat," she said. "It's like a fairyland."

Come on, Den. Don't miss this. We both deserve a night just for us.

Her eyes drifted from couple to couple. Some fit well together and others . . . not so much. When she checked out her friends with the same critical eye, she knew they were right for each other. Simi laughed at something Peter said and it wasn't forced. They were genuinely enjoying each other's company. If Peter's mom had still been in town this night probably wouldn't have happened.

As usual, Simi was her own person when it came to clothes, clad in a short harlequin print dress and hot pink tights that made her look like an escapee from a punk rock band. Her hair was a mish-mash of black, silver, and pink, but when put all together it looked great. Peter was in a black suit and a tie that matched Simi's tights. His hair was spiked at the ends and he looked really sharp, despite the slight bruising from his brush-up with Allan's fist.

Suddenly nervous, Riley fussed with the flowers in her hair, delicate pink orchids with baby's breath, a present from Beck that had arrived earlier this afternoon.

Stop worrying. He wouldn't have sent them unless he meant to be here.

Her friends were watching her now, reluctant to leave her on her own.

"Go on. I'll wait here. I'll be fine," she said, fibbing.

"Find us when he shows up, okay?" Simi said.

"I will."

They wandered off, occasionally stopping to talk to other students. Riley spied Brandy and her date, some really tall guy, near the hallway that led to the ballroom. He was way cute and Riley wondered where she'd found him. Farther down the hall was their class' resident vampire wannabe, the guy Riley had dubbed Vlad. He was in a classy tux and his date was clad in a long black gown. Her blond hair hung in waves down her back and there wasn't a single tattoo or piercing in sight. When Vlad smiled, his fake vampire teeth were noticeably missing. Maybe his date had given him the word on those.

When her eyes lit on another guy, her stomach lurched. *Allan.* He was staring at her. Before she had a chance to escape, her ex was in front of her.

"Face it, you've been dumped. How does it feel?" he chided.

Now was not the time to get into it with this guy.

Knowing it was a waste of time to talk to him, Riley took off across the atrium. She wasn't so much afraid of Allan's fists anymore as what harm he could do to her friends. The more she pushed back the more volatile he would become. One of these days there would be a showdown, and he'd be surprised to find that she wasn't the same girl he'd assaulted two years before.

To Riley's delight, the fairyland theme carried over into the ball-room where gauzy wings hung from the ceiling, shimmering in the muted lights. The tables were laced with silvery ribbons and bal-loons were tied to the chairs. An iridescent bubble floated by her nose, created by a special machine near the front of the room. Luck-ily Simi's choice of bizarre hair color proved a boon as she and Peter were easy to find in the packed ballroom.

When Riley joined them, they all traded looks and the message was passed: no Beck.

"The Neanderthal find you?" Peter asked.

"He did," Riley replied. "I'll leave before I'll dance with him." Which would make her evening a total wreck.

"Did you see Vlad? He looks human tonight. Who'd have thought that?"

Riley's eyes wandering over the crowd in search of a particular pair of broad shoulders and enchanting eyes.

Still no Beck.

She could call him, but what if he was actively trapping? That distraction could get him hurt. Especially when he was trying to capture a pack of Threes.

He said he'd be here. He lives up to his promises. Just chill, will you?

Another song started and Peter and Simi headed toward the dance floor. Out of the corner of her eye Riley could see Allan working his way through the crowd, intending to make his move. He never learned.

She gave him her back and prepared herself. When a hand touched her elbow, she turned, ready to deliver a tongue lashing.

The scorching words died in her throat. It was her hero.

Beck's face was flushed like he'd been running. "Hey," he said, taking a deep breath to calm himself. "I made it." His eyes ran the length of her and then widened in appreciation. "Look at you. That dress is . . . I've never seen anything like it before. Yer so beautiful, Riley."

He's in a whole roomful of pretty girls and all he sees is me? How awesome is that?

Riley would replay this scene for the rest of her life. Him. Her. All of it.

"I'm sorry I'm late," he added. "We got all three of them and nobody was hurt."

That was really good news. "You're forgiven," she said, touching the lapel of his jacket. "That's a new suit. It's really nice." It fit better than his old one, accented his muscular build.

He smiled, pleased by the praise. "Figured the other one had seen too much sorrow. This is a new beginnin' for us, so I wanted to do it right."

Riley carefully straightened his tie. "This matches my dress. How did that happen?"

"Oh, I might have had some help with that," Beck said. "So, how's about we go dance, pretty lady?" He offered his arm and she took it.

"Yes . . ." *Forever.*

✛

Beck had been so wired it took him some time to unwind. By the end of the first fast dance, he felt better. It'd all worked out, even if it had been insane right from the start.

After the dance, they joined Simi and Peter at a table where the females promptly took off to that most mysterious place in the universe: the girls' restroom.

"Dude," Peter said, executing a fist bump. "Good to see you. I kept telling her you'd be here."

"Thanks. It was a pain to be late, but I had no choice."

"Does she know Simi gave you the prom flyer?"

"No. Best we leave it that way," Beck replied. "It worked out perfectly."

Peter's eyes roamed across the dance floor and when he followed his gaze it ended on Allan.

"He botherin' her tonight?"

"A little, but she can handle him now. He tries to nail her and she'll bust him one."

Beck nodded. "Heard you did the same."

"Yeah, I got my hit in right before he flattened me. But I don't regret it."

Beck shot the offender a visual warning that said serious agony was his for the taking if he kept bothering Riley. Allan scowled, then backed off, no doubt hunting for some other poor girl to thump.

Peter lowered his voice. "It's probably none of my business, but is this a onetime date or . . . I mean, if this is just a drive-by, I'd better find some protective armor, you know?"

"It all depends on Riley," Beck said, then took a sip of the punch. It was too fruity for his liking and he set it back on the table. "I'd like this to be the start of somethin' good. I'm tired of messin' around with girls that aren't worth the trouble."

Peter nodded his approval, accompanied by a huge grin. "All right! No armor needed. Just don't lie to her or treat her like a kid, and you'll be fine."

"Yeah, already learned those lessons." *The hard way.*

When his date and Simi returned Beck found himself staring at Riley in awe, wondering what he'd done to deserve the honor of escorting Paul Blackthorne's daughter to the prom. He'd known she was pretty, even when covered in demon pee and wearing ruined jeans, but that dress hugged every curve, setting his blood on fire. Her glossy brown hair curled around her shoulders and he wanted nothing more than to touch those curls. Touch her.

Beck behaved himself, though it was really difficult, especially during the slow dances when they were so tantalizingly close. He savored the feel of her against his body, the light scent of her perfume, the look in her eyes that told him he was the center of her universe. It was a new and totally overwhelming experience.

I could get used to this.

Beck finally gathered his courage during their last slow dance. Moving his lips close to her ear, he whispered, "Thank you for believin' in me."

She smiled up at him. "I knew you were worth the effort, even when you got yourself lost in that old swamp."

He made sure the kiss they shared wasn't hurried: If it got them thrown out of the dance, he didn't care. When it ended, he sighed in wonder.

He was sure that somewhere up in Heaven, Riley's parents were giving them a thumbs-up.

✛

The drive back to Stewart's went too quickly for both of them. Riley could sense Beck didn't want the evening to end, and neither did she. Tomorrow it would be back to the homework, *Demonland*, and Ori, but tonight was just for the two of them.

Beck played the gentleman, opening the truck door for her. As they walked to the house, they paused every few steps and traded kisses.

"I should go," he said. "Don't need someone complainin' to Stewart that we were makin' out on his front porch."

Riley laughed lightly. "He's in bed. He told me that he'd leave a fire going for us if we wanted to come in for a while. "

Beck arched an eyebrow in surprise. "I'm likin' that old man more every day."

✛

While her date added a log to the glowing embers, Riley settled on the couch, a thick afghan over her legs. It wasn't sexy, but she was used to heavier clothes.

"Cold?" Beck asked as he settled next to her.

"A little. He keeps it like Scotland in here. Chilly."

"Then I'm not doin' my job right."

"What?" she asked, puzzled.

The kiss that followed helped her warm up considerably.

"Better?" he asked. There was a bad-boy grin now.

"Getting better."

The next kiss made her toasty indeed.

"You still cold?" he asked, teasing.

"A little," she fibbed.

He bent to the task and this kiss was longer and deeper than the ones before, their tongues lightly touching. The kiss took on an intensity of its own as Beck slid his hand underneath a breast and cupped it. He didn't appear to have noticed he'd done it until the kiss ended.

"Whoa, sorry," he said, pulling the offending hand away. "That was out of bounds. My bad."

Riley couldn't hold back the grin. "If you get out of line, I'll let you know."

Beck sighed. "It's just that, well, I've always been in a hurry to get a girl in bed, mostly because that's all that mattered. Never figured there was much past that." He ran a finger down her cheek. "Not this time. I don't want to push you into anythin'. We do it right, so it'll last."

He's totally serious about us.

Riley curled up against him, silent as she thought that through.

"Oh, damn, now I've upset you," he murmured.

"You're fine, Den. I was realizing how this is so different for both of us."

"I hope so. You've trusted other guys and got hurt and—"

She put her fingers over his mouth to stop him. "We'll work it out. We'll know when the time is right."

They cuddled for a time. Then he stirred again. "You ever think of what yer gonna do after you graduate from high school?"

Why is he asking that? "I'd like to go to college, but it can't be full time, not and keep trapping. What about you?"

"I want to get my master's license. That's about as far as I've thought ahead. Well, at least when it comes to trappin'."

She stilled her breath. What else had he been thinking about?

When he said nothing more, she laid her head on his chest, feeling his breath in her hair and the soft touch of his fingers on her shoulder.

If only one moment of her life could be preserved for eternity, Riley would choose this one.

⁜

It was close to midnight when she walked him to the front door, wondering what might have happened if she was still in her own apartment. Would she have asked him to stay until morning? Wasn't it too soon to be thinking about that?

Their final kiss was achingly tender. "Thank you for making a dream come true," she whispered.

"That goes both ways." He touched her cheek with fondness. "You sleep well. I'll be dreamin' about you, don't you doubt it."

After he'd departed, Riley floated up the stairs to her own bed; her near-perfect evening with Denver Beck was over.

No matter what tomorrow threw at them, they'd always have this one night.

TWENTY-EIGHT

As if to punish her for the romantic time with her beau, Ori summoned Riley out of her dreams about an hour after she'd gone to bed. The first stop was somewhere in Atlanta, then they were in Las Vegas and on to Seattle, where a cold rain pelted down on her in the dark night. Once all the demons were dead, she was coated in steaming black blood, the fiends' death shrieks still reverberating in her ears.

"I can't do this anymore," she pleaded. "Please . . ."

Ori glared at her as the rain poured from the heavens. "You should have been able to kill all of them on your own by now, but you're too busy thinking about that accursed trapper and—"

"Why are you doing this to me?" she demanded, heaving herself to her feet. "Are you jealous of Beck? Is that it? God, if you hate me that much, just kill me!"

Something altered in the angel's deep eyes. It wasn't jealousy she saw there, but cold resolve. Riley took a few steps backward, suddenly afraid.

"You forget your place. It is I who owns your soul, not the other way around."

"If I am so pathetic, then why are you bothering with me?"

"Because there was no other choice." Then just as suddenly as it came, his anger fled. "We have little time left. I want you to . . ." He shook his head. "The time may come when I am not able to protect you. You have to learn how to fight, how to survive or all of this will have been for nothing." He waved a hand dismissively. "We're done for tonight."

Riley found herself on the floor of her room. There was no demon blood on her, her clothes as clean as if she'd pulled them out of the dryer, but she could not cast aside the horrific images in her mind. No angelic power could erase the growing sense of dread deep inside her heart.

⁙

Like the previous day, Riley's fellow students were all buzzing about the dance, who was there with whom, who wore what, and who got drunk and passed out in the girls' (or boys') restroom. Because there was always one or two of those.

Peter nudged her with an elbow. "Hey? Anyone in there?"

"Sorry. It was a late night." Not willing to share anything about her ordeal with the angel, she went for a more pleasant memory. "Beck and I sat in front of the fireplace until about midnight, then he went home. It was so . . . perfect."

"Please tell me there were abundant displays of affection."

That got her to smile. "Of course there were. How about you and Simi?"

"We went to the coffee shop to get her caffeine fix and we talked until it closed," her friend replied. "She's got a really unusual mind, but I like that. Then I drove her home. And yes, there were PDAs."

"Wait until your dad wants to meet her."

"That's in the works," he said, not sounding happy about that. "He is *so* going to freak out when he sees her hair." Peter popped a couple of knuckles, demonstrating how much he was concerned about that *meet the parent* encounter.

"It'll work out. She's crazy, but she's cool. I bet your dad will see that."

Riley felt the weight of someone's stare. It was Allan and from his expression he was jonesing for payback.

"Okay, people, let's dig into the homework," Mrs. Haggerty called out.

Riley pulled out her sheet of math questions and then smiled to herself as Beck's last kiss danced into her mind. When the teacher called her name to answer question number seven, she reluctantly returned to the real world.

⚜

After class, Riley and Mrs. Haggerty worked on a math problem she couldn't get. By the time they left the building, the rest of the students had split.

"Did you enjoy the prom?" the teacher asked as she locked the doors behind them.

"Definitely. It was great."

"I saw the young man you were with. Very handsome. Is he a trapper too?"

Riley nodded. "Yeah, he used to trap with my dad."

"I'm glad you found someone. After your father died, I was worried. I'm less worried now. You be careful, okay?"

"I will. Good night, Mrs. Haggerty."

Riley had just unlocked her car door when her cell phone lit up.

"Hey there, Princess. How's it goin'?"

It was her fave guy. "It's good. I just got out of class. What's the plan for tonight?"

"I thought maybe we could have some supper together. Mama Z's barbecue?"

"That works."

They coordinated the time and the call ended along with his

promise to make up for being late the night before. As Riley began to calculate how many kisses would equal a proper apology, a noise came from behind her. Then the crunch of footsteps on gravel. She turned just in time to see Allan marching toward her.

Before she could react, he caught her arm and swung her away from the car. The door slammed shut as he placed himself between her and the vehicle.

"You blew me off," he said. "You didn't answer my calls and now you're all over that hick. I saw you making out with him at the dance. Why are you doing this to me?"

Riley shook her arm to make him let go. "You hit me, remember? You socked me in the jaw because I wouldn't steal a computer for you and you're surprised I want nothing to do with you?"

"You're making a big deal out of nothing. I know what you're doing—you're dating that hick just to get back at me," he said, his voice rising. Both his hands were clasped into fists now.

Beck would expect Riley at the restaurant in a few minutes. If she showed up with bruises . . . Beck didn't need jail time because of this loser.

"This is all your fault," Allan continued. "I didn't want to hit you, but you made me mad. If you'd just done what I told you—"

Riley's fury soared. "It was *never* my fault. You. Hit. Me."

"You're making me look like a fool in front of everyone. I bet your hick would dump you if he thought you were cheating on him. Or if you weren't pretty anymore."

Her blood chilled at the threat, knowing what damage his fists could do. She set the backpack on the ground and slid the steel pipe free.

"You're never hurting me again. Don't even try."

"You need to learn some respect," Allan said, his eyes afire and his jaw clenched. "Then maybe you'll know what it feels like to be me."

As Riley braced herself, trying to figure out how to escape, Allan went slack, unmoving, like a statue.

She felt the angel's presence and shifted positions so she could see them both.

"You can strike this one, but he won't understand pain," Ori said. "He's had too much of it for one life."

"What do you mean?" she asked, her heart pounding hard.

"Where do you think he learned to use his fists? His father beats him and his mother. He is only doing what he has been taught."

Riley had never even considered that. She gestured at her ex. "So what now? You can't leave him like this forever."

"I could kill him for you," the Fallen offered. "End his misery."

She jolted at the suggestion. "No! I mean, he's bad and all that, but..."

A nod returned as if she'd passed some test.

"Perhaps he needs to see his future a bit more clearly," Ori replied. He snapped his fingers and her abuser came to life.

"What the hell is going on?" Allan demanded, his eyes riveted on Ori now.

"Well, if you really want to know..."

The pair vanished in a single flash of white light.

"Show-off," she muttered, blinking eyes to clear them. Fortunately the parking lot was empty. She'd just jammed the pipe in her backpack when they returned. This time Allan was no longer full of rage, but on his knees sobbing hysterically, his clothes smelling suspiciously of sulfur.

"You didn't—" she began.

"Take him to Hell? Of course I did. If this worthless mortal wishes to continue on this path, he should know where he's headed. I'm surprised his soul is still his own, he's so ripe for the picking."

Riley swallowed, hard. She was headed to the same address when she died, but Ori had never given her the tour.

"Your day will come," her demi-lord replied.

Allan finally raised his head and when he saw the angel, he flailed backward, crying out in abject terror.

"You understand now?" Ori asked, his wings arching outward, making himself even more threatening.

A panicked nod returned as torrents of tears ran down her ex's ruddy cheeks.

"Then cease your evil ways, Allan Benjamin Blazek. You are *not* your father. Be better than that despicable piece of clay!" He pointed into the distance. "Depart!"

Allan stumbled to his feet, then staggered away, still crying. After a short distance, he shot a panicked glance over this shoulder and picked up speed.

"Is he going to be okay?" Riley asked as she watched the retreating figure.

Ori gave her a sidelong glance. "You're concerned about your abuser?"

"Yeah. He's a mean jerk, but . . . he was scared out of his mind."

"That you would ask such a question is exactly why you don't deserve to be in Hell," Ori replied. With another flash the Fallen angel was gone.

Even if she didn't deserve eternal damnation, it was hers. Nothing was going to change that.

⁜

Each night Riley crawled into her bed, she uttered a simple prayer: Do not let the angel take me away tonight, and each time that prayer was ignored. Despite Ori's earlier appearance at the school, tonight was no different. This time she found herself in one of Demon Central's back alleys, minus the angel. That was new. He was usually there to critique her performance as they dispatched Lucifer's enemies.

The scene gradually came into focus: There were three people in the alley, a young man in jeans and a sweatshirt and two women. The shorter of the two females wore a miniskirt and a black bustier and appeared younger than Riley. The other one was taller, with numerous body piercings and an obsession with black leather, her pure white hair cropped short.

What am I doing here?

Look closer, Ori said in her mind.

It was then Riley began to notice the smaller details, like how the guy wasn't on this planet, his expression blank and his jaw slack. Then came more revelations: The two "women" were Mezmers, Grade Four Hypno-Fiends, and the dude their victim. If left in their clutches, he'd be minus his soul very soon, along with his life.

The more powerful one nearly claimed Beck's soul, Ori explained.

So that was why Riley was here. This was payback.

She stepped closer and that attracted the shorter demon's attention.

"Blackthorne's daughter," the Mezmer growled.

The taller demon turned toward her now, sniffing the air in disgust.

"Where is your demi-lord, foul child? Why is the Divine not here to protect you? Have you displeased him? Has he sent you to your death?"

Those were all very good questions.

When Riley didn't reply, the fiend broke contact with her victim. "I shall rend your flesh," it rasped. "If the Prince's lap dog comes to spare you, I shall destroy him."

These two must be part of Sartael's crew.

"Not on Lucifer's team, huh?" Riley chided.

The younger demon cried out at the use of its master's name. The older demon only winced, which meant it was more powerful than Riley had first imagined. But then it would have to be if it nearly claimed Beck's soul.

She watched with fascinated horror as the elder demon's disguise melted away, revealing the grotesque Hellspawn beneath. It stood a head taller than Riley, with beige skin and an impressive set of horns. Its blazing eyes fired crimson in the night. Curiously, wing folds had begun to form between its body and arms.

This thing's almost an Archfiend.

Which is why it must die, Ori replied. *Kill it.*

There are two of them.

So?

The young man remained oblivious to the fact the one of the "ladies" now looked like someone's idea of a low-budget horror movie.

Riley felt a prickle of discomfort in the palm of her right hand as the fire extended down her fingers, joint by joint and then flamed out of the end of them as the ethereal sword took shape. The younger demon hissed in fear and reverted to its natural form.

"Ah, crap." The cat was definitely out of the bag.

"What is this?" the older abomination demanded. "How is it that you wield the Divine Fire?"

"Just lucky, I guess."

Kill the stronger one first.

"You think?" Riley muttered.

She and the elder demon squared off, working in a wide circle around each other, Riley's nerves at the breaking point. Ori was throwing her to the wolves. Or the demons, in this case.

Fortunately, the other Mezmer stayed out of the fight, nervously chewing on one of its claws.

Do not trust it, Ori cautioned. *Do not show it your back.*

Riley was fed up with the running commentary in her head. *Why are you making me do this?*

Time for you to carry your own weight. Either you kill it or you die tonight.

"No way," Riley said, more to herself than the voice in her mind. She had too much to live for and she refused to give up now that she and Beck had finally gotten their hearts in sync.

The elder demon gestured at the clueless guy. "Kill it and feed on its corpse."

The younger fiend moved to fulfill its superior's orders.

"No! Stop!" Riley knew it was a trap, but she had no choice. When she broke formation to intercept the lesser demon, its companion struck. The first swipe of its claw cut a line of pain across Riley's left shoulder and her arm immediately went numb.

Move! Ori shouted.

Riley ducked another broad slash and retaliated with one of her own. It sliced deep into the elder demon's muscled chest, but not deep enough to slow it.

The Four wore a cunning smile now. "I know of a mortal who cares for you. The trapper I nearly possessed. I saw you in his mind."

"Goody for you," Riley said, still circling. *How do I stop this thing?*

There was no reply from the angel. She was truly on her own.

"After I kill you, I shall seek and destroy the trapper," the fiend taunted. "I shall feast on his body and his soul shall be mine."

Riley's composure fled and she charged forward. The demon responded instantly, leaping toward her with teeth and claws bared. She raised the sword to repel its attack and the creature tried to redirect its lunge, but it was moving too fast and the blade impaled it before its talons could reach her. An ear-splitting shriek filled the air as they hung for a second, frozen in battle. Then the demon exploded into a seething cloud of boiling flames, followed by a choking cloud of black ash.

Riley clamped her mouth shut to avoid getting a lungful of the stuff.

Behind you!

She whirled and countered the smaller demon's halfhearted attack, wounding it. It fell on its knees, wailing in Hellspeak, begging for mercy, offering its allegiance for eternity if she would spare its life.

Ori materialized near her.

"Now you show up," she said, bent over, trying to catch her breath.

"You did the job as required," he said. "Though that was sloppy."

He never gave her any praise. Not once.

With a gesture, Ori restored the young man to his senses. "Go, mortal. Tonight is not your night to die."

The man bolted down the alley and never looked back.

The smaller demon continued to whine, bowing its head to the ground in abject obeisance.

"If you do not kill it, it will be yours to command," Ori explained. "Is that what you want? Do you wish to become a mistress of demons?"

"What? No!" Riley exclaimed. "Let it go!"

"That is not possible now." He closed on the wailing fiend, then raised his sword. Riley averted her eyes, but still heard the sickening sizzle as Ori's blade sliced through the demon's flesh, bisecting the body.

Her stomach felt as if it was about to empty, the adrenaline rush history.

"I want to go home now," she said wearily. "I don't want to kill anymore."

The angel shook his head. "There are more Hellspawn in this world that have need of your sword."

Riley turned on him, no longer fearing his wrath. "I am not some heartless executioner like you. I can't keep doing this."

"In that you are wrong," he said patiently. "The moment you gave me your soul, you lost your choice in the matter."

⊹

The night's sleep trashed by recurring nightmares of murderous Mezmers, Riley knew she had to talk to someone or lose it entirely. She didn't dare tell Beck about what she and the angel were up to, at least not yet, and confiding to the masters would lead to repercussions with Rome for both her and Stewart.

That left her friend Ayden: The witch had always given her sound advice and Riley desperately needed more of the same.

It took time to score a parking spot near Centennial Park as she'd never have Peter's talent in that regard. She docked her car in the lot across from the ruins of the Tabernacle and surveyed the scene. It had changed since the last time she'd been in the area. Giant monoliths sat at irregular intervals, testimony to a bulldozer's industrious efforts. It seemed sacrilegious to clear away the building, but the land was probably worth something to somebody.

They better not build anything dumb.

Once she'd locked the car and hefted her backpack onto her shoulders, she was drawn across the street into the ruins. The ground was uneven, so she moved carefully. Trying to find landmarks in the rubble was impossible, so she wandered around aimlessly, recalling that terrible night, the demons and men who'd died. Someone had laid flowers at the base of one of the brick mounds, a shrine of sorts. She knelt and touched the bouquet. A card attached said it was for Ethan, one of the apprentices who'd been lost in the fire and it was signed *Love, Janine.* Probably his fiancée.

Nearly overwhelmed by the enormity of the loss, Riley rose, eager to get away from this place. As she turned away, the toe of her tennis shoe caught on a piece of wood, shifting some of the debris. Riley stared at a piece of leather cord that snaked from underneath the rubble and she knew what it was even before she unearthed it. Though scorched, Simon's initials were still visible on the back of his cross. Somehow the symbol of his faith had survived the disaster.

Riley dusted it off, her hand coming away black with soot. If she returned it to him now he might not take it, still shaken by all he'd endured. Instead, she tucked it into her pack for safekeeping hopeful that someday Simon Adler would find solace in his faith again and he'd welcome the cross's return.

⊹

The Bell, Book and Broomstick bustled with customers checking out the ample supplies of incense, crystals, and various potions. Ayden was assisting a woman who kept insisting she wanted a love charm. The witch patiently cautioned her how such magic often had unintended consequences but the customer wasn't listening.

"I don't see why this is a problem," the woman said. "I just want to him fall in love with me."

"And then what?" Ayden asked, an eyebrow raised in irritation. "What happens when you decide you don't love him anymore? You've bound his will to yours."

"I'll tell him it's over. No big deal."

Fortunately, the woman took off a short time later, minus anything resembling a love potion. She'd claimed she knew somewhere else she could buy one.

"That one's about to learn a nasty lesson," the witch replied. Her curly auburn hair was up in a loose bun, displaying her neck and the chest tattoo that extended into her bodice. Before it'd been a line of solemn fairies marching into battle but now it had reverted to the full dragon tattoo.

"Do you change your tattoo or does it do it itself?" Riley asked, intrigued.

"Once I set the magic it alters as it sees fit. Usually it picks up what's going on around it." She glanced down. "Hmm . . . I wonder what that means."

"Nothing good." Riley gave a quick look around. "I need to talk. Any way you can get free?"

"Sure. I need a break anyway. Let me get my cloak."

As they walked to the tent that served hot cider, Ayden brought her up to speed on the witch/necromancer politics and what Riley had missed when she'd been in South Georgia.

"We have a truce in place. Ozymandias laid down the law to a few of the hotheaded necros and they backed down."

"Ozy? The Dark Lord himself? Why he's involved?"

"Mort thinks the guy's trying to atone for the disaster he unleashed upon us. Ozymandias has let it be known that he will personally toast any summoner who calls up demons."

"That's harsh."

"It did the trick," the witch admitted. "It took my people longer to cool down, but right now everybody's playing nice. I'm hoping it will last."

Her friend led her to the same tent they'd visited a while back and bought two mugs of steaming cider. They settled in the back on oversized pillows.

"I saw the news reports about what happened in the swamp," Ayden said. "That had to be rough going."

"Pretty much. But not everything sucks. Beck and I went to the prom the other night and it was *totally* awesome."

"That's news I can live with," the witch replied, smiling.

Riley adjusted the cup in her fingers. "I made a mistake with Ori, you know . . . sleeping with him. If Den and I . . . What if it's all wrong?"

"Does your love for Beck seem the same as you had for the angel?"

Riley shook her head before Ayden finished the question. "This feels . . . real, you know? We've been through so much and yet when I'm with him I'm complete. It's as if he holds all the pieces of me I've lost along the way. Ori was cool, but what we had was too surreal. Too perfect."

"Sounds like you've got your head on straight this time. So what's the problem?"

"I don't want to screw this up."

"Love without risk?" Ayden said. "It doesn't exist. There are no sure outcomes. You do your best and hope not to get hurt too badly. If you survive unscathed, you're doing really well."

"Been there, done that?" Riley asked, studying her friend anew.

"You could say that."

It was time to come clean. "I've got another problem." Riley let her gaze wander to the tent's red silk as she explained exactly what was going on with her and Ori. How the angel was alive, how her new boyfriend wasn't aware of her latest occupation: demon slayer's apprentice.

Ayden was frowning now. "You have to tell Beck everything. You can't hide this from him. He has to know."

"But what if he can't deal? He's jealous of Ori and if he finds out I'm spending almost every night with the angel—"

"He should know that now, before you commit more than your heart to this union."

It was sound advice, though it wasn't what Riley wanted to hear. *She's right.* Riley had expected Beck to lay out all his secrets, she had to do the same or their relationship would never survive.

"Tell the masters, especially Stewart," Ayden advised. "You can't handle this on your own."

"I've done pretty well so far," Riley replied, irritated.

"You have, but now it's time for backup. Perhaps Stewart will know why the angel is doing this to you. He always sees the bigger picture."

Riley reluctantly nodded. "I'll tell Beck tonight. Then . . ."

If he truly loved her, he'd be there for her. If he couldn't deal . . .

Hell might as well claim me now.

TWENTY-NINE

That afternoon's class was uneventful, an anticlimax to the whole Allan/Ori drama. Her ex was AWOL and the word was that he'd called in sick. Riley suspected his class transfer was already in the works.

She actually felt bad for him. He'd never said his dad beat him, he just demanded the world bend to his will, probably because it wasn't that way at home. Maybe Ori's tour of Hell would do him some good. If not, at least they'd tried.

I can't save everyone. So far she hadn't even figured out how to save herself.

⁜

When Riley left class she found a voice mail from Harper waiting for her on her cell phone. The news wasn't good: Both his new apprentices were history. Lambert was gone because he'd smart-mouthed Harper one too many times and Fleming had been tossed out because he'd been the "mole" planted by the television producer. The other message was from Beck, inviting Riley to his place. Though that invitation should have been greeted with considerable enthusiasm and seriously steamy daydreams, Riley went directly into a bad case of nerves.

I have to tell him, but what if he loses it?

Unfortunately, there was only one way to find out.

⁜

Once *Riley arrived* at Beck's house, she found her courage flagging even though she'd given herself a pep talk on the way over. After trading a kiss, they settled at the kitchen table. Riley tried to do her homework while Beck sat across from her working on his reading and writing exercises. He wore a clean shirt and she caught the faint scent of aftershave, evidence he'd been looking forward to an evening she was about to ruin.

Just tell him. She opened her mouth then closed it, fearful of losing everything that mattered in her life.

He caught her looking at him. "Yer too quiet," he said. "What's goin' on?"

"Just doing my homework," she replied, hoping he'd accept that lie.

"No, it's not that." Brows furrowed, he leaned forward, resting his elbows on the table. "Tell me what's botherin' you. That's part of this whole goin' together thing."

"Guys don't talk stuff out," she replied, waving him off.

"It's the angel, isn't it?"

Riley slammed down her pen, upset that he could read her so easily.

"Why does everything have to revolve around Ori?"

"Because it does as long as he's yer demi-lord," he replied, his jaw tensing.

"I can't undo that, Beck," she said. "It's not a 'Gee, I made a mistake, can I have my soul back now?'"

"I know that," he said, testily. "But I refuse to let that Fallen come between us."

"I'm not cheating on you."

"I never said that," he said, his voice equally sharp. "Somethin's got you spooked. I trusted you with my problems, you have to trust me. It's not just one-way."

Riley rubbed her face in profound weariness.

"Please let me help you," he said.

His tone was gentler now, not as confrontational. He really cared.

"I killed a Four last night. It was the one who almost took your soul."

"What?" Beck blurted. "You shouldn't have been anywhere near that thing. If it got into yer mind . . ."

"And do what? My soul's gone, Beck. The worst it could do was kill me."

"Why were you after it?"

"I was hunting with Ori."

Beck took a long and deliberate inhalation, no doubt to short-circuit his anger. It wasn't working as his fists were clenched now.

"So what's really goin' on?"

"He's teaching me how to slay demons. I don't have a choice in the matter."

"Why?"

"He said it's because he owns my soul. He says I have to learn how to kill them to stay alive."

"Oh, sweet Jesus," Beck muttered.

Now that the truth was out, Riley wanted to tell him everything.

"He calls me out at night. One minute I'm sleeping and then I wake up somewhere else. My hand . . ." She stared down at the right palm. "That fiery sword he used at the cemetery? I have one like it, except it's more . . . me-sized. He said it's an extension of his angelic power."

Beck's mouth dropped open in shock.

"Usually he's right there bitching at me about how I'm not doing anything right, but last night he didn't show up until after I'd killed the first Mezmer. He took out the weaker one."

"Yer sure yer not dreamin' all this?" he asked, skeptical.

"It's real, Beck." *Too real.*

"Did he do this kind of crap with Paul?"

"No, it's just me."

"Damn that bastard!" Beck stormed, slamming a fist down on the table, nearly knocking over his cup of coffee.

Riley knew he'd never hurt her, but she still put some space between them, retreating to the picture window. The street was dark now, demarked by the occasional streetlight. Someone was rolling a trash can to the curb.

Behind her she heard Beck swear under his breath. "Why didn't you tell me this was happenin'?" he demanded.

"I..." She choked back a sob. "I was ... scared I'd lose you just when ... we ..."

There was a long silence, then a chair slid back and footsteps came toward her.

Was he going to open the front door and tell her to leave? Tell her never to come back like he had the last time, but this time it would be for keeps?

She tensed as Beck's strong arms curved around her waist possessively and drew her back against him. His comforting warmth flowed into her, strengthening her.

"Ah, girl, I'm not goin' anywhere without you. No way some damned angel's gonna break us up. No one in Heaven or Hell has that kind of power."

Beck was drawing her closer, not pushing her away. She knew right then that she'd been a fool to think otherwise.

"No matter what happens, I love you," he whispered.

He'd never used the *L* word before.

She wasn't in Hell yet. She still had time to live.

Riley turned in his arms and gazed into his rich brown eyes. All she wanted was for him to kiss her, touch her, make love to her.

"I don't want to go home tonight," she said, her voice quavering. "I want to stay here ... with you."

Beck tipped her chin up. "You mean ... you want us to ..."

"Yes. I'm so scared, Den. The only place I feel safe is with you."

Their foreheads touched. "Same with me," he murmured. "But if we . . . it would change everythin' between us. There would be no goin' back."

She leaned away until she could see his eyes again. "I don't ever want to go back to the way it was. I love you." *I trust you.*

He pushed a lock of hair behind her ear, his gaze remarkably tender. "I want nothin' more than to scoop you up in my arms and carry you to my bed."

"And then . . ." she whispered, her heartbeat beating faster now. What would it be like to feel his skin against hers?

"Then I'd show you what it means to be loved by a Southern boy." His face filled with a sultry grin. "It wouldn't be quick. No, it'd probably take all night."

For a second, Riley forgot how to breathe.

"So if yer sayin' that's what you want—" he began.

She cut off his final words with a kiss, one nearly as possessive and needy as the one she'd given him at the bus station. He wrapped his arms around her and pulled her tightly against him. Riley could feel his pulse quicken. When they broke apart, his eyes shone with unbridled desire.

Beck swept her up his arms. When she protested she could walk to the bedroom, he refused to put her down.

"Why do you think I lift weights?" He laughed, carrying her down the hall.

He laid her on the bed, then stood to strip off his shirt. His muscles moved in unison as the garment hit the floor, revealing a patchwork of healing bug bites. Then he remembered his boots and parked himself on the edge of the bed to unlace them, grumbling under his breath at the delay.

"I thought you had a lot of practice at this," Riley jested, trying to cope with her sudden case of nerves.

"I do. Just not with you." The boots landed on the floor with pronounced thumps as she toed off her tennis shoes.

Beck rolled over on the bed, caging her in his arms. The first kiss was hesitant. The second grew more bold and uninhibited. When she didn't response as he'd expected, he pulled back. "What's wrong?"

Lost in the heady rush of emotions, Riley had forgotten something important.

"Ah, we can't do this. I don't have any . . . ah, protection."

"Already taken care of," he replied. "There's a box of rubbers in the nightstand."

She frowned up at him. "I thought you didn't bring girls here."

"I never have, until tonight." He gave her his best bad-boy smile. "I always knew you'd come after me eventually."

"You arrogant little—" His kiss cut her off.

⁘

Beck wasn't feeling arrogant. He was way nervous. He'd been with a lot of women, but none of them were Riley. It wasn't that she didn't know about the loving, what happened between a guy and a gal, but this was her first time with him and he wanted nothing less than to erase her memory of that night with the angel. He wanted Riley to be his, alone.

As she ran her hand though his hair, he leaned close, inhaling the scent of her light perfume. This was his woman, the one who possessed a heart of steel. She loved him unconditionally.

He began with light kisses on her forehead and cheeks, savoring the ability to touch her so freely. He'd wanted to for so long, often sneaking glances at her when she wasn't watching, thinking of what it would be like. With all that they had gone through, this would be more than a meeting of the flesh. Beck knew they were forging together their very souls.

⁘

When the last pieces of clothing were removed, Riley's nerves flared to life. Beck had been with so many girls. What would he think of her? Would he find her too fat or too thin or . . .

As if he knew her worries, Beck placed a delicate kiss in the center of her forehead. "You are the most beautiful woman I have ever been with," he said.

"Really?"

"Without a doubt," he replied.

At his urging, she shyly began to explore his body, running her hands down his back, encountering the scars his life had left behind. Her guy wasn't perfect, not like the angel, but each wound told the story of his journey to her and that made her love him even more.

In return, he seemed to know where to touch her, as if they'd been lovers before. Kiss by kiss, caress by caress, he stoked the rampant fire within her. She had never felt so alive, so true to herself as in this moment. As Beck leaned over to the nightstand, Riley closed her eyes. No matter what befell them after this night, they'd always be together, their hearts as entwined as their bodies would soon be.

When he turned back toward her, he kissed her deeply. "Don't ever doubt that I love you," he said, cupping her chin in his strong hands. "That will never change."

Beck's taut body covered hers, alive and vital, charged with desire. And then they became one.

✛

Riley lay with her head against Beck's bare chest, listening to his heart. Their joining had been full of discovery, heady and passionate, the way it was supposed to be between lovers.

A few of his chest hairs tickled her nose, so she smoothed them down with a hand. That earned her a pleased hum from Beck.

"You'll stay all night, right?" he asked.

Riley nodded, snuggling closer to him. Nothing in this world was going to pull her away, except maybe the angel. That possibility she didn't want to consider.

If she wasn't moving from Beck's bed, she'd better call Stewart.

When she said as much, Beck pulled on a pair of sweatpants and headed down the hall. A short time later he returned with her phone. As she dialed he retreated to the bathroom.

Coward. Not that the Scotsman would be upset by this change in their relationship, but still . . .

"Master Stewart. Atlanta Guild," the master's tired voice announced.

There was no point in shading the truth as he'd see right through any white lie. "Hi, ah, it's Riley. I don't want you to worry about me, but I'm staying at Beck's tonight."

"Lots of homework, huh?" he said, mischievously.

"Ah, yeah."

He chuckled into the phone. "I'll not be worried if yer with him. Just be adult about it and take the proper precautions. Ya don't need a wee bairn this soon."

Riley's cheeks burned in embarrassment. "Got it."

"Good night ta ya, then."

As she set the phone on the nightstand, Beck returned, settling on the edge of the bed. When Riley relayed the public service message, trying hard to imitate the Scotsman's broad accent, he laughed at her pitiful attempt.

"I didn't think Stewart would be upset. He knew we were in love a lot sooner that we did."

In Beck's hand was a flat white box about two inches square. When she gave him a quizzical look, he opened it, removed something, and then set the box aside. Resting in his palm was a silver band, interlaced with ivy leaves.

Riley's breath caught.

Beck shifted the ring to between his thumb and index finger, admiring it.

"It's too soon to ask you . . . to . . . ah . . ." He groaned and shook his head. "I'm not doin' this right." The hand holding the ring was trembling now. "This is my grandmamma's wedding ring. She and my granddaddy were married for over forty-five years."

"That's a long time, Den."

"Yeah, and they never stopped lovin' each other. I miss them so much." Beck took a deep breath. "A few days before my gran passed over, she gave this ring to me. She said that the ivy means faithfulness, and that when I found the right woman, I should give it her. I want you to know that this isn't a one-night thing for me. I'm in this for the long haul."

"Same here," she murmured.

He reached for Riley's right hand and then hesitated as if there was one last hurdle to overcome. He took a very deep breath and let it out slowly. "Will you wear my ring so all the world knows yer mine?"

Beck wasn't asking for her hand in marriage, but it was so close he might as well be. Riley was deeply touched and she struggled to find the right words.

"Yes," she began. "I'd be proud to."

With a pleased smile, Beck slid the circlet onto her right ring finger. It fit pretty well. The band wasn't shiny and new, but that didn't trouble her. This symbol of love had endured for over four decades. That Beck would want her to have it revealed the depth of his commitment.

"Looks good on you," he said, smiling wider now. "I know it's not fancy, but maybe someday you'll do me the honor of . . . well, movin' it to the other hand."

Yet again, he'd captured her heart.

"That could happen," she said, touching his face fondly.

He grasped her hand. "I've never given this ring to any other girl before."

Wow. "You've blown me away, Den."

"That was the whole idea." He gently laid her back on the bed, threading his fingers in hers. "I don't know how long we have together, but I want to make every day count."

Tears bloomed. "You're an awesome man, you know?"

"Only when I'm with you."

✛

To Beck's profound relief, the angel had not summoned Riley during their first evening together. He knew that respite wouldn't last and he wasn't sure how to handle the problem. Actually, he did. He wanted to tear the bastard's wings off and bury his steel pipe deep in Ori's chest. Despite that desire, he had to know what was really going on.

When Riley came to his house the next night, he invited her to his bed, then laid down the law.

"I'll watch over you tonight," he said firmly. "I won't let him take you from me."

"You won't be able to stop him."

"Then I'll go with you. Fight by yer side. I am not gonna let him get you killed."

They'd said no more after that, knowing they were wasting their breath. Everything felt more urgent now, as if every hour might be their last. After they made love, they rested. Then Riley dressed and crawled back into bed with him, a sobering admission that her life was not her own. Beck dressed as well, then held her close against his body as she drifted into an uneasy sleep.

When his neck began to cramp, he rolled over onto his back. Unwilling to break contact, his hand sought hers. She murmured his name in her sleep and that pleased him.

The angel may own your soul, but he doesn't own your heart. I will not let him hurt you ever again. I will kill him first or I'll die tryin'.

Even with his best efforts to remain on guard, Beck finally fell asleep with his lover by his side. When he roused a couple of hours later, he rolled over toward Riley, seeking her comforting warmth. She was gone. He jolted out of bed and called her name, but there was no reply. A quick search of the house proved the angel had stolen her away.

With a cry of anguish, Beck retreated to his bedroom to await her return.

THIRTY

Riley had expected a return trip to some alley in Demon Central, but nothing looked familiar. In fact, this wasn't like any place she'd ever seen. In the distance was a wall of flames, undulating crimson and yellow, and a smell hung in the air, sharply caustic. *Sulfur.*

This was Hell.

"Why are we here?" she demanded. She wasn't dead, or at least she didn't think she was. The last thing she remembered was falling asleep next to Beck.

"We have been summoned before my master," was Ori's chilly reply.

"But—"

"Keep up," he ordered, moving forward at a pace that made it difficult to comply. "You fall behind, you'll remain here."

When Riley sprinted to catch up with him, they quickly reached the wall of flames. Too quickly for the distance involved. Time and space were different here.

The wall wasn't actually composed of fire: Each flame was caught within a tiny shard of glass and millions of them they billowed upward in a solid curtain. "What are those things?"

"The souls of the damned," Ori replied. He stood beside her now, in his full angelic glory. "How many are there?" he said, as if she'd posed the question. "Even the Prince has lost count."

"I can't go through that. It'll cut me to pieces."

"You are under my protection. You will not be harmed."

"What if Lucifer decides otherwise?"

He frowned, but offered his hand nonetheless. Riley took it and jammed her eyes shut as they traversed the sheet of flaming souls. She waited for the shards to flay her flesh, to strip her to the bone but the pain never came.

"If nothing more, you should know you can trust me," the angel said reproachfully. "Yet you trust that trapper. I do not understand."

"I love him."

"You once loved me, did you not?"

"Yes, but that was different," Riley replied. "We both know why that didn't last."

"If you think I took pleasure in what I had to do, you would be wrong. It was the only way to keep you safe."

"If I'm safe, then why am I in Hell?" she asked.

Ori's shoulders tightened. "Because I refused to give up your soul. Now we both must pay the price for that defiance."

He ceased speaking after that, pressing her to move faster now, as if to make up for lost time. The landscape became more like Riley's idea of Hell, a bleak, desolate terrain pockmarked by craters, like the moon. Dense steam poured out of them along with the nauseating stench of rotten eggs. She covered her nose with her palm, trying not to gag.

Ori eyed her. "What does it look like to you?" She described it to him. "To each it is different. Your mind provides your own version of Hell. My Hell is different."

She wanted to ask what his was like, but something told her not to pose that question.

They soon reached a wide stone gate where two Archfiends stood guard on either side of the portal, each armed with curved swords. They eyed Riley with their goat-slit eyes.

As Ori passed they bowed, but not very deep, as if such deference was expected but not warranted. In her mind she heard the fiends talking to each other, speaking of the delicate morsel that the Divine had plucked from the mortal world and how he had not offered that morsel to his master. That now he was a traitor to the Prince.

"Do not listen to them," Ori said, steering her down a damp tunnel where verdant moss carpeted the walls. Right before the tunnel ended, a bizarre mouselike creature with tiny spikes skittered ahead of them. As they entered an open area, a dense fog greeted them, as if somehow they'd been transported to the seashore.

"These are the shades of the damned," Ori said. "They're quite thick here. Some you might recognize."

God, I hope not.

"So many," she whispered as individual faces swam by her, quickly replaced by another and then another.

"Some are here for eternity. Others pass through once their souls are cleansed of their sins."

"You mean Hell's not a forever thing?" she asked, surprised.

"It depends on the deeds of the deceased."

"What about . . . me?"

The angel did not reply.

⊹

The demon sat at an antique wooden desk laden with stacked IN and OUT trays, like you'd find in any earthly office. He, or at least Riley thought it was male, had a quill pen wedged behind his fan-shaped ear. This was a clerk. A Hellish one. She wondered how many of them it took to handle Lucifer's infernal business.

"State your name and purpose," the demon said.

"You know who I am, Asbantarus," Ori replied crisply. "The Prince has summoned me. I bring with me the living mortal, Riley Anora Blackthorne."

The demon's goat eyes checked out Riley and then he nodded. With a wave of a scaly hand, a door appeared in the solid rock wall behind the desk.

They were about to enter Lucifer's court. Surely the Prince wouldn't let her leave after this. Who had ever gone to Hell and come back to tell the tale?

"Come," Ori said. "We must not keep him waiting any further."

When she didn't move, he took hold of her hand and pulled her forward like a naughty child. Once she was moving on her own the Fallen released her.

Riley thought throne rooms were supposed to be big and opulent. This space resembled a school gymnasium, minus the basketball hoops and the bleachers. It smelled about as bad.

She had expected something more medieval: rows of banquet tables laden with the corpses of the damned, blazing torches in wall sconces. There were no bodies or tables, and instead of the sconces there was some sort of subtle light dancing along the walls. When she peered closer she realized they were souls, expending themselves to provide Hell's interior lighting design.

That's totally sick.

Though Riley didn't try to count them, there had to be at least a hundred or more demons here. *No wonder the place stinks.* They varied from the small to the large, all hideous. There were Mezmers and Gastro-Fiends and a number of Archfiends. Some were Hellspawn she'd never seen before—like the one that oozed across the floor in a wave of crimson steam.

"Can they hear what I think?' she whispered.

"No. I'm shielding your thoughts from the fiends. You'll get yourself killed otherwise."

Lucifer sat in a carved ebony chair at the far end of the room where two massive Grade Five Geo-Fiends stood guard over him, their horned heads ending only a few feet below the curved stone ceiling.

Demonic growls rose around them as Ori strode toward his lord and master. He'd killed enough of them over the eons that he was hated by their kind.

The Fallen angel paused about fifteen feet from Lucifer, but did not go down on one knee or bow. In the past Ori had shown nothing but deference to the Prince of Hell.

What is going on here?

Riley didn't know what to do, so she stood by Ori's side, wishing that this was just a bad dream and that Beck would wake her up and hold her and it would be all right. She clasped her hands together, rolling his ring back and forth on her finger, frightened to her very bones.

When Lucifer's midnight-blue eyes tracked to her, she couldn't help but shudder. They did not speak of welcome, but of malice.

This was no dream.

The chief of the Fallen was clad in armor, such as she'd seen him wear at the battle in the cemetery. A sword lay across his thighs, unsheathed. Did he feel so vulnerable that he had to be fully armed in his own realm? Or was this for Ori's benefit?

"You requested my presence, my Prince?" her escort said.

Lucifer leaned back on his throne, stroking his chin in thought. "I have been hearing rumors that you are not happy with your tasks."

His voice was different than when she'd last seen him in the cemetery, more guttural. There was none of the suave trickster on display now. Was this the real Lucifer or just another persona he donned when the need arose?

"Well? Are these rumors true?"

"You know what I think on the matter," Ori replied.

"Yes, you've been extremely candid about that. I see your latest conquest is at your heels." Lucifer straightened up now, eyes blazing. "How *dare* you bring the whelp of a master demon trapper to stand in my presence?"

She frowned up at Ori. "You said he wanted me here."

Her demi-lord ignored her. "This mortal's soul is in my charge and I do not trust leaving her without my protection. Some might feel the need to harm her."

"For good reason," Lucifer replied. "Perhaps I should break the bond between you and gift her to one of my other, more *loyal*, servants."

Break the bond? Can he do that? Of course, he could.

Demons in the back of the hall laughed and hooted, the sounds scorching like acid in her veins. She twisted Beck's ring again, trying to find some courage from the simple piece of metal.

When Ori did not rise to the bait, Lucifer settled back on his throne. "Deliver your report," he ordered.

Ori began to detail the executions, listing out the long demon names, one after another. The Prince remained motionless, his bottomless eyes riveted on Riley. Sweat broke out on her forehead, though it wasn't particularly hot, and her skin began to itch like it was peeling from the inside out. She desperately wanted to scratch herself, but forced her hands to remain clasped.

Lucifer waved Ori to silence. "What of you, Blackthorne's daughter? What have you been about?"

"Ah . . . I've been acting as his second," she offered. At least that's what she hoped he wanted to hear.

A chorus of hisses erupted from the demons telling her that wasn't the right answer.

Lucifer shot up from his throne, sword in hand.

"How dare you teach a mortal to slay my servants?" he roared, his voice booming off the cavern walls.

"You refused to provide me assistance. You said I should use my imagination to destroy your enemies. So I have. I can kill twice the amount of traitorous demons if I have a second."

"That is no excuse! You have given this mortal a taste of Divine power. You have favored her since the first time you saw her."

"You were the one who ordered me to guard Blackthorne's daughter," Ori parried back.

"An order you have taken to the extreme. When you were dying, you could have saved your own life, yet you refused to take hers to do so. Why?"

Stunned, Riley looked over at the angel. "Is that true?"

"Yes," Ori conceded, answering her, not his master. "As your soul is mine, I could have drained your life energy to heal myself. I refused."

Ohmigod.

"It was I who healed you," Lucifer continued, striding up and down in front of them, his fury translating into motion. "Yet I see no gratitude for that gesture, my *servant*."

Ori stiffened. "I sought the nothingness of death and you refused me that honor. I do what you command me, my Prince, but there is no love in the task."

Lucifer came to a halt and laid his sword over an armor-clad shoulder.

"It is whispered that you seek my throne," he said, his words slitting like razors. "That you wish to overthrow *the tyrant*. What say you to that?"

Ori did not reply. Behind them, the demons grew restless, scenting blood on the wind.

We are so dead. There was no way the Prince could back down now. She'd just disappear and Beck wouldn't know what happened to her.

No, not this way. Please. I want to see him one more time.

A tortured howl erupted from somewhere in the vast room. Lucifer issued an order and the fiends parted, revealing a battered figure that knelt inside a broad circle sketched onto the stone, some sort of magical prison. The creature's garments hung on its body, filthy and tattered, and there were thick metal chains looped around its body. Those chains were not stationary, but moved, sliding across the abraded flesh.

Sartael.

The Archangel's mad eyes sought hers and he howled again, shouting curses at her in Hellspeak.

"Your enemy has missed you," Lucifer said dryly. He returned to his throne, the sword across his thighs again. "Do you understand the precipice upon which you teeter, my servant? Do you doubt that could be you in those chains?"

"Yes, I understand, master," Ori replied through gritted teeth.

Lucifer's attention went to her and he grinned savagely. "Do not think that fate is for Ori alone . . ."

Riley began to quake in terror, her lungs tightening with each sulfurous breath. She pulled her eyes away from Sartael's endless torture and riveted them on the feet of one of the massive Fives in front of her, the claws on its toes as long as her arm.

Lucifer rose from his simple throne, his dark wings fully visible now. Lightning danced along the walls, arcing into the vaulted ceiling and then down to ground itself in the throne behind him.

He pointed at Ori with the tip of his sword. "Seek my enemies and destroy them. Side with them and your punishment will be eternal. This is your last warning. Now begone!"

THIRTY-ONE

A hysterical sob brought Beck out of his dark thoughts. He leapt toward Riley as she wavered on her feet at the end of the bed. Taking her in his arms, he gasped at the overwhelming stench of sulfur.

She shook like a frightened kitten, sobbing uncontrollably, each breath a tortured wheeze.

"I'm here, girl."

Her eyes were consumed with abject fear, tears flowing from them in torrents.

"Hell..."

Beck hefted Riley in his arms and carried her into the bathroom where he sat her on the edge of the bathtub. She instinctively bent over, trying to pull as much oxygen as possible. The next breath grew tighter and he began to panic. What if she stopped breathing? What would he do?

He opened the window and then turned on the shower, hoping the fresh air and humidity might help. It was then he saw her right hand, the one with Hell's inscription glowing a pale white. *My God.*

He knelt in front of her, making eye contact with the terrified girl.

"Take a slow breath. Okay, now another one. That's good," he said, coaching her. Over time and with his patient coaxing, her breathing improved. When he felt she was doing better, he reached for the top button of her shirt. "Ya need a shower. It'll warm ya up. Get rid of that . . . smell."

Riley nodded and allowed him to help her undress. When only her underwear remained, he backed off.

"I'll let ya do the rest, okay?" he said. "I'll go make ya some hot chocolate. Ya need anything, call out."

Beck reluctantly left her on her own. When he heard the shower door roll closed, he sagged against the wall outside the bathroom door.

Why had she been in Hell? What had Ori done to her?

I have to stop this. But how?

Riley took her time in the shower, like he'd hoped. When she stepped out, he had a warmed towel waiting and covered her so she wouldn't feel so exposed in front of him. Then he had her stand in front of the sink as he gently towel-dried her hair and combed it. Those simple actions and the mug of hot chocolate seemed to calm her.

Every time life sucker-punched her she'd pulled herself up and kept going. It was one of the many traits he admired about her. But even Riley had a breaking point, and it appeared she'd just reached it.

"That's better," he said, trying to sound upbeat. "You smell like my girl again."

Her reddened eyes met his in the mirror, her hands shaking so badly she could barely hold the mug.

"Lucifer summoned us," she said in a roughened voice. "He was furious. He thinks Ori is after his throne."

Beck forced himself not to react, unwilling to frighten her further. Instead, he urged her to drink more of the beverage. After she did, he placed the mug in the sink. "Let's get you to bed. It'll be warmer there."

Riley offered no protest, but allowed him to dress her in one of his long T-shirts and then tuck her under the covers. He climbed in next to her and she clung to him.

If the Prince believed Ori a traitor, he'd kill her demi-lord and claim Riley's soul. Who knew what torment she'd face at Lucifer's hands or at the whim of his demons?

"Tell me what happened, all of it," he said.

In a halting voice Riley gave him the story, how she'd seen the demons and the dead souls and Sartael in chains.

"I know what it's like now," she said, her voice so faint he could barely hear her. "I'm going there when I die." She sobbed into his chest. "God, I'm so afraid. I don't know what to do anymore."

Beck did. "In the mornin' we'll go to the masters, tell them everythin'. They'll know how to handle this."

"No," she replied, shaking her head. "Stewart will have to tell Rome that I slept with Ori. They'll . . . lock me up or . . . something. I'll never see you again."

"I think Rome's already got a good idea of what happened between you and the angel and they don't want to push it. Not after you kept the world from bein' torn apart."

She shook her head again. "The masters won't be able to do anything. Ori is going down and I'll go with him. You know those chains Lucifer put on Sartael? There's a set waiting for me."

He felt the panic start to work on him, like it did before every battle. The unrelenting doubts, the rampaging fear, the utter helplessness.

Not goin' there. She needs me. I have to be strong for her.

As tears rolled down her cheek, Riley began to fumble with the ring on her finger, trying to remove it. Beck knew he couldn't let her take that step. He took both her hands in his.

"No, pushin' me away is not the answer. What we have is more than just for when things are goin' right. It's *forever*, Riley."

Her eyes sought his. "They'll kill you, Beck. I can't face that."

"I don't give a damn about bein' alive if yer not with me. I love you and no Fallen angel is gonna take you away from me. You hear?"

"But—"

"No! You didn't walk away when I was dyin' in the swamp and I'm not leavin' you now. We face this together. That's the only way it's gonna be."

There was gratitude in her eyes now. "I love you," she whispered.

"I know. We'll make it through this," he insisted. "You and me, we're stronger than Hell. Love always is."

Riley pulled her hands out of his, but made no further attempt to remove the ring.

"You really think the masters can help us?" There was more strength in her voice now, like she was tapping her last reserve of courage.

Beck kept his sigh of relief to himself. "We'll find out in the mornin'," he replied. "Now you get some rest."

"No. I don't want sleep." Riley kissed him on the lips and pulled him closer. "Make me believe we'll still be together when this is over."

"We will be together, Riley, one way or another. I promise."

Even if he had to kill every demon in Hell to make that a reality.

THIRTY-TWO

Beck was out of bed at dawn, his mind too full of worries to rest. As he pulled on his clothes, he tried not to make any noise so Riley could continue to sleep. She had rolled over now, her hair draped on the pillow. His heart ached at the sight of her so soft and vulnerable.

God, I love you.

If he didn't figure out how to shield her from Hell's politics, she wouldn't be with him much longer. He knew exactly what his life would become without her: It was just a matter of buying enough booze and picking which gutter he wanted to die in.

Beck pulled the door closed and then made a pit stop in the bathroom. After putting her clothes into the washer to remove the sulfuric stench, he allowed himself to stall by making the coffee. After that there was nothing left to do but pick up the phone and call Stewart. He dialed the master, in some ways feeling like he was betraying the girl he loved. Once Stewart answered, Beck nearly choked up.

"Riley's in big trouble and we desperately need the Guild's help, sir."

There was a momentary pause. "This have somethin' ta do with that Fallen angel?" the master asked.

How did you know that? "Yes, it does."

"Bring Riley here at nine. I'll call Harper." The line went dead.

Beck set the phone down on the table, replaying the conversation in his head. How was it that Stewart always seemed to be one step ahead of them?

The Vatican would probably take Riley to Rome for her own protection, though Beck questioned whether the Church could shield her from the Prince's wrath.

What if I never see her again?

At this point he'd do anything to keep her alive, even turning her care over to someone else.

As he reached for a cup, his balance faltered, then his head spun. He reached out to grab the counter to keep from falling, but it had vanished. When Beck's senses came back online, he was no longer in his kitchen, but in a verdant pasture. The sky was a bright blue and the weather sunny and warm, like midsummer. It certainly wasn't Atlanta in early March.

"What the hell is this?"

Then he spied the angel under a broad oak tree, his enemy's wings clearly visible. Spitting out an oath, Beck marched toward him, eager to vent his frustration and fury on Riley's seducer.

The angel watched him approach without concern.

"Killing me will not help Riley Anora Blackthorne," Ori said.

Beck ground to a halt, love and revenge waging war within him. "What the hell are you playin' at? Where are we?"

"A place of my own making. I like being somewhere no one else can overhear us."

Which meant if this bastard decided to kill Beck, no one would ever know.

"That too," the angel replied.

"You can read my mind."

"Sometimes. Right now you're so emotional, it's child's play."

Beck growled, but held his ground. "Why are you takin' my girl out of my arms every night and tryin' to get her killed?"

In lieu of a reply, Ori settled under the tree, propped a foot up, and laid his forearm on his knee. The gesture seemed so human. But then this Divine had been around mortals for a long time and it was only natural he'd begin to copy their behavior.

"I'm waitin' for an answer," Beck said.

The Fallen's dark eyes turned toward him. "Our realm is in turmoil because my master did not kill Sartael when he had the chance."

Beck frowned. "Lucifer is not a wimp. If he thought one of his angels was a threat, that sucker would be dead."

"Only if and when that death suited his plans." Ori plucked a long blade of grass and twisted it thoughtfully between his fingers.

When the angel said nothing further, Beck took a position under the tree, but left considerable space between himself and his enemy. The wind ruffled the grass around him in rolling waves.

He sighed heavily. "Lucifer's a lot like Stewart," he mused aloud. "He does nothin' without a strategy behind it. Which means . . ." Beck began to see other possibilities. "Something must have made the Fallen angels uneasy with their master." He suspected that *something* was sitting near him. "Why are you alive? Last I saw you were dyin', leakin' blue blood everywhere."

The sudden fury in Ori's dark eyes made Beck tense up in response. "My master refused me the right to die."

"What happens when one of yer kind dies?"

"We are sent to Oblivion. Nothingness. You mortals call it Limbo. It's a great void—no sound, no light, nothing. If we have paid our debt, we may be summoned back to our Creator. If not . . . we're alone for eternity."

The angel wasn't making much sense. "Why would you want to die if that's where yer headed?" Beck quizzed.

"Eternity in nothingness is what I deserve," Ori replied, quieter now. "I am weary of . . . life."

Beck had never considered that possibility. If you were nearly eternal, perhaps you could grow tired of each new day.

He was getting closer to the real issue, he could feel it. "What do the other angels think about Lucifer not letting you die?"

"Most are angry I have not been given the choice to end my life."

"Angry enough to side with Sartael and his crazy demons?"

"Perhaps."

Beck huffed. "Yer bein' played, angel. Both the Prince and that crazy-assed Archangel are usin' you as the tinder for this war."

"I know." Ori's brows furrowed as he tossed the blade of grass aside. "That is why I have been training Riley so hard. It is vital she survives. Soon Sartael's fiends will free him, and when that happens, he will not remain in Hell. He will return to the one place in your world that has shown him defeat. Where do you think that might be?"

"Atlanta," Beck said, his heart sinking.

"Need I warn you what he intends to do with those who vanquished him? The trappers? The necromancers and witches? Or the daughter of the master who put him in those chains?"

Beck shook his head. It all made sense now. "Does Riley know any of this?"

"No. All she needs to know is how to survive. When Sartael begins the battle anew, I will try to kill him, but he has many demons in thrall and draws power from all of them. If he is injured, he can heal himself by pulling on their life energy. He will most likely defeat me."

"Damn..." Beck muttered, running a hand through his hair. The air grew stickier now and his shirt clung to his back. "What about the other Fallen? What will they do?"

"Unknown. My job is to try to kill Sartael as quickly as possible so that my kind do not step into the war against their master."

"Why are you tellin' me all this?"

The angel rose. His face was hard, jaw set. "Your task is to keep Blackthorne's daughter alive. That is all that matters to me."

"What? Why would you care?" Beck demanded, leaping to his feet. "Are you in love with her?"

"Not in the way you are, trapper. I love what I see in her eyes, for there is a glimpse of Heaven there. I told her that once, but she thought I lied so I could seduce her." Ori shook his head sadly. "It was the truth."

"If you die, her soul is still goin' to the Prince."

Ori cocked his head. "No. If I die before Riley Anora Blackthorne, her soul is freed from Hell. That was part of our deal. If Sartael learns of this, he will ensure I do not die."

"Who knows so far?"

"Only Lucifer. Riley drove a hard bargain, but that won't matter when Sartael comes to Atlanta. He will destroy her."

"He has to get through me first," Beck replied. "I know I'm not some high-and-mighty angel like you are, but I'll do my best to keep her alive."

"You swear that on your soul?" Ori retorted.

Beck stilled. *So that's the trap.*

"If you fail to keep Riley alive, your soul will belong to Hell."

"In exchange for what?"

The corners of Ori's mouth rose into a smile. "I can see why a grand master has taken you under his wing. You have little fear."

"Just answer the question."

"I'm willing to share knowledge that is forbidden to mortals. I'm going to tell you how to kill a Divine."

Beck jolted in surprise. "What keeps me from doin' the same to you?"

"I am trusting that you love Riley more than you desire revenge."

Ori had read him right.

"Damn you," Beck muttered, knowing he'd been cornered. "Tell me what I need to know. If Riley dies, it won't matter where I go. My life will be Hell anyway."

⊹

As they walked in tandem down the hallway to Stewart's den, Riley tightened her grip on Beck's hand.

"Frightened?" he asked.

"Totally. I'd be losing it if you weren't here with me."

"Then I'm doin' my job," he said and gave her hand a reassuring squeeze.

Both masters were waiting, just as Beck had warned her. Harper had a cup of coffee in his hand, his scar pulled tight along the side of his face. He nodded at her, but she saw none of the animosity she'd faced in the past.

Stewart was in his favorite chair, but his posture spoke of considerable tension.

"Lass," he said. "Have a seat and then tell us what's goin' on. Leave nothin' out, ya ken? Then we'll see if there's anythin' we can do for ya."

When Riley sat on the couch, Beck unfolded an afghan and wrapped her in it, a loving gesture. In his own way, he was telling the masters that if they thought they were going to throw her to the wolves, he would be in their faces.

"Go on," Beck urged. "You and me can't do this alone."

Once Riley began, the story of her and the Fallen angel burst from her like a storm-swollen river. She left nothing out: how they'd sealed the deal in the cemetery for her soul so Ori could fight Sartael and the unique terms of the arrangement. What that meant for both her and the angel.

As Riley spoke, she stared at the marks on her palms, not at the faces of the two men who held her fate in their hands. She was afraid of what she'd see there.

"Ori showed up after I returned from Sadlersville," she continued. "He's been teaching me how to kill demons. Last night . . . we were summoned to Hell."

There was weighty silence after she finished and Riley forced her eyes up, toward the masters. Harper was staring down into his cup and Stewart's face was pensive.

"I know you have to tell the Vatican," she said. "I don't want them to blame you, Master Stewart. It was me . . . I made the mistakes."

"You never had a chance," Harper said, his eyes rising to meet hers. "Once your father sold his soul, they went right after you." He sighed. "Truth is, I would have done the same for my son."

It was as close to an apology as she'd ever receive.

Stewart stirred. "We'll need ta talk this out, lass. Go get some rest. We'll let ya know what we decide."

Beck gave her a kiss on the cheek and then she moved out of the room and down the hall, defeat in every step.

"How long have ya known about the angel?" Stewart asked.

Beck eased the door closed. "Only a couple days. How about you?"

"I spoke with her demi-lord right after the pair of ya went ta South Georgia. I called Harper the same day ta let him know what was in the wind."

Beck frowned at the pair of them. "Why didn't you tell me?"

"Because there were other things the pair of ya needed ta sort out before ya faced this immense challenge. Am I right?"

Beck nodded wearily and sank on the couch. "Yeah, I suppose."

"Has the angel talked ta ya yet?"

This was not what he'd expected, and it angered him. Agitated, Beck jabbed his fingers through his hair, then sank wearily onto the couch. *They knew all along and never told me.*

"Lad?" Stewart pressed.

"Yeah, this mornin' the angel pulled me out of my own home like I was some damned puppet."

"Then ya know we're in grave danger. The angels are verra angry with Lucifer right now. Not all of them care for Ori in any fashion, but Lucifer denying him the right ta die tells them they're little more than pawns, no better than the demons, who they detest. That was Lucifer's mistake. He got too clever for his own good."

"Ori believes Sartael will be freed tonight, when that reverend tries to cast out the demons," Beck said.

Neither master looked surprised. "We've already got our people ready," Harper said. "The necromancers are on board and maybe a witch or two. They know their job is to deal with the demons while Ori tries to kill Sartael."

"Ya understand yer role, lad?" Stewart asked, his eyes riveted on Beck now.

"Yes. I'm to keep Riley alive and maybe even take down Sartael if I get lucky."

"Wouldn't count on the latter," Harper said. Stewart didn't reply, his eyes still locked on Beck.

How much else does he know that he's not tellin' us?

Beck snorted. "So let me get this right—we're gonna be sidin' with one part of Hell against the other."

"The lesser of two evils, my friend," Stewart replied.

At least my will is up to date.

⁛

Brunch was as sumptuous as usual, but Riley had no appetite, and she stared at the eggs on her plate as they grew cold. Mrs. Ayers fussed a bit, then gave up and left her alone.

Shortly after that she was joined by Master Stewart, who slid out a chair and sat across from her. Riley knew him well enough to know that what he was about to tell her wasn't good news.

"The Vatican wants me in Rome, right?"

"Aye. They're hopeful that they can get ya out of harm's way."

"That's not going to work. Ori will call me to him whenever he wants. It won't matter where I am." She pushed her plate away. "How soon do I have to leave?"

"A few days," Stewart said. "They have ta make arrangements and I've told them not ta be in a hurry."

His somber tone made her look up. "Why?"

Stewart laid his hands on the table, fingers spread. "Whatever is brewin' in Hell will be goin' down before ya leave. I have that on good authority."

"But who . . ." *Ori.* He was totally plugged into Hell's politics. Or was it the Prince who'd been keeping Stewart in the loop?

Had she been wrong about the master? Had he really been working for Lucifer all along?

"I'm not on Hell's payroll," he replied, as if he'd heard her thoughts. "As a grand master I am tasked ta preserve the balance between good and evil. Sometimes that means I work with those I would consider my enemies."

"Like Lucifer and Ori."

Stewart nodded in return. "When Sartael is freed he will return ta this city ta exact his revenge. There will be a bloodbath."

"Then have the Vatican's guys come back to Atlanta."

"Nay, it's our job and, truth be known, there isn't time for the demon hunters ta get here anyway."

The hunters could move pretty quickly, which meant . . .

"How soon is this going to happen?"

"Tonight. It's for the best. The longer the war brews in Hell, the worse it will be. Many of the demons and the Fallen haven't chosen sides yet. We want to keep it that way."

"In case they go Team Sartael," Riley replied.

"Aye. I've known all along that Ori was trainin' ya, and I reluctantly agreed with that. He is tryin' ta keep ya alive."

He knew what was happening and he didn't stop it?

It appeared that just about everyone had been playing her for a sucker.

⁑

It was early afternoon when Beck tapped on the door to Stewart's house. To his relief, Riley answered and beckoned him in.

"I thought, well . . ." he began, then faltered, unsure of how to ask for what he needed between them.

Riley didn't reply, but took his hand and led him up the stairs to her room. As he set his backpack on the floor, she shut the door behind them. Then locked it.

She wanted the same as he did—the chance to spend their last few hours together, as lovers would.

This time she took the lead, slowly removing his clothes, garment by garment. Every touch spoke of love and of sadness yet to be experienced, of the potential for unthinkable loss.

Riley was not as experienced as most of the girls he'd been with, curiously awkward and shy, but that did not matter to him. She was claiming him as her own, and it humbled him. If this was their last day on earth, he could think of no better way to spend it than with the woman he loved.

⁘

"Why did we waste so much time?" he whispered later. "I think of all the nights we could have shared. Why was I so stubborn?"

"We both were," Riley replied. "We were too scared of being hurt again."

He fell silent for a few minutes, pondering his life and the twists and turns it'd made along the way. "I went to see Louisa and her husband before I left Sadlersville. While we were talkin', her baby began to kick somethin' fierce." He slid his hand onto Riley's bare abdomen. "I got to thinkin' that a few years down the line, when yer older, what if that was our baby and I could feel it right here under my hand. Feel the life we'd created."

Riley's eyes moistened. "Girl or boy?"

"Doesn't matter. If it's a girl, we can name her after my gran. Her name was Emily Rose."

"Hmm . . . I like that. Maybe the boy could be Paul Arthur, like my dad."

"Yeah, that works. But that's all way down the line, isn't it?" *It might never come to pass.*

Her breath caught and then in a swift motion, she slid out of his arms and off the bed.

"What's wrong?" he asked.

"Nothing," she said softly, hunting for something in her pack. Once she returned to bed, Riley modestly tucked the sheet up to cover her breasts.

"When I was in front of Lucifer, I held on to your ring. It was as if you were there with me and I didn't feel so alone." She took a deep breath, like she was working up her courage. "There's a lot of darkness coming our way, Den. I want you to have a little bit of light of your own."

She offered him a small white box. Inside was a thick leather cord and attached to the cord, a band of silver he knew so well.

"It's Paul's wedding ring," he said, looking back up at her in amazement.

Riley touched it with fondness. "Your fingers are bigger than my dad's, so I thought you could wear it around your neck instead."

She had offered him one of her most prized possessions, just as he'd given her one of his. The gesture so touched his heart, speech failed him.

Beck set the box aside and slipped the cord over his head. Now the band rested on his chest, a reminder of a dear friend and the promise that one day it would be more than Paul's ring.

He gathered Riley into his arms and held her tight as the last of his defenses crumbled and turned to dust.

THIRTY-THREE

People began to gather in the heart of Demon Central just after dark. In that way Atlanta was no different than any other town: They loved to see other folks making idiots of themselves. From what Beck could tell, the swelling crowd fell into three distinct camps: the cautious, the hecklers, and the true believers.

He belonged with the first group, curious how one guy, in this case Reverend Lopez, was supposed to exorcise every single demon in the entire city at the same time. Just how would that happen? Where would they go?

"What do you think about this?" he asked, looking over at Jackson.

His fellow trapper shrugged. "Part of me would love to have it work. The other part of me is thinking about the mortgage payment I have due in a couple of weeks."

Beck understood that. No demons meant no need for demon trappers.

They were in one of the largest open sections in the heart of Five Points. As usual, it was ringed with trash and Dumpsters and scrap metal. Usually folks didn't try to collect it, what with the Threes on the prowl, but tonight might be a different story. Strength in numbers and all that.

Lightweight fencing had been set up as a barricade to keep the crowd at bay. Inside the fence was the A-list crowd—a few local church leaders, someone from the mayor's office, and other dignitaries. They might think Reverend Lopez's demon-exorcising plan was a load of crap, but if it worked they wanted to be the first to sing his praises in front of the news cameras.

Beck had already spied Justine, who would always be in the middle of anything that made news. They traded nods but nothing more. Now, as he studied her, he realized she'd helped him find a future with Riley, even if it had been totally self-serving on her part. Not that he was going to thank her or anything.

A few off-duty cops milled around to keep the peace and sprinkled among the crowd were most of the Atlanta Guild, at least those who weren't recuperating from the Oakland battle. Beck noted Simon, Reynolds, McGuire, Remmers, and a few of the others. Each had a weapon, usually a steel pipe or a sword wrapped in some sort of covering so as to not spook the locals.

Harper had definitely called in the big guns, as well. Besides himself and Stewart, the magical folks were well represented. Mort stood next to the taller Ayden and they were laughing about something. Nearby was none other than Lord Ozymandias, clad in his black cloak and leaning on his staff. Though Beck detested the summoner for what he'd done to Paul, he was pleased they had serious magical backup.

He saw Riley weaving her way toward him and the unrestrained love they'd shared this afternoon sang like vibrant chord between them. He had put his soul on the line for her, but then she'd done the same for him and others.

As Riley moved closer to him, she paused near the magic users, collecting hugs from both Ayden and Mort. Beck could tell the moment she noticed Ozymandias—her body stiffened. The summoner inclined his head and then looked away.

She joined Beck a short time later. After greeting Jackson, she whispered, "What is Ozy doing here?"

"Just watchin' our backs in case Hell accepts this invitation."

To distract her, he slipped his hand around her waist and dropped a kiss on her cheek. Her skin was unnaturally warm, though it hadn't been that way this afternoon.

"You okay?" he asked, concerned.

A slight shake of the head. "It's like I've got a fever. It started about an hour ago."

Someone called out Riley's name and she turned to find Peter walking toward her. Her friend wore a hundred-watt smile, like he'd won the lottery.

"What are you doing here?" she demanded.

He ignored her sharp tone. "I wanted to see the *Demonland* set and whatever this exorcist dude is up to. Thought it'd be fun. I met Blaze, can you believe it? She's ah-mazing."

"That's all great, Peter, but you should go home . . . now."

"What? Why?" he asked, confused.

Before she could answer, a cheer went up as a man in a dark suit crossed the open space and climbed onto a makeshift stage. The demon exorcist had arrived.

It was the first time Riley had seen Reverend Lopez and she had to admit he cut a commanding figure. At a little over six feet tall, he wore a black suit and his dark hair was perfectly styled and in his hand was a worn Bible. Just his presence told her that if anyone could cast out demons, this would be the guy to do it.

"Atlanta!" he called out. "Tonight, I will save you from eternal damnation. I'm not here to negotiate with Hell. I'm here to kick Lucifer and his servants out of this city."

There was a throaty cheer from behind the fencing.

"This sounds like a revival to me," Beck said.

The exorcist waved his hands to quiet the crowd's enthusiasm.

"Now I've heard that some of you think I'm crazy, but I'll prove that Heaven can exist here on earth. But first, let's have a prayer."

Riley bowed her head, not because the reverend had asked them to, but because it felt right. If Sartael and his demons were on their way, this might be her last time to send a personal message to God. She doubted prayer was an option in Hell.

Please keep Beck safe. Let him have those kids he wants, even if they're not with me. I'm lost, but he deserves a good life.

As if he knew what she was thinking, Beck's hand tightened around her waist protectively.

The prayer ended and Lopez took a few steps closer to the crowd. "Are you ready to reclaim your city?" he cried.

More cheering now. As he continued to raise the crowd's enthusiasm to a fever pitch, Riley's eyes moved to her fellow trappers, one by one. They were vigilant, not caught up in the moment. Simon's bright blond hair was easy to spot where he stood next to Harper, a sheathed sword in his hand. When he saw her, he nodded in return.

"By the power given to me by the Almighty himself," Lopez drawled. "I call forth all the Hellspawn in this city. Come forth, servants of darkness. Come forth and meet thy Holy Master—"

The earth shook, and though Lopez paled, he kept exhorting the demons to come forth. The tremors ceased, causing many in the crowd to sigh in relief.

The time grows near, Ori whispered in her mind.

Riley's body ignited in a flood of heat and she gasped at the sensation. The tattoo on her right palm began to pulsate, the call to battle. Very shortly the sword would appear, and the entire world would know her secret.

I summon you to my side, Riley Anora Blackthorne.

Shaking now, she tipped up on her toes and placed a lingering kiss on Beck's lips.

"I love you, Den," she said, touching his face with the back of her glowing hand. "Stay alive, you hear?"

"You too. Let's get this settled once and for all. I've had enough of this crap." As Beck reached to touch her, a tremor shot through her soul. Hellish voices roared in her ears, proclaiming war.

Sartael has been freed.

Before she had the chance to warn Peter, cries of shock came from around them as the crowd parted in panic. A lone figure strode forward through their midst, wings unfurled, sword blazing white hot in the night air.

Ori. The angel was definitely out of the closet.

When the tingle in her fingers became an inferno, Riley didn't bother to look down. Her sword was fully formed now.

"What the heck is—" Peter began

"Go home. Go be with your family."

He blinked. "End of the World stuff, *again?*" he moaned.

"Yeah. I love you. Keep yourself safe, okay?"

Before she could stop him, he gave her a hug, then stepped back. "Same to you," he said solemnly.

Riley strode through the crowd to join up with the angel. Though she had no wings, the fiery sword in her hand told the story to those who understood: Ori was her demi-lord and she was in Hell's yoke.

As she passed Simon, she caught his expression, a mix of awe and immense sadness.

You were right about me, but for the wrong reasons.

When she and Ori took positions in front of the stage, Lopez stammered to a halt, caught by the sight of the winged warrior and his young female apprentice.

"Who are you?" he demanded.

"I am Ori, the Prince's chief executioner," Ori replied in a voice that had to have carried to the ends of the earth.

"Have you come to kill me?"

"No, you are not my enemy," the angel replied.

The air around them grew volatile, explosive. When a jagged spear of lightning impacted a nearby building, throwing sparks high into the night, the crowd reacted with shrieks and the sound of running footsteps.

Ori raised his eyes to the heavens. "Sartael is nigh." He turned and gazed over a shoulder, his eyes locking on Beck. "Remember your promise, trapper."

Her boyfriend nodded grimly.

"What promise?" Riley asked. "What did you—"

A near-deafening boom shattered the air above them, causing her to jump in startled surprise. Just like at the cemetery, their enemy descended to the ground clad in his simple black monk's robe, his gray wings flapping noiselessly. There was no evidence of the wounds Sartael had sustained in Hell and his clothes were intact.

"It's the Devil!" someone shouted.

No, but just about as bad.

Ori's blade dipped downward as if he was acknowledging a superior. Sartael noted the gesture, his eyes glowing with an unnatural light.

"We meet again, old friend." Sartael's feet lightly touched the earth. His attention moved to Riley. "What is this? How does she wield the Divine fire?"

"What do you offer in exchange for my allegiance?" Ori asked.

"What do you wish?"

"Death. I wish the respite that nothingness will bring. And the promise of safety for the soul I hold."

Sartael's eyebrows rose. "If you serve me, I shall allow you to die. In fact, I will ensure you do so."

"What of Riley Anora Blackthorne?" Ori asked.

Sartael's attention moved to her and Riley shivered at the madness in his blue eyes.

"I will hold her safe," Lucifer's enemy promised.

He's lying. He will put us both in chains and you know it.

There was a sigh in her mind. *Yes, he will.*

"I detest my master's endless schemes," Ori said, his voice louder now. "But he is not you, Sartael."

For a moment their rival appeared confused as to whether this was praise or not.

"Swear your allegiance, Ori, and that of the mortal soul you hold, and I shall free you. Lucifer's reign is ending. Even now, in Hell, my demons are cutting through his forces. Join with me. Rule with me. We shall challenge Heaven and retake what is ours. Then you shall regain that peace you so desire." Sartael's eyes were still on Riley, though, and they made her skin crawl.

Her angel gave her a quick glance. "Yes, Sartael, I shall join you . . . *in the nothingness.* I hate Lucifer for denying me final death, but you are a traitor to our master and I will not allow you to destroy this city or those in my care."

I will not permit him to harm you, Riley Anora Blackthorne. You are the closest to Heaven I shall ever be, now that I am Fallen.

It took Sartael a moment to comprehend that once again Ori wasn't going to play his game.

He reared back, furious. "You've always been willing to lick Lucifer's boots. I will devour your heart after I rip it from your chest. And I will do worse to the soul you hold, for her father betrayed me."

Remember what I taught you, Riley.

I will, angel. Good hunting.

"Shall we, *old friend?*" Ori said, raising his sword.

The Divines' swords clashed on impact as they rose into the air to fight one last time. Riley backed off, knowing this really wasn't her battle. Tense, she swept the scene, looking for threats: The mad Archangel never did anything without backup.

Beck and the other trappers were also on the alert. He caught her eye and nodded. His said all that mattered.

I love you, too.

The reverend kept intoning Bible verses, not quite comprehending that this war had little to do with Heaven. Standing near him was one of the cameramen from the *Demonland* crew, filming for all he was worth.

That's just what we need.

"Heads up, lads," Stewart called out.

Grade Three demons poured over the crumbled walls in a solid wave. Riley froze, then she forced herself to shake off the fear. No matter how she looked at it, she was dead one way or another and that macabre reality gave her courage. Some of it was bravado, but it felt right, so Riley made it her own. It was either that or totally freak out.

As she moved forward to challenge one of the Threes, the ground near Lopez began to heave in rolling waves. After a final prayer, he ran for it, and not a moment too soon. Out of the broken earth rose a towering figure, a Geo-Fiend, seven feet worth of unbridled menace, topped by a bull's head. Its blazing red eyes went directly to Riley.

"Blackthorne's daughter!" it cried.

Here we go again . . .

It was the shorter figures clustered around the Five who were the really bad news. Riley did a quick head count: nine Archfiends, in all their evil glory. That was three times the number they'd had to face in the cemetery and this time, there were no demon hunters to help them.

A figure in a swirling black cloak stepped forward as magic burst from the tip of his upraised staff and encompassed the closest Archfiend. The demon burst apart in brilliant curls of flame.

"Go, Ozy!" she cried. *That totally rocks.*

The Five roared its fury, but it didn't move, allowing the Archfiends to break ranks and flank the necromancer. Ozymandias might be the most powerful summoner in the city, but there was no way he could take down eight of these fiends at once.

Beck was next to her now, his blade unsheathed.

"Looks like Ozy needs our help," she said. The same necro who had stolen her father away from her.

"This really bites, you know?" Beck replied.

"Same here."

They took off at a run.

THIRTY-FOUR

As Beck made for the Archfiend farthest to the left, Riley veered to the right, making sure to give the necro and his magic as much room as possible. The fiend she chose was a smaller one, but just as vicious as any of its kind. Its three pairs of bloodred eyes glared at her from a domed skull and the four sickle-shaped teeth had been sharpened to needle points. With a furious flap of its wings, it leapt into the air above her, its smoking sword aimed to decapitate her.

As Ori had taught her, she dropped and rolled out of the way of the blade, then spun and cut at the closest wing. The first pass she missed the demon entirely and the fiend chided her.

"I will drink your blood this night," it crowed.

The second dive brought it closer, as if it'd decided she was no serious threat. One of the wingtip claws caught the back of her jacket, ripping it.

Furious, Riley swung at it, but missed again. Stumbling a few steps, she tried to regain her balance. Instinct made her turn and she buried the burning blade deep into the fiend's chest as it dove at her. It shrieked, then weaved erratically in the air, black smoking blood pouring from the wound. With a dying howl, it fell and the ground shook from the impact.

"Riley!" Simon called out.

She ducked as a blade swung so close she could feel the fire singe her skin. Her ex advanced on the larger Archfiend.

"Come on, I'm the one you want," he called out, giving her time to recover her footing.

They double-teamed the monster, driving it backward. When it rose in the air to dive at them, they'd split apart and it couldn't decide which one to target. Unfortunately, the Archfiend learned the trick too quickly. When it rose again, it tracked toward Simon, sailing low across the ground, its curved blade positioned to slice him in half.

Riley rushed underneath the wings. As the fiend passed over her, she raised her blade and it severed one of the main wing tendons. Unable to fly, the demon tried to compensate, but it crashed into Simon. The trapper's sword fell from his hand as they rolled over and over in a jumble of wings and legs.

As Riley ran to help him, another Archfiend blocked her way. She hacked at it, parrying thrusts, but her moves weren't as fast as before.

"Your demi-lord weakens," the demon taunted.

Riley aimed a blow at its wing, then pivoted at the last second. The blade caught the Archfiend in the throat and it reeled back. It wasn't a mortal wound, but it bought her time to reach Simon. Somehow he'd regained his feet and was once again battling his own foe.

With a cry of triumph, he decapitated his Archfiend, the demon's head rolling away, stunned surprise its last expression. Nearby another fiend fell under Jackson's sword, though he cradled a broken arm next to his body.

Though Beck was bloodied, he was gaining ground against one of the Archfiends. The two masters, along with the other trappers, were addressing the Threes, reducing their ranks as if they were at a slaughterhouse. Fighting next to them was Ayden, her blade slashing with deadly precision. Blue flashes of magic lit up every now and then like oversized fireflies.

There was a scream and Riley turned to discover that a group of bystanders were trapped against the remains of a building, with no escape. Moving closer to them was a pack of Gastro-Fiends, their claws bloodied, with an Archfiend in the lead.

"No!"

She'd taken only a few steps when a winged figure appeared in between the frightened citizens and the ravenous demons. It was a Fallen, with ash-gray wingtips and brilliant blue eyes.

Please don't be one of Sartael's guys.

The angel observed her coolly, then shook his head. Then he barked something in Hellspeak at the Threes and the Archfiend leading them. The demons' leader shouted something back and the war was on. It was no contest as one by one the demons fell under the angel's blinding white sword. When they were all dead, he remained in position, guarding the mortals, his face solemn. Behind him, people wept and some were on their knees, praying.

"Thanks," she whispered. "Whoever you are."

I am Gusion and I am heeding the call of an old friend.

A cry of rage brought her attention back to Ori and their enemy. They were no longer in the air, but fighting across the wreckage of Demon Central. Her demi-lord was losing the battle, growing steadily slower with each sword thrust. Sartael, on the other hand, seemed as strong as ever.

The ethereal blade in Riley's hand vanished, evidence that Ori wasn't going to last much longer. If he had shared his power with her, could the Archangel pull strength from his demons? *Of course he can.*

It was time to do some good old-fashioned trapping.

When Riley sprinted to where her pack lay on the ground, she found Peter crouched near the makeshift fence.

"Why are you still here?" she demanded.

"Because you are," Peter replied, his chin out, defiant.

"Ah, geez. Okay, then you can help me."

She pointed at a trapping bag that sat a short distance away, though she had no idea who it belonged to. "Pull out all of the blue spheres. Hurry!"

Digging through the duffel bag, her friend did as she asked while Riley did the same to her pack.

Peter held up two orbs. "Now what?" When Riley told him exactly what he needed to do, he nodded.

A feminine hand extended in their direction. It was attached to Blaze, her hair askew and a dark smudge on her cheek.

"I'll help too," she said. "These things have to be stopped."

Riley gaped at the actress. "This isn't a TV show."

"Duh," the actress replied, waggling her fingers now. "Hand them over."

Riley reluctantly dropped the spheres into the woman's palm. "Let's go kick some demon butt, people."

Peter sped off, dodged a rampaging Three, then tracked along the temporary fence on the other side of the battlefield. Blaze did the same in the opposite direction. Once they were in place, Riley gave them the signal.

Spheres hit the ground, broke open, and energetic blue lines of magic leapt to the fence. The magic seemed to take a deep breath, then zipped along the metal, wire by wire.

Now it was Riley's turn. She sprinted to her sections of the fence, dropping the magical spheres as she went. When all four sides were engaged, the Geo-Fiend would be grounded and Sartael would be deprived of some of his power.

Or at least that was the plan.

The final run of grounding magic connected all four sections of the metal together and began to pull the demon toward the earth. The Five reacted like they always did, shrieking and trying to rise higher to avoid contact with the ground.

Hail hammered down and erratic winds buffeted the trappers. When a Three began a run at her, it went down with one sweep of Stewart's massive claymore. Another died a short time later when Ayden stepped in its way.

Abruptly the grounding magic ended and the fiend began to rise again. It turned its blazing eyes on the two masters, lightning sparking out its claws.

Stewart swung his sword, loosening up his shoulders. He was singing a song in Gaelic, she thought. Harper stood next to him, sweat on his forehead. One by one the trappers lined up, facing down the Five.

Behind her she could feel Ori fading away, his life force dwindling.

Unexpectedly, Mort stepped in front of the trappers, his hands seething in magic. Next to him was Ozymandias, who seemed to be coaching him on how to handle the incantation. With a bright snap, the magic shot out of the junior necromancer's fingers and enveloped the Geo-Fiend. The fiend fought against the spell, but slowly the winds dropped and the hail ended.

A shout of joy erupted from the trappers when the Five fell to the ground, its power draining away. It bellowed and struggled as another earth tremor leveled one of the decrepit buildings nearby.

Without warning, two massive claws erupted from the ground and clamped themselves around the torso of the Geo-Fiend. It flailed against its captor, its ruby eyes reflecting endless terror.

"Traitor to the end," a voice called out, and then the fiend was dragged deep into the hole, wailing its death cry.

Lucifer had begun his purge of Hell.

Riley . . .

Ori was on his knees now, face white, his chest a mass of blue blood. His flaming blade faltered and died.

"No!" she shouted, racing toward him. She skidded to a halt and fell to her knees next to him.

As she cradled the angel, Beck took a defensive position between them and Sartael, sword at the ready. In his own way, he was granting Riley time to say good-bye to her first lover.

"Valiant Light," Ori whispered, trying in vain to touch her face, but he could not raise his injured arm high enough.

She became aware of an angel kneeling next to them. It was Gusion, the one who had fought the demons.

"I am sorry, old friend, but our Prince has not granted you death," the angel said.

Ori was murmuring in some archaic language, his face full of pleading. His wounds began to heal and he cried out in anguish. "No! Release me! I beg of you!"

Riley's eyes met Gusion's.

"That is a favor I do not have the power to grant, my friend," the angel said.

Favor?

"Lucifer," Riley called out, not bothering to raise her voice. She knew he could hear her. "I did as you asked. I freed Ori and now it's your turn. I call in my favor with you, Prince of Hell. Release your servant and let Ori die. Let him find peace."

Ori's eyes widened as he choked hard.

"Lucifer!" she called out again. "Honor your promise!"

The Prince swore in her mind. Then came the words she'd hoped to hear.

Your favor has been paid. My servant will die. I hope you're happy now.

"Yes," she said, without hesitation. "I am."

Ori's wounds began to bleed again, torrents of blue blood flowing onto her hands and onto her lap. He smiled at her weakly. "Thank you."

Riley's tears spilled down her cheeks. "Find the Light, Ori. Never stop looking. You were never meant to stay in Hell."

A faint nod. *I release your soul, Riley Anora Blackthorne. Watch the sunrise . . . and think of me.*

A soft stream of an unknown language passed Ori's pale lips with his final breath. A prayer for forgiveness, perhaps?

As Riley held him, she knew that in some way she still loved him. He had shaded the truth on occasion, but he never lied to her. He had saved her life and that of Beck's.

The angel's body grew fainter until all that remained were the stark patches of blue blood on her hands and arms. She looked up at Gusion and saw a single tear track down his face.

"He is at peace. I envy him," the angel said.

This time Ori was gone forever.

✠

Beck's foe smirked at him, Sartael's breath unusually labored. "Step aside, Denver Beck, and I will grant you any wish you choose. The master's whelp is not worth your life."

"You got nothin' I want."

"I can free your mother's soul from Hell."

Beck hesitated, then shook his head. "No deal. This ends here, for both of us."

As his foe's blade came uncomfortably close, Beck reared back. He was tiring, but then, surprisingly, so was his opponent. With his cohort of demons out of commission, both here and in Hell, Sartael had only his own power to draw upon. Still, that was enough to kill a trapper ten times over.

Sartael's next blow sent Beck's sword flying and he retreated, desperate for a weapon. With a shout, Simon tossed him his sword.

"Thanks!"

He waded back in. "What's with you, angel?" Beck called out. "Figured you'd have leveled the city by now."

Sartael redoubled his blows, sending waves of pain through to Beck's arm and shoulders. With a prayer on his lips, Beck drove his own sword toward the Archangel, but Sartael's blade struck him first, slicing deep into his upper left chest.

Beck screamed in agony, his left arm going numb in a heartbeat. He fell backward, the wound spreading shards of ice along every vein, as if he was being frozen alive.

As the Archangel moved closer now, keen to impale him, there were shouts from some of the trappers. None of them would be close enough to save him.

A dirty figure rose, Beck's sword in her hand and hate in her eyes. "Stupid child. Bow down to me and I'll spare you!" Sartael ordered.

"Like Beck said, it ends here."

Riley was facing down one of God's most deadly creations, and without Ori's protection, Sartael would cut her down like a stalk of ripe wheat. The Archangel closed in for the kill.

With one final burst of strength, Beck made it to his feet and took his place next his woman, though he had no weapon.

"Lad!" Stewart called out and the master's sword skidded to a halt near Beck's boot. It took every ounce of his energy to pick it up and it felt as if it weighed more than he did. Beck could barely hold it in his right hand, his left almost useless. He forced the numbed fingers around the hilt and clasped his good hand over the top of them.

"All or nothing," Riley said.

"All or nothin'" he repeated, his throat dry and his heart bursting in his chest.

Please, God, give us a chance. Just one chance.

The Archangel's strike was faster than Beck had anticipated. It struck his blade first, then slid off and knocked Riley's from her grasp. She cried out when the flames came too close to her face and she staggered back, blinded. A quick clip of Sartael's wing knocked her aside.

"You son of a bitch!" Beck shouted and dove forward in his last, desperate bid to kill their enemy. Stewart's powerful sword drove home deep in the center of the Archangel's chest, exactly where Ori had told him to strike. Using all of his power, Beck pulled the blade to the right, destroying the Fallen's heart like a ripe fruit.

The Archangel reeled backward, shocked, as blood pumped out from his chest and soaked into his monk's robe. He reached out with a hand, trying to pull energy from those in Hell who were his to command. The blood continued to pour out, faster now.

Lucifer had cut his lifeline.

"No! You cannot deny me!" he cried. His eyes sought Riley and a cruel smile formed. "Blackthorne's daughter will serve me just as well." His hand went toward Riley and she began to flail on the ground, crying out in agony as brilliant white light flowed from her to the wounded angel.

But a figure stepped between then, cutting the flow of healing energy from its source.

"Gusion. Why do you do this?" Sartael demanded. "I cannot heal without—" He wheezed, each breath tighter now. "Why?"

"As a favor to an old friend who is no more," Gusion replied. The angel gestured to Beck. "He is yours, mortal. It is between you two now. Whoever is better will win."

Sartael swung at Beck, but missed. Beck did not, his slice a perfect union of holy steel and righteous anger. The instant the blade slid laterally across his enemy's neck, severing it from the body, the corpse and the head fell into the heap on the dirty ground. It immediately ignited into a mass of black, roiling flames, but there was no smoke, no stench of burning flesh, only absolute destruction. Lucifer's rival was no more.

Beck had kept his promise to Riley's angel.

He lost his ability to stand, his strength gone. Arms held him and there was dampness on his cheeks. He wondered if it was raining.

"Promise me you'll live," Riley begged.

"I love . . . you." It was the best he could do, for there were no promises left.

As Beck slid into utter darkness, fell voices assailed him, carving through his soul like a barbed whip does tender flesh. Scores of demons called to him, naming his fate.

Angel killer.

Destroyer of Divines.

Hell is your home now.

THIRTY-FIVE

Riley was oblivious to anything but the man in her arms, though her face and eyes burned so badly tears flooded without restraint. Why wasn't anyone helping him?

It seemed like forever before someone touched her arm.

"Riley?" Harper said. "Let go of Beck so we can treat him."

She didn't want to let go, but she did anyway, hearing unusual compassion in her master's voice. When someone took hold of her hand, she forced her eyes open, even though they felt as if they'd been bathed in acid. Peter knelt next to her, unharmed.

"He can't die. Not after all this," she pleaded. Her friend's reply was a tight hug.

Through the sheen of tears, she watched as Harper gently peeled back Beck's jacket and then his shirt. The wound was high on his chest, but it wasn't bleeding. In fact, it had sealed over as if it had already healed. This was something different. Something very frightening.

When her eyes met Harper's, his had saddened. "This isn't good, Riley," he said. Then he was up on his feet, talking to Stewart in hushed tones.

"Aye," the Scotsman said in reply. "The lad will want ta be in his own bed when . . . Remmers, ya and Simon carry him ta my car and take him ta his house."

"Shouldn't he go to the hospital?" Remmers asked.

"There is . . . no need," the old master replied, his eyes meeting Riley's.

It was then she knew that the man she loved was dying.

✢

Riley remembered little of the journey, other than sitting in the back of the car with Beck's head in her lap. The longer they drove, the more his color grew ashen, his breathing increasingly shallow. She hung on every one of those breaths, afraid that it would be his last.

He can't die. Not now.

After Peter helped her disable the alarm—she had trouble seeing the keypad—the trappers carried Beck to his bed. Simon stripped off his boots and Remmers helped remove the injured man's outer clothes. Once Beck was settled under the covers, Riley sat near him, holding his hand.

As she bent down to kiss him, the scent of his aftershave caught her nose. It brought back memories of them in this very bed, laughing, making love, talking about their future.

Through her fog of grief, snippets of conversation came from the front of the house. One of the voices belonged to Carmela, the Guild's doctor.

"I want to examine him," she insisted.

"Aye, I understand, but there is nothin' ya can do for him," Stewart said. "Mortals are not supposed ta kill an Archangel. Angelic wounds are unlike any other and the healin' must come from within him, not from without. There is nothin' ya can do for him."

"My God," the doctor murmured. "What are his chances?"

"Astronomically poor," Stewart replied, his voice catching. "We'll know within twenty-four hours."

Riley lowered her face to Beck's ear. "I don't care about those odds. Those mean nothing to me. All I know is that Rennie and I need you, so don't you dare die on us, you hear? Don't. You. Die."

Then she closed her eyes and began to pray.

⁜

Later, when Carmela insisted on examining her, Riley tried to push the woman away until Stewart intervened and she had no choice in the matter.

The doctor's touch was gentle. "Your face has a bad burn from the angel's sword. I'll give you some ointment for that. As for your eyes . . . I've got some drops. Use them every two hours. A cold compress wouldn't hurt either. If your eyesight isn't better by tomorrow, you'll need to see a specialist."

Riley nodded, but none of that mattered. There was nothing in this world she wanted to see without the man she loved at her side.

⁜

As time passed, Beck began to murmur in a nonsensical language, like the one Ori had spoken right before he'd died. Stewart said it was the mother tongue of the angels, but how would he know?

Sometime near midnight, Father Harrison joined her for the vigil. It felt good to have him here, even if she wasn't Catholic. He had a way of offering hope even when you were surrounded by impenetrable darkness.

"I spoke with Father Rosetti an hour ago," he said. "They're offering a healing mass for Beck at St. Peter's Basilica in the morning. And there are prayer chains active throughout Atlanta."

Maybe God would listen to all those people if He didn't listen to her.

"What about the demon exorcist guy?" she asked. "Is he alive?"

"Yes. He's not saying much. I think he's as frightened as everyone else."

"No need to be. Not anymore." *Sartael is dead.*

✢

Hours passed. Friends came and went: Fireman Jack, Peter, Simi, then Ayden and Mort. Even Justine called to wish Beck well.

Every now and then someone would bring Riley a drink—water or juice. She took what was offered, but refused anything else in the way of food. Sometimes she'd talk to Beck like he could hear her. Other times she'd just hold his hand and will him to live.

Toward dawn, he grew more agitated, calling out in delirium. At his cries, Stewart stirred from the chair on the other side of the bed. The old master hadn't left the house since the battle, still wearing the same bloodstained clothes from the night before.

"What is happening to him?" Riley asked.

"He's bein' tormented . . . in Hell. It's the fate of anyone who kills a Fallen."

She jolted back in surprise. "He doesn't belong there. They don't own his soul."

"Aye, but that's what's happenin'." He looked over at the injured trapper. "Despite how bad it looks, he has somethin' ta fight for now. Yer the lighthouse in his storm, lass."

"Will it be enough?"

"That's up ta God."

She'd used her one favor for Ori, not realizing that Beck would be in dire need as well. She knew what the angel would have done—he would have insisted her favor be given to the mortal she loved.

Which is why you deserve to be in Heaven, Ori.

"Maybe if I talk to Lucifer . . ."

"I know ya love this lad more than yer own life," Stewart replied, "but if yer thinkin' of makin' a deal with the Prince ta save him, that would be a mistake. Beck has ta do this himself. Ya ken?"

Her eyes began to cloud. "No, I don't *ken*. Everyone gets what they want. For once, why can't I?"

"It *has* ta be his battle. I know that makes little sense ta ya, but that's the way of it."

She really didn't want to believe the old master, but in her heart she knew he was right. If she did make a deal with Hell to save Beck's life, it would never be the same between them.

Riley bent over and laid her head on her boyfriend's chest, tears bathing her cheeks.

"Come on, Backwoods Boy," she said fiercely. "Don't let them win. Don't let them take you away from me."

As she sobbed, Stewart's hand touched her shoulder. It shook as the older man wept with her.

⊹

Beck heard her calling to him. Though Riley urged him to live, he felt so alone in this barren place. He should have known he'd been damned either way—if he killed Sartael or not. Hell never played fair.

When he was a kid, the preachers always conjured up gruesome descriptions of fiery pits full of boiling sinners or maniacal demons cutting people into pieces and roasting them over open flames.

This Hell wasn't like that. At least not the part he was in. There were demons here, but he felt them more than saw them. They pressed around him, touching him, cursing him for daring to venture into their realm. It was like being clawed to death by invisible rats.

That was bad, but what really frightened him were the faces of the damned in the walls and the ceiling of the long corridor in front of him. The tormented eyes followed him as their mouths cried out to him. Some insisted they were here by mistake. Others, more cunning, offered to help him if he would just free them. All he needed to do was touch the entombed face and then they'd show him the way out. Beck knew better than that. He heard the lies, so he kept walking, praying that the corridor would end and he would find himself outside of purgatory.

The Prince of Hell materialized out of nowhere. There were wide swatches of black demon blood smeared across his armor, but he wasn't carrying a sword.

"Denver Beck. Welcome to my domain," he said magnanimously. "What do you think of it?"

Beck kept walking. The ache in his left shoulder grew, a hundredfold now, throbbing with each rapid heartbeat. He was miserably cold, like he was already in the grave, though the air around him was filled with steamy mist.

"I can send you home," the Prince continued. "You could be back with Blackthorne's daughter this very instant. Just say the word."

Beck forced one foot ahead of the other. The Prince didn't bother to catch up with him, but just appeared farther down the hallway in front of him.

"I don't see one of Heaven's angels offering to help you out," Lucifer said slyly.

Beck came to a halt in front of Hell's ruler. "I may not have any more time with the woman I love, but my soul is still my own. That's not gonna change. So go torment some other poor bastard."

"What will it matter? You're here, whether your soul is yours or not."

"It's a pride thing," Beck said. "Now leave me be, angel."

"Well, I did try," Lucifer said lightly. "It is my job, after all."

Then the Prince vanished, leaving him with only the voices of the damned for company.

⁜

An eternity later, Beck began to rethink the proposal. He could be free of this place, with Riley, and no one would ever know he'd bargained his soul to save himself. They could get married and have kids and . . .

She had given up her soul to save the world. Why couldn't he do it to save himself?

The damned all began to shout at once, a roaring sound that beat at him like a solid wall of sound. Beck covered his ears, trying to shut them out, to prevent them from driving him mad.

"God, help me!" he cried out.

Someone touched him on the shoulder and he jumped in surprise.

"Momma?"

His mother wore the dress Riley had chosen for the burial and her eyes burned with that same eerie fire like those in the walls.

"Come, boy," she said, offering her bony hand. "Ya don't belong here."

"I'm not givin' up my soul."

"I know that. Come on!"

He didn't dare trust her. She had lied and hurt him all her life, left him to die in the swamp. And yet here, in this purgatory, he had no one else to trust.

"Come on, Denver. Don't be a fool," she said. "The girl is waitin' for ya."

The moment he offered his hand, Sadie yanked him forward. They moved at incredible speed, their feet never touching the floor, as the faces in the corridor blurred to gray.

Sadie abruptly halted. The area in front of them held . . . nothing. No faces, no walls or ceiling. Oblivion. She pointed into that endless nothingness. "Go there."

"I don't understand," he said.

"Yer not dead, boy. If ya fight hard enough, ya might make it back alive."

That was the one thing he did know how to do: He'd fought all his life.

"Come with me," he said, tugging on her hand.

She pulled herself free. "I can't, Denver. I belong here."

This might be the last time he'd see her. "I love ya," he said. "I know ya never loved me, but that didn't matter."

Her face tightened. "I know. I see what it all means now. I'm sorry, Denver. I truly am."

The shade that was Sadie Beck faded away.

"Good-bye, Momma," he said.

It seemed colder now and Beck shivered from head to toe. With uneasy steps, he moved forward, his hand clasping Paul's ring so tightly it dug into his skin.

He just had to trust his mother one last time.

Maybe this time it wouldn't be a lie.

THIRTY-SIX

When Beck's eyes jerked open, a soft light touched them. He blinked a few times and the scene became clearer. It was morning and he was in his own bedroom and someone was sitting in a chair near the bed, reading aloud. The words were from the Bible, he thought. *Psalms.* When he cleared his throat to try to speak the man looked up.

"Lad?" Stewart said, dark, heavy bags under his eyes. "Oh, thank God." The master placed the book on the nightstand and leaned closer. "How are ya feelin'?"

"I hurt like hell," Beck said. He cautiously shifted his left arm and was pleased to find it was no longer numb.

Someone was missing. Panicking, he tried to rise off the mattress and failed. "Riley? Where is she? Is she hurt?" *If she's dead . . .*

"Riley's friends are tryin' ta force some food down her. She's barely left yer side since ya were wounded."

She's alive. Oh, thank God. Beck took a deep breath to calm himself. "It was so weird. I . . . was in Hell, for real."

"Aye, ya would have been. We'll talk of that when yer stronger." Stewart gently placed his hand on Beck's uninjured shoulder. "I'm verra proud of ya, lad. Well done. Now I'd best go tell yer lady the good news or she'll have my head."

When the master reached the kitchen, Beck heard voices, one of them Riley's. She was telling someone exactly where they could put the sandwich they'd made for her.

Yeah, that's my girl.

Stewart announced the news, and for a moment there was profound silence, then a whoop of joy followed by someone racing down the hall. Riley didn't launch herself onto the bed like he'd figured, but sat next to him, looking the worse for wear. Her face was blotchy, crimson in places, and she wore a pair of sunglasses . . . inside the house.

She pulled off the glasses and set them aside, revealing swollen eyes and puffy cheeks.

"You okay?" he asked. "Yer eyes . . ."

"Are getting better," she replied, her voice huskier than usual. "That'll teach me to get close to a fiery sword."

Still troubled, he gestured with his uninjured arm for her to lay her head on his chest. It wasn't comfortable, but he didn't care. He heard her sigh as he stroked her hair, savoring that simple pleasure.

Sartael is dead. He'll never hurt us again. And I killed him.

Beck couldn't suppress the well-earned grin.

There was a shuffling in the doorway and he discovered four smiling faces watching them. One belonged to Jackson, his arm in a cast, then Riley's friends Peter and Simi, and finally, Stewart. Eight thumbs shot upward in unison.

"Thanks, guys," he said, overwhelmed.

There were congratulations, then Stewart shooed them off. "All right the lot of ya, out! They need their privacy. We can celebrate later."

The old guy understands.

The instant the front door closed, Riley raised her head, blinking her eyes repeatedly. "I thought I'd lost you," she said, running her fingers through his hair.

"We Georgia boys are . . . hard to kill." His mind flashed back to his mother. How she'd led him out of Hell and that she'd had to stay behind. "Sadie helped."

"What?"

He shook his head. There was no way he could explain that.

"Thank you for coming back to me," she murmured.

"Wouldn't have it any other way," he said.

Beck raised his eyes to the ceiling, as if somehow he could see Heaven.

You never listened to me before, but this time you did. I won't ever forget that.

Then the tears he'd been holding back began to trickle down his face as he wept along with the woman he loved.

⁘

The next three days proved harder than Riley had expected. Though he was regaining his strength, Beck's mood would veer from morose to jubilant and back into depression in a fraction of a second. One minute he wanted to hold her, the next he wanted his space. That irrationality made for a few tense scenes.

Stewart insisted the patient's behavior was normal, but after the love of her life had snarled at her about the taste of the meal she'd lovingly made for him, Riley's patience snapped. She retreated and called in reinforcements.

The master took over, tactfully suggesting she catch up on her homework while he tried to maneuver the patient back on an even keel. Riley decamped from Beck's house and left the grump behind with few regrets.

⁘

Beck wasn't in the mood for a social call, his nerves as brittle as a thin sheet of pond ice in the spring. He was on the couch now, tired of the bed, but the change of location hadn't helped his mood.

"I don't need you here," he grumbled, eyeing Stewart as the master eased himself into a chair.

"Ya need ta talk about what's goin' on in yer head. Yer the kind who bottles things up. That's not healthy."

"No reason to talk about it," Beck replied. How could he ever explain what had happened with his mother?

"Come on, lad, tell me what ya saw while ya were ill."

"Just dreams," Beck said dismissively. "Nightmares."

"Of Hell, am I right?"

Beck cautiously straightened up, mindful of his sore shoulder. The sling only did so much to reduce the discomfort. "Why are you really here?"

A thoughtful smile appeared on his guest. "I'm here ta see that ya keep yer sanity after all ya've been through. It would be a damned waste ta have ya go crazy now."

"You tell me what happened." *Why Sadie saved me.*

"Yer wound exposed ya ta the power of the Divine. Because Sartael was a Fallen, ya were sent ta Hell to pay the price for slayin' an angel."

"But I didn't stay there."

"Aye. So who showed ya the way out?"

Beck stared at the master in profound shock. "How did you know that?"

"I think the best way ta answer that is with a wee story." Stewart eased back in his chair. "A couple decades back a master trapper killed a Geo-Fiend. He was feelin' pretty damned proud of himself until a Fallen angel showed up. It was the Five's demi-lord, ya see, and it was angry at losin' such a powerful servant. The angel and the master fought, and by the grace of God, this lad killed the Fallen, though he was badly injured."

"So this guy went to Hell like I did?"

"Aye. He wandered in this endless maze of thorns, teeterin' on the edge between life and death. When he cried out for help, one of the damned souls came ta him. It was an old friend who'd gone down the wrong path many years before. That friend helped the trapper find his way out of the maze and back ta the light."

My God.

"It was . . . Sadie, my momma," Beck admitted. "She took my hand

and showed me the way out. There was no way I could save her. She's there until . . ."

"God decides she isn't."

Beck searched the master's face. "Why did she do that? She could have left me down there to burn with her."

"She may not have been able ta show ya love in this life, but once we cross over, we see things more clearly. All the lies we wrap ourselves in are stripped away." Stewart paused. "Yer mother came through when it really counted. If for nothin' more, remember her kindly for that."

"I will." Beck slowly pieced together the connections. "That leg wound of yers. It wasn't from an Archfiend, was it?" The master shook his head. "You killed the angel, that's how you know about Hell, about bein' lost there."

"Aye."

There was something more here, Beck could feel it. The final connection snapped into place.

"To be a master demon trapper, the Guild says you have to kill or capture an Archfiend. To be a grand master . . . you have to do that with an angel?" Beck asked.

"Ya have ta kill them. There's no capturin' those things," Stewart replied. "There are only a handful of us grand masters in the world." The Scotsman smiled broadly. "And now there's one more."

Beck could barely comprehend what he'd just heard. "You mean . . . I . . ."

"There will be extensive trainin' and a lot of bookwork, but ya have what it takes ta be one of us. I knew ya had the talent ta become a damned fine master. But now, lad . . . yer much more than that."

"A grand master," Beck whispered.

"Now it's not an easy life. We have duties that are . . . so verra painful sometimes, but we do what we can ta maintain the balance between the dark and light. That will be yer job too, if ya care ta join us."

"But . . ." He had to come clean. "I can't read and write that good," Beck admitted.

"That's somethin' ya can learn. What's important is that yer wise beyond yer years. Ya've seen death close up, ya've killed and know the toll it takes. Ya know what true love is. That's as much of the job as anythin'."

"A grand master," Beck repeated. Then he frowned. "How will this all happen?"

"Once ya've made master here in the States, ya'll go ta Scotland for a few months' trainin'. Then every year after that ya'll return for more education, sometimes there, sometimes in other parts of the world."

He'd have to leave Riley behind and . . . "How long would I be gone?"

"I know where yer headed. Ya'll not want ta be away from yer pretty lass for that long, so we'll have her come visit ya as needed. I can tell ya, there's nothin' more romantic than a walk in the hills of my homeland, especially if ya have a certain question ya might want ta ask."

Beck's eyes rose and he found himself smiling at the notion. "I might have one of those. Does Riley know any of this?"

"Nay, but I'll be tellin' her soon enough. I believe she'll be as proud of ya as I am."

Beck shook his head in amazement. "I can't believe it. This all happened because one crazy Archangel decided he wanted to rule in Hell."

"That was a bit of it, but not the most important part," Stewart retorted. "This all happened because one poor and abused lad refused ta accept that was his lot in life. Ya sought somethin' better. Now ya'll have it."

THIRTY-SEVEN

While Stewart jousted with her grouchy boyfriend, Riley took refuge in paradise. Or at least the coffee shop. Her favorite booth was empty so she spread out her homework and started working. Memories kept intruding, especially those that involved Ori. She found she missed him more than she'd anticipated.

Her eyes were still bugging her so she put in more drops and those seemed to help. Digging into both the hot chocolate and the homework, she found it hard to concentrate. How was Beck doing? Would the master set him right?

She'd just finished her sociology assignment about the Maori when Stewart's call came through.

"Lass? Beck's doin' better. We got some things settled and now he knows the lay of the land. He said he'd call ya when he was ready ta talk."

"Oh good. He was *so* bitchy and I didn't know what to do."

"There is one more thing . . ."

As she listened in increasing astonishment, Stewart explained exactly where Beck's future lay, that her boyfriend was now qualified to join the ranks of the grand masters.

Riley's mind reeled. "He knows this?"

"Aye. He's still tryin' ta handle the news. I thought ya should know."

"Ohmigod. That's like . . . *really* big."

"That it is. Beck will need yer help with the readin' and the studyin', but I have no doubt he'll do just fine. He's a smart lad, even if he claims not ta be."

"This is so awesome." *Beck has to be blown away.*

"As for yer situation, I chatted with Rome this mornin'," Stewart continued. "They're comfortable with the way things are now. They've lifted yer restrictions so ya can live wherever ya wish. They do recommend that ya don't mess around with any Fallen in the future."

"That I can live with."

"When things settle down, I'd like to talk ta ya about compilin' the history of Atlanta's Demon Trappers. We don't have a historian and it's time we did. The job would pay a small stipend, enough ta help ya with some of yer expenses."

Riley's dad, the history teacher, would have jumped at that chance. "I'll do it. Thank you, sir."

"It's Angus. We know each other well enough ya should call me by my Christian name."

"Thanks, Angus. You rock. I mean that."

⁂

It proved really hard not to call Beck and celebrate his incredible news, but she took Stewart's advice and curbed her impatience. Her guy would call when he was ready.

She'd moved on to her history homework with an occasional *ohmigod, I can't believe it* moment thrown in, when Simon entered the coffee shop. When he saw her, he headed to the booth.

"Hey," she said, unsure of where they stood.

"I'd like to talk. Is that okay?" he said, more solemn than usual.

"Sure." Riley closed the book in front of her, wondering what was on his mind.

"Would you like some more hot chocolate?"

She nodded, if nothing more than to gain time to prepare for what was to come. He didn't seem angry or hostile, so maybe this would be a good talk rather than one that they'd both regret.

Riley watched as Simon waited at the counter to place their order. He appeared so much older now, though only a few months had passed since that night they'd first met at the Tabernacle. Older, stronger, more scarred. She felt the same way.

Her ex-boyfriend slid into the booth after handing over her drink. When he didn't speak right off, she savored the chocolate curls on the top of the abundant whipped cream.

Finally he cleared his throat and asked her about her eyes. They both agreed she looked as if she'd fallen asleep in a tanning bed. Then he asked about Beck and she let him know everything was good there as well, without revealing her boyfriend's latest news. That was his to announce.

The pleasantries over, Simon moved on to what was really on his mind. "I passed my journeyman's exam. I heard this morning."

"That's great, Simon. Congratulations," she said, meaning every word.

"Yeah, it is."

"Ah, you don't sound happy."

"It's all changed now. It's an accomplishment, but not like it once would have been." His slender fingers wrapped around the ceramic cup. "I . . . will be here for another couple weeks and then I'm leaving Atlanta. I need to spend some time away. I need to get my head on right."

"Oh," Riley replied, caught off guard. "Where are you going?"

"I want to visit some holy sites. Rome, for sure. Lourdes. I'll go to Israel and then . . ." He hesitated, though his eyes were alight now. "India. I want to talk to some of their holy men. And Tibet, maybe. The monks might have some insights." He paused to take a sip of the coffee. "Ayden suggested I spend some time at a couple of stone circles while I'm in Ireland."

The old Simon would have never listened to the witch or been willing to go near places or people that didn't share his faith. This was a huge step.

"While you're at it, spend some time with a rabbi or an imam," Riley suggested. "Maybe one of those folks will help put things into perspective for you. If I didn't have a reason to stay here, I'd join you."

"That reason is Beck, isn't it?" Simon asked, their eyes meeting now.

"Yes. We're in love. It's . . . good."

"I'm pleased to hear that," he replied. "We never got a chance."

"No, we never did."

It took a bit of work, but she extracted his charred cross from the bottom of her backpack. "I found this at the Tabernacle the other day. I thought you'd want it."

Simon reached for it, then pulled his hand back. "Keep it for me, will you? If . . . Maybe someday I can take it back and have it mean what it once did."

"No, if you ever wear it again, it'll mean something completely new. Then you will have passed your test."

When she took his hand, he gently flipped hers over. "The mark from Hell is gone," he observed. "What about your soul?"

"It's mine again." Riley turned over her left hand. "The one from Heaven is still here. Guess they're not finished with me yet." They clasped hands. "When you're on the road, write to me, will you? I want to know how it's going for you. I'm serious."

"I will. You understand better than anyone else."

They held hands for a little longer before Simon left her behind, pensive as always.

If you regain your faith you're going to be one awesome weapon against the darkness. You know how they play their games. They will never defeat you again.

Perhaps that was what Heaven had in mind all along.

✣

After Stewart left, Beck sat unmoving for a long time, working things out in his head. As the afternoon faded to twilight he didn't bother to turn on a lamp. He didn't fear the dark now that he'd been to Hell and seen the worst.

Finally he reached for the phone and dialed Riley. "Hey, Princess." He sighed. "I'm missin' you."

"I'm missing you too . . . Grand Master Beck."

He closed his eyes in thought. "Not there yet."

"But you will be one day, Den."

"So it seems. Now come on home. I need you here." *Everythin' is better when yer near me.*

"I'll be there in a little bit."

THIRTY-EIGHT

It was nearly ten days before Beck was well enough to leave the house. Though Riley had intended to make the trip to the cemetery on her own, he insisted on accompanying her. And then insisted on walking from the west entrance, rather than having her drive to the mausoleum.

"I need to build myself back up," he said. "I got plans and they don't involve lyin' around in a bed the rest of my life."

"Dude, you're going to be trashed when this is over."

He didn't disagree, but kept moving down the asphalt path, albeit at a slower pace.

It was right after sunrise—she hadn't wanted Beck out much earlier—and the cemetery was tranquil. The mornings were much warmer now and the flowers beds alive with the merry colors of daffodils and crocuses. In the distance rain clouds were moving in, but at present the sun lit their way.

They held hands as they walked, trading small talk. When they reached her family's mausoleum, Beck sank onto the steps, exhausted. As he rested, Riley tidied up her parents' graves and laid the bouquets of flowers she'd bought on each patch of earth. Soon she'd need to have a marker made for her father, one that would be in harmony with her mom's. His bones weren't there, of course, but that didn't matter. She wanted people to know who he was and that he was loved even in death.

She returned to sit next to Beck. He was breathing easier now, less winded.

"I wish there was some marker for Ori, you know?"

"Where do you think he is?"

She shrugged. "Probably somewhere in the darkness and that makes me sad. He so needs to see the light."

A robin flitted from one tree to the next as traffic noises came from the city to the west. Then the noises stilled. Riley rose, checking out the landscape. Someone was watching them.

"What's wrong?" Beck asked.

She felt a familiar presence. "It's Lucifer."

The Prince of Hell stood near the spot where Ori had once been a statue. His armor was gone, replaced by black jeans and a shirt. He appeared more like she remembered him, not like the ferocious ruler she'd seen in Hell. If she was right, there was more silver in his hair now, as if somehow Prince of Demons had aged during this ordeal.

Riley descended the stairs, nervous at being in his presence once again.

"Thank you for honoring the favor you owed me," she said. It never hurt to be polite, even to the chief of the Fallen.

"I never should have given you that boon," Lucifer replied tartly. "I knew Ori would eventually win your soul, but I thought he would promptly offer it to me. Instead, he accepted your outrageous bargain, which means you're now free of Hell. For the time being, of course."

Riley drew in a quick breath. "Ori did what was right."

"He did as I commanded, but his heart was in service to another master," Lucifer said coolly. "He never should have left Heaven. I knew it was a mistake for him to join me in exile."

Lucifer moved his attention to her boyfriend, studying him with renewed interest. "Ah, the angel killer. You're legendary in Hell now,

Denver Beck. Does it not trouble you that you murdered a Divine, one of *His* creation?"

"I'm good with it," Beck replied bluntly. "Sartael was an evil bastard who killed innocent folks just to feed his madness. I won't ever regret putting him down."

A knowing nod returned and Lucifer's attention turned to Riley. "I can anticipate your next question, Blackthorne's daughter: Ori currently resides in the void, as I cannot ensure he goes to Heaven. That is not in my purview."

"He needs to be somewhere he can see the light," Riley said. "It meant so much to him. It would give him hope."

"What are you willing to pay in return for this freedom?"

Riley had known it would come to that. "Nothing. As I see it, you owe us. We helped you get rid of a dangerous rival who caused nothing but trouble in your realm."

"I would have destroyed Sartael eventually."

"True," Beck replied, "but we just made it quicker. Now you can get on with ruling Hell."

"You're not willing to offer your soul for Ori's freedom?" the Prince pushed.

"No," they both replied at once.

"We've paid enough as it is," Beck added, gesturing toward Paul's grave.

Lucifer sighed wearily. "I must be losing my touch." He idly waved a hand. "It is done. My *former* servant Ori is free so that he may watch the sunrise each morning, however that will benefit him."

"Thank you," Riley whispered.

"Mark me, he may one day be forgiven and return to Heaven, though I doubt he'll find comfort there. The others of our kind do not share in the endless well of mercy."

Beck rose wearily. "You planned this all along, didn't you? Ever since Paul's soul became yours."

"I saw certain possibilities when Sartael began to work against me," the chief of the Fallen replied. "I suspected his servants would try to free him, so I let them. That way I knew who they were and then they could be destroyed."

"But you didn't destroy them. You left that to us," Beck said.

"The ones that accompanied Sartael, yes. The ones still in my realm?" Lucifer's eyes glittered. "I took care of those *personally*. The question of who rules in Hell has been answered . . . in blood."

A shiver crept up Riley's spine.

"Which, I suspect, was the whole point of the exercise," Lucifer continued. "When I rebelled, my punishment was to have my own kingdom, with my own servants, so that I could learn exactly what it meant to rule over others. How it is not as simple as issuing commands and expecting loyalty in return. How servants can turn on you so very easily."

"Would you go back to Heaven if you could?" Beck asked.

Lucifer's jaw tightened. "Ah, that age-old question: Is it better to reign in Hell than to serve in Heaven? I do not know the answer. I *detest* the demons and all their corrupt intrigues. They are truly abominations. Yet, I am master in my world, for good or ill. I shall remain so until my role is deemed complete."

"At the end of days," Riley said.

The Prince's expression flattened. "We are done here, Blackthorne's daughter. Your favor has been fulfilled. Best not to summon me in the future or you *will* regret it." Lucifer gave her one last long look, then vanished. The birds began to chirp again, as if relieved at his departure.

"He's not done with us," Riley observed.

"Didn't figure so," Beck said. "At least we have a good idea how he plays his games now."

"If you had to, could you kill him?" she asked.

Her boyfriend shook his head. "Sartael's arrogance was his weakness. Lucifer's more calculatin' and he'd be difficult to defeat. And if I did, who would take his place? Another Sartael?"

"True." She caressed his cheek. "You're getting more like Stewart every day."

"Don't think that's too bad," Beck admitted. "But I'm not puttin' on one of those skirt things he wears."

"You'd be hot in a kilt, dude."

"Not happenin'. No way."

Beck turned back toward the mausoleum. "Rest in peace, Paul," he said. "I'll watch over yer girl for you."

"Don't worry, Dad, I'll keep Beck in line. Like you did."

He acted as if he hadn't heard her. Instead, he stared up at the roof of the structure, entranced.

"What are you doing?"

"Checking out the new gargoyle," he said.

"Yeah, they're way creepy." Then it hit her that he'd said *new* gargoyle.

She followed his gaze and gasped. There had always been four lion-faced grotesques on the mausoleum, one for each corner. Now there was a fifth. It was slightly bigger than the others, wings rounded and with a face she knew intimately. It was precisely positioned to the east so it could catch the dawn's rays.

"Ohmigod, its Ori." Lucifer had turned him into a gargoyle. Or put his soul in one.

"Good view of the sunrise," Beck said. "He could do worse."

"He'll be there for centuries, at least until the building is no more. Then maybe they'll let him back in Heaven."

"Or not," Beck replied. "You heard Lucifer's warning about that."

"Well, at least he's at peace right now," she replied. *Like my dad.*

"Makes you wonder how many of those things used to be angels," Beck said.

"No wonder they creep me out."

⊹

When they returned from the cemetery, Beck went to sleep, worn out from the exercise. Riley took that opportunity to pound out a term paper. It was nearly one when he awoke and invited her to his bed. There, with the sound of rain on the roof, they made love for the first time since he'd been injured. It was a tender, careful joining, a rebirth for both of them.

After their passion had ebbed, Beck felt a profound peace settle inside of him. He knew it was because of the woman lying next to him.

"I love you, Princess," he whispered.

"I love you, Hero."

"I'm no—" Her finger silenced him.

"You've always been my hero, Denver Beck. Just accept that, and it'll make the next forty-five years a lot easier."

He knew better than to argue.

THIRTY-NINE

Four months later

As Riley waited for the new apprentices to get themselves organized, she loitered outside the law library, the exact one she'd damaged a few months before. The librarian had another Biblio-Fiend in residence and she'd insisted that Paul's daughter be the one to trap it.

The universe had a truly bizarre sense of humor.

This time she wouldn't be working solo: It was her job as a newly minted journeyman trapper to help train the latest batch of apprentices. They were a mixed lot: The eldest was forty years old, a former DJ at a radio station. The next youngest was in his late twenties and a computer wizard. Harper had already decided this guy was going to excel at trapping Techno-Fiends. The third was a redheaded girl in her early twenties, proving Riley's stint as the only female in the Atlanta Guild was drawing to a close. She had blazed the trail and now it was time for others to make their mark.

The three were lined up in front of her, but there was no smirking or disdain. Ever since video footage of her battling an Archangel had found its way onto the Internet, she was someone to be taken seriously. In fact, there were rumors that Hollywood wanted to do a spin-off of *Demonland*, the lead character being somebody a lot like Riley Blackthorne.

Just what I need.

As she was about to lead her charges into the library, her cell phone rang. She'd been expecting this call: Beck was about to sit the National Guild's exam for master demon trapper.

"Give me a sec, guys," she said, then stepped away from them for privacy.

"Hey, lady," Beck called down the line. "Lie to me and tell me this is goin' to go okay."

"You'll be fine. You've memorized the exam's questions, you know the answers, and they'll give you plenty of time to answer them." They'd even allowed him to type his answers into a computer, since writing was so painfully slow for him. "You will pass this, Beck. No question in my mind."

"God, I hope so. I've never been this nervous. Well, except when I asked ya to wear my ring."

He really was worried if he was back to using "ya."

"Take your time and ask if you don't understand something," Riley advised. "The masters want you to pass, so don't worry."

A long sigh came down the phone. "I wish I had yer confidence."

"Dude, you took out an Archangel. An exam is nothing, okay?"

"I hope so."

"Once you're done, we'll go out for food and celebrate."

Beck perked up. "Yeah, that'd be good. Maybe I'll have a couple of beers and we can play a few games of pool."

Armageddon Lounge, here we come. Dating a Georgia boy wasn't for wimps.

"Sounds good. Now go kick some butt."

"Love ya, Riley girl."

"Love you, Den. Later."

✠

The library didn't look much different and neither did the librarian. The former was in good shape—bookshelves all in perfect alignment—while the latter was as neatly dressed as always.

"Any chance of a recurrence of your last visit's issues?" the woman asked.

"No. That Grade Five demon is dead and none of the others would dare try that stunt now."

Once the paperwork was completed, Riley channeled her father the teacher.

"So pay attention, guys . . . people, because I will be quizzing you at the end."

Riley walked them to the door of the Rare Books room and laid down a double line of Holy Water, one inside and one outside the room, because you could never be too paranoid.

Then she went in search of the demon in question. Once she'd found evidence of its destruction, she lined her charges up in a neat row. The plastic cup came out of her backpack.

"You trap with a sippy cup?" the older guy said, taken aback.

"Demon trappers have jack for a budget so you use what you can find. A Grade One demon fits inside one of these and if you screw the lid on correctly, it can't get out."

"And if you don't screw on the lid right?"

He'd taken the bait like she'd hoped. "Then it'll get loose while you're driving and you just might *nearly* rear-end a cop. Been there, done that. Learn from my mistakes."

Riley heard a chuckle from one of the nearby tables. It was the hunky guy who'd dissed her after the trapping debacle. She frowned him into silence and went back to the hands-on instruction.

"See there, between the Constitutional law book and the one on civil procedure?" she said, pointing upward.

All three of her newbies followed her finger and then stared in fascination at the Biblio-Fiend rending his way through a volume devoted to maritime law.

"It's . . . way ugly," the girl trapper whispered.

The demon hissed in response and Riley knew what was coming next.

"You might want to step back," she warned. Two streams came at them: one of green demon pee and the other of Hellish obscenities.

"Eww. That stinks," the young guy said, pinching the bridge of his nose.

"Lesson number two," Riley began. "Demon trapping is never like you see on television. It's a dirty job."

"But someone has to do it?" the younger dude suggested.

"Yeah. And now it's your job. Let's get this pest out of here before he does any more damage."

It went down like clockwork: Deploy Herman Melville's demon-stunning prose, collect comatose fiend, and drop it into sippy cup, tighten down the lid.

"Sweeet!" the girl trapper replied. "When do we get to do that?"

"Next week. Read up on Biblio-Fiends in your manual and then we'll start having you guys trap these things."

The older apprentice eyed her. "It can't be that easy. There has to be a catch."

Riley was really beginning to like this dude. He had just enough life experience to be cynical.

"Yes, there is a catch or two. Let's get the paperwork signed and then I'll tell you exactly what happens when you screw things up."

"Another been there, done that?" the guy asked.

"Totally."

The Biblio flipped off the girl trapper and swore at her, which earned it a laugh in response. Then it glared up at Riley.

"Blackthorne's daughter," it said, using both middle fingers this time.

"Why does it do that?" one of the apprentices asked.

"Because Hell isn't very fond of me."

Which was an understatement.

✛

As the apprentices chattered among themselves, Riley followed them out of the library. This time there were no EMT units or news vans, no upset Backwoods Boy or frantic phone calls from her father. Just a quiet campus on a gloriously warm late July morning.

Life had come full circle.

Riley found herself smiling at how things had turned out. In one month's time Beck would be off to Scotland to begin the first phase of his grand master training. Uncharacteristically, he'd obsessed about every little detail, alternately jazzed and incredibly spooked. To put his mind at ease, she'd agreed to house-sit while he was gone, watching over Rennie. Relieved, Beck had hinted that maybe they should make that a permanent arrangement when he returned, then invited her to come visit him during his training. She knew what he had in mind.

He'll propose in Scotland on my birthday.

There was no doubt as to what her answer would be.

When Riley's life had been so terribly bad and there seemed no end to trouble, misery upon misery heaped on her, her father had always reassured her that everything would be okay. For a long time *okay* was as good as it could be.

Now all those dark days and nights had spun themselves into a promising future that shone like newly minted gold. She was a journeyman trapper and caretaker of Denver Beck's heart. Even Hell knew her name.

Blackthorne's daughter would never settle for "okay" ever again.

From now on, it's awesome or nothing.